CUSTER
AT THE
ALAMO

AN ALTERNATE HISTORY ADVENTURE

by Gregory Urbach

ISBN: 1-4922-3621-7
ISBN 13: 978-1-4922-3621-4
Library of Congress Control Number: 2013916034
CreateSpace Independent Publishing Platform
North Charleston, South Carolina

TABLE OF CONTENTS

Chapter 1   Little Big Horn June 25, 1876 1

Chapter 2   Encounter on the Rio Grande 25

Chapter 3   Trouble in Béjar 55

Chapter 4   Commanding the Alamo 75

Chapter 5   Ignominious Retreat 101

Chapter 6   Negotiating With an Enemy 127

Chapter 7   The Battle of Cibolo Creek 149

Chapter 8   Crockett's Secret Mission 171

Chapter 9   Return to Béjar 195

Chapter 10   A Line in the Sand 219

Chapter 11   Picks, Shovels and Bowie Knives 243

Chapter 12   Santa Anna's Decision 269

Chapter 13   By Dawn's Early Light 293

Chapter 14   The Price of Glory 325

Acknowledgements 347

References   349

Cover by Doug Stambaugh
Matthew Bernstein, story editor
Back cover map by Adam Lovell
Website design by Candace Lovell
Illustrations by Kwei-lin Lum, Chris Stewart,
Matthew Bernstein and Greg Urbach

LIST OF ILLUSTRATIONS

Comanche Village, 1940's vending card, artist unknown iii

Custer & Crockett by Doug Stambaugh iv

Map of the Little Big Horn by Lt. Edward Godfrey, 1877 v

Fall of the Alamo by Robert Jenkins Onderdonk, 1903 ix

Custer's Last Stand by Elk Eber, 1880 ix

Battle of the Little Big Horn x

Battle of the Rio Grande 24

Custer's March to the Alamo 54

Diagram of the Alamo 73

The Ruins of the Alamo by Edward Everett, 1848 100

The Battle of Cibolo Creek 147

San Antonio de Béjar 218

Alamo Battle Position 1 267

Alamo Battle Position 2 292

Alamo Battle, The Final Position 324

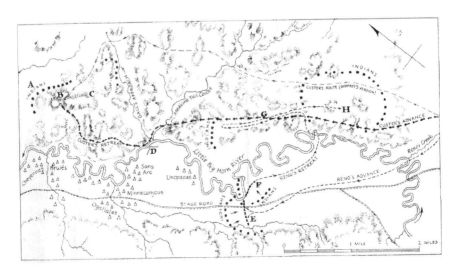

FOREWORD

Following the failure of the Bay of Pigs invasion in 1961, President John F. Kennedy said, "Victory has a hundred fathers and defeat is an orphan." The same might be said for anyone foolish enough to write a historical novel about the Alamo and the Little Big Horn. Like many baby boomers who grew up under the influence of Walt Disney's *Davy Crockett, King of the Wild Frontier*, I have studied the Alamo and often blindly believed all of the various myths surrounding that historic battle. And like many who came of age in the 1970s, I often believed the revisionist propaganda that made George Armstrong Custer the great villain of the Indian Wars. Real history is, of course, more complicated.

It is hard to blame people for getting so much false information in an age where politics trumps the truth. In July of 2011, I had the misfortune to watch a so-called professor on public cable access, presumably representing California State University, Dominguez Hills. This professor was teaching about the culture clash along America's southern border and touched on the Texas Revolution of 1836. In the process, he claimed David Crockett was from Kentucky, that he had been forced to flee from the United States, that he was an enemy of indigenous peoples, that he had brought slaves with him to Texas, and that Crockett envisioned Texas as a slave empire.

For the record, David Crockett was from Tennessee, not Kentucky. He was not forced to flee the United States; he left Tennessee after losing a re-election bid for Congress, where he had served three terms. Far from being an enemy of indigenous peoples, Crockett's political career was destroyed when he bravely supported the Cherokee Nation against President Andrew Jackson's infamous *Indian Removal Act*. Crockett did not bring slaves with him to Texas, nor is he on record as an advocate for a Texan slave empire. Can we blame kids for being so ignorant when college professors show such contempt for basic historical facts?

George Custer's reputation has also been submerged by political correctness. Far from the hair-brained, Indian hating egomaniac we see in movies, Custer was an intelligent and dedicated soldier. And he was far more principled than the corrupt politicians who sent the Seventh Cavalry to Montana in the spring of 1876. Custer not only made more peace agreements with the Indians than he fought battles, but his army career was damaged when he spoke up against the miserable way Washington was abusing native peoples. Custer himself is quoted as saying, "If I were an Indian, I often think, I would prefer to cast my lot among those of my people adhered to the free open plains rather than submit to the confined limits of a reservation."

This is not to say that Custer wasn't a man of the 19th century, with all of its prejudices and misconceptions, but he was better than most. And he had many friends among various Indian tribes.

I have no doubt that this novel will contain many errors, and many interpretations that honest people may disagree with. And it will likely inflame those who get their history lessons from television. For the errors, I apologize. But *Custer at the Alamo* is not, in the final analysis, intended to be a history book. This is an adventure story.

Gregory Urbach
Reseda, California

On these walls, we take our stand;
Our duty now made clear.
Life's sweet hopes can't blunt our cause
Nor Tyranny of fear.

On the hill, the arrows fly;
Soldiers dying side by side.
There is no future, just the past;
Fighting bravely to the last.

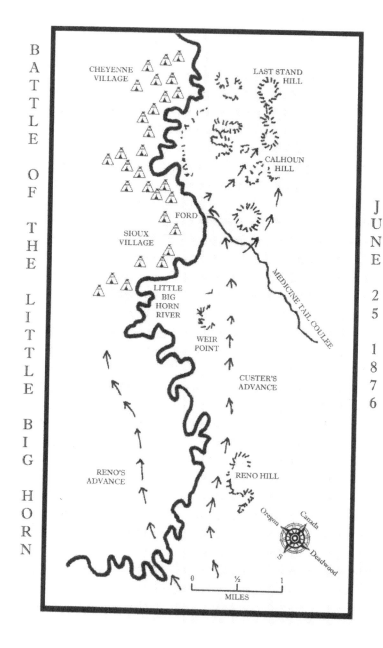

BATTLE OF THE LITTLE BIG HORN

JUNE 25 1876

CHEYENNE VILLAGE

LAST STAND HILL

CALHOUN HILL

FORD

SIOUX VILLAGE

LITTLE BIG HORN RIVER

MEDICINE TAIL COULEE

WEIR POINT

CUSTER'S ADVANCE

RENO'S ADVANCE

RENO HILL

Oregon
Canada
S
Deadwood

0   ½   1
MILES

CHAPTER ONE

LITTLE BIG HORN
JUNE 25, 1876

Once I was called Tatanka Iyotake, a leader of the Strong Hearts, medicine chief of the Sioux Nation. A man powerful in the ways of Wakan Tanka, the Great Spirit. We had fought the wasichu for many years, forced them from our sacred Black Hills, and some had signed a treaty to live in peace. But the white men came back. Always they come back.

We were gathering for one last hunt when the white general Crook attacked. We drove him away and traveled up the Rosebud River to celebrate. There I performed the Sun Dance, cutting a hundred strips of flesh from my body. In return, I received a vision of that which would come. The people rejoiced. Though another army of white soldiers were approaching, they would fall into our camp and perish. I did not tell my people of the vision's end, of our eventual defeat, or of the reservations. I did not tell them of the starvation and humiliation yet to come. Destroying this second group of bluecoats would mean the end of the Sioux nation for all time.

What could be done? What offering might Wakan Tanka accept to forge a different path? I began to pray as we crossed over the Wolf Mountains into the valley of the Greasy Grass, each day growing more pensive. Our numbers *increased as young men left the reservations to join us, the warriors soon numbering in the thousands. Never had the People gathered in such strength.*

On a quiet afternoon, the trouble began. Gunshots at the southern end of the encampment. The final battle had begun, a battle we would win but destroy our way of life. I did not reach for a weapon, nor even leave my teepee. I searched the mystic lands for wisdom from the Great Spirit. Deep into my heart, I looked for hope. A path not taken. Then a strange mist arose, lifting me, guiding me, but not in a direction I understood. Was this to be Wakan Tanka's answer?

A JOURNEY THROUGH GRAY CLOUDS

My name is George Armstrong Custer, once a major general in the United State Army during my country's Civil War. Because I've been known to embellish upon my accomplishments, there are some who may doubt the veracity of this account. I cannot explain the recent events that have led to this chronicle. I don't think there is an explanation. All I can do is relate the story to the best of my ability, and let history be the judge.

JUNE 25, 1876 - MONTANA TERRITORY

"They're down there, General," Lt. Varnum said as we studied the misty valley from a vantage point called the Crow's Nest.

The Little Big Horn was still a good fifteen miles away, a morning haze rising from the distant river. Even though I had borrowed Lt. DeRudio's Austrian binoculars, I could detect no evidence of a village.

"I don't see them. Not a one," I said. Not that I doubted Varnum's judgment, but I needed to know what we were up against.

I had pushed the command hard for three days, riding up the Rosebud River from the Yellowstone before crossing the divide over the Wolf Mountains. The Sioux and Cheyenne were nearby, gathered in strength but ready to flee the moment they realized the Seventh Cavalry was following their trail. I could not allow that. This needed to be a short war, brutal if necessary. A scattering of the hostiles would lead to the massacre of white settlers throughout the Powder River country and, inevitably, to the decimation of the Indians themselves.

Since my final conference with General Terry on the Yellowstone, we had traveled south through empty badlands. Six hundred cavalry and an unruly pack train driven by hired teamsters. Fifty Crow and Arikara Indians scouted our path. Needing to travel fast over rough ground, we had taken no wagons. I even rejected the two Gatling guns I'd been offered, afraid they would slow our march.

The late June weather was brutally hot, the Montana landscape already turned dry. Sagebrush and weedy gullies often hindered our passage. The only trees tall enough for shelter grew near the twisting creek that we were forced to cross several times.

The Wolf Mountains are low series of hills, the creek water so alkaline that we struggled to find a clean spring. The mules kept losing their packs, causing a good deal of cursing, but we had no trouble following the trail left behind by the Sioux. The wide path crossed from the Rosebud into the Valley of the Little Big Horn, the terrain torn up by heavy lodge poles and thousands of ponies. I guessed that several tribes lay ahead of us, mostly Lakota and perhaps a few Cheyenne.

We paused for several hours at the crest of the mountains. I would rest the command for a day, scout the enemy location, and attack at dawn on the 26th. That should give General Terry and Colonel Gibbon time to come downriver from the north and block any attempt at escape.

Varnum and I were still at the Crow's Nest, searching for signs of the elusive village, when I received word of a most disturbing nature.

"General, compliments of Captain Custer," Corporal Voss reported, a reliable young man acting as the regiment's chief trumpeter. "The captain says we've been spotted."

"How is that?" I asked, startled by the bad news.

"Lost some packs on the back trail. We was retrieving 'em when a bunch of hostiles saw us from a hill," Voss said.

I instantly realized there was no longer time to scout the village or wait for General Terry. If I was going to catch the Indians before they fled into the mountains, we would need to advance at once.

"So much for a surprise attack," Lt. Varnum lamented.

"We haven't lost the initiative yet," I replied. "Voss, my compliments to Captain Custer. Tell him to bring the entire command forward on the double."

By noon the Seventh Cavalry was in motion with barely a few hours rest. We crossed the divide and started down the long slope toward the Little Big Horn, reaching a lone teepee a few miles above the valley. A dead warrior lay inside, dressed in his finest regalia.

Though I had not been able to see the hostile village from the Crow's Nest, my scouts assured me they were waiting for us down in the grasslands, hidden by a series of steep bluffs. I sent Captain Benteen to the left with companies H, D and K to prevent the Indians from escaping into the foothills. Benteen and I had not been on favorable terms for many years. Though a good soldier, he was also a back-stabbing complainer, always seeking to cause trouble. But I wanted Captain Keogh with me, so Benteen, as the senior captain, won the assignment.

As Benteen split off with a hundred and twenty troopers, I preceded along a shallow creek until a group of mounted Sioux suddenly appeared on the trail ahead. They were not dressed in war paint or carrying their traditional weapons. It could be a hunting party, but they would soon sound the alarm.

I could not afford to delay, ordering Major Reno to cross the river and charge the village with three companies. This would panic the Indians and allow me, with five companies, to attack in flank and complete the rout. By nightfall the campaign would be over. I was already looking forward to seeing my beloved Libbie again. Maybe we would spend the holidays with the family in Monroe, or go to New York City for the winter.

"Autie!" my younger brother yelled.

Tom knew he wasn't supposed to address me informally in the field. My official rank was lieutenant colonel. Twelve years before, during the Civil War, I had achieved the rank of major general at the rambunctious age of twenty-five. But it was a brevet rank, subject to reduction when the war ended.

Tom had never been much for formality, however. Six years my junior, ruggedly handsome and largely self-educated, he had joined the Union Army as a private, only sixteen years old. By 1864 he held the volunteer rank of 2nd lieutenant, and by the end of the war, he had earned the brevet rank of lieutenant colonel. Now he was my aide-de-camp, newly promoted to captain only a year before.

There were times I envied my little brother. Tom seemed to have all the qualities I lacked, like cool judgment and a popular style of leadership. He also had one of my best qualities, having won the Medal of Honor during the Civil War. Twice. While winning the second award, he had been shot in the face at point blank range, leaving a long scar on his jaw. And even then, he refused to leave the battlefield. Tom bowed to no man when it came to courage.

"Autie, over here!" Tom shouted, waving from the back of his horse. "We can see the valley from this peak!"

I gave my brown sorrel a good kick in the flanks and followed Tom up a steep slope to a high point along the trail. I was followed by my adjutant, Lieutenant William Cooke, called Queen's Own because of his Canadian birth. Cooke was thirty years old, and, like Tom, a veteran of the Civil War. The day had turned unmercifully hot, the dust terrible, and the long marches necessary to bring us to the battlefield had the entire command exhausted. But we were still the Seventh Cavalry, the finest unit in the United States Army, so I figured we had plenty of fight left in us. I quickly realized we were going to need it.

"Goddamn, George, there must be ten thousand Indians down there," Lieutenant Cooke said, scratching his long bushy sideburns.

We had reached a rocky outcrop east of the Little Big Horn River atop a string of hundred foot bluffs. Cooke knew I didn't care for his swearing, but I overlooked the indiscretion.

"Not quite that many, Bill," I replied, though it wasn't a bad guess.

I turned to look back at our line of march. Coming down from the divide, the village had been hidden from view. Now the size of the enemy encampment was all too clear. The Indian agents, those grasping, corrupt bastards appointed by Ulysses S. Grant, had told us that only eight hundred Indians had left the reservations, but here were six times that number. The village stretched along this twisting tributary of the Big Horn River for at least a mile. Probably a thousand lodges. It was without doubt the largest gathering of Indians ever seen on the western plains. And I had blindly stumbled right into it.

I recalled my conversation with General Terry, a final conference on the paddle-wheeler *Far West* up on the Yellowstone. The Indians had been ordered to report to the reservations, and failing that, would be rounded up and sent back by force. Sitting Bull and the other non-treaty tribes had chosen to resist, making it the army's job to enforce the government's policy. General Crook was approaching from the south. Colonel Gibbon had come from Fort Ellis to the west, the Seventh Cavalry from Fort Lincoln to the east. We had endured five weeks of hard riding, trying to find Indians that didn't want to be found.

Well, now we had found them. No telling what had happened to General Crook. Colonel Gibbon was two days away, beyond supporting distance. If the hostiles were going to be defeated, the Seventh would need to do it alone.

"Reno's charging the upper end of the village, if you can call that lazy-ass attack a charge," Tom said. "Where the hell is Benteen?"

Down to our left, Major Reno was making a half-hearted assault on the village with his three companies. Reno had a brave Civil War record but didn't know squat about fighting Indians, and I suspect he had an unspoken fear of the savage red man. One generally shared by those who had seen the mutilated bodies of their victims.

Reno's approach had taken the Indians off-guard, but now they were stirred up madder than a hornet's nest, riding out against him in force on their war ponies. If Reno stopped his charge, if he gave up the initiative, not one of his hundred and twenty men would leave the valley alive.

I waved back to the ravine where my five companies were waiting. Two hundred and ten tired but brave soldiers anxious to get into the fight. The men cheered. They wanted to go home as much as I did.

Mitch Bouyer rode up. A grizzly half-breed scout, part French Canadian and part Santee Sioux, there was nothing about Indians that Mitch didn't know. With Bouyer came Sergeant Jimmy Butler of L Troop, the best marksmen in the regiment, and Mark Kellogg, a reporter for the *Bismarck Tribune*. Corporal Voss rode nearby with his trumpet, as did Sergeant Bobby Hughes, bearing my personal red and blue silk guidon.

"Told ya thar were too many Injuns, Gen'ral," Bouyer said, leaning forward on his saddle horn while chewing on a chaw of tobacco. Another habit I didn't approve of.

"We still have a chance," I said. "We'll charge the northern end of the village and ride through them. Where can we cross the river?"

Bouyer laughed, which annoyed the hell out of me.

"There's a ford 'bout two miles downriver, but we'll never make it across. The Sioux is gonna chase our butts up into the hills and chop us to pieces. Literally, sir. Chop us all to hell. We had better skedaddle if you wanna see another sunrise," Bouyer said.

"We will attack," I said.

I twisted in my saddle and motioned for the command to move out. We were being screened by the bluffs. With luck, which I've always been blessed with, we'd be in the village before they knew what hit them.

"Autie, you know this isn't going to work, don't you?" Tom whispered, riding close at my side.

"We're committed, Tom. It's got to work," I said.

"We can still fall back. Regroup," Tom suggested.

"If we retreat, the Indians will scatter. White settlers will be murdered from the Yellowstone to Deadwood. Civilian militias will massacre the Indians in retaliation, and not just the warriors. The squaws and children, too, like Chivington did at Sand Creek. Either we end this war today or get three months of blood. Is that what you want?"

"You'd rather be fighting with them, wouldn't you?" Tom asked, and not for the first time.

"If I was an Indian, I'd fight for my land and people. Just like you would. But we're not Indians. We're officers in the United States army," I answered.

I turned Vic around and rode down from the bluff into the ravine behind the ridge. Most of the command was already moving ahead. Cooke and Bouyer were waiting for me along with a young Italian private. Martini, I think he was called. Cooke gave Martini a written order for Captain Benteen to come on quick. His three companies were badly needed if we were to have any hope of success. Tom took a saddlebag of ammunition off Martini's horse.

"Gentlemen, to hell or glory," I said.

We rode hard to catch up with the command. Within minutes I heard heavy gunfire up ahead. Not just the Model 1873 Springfield carbines issued to the cavalry by the quartermaster, but rapid fire weapons. Winchester and Henry rifles. The Indians not only outnumbered us, they had repeating rifles, too.

From the top of a long draw that Bouyer called Medicine Tail Coulee, I saw we were already in trouble. Companies C and E, led by Captain Yates, were being repulsed at the river. The remaining three companies were climbing a ridge to the north struggling for high ground. Hundreds of Indians were pouring from the village on foot and horseback.

My headquarters staff charged on the heels of F Company, anxious to lead our comrades or share their fate. If nothing else, we were better armed than the average soldiers. I carried my .50-caliber Remington hunting rifle. Tom and Bill Cooke carried lever action 1873 Winchesters, as did most of my officers. Sergeant Butler carried a custom-designed .45/70 Sharps. Kellogg was a good shot with his Spencer rifle, while Bouyer insisted on keeping his old buffalo gun. It kicked like a sassy mule but could take a man's head off at six hundred yards. I also rode with two ivory-handled English Bulldog revolvers, one of which I drew as we rode toward the river.

I must admit, the odds didn't look good. But I had a plan. I always have a plan. If we could only . . . ?

Suddenly a swirl of dust kicked up. No, not dust, but a cloud. Gray at first, then black. I reined Vic in, the cloud so thick I could no longer see the trail. I shouted for Tom but couldn't hear him. The gunfire increased, coming so fast and loud it seemed impossible anyone could live through such a storm. I heard a swishing sound, like the air above my head was being cut with whistling arrows. And then more arrows, hundreds more, raining all around me. Men were screaming. Horses were neighing in their death throes.

Then, from the dust and confusion, there was a vision . . . no, a premonition. I saw myself standing on a weed-covered hillside surrounded by overwhelming numbers of Sioux and Cheyenne. My revolvers were so hot I could barely hold them, the ammunition nearly gone. Dozens of wounded soldiers lay around me in a circle of dead horses. Tom was yelling at me to get down as I stood near the colorful guidon Elizabeth had sewn for me, the tattered banner hanging limp in the airless heat. I looked back down the bleak treeless ridge, wondering where Benteen was. All I saw was a broken line of fallen soldiers. Why hadn't Benteen come to our support? Or Reno? Couldn't they hear the gunfire? The volley fire we'd used as a signal? Suddenly I felt a thud in my chest and fell over backwards, landing on a dead trooper. The shooting slackened off until all that remained was a deathly quiet and the smell of late spring grass.

The cloud drifted away. I was no longer on the blood-soaked hill. The day was no longer hot. And there were no Indians, only me and my horse. Vic kicked his white hooves and snorted, just as spooked as I was. The harsh wind was cold, damp with winter rain. I buttoned up my buckskin jacket and tucked my red scarf tighter around my neck. The mountains were gone, replaced by a broad, barren prairie.

Damned if it wasn't the most bizarre thing. I couldn't help wondering if I'd been killed, cast into some sort of purgatory for my sins. I'd lived a boastful life filled with a lust for glory, and though I loved my Libbie dearly, I had not been blind to the flirtations of pretty women. But that explanation made no sense. I have never believed in supernatural occurrences.

I wasn't dressed for winter. Like most of my officers, I wore a fringed leather jacket and buckskin pants, a blue campaign blouse, and a white wide-brimmed trail hat now stained gray with sweat. Except for my saddlebags, all of my kit was back with the mule train. A freezing blast of wind made me wish I hadn't cut my hair so short. That is, the hair I had left. My hairline had been receding for several years.

Wherever I was, it seemed a long way from where I'd started. I was born in New Rumley, Ohio, in 1839, and for awhile, I taught grade school. Maybe I would have stayed a school teacher if not for West Point, but I grew up reading of history's great heroes and always believed myself cut out for a special destiny. In 1857, a few months before my eighteen birthday, I entered the Academy by appointment of my local congressman, and though I graduated 34th in a class of 34, no one thought me stupid, merely undisciplined. I went straight from graduation to the First Battle of Bull Run, a green second lieutenant with more sass than sense.

That was fifteen years ago. Fifteen years of Civil War, garrison duty in Texas, suppressing the Ku Klux Klan in Kentucky, and fighting Indians on the plains. I'd spent eleven of those years as a Lt. Colonel with little chance of promotion. I retained the privilege of being called a general, my brevet rank during the war, but everyone knew my army career had reached a dead-end. Even my financial prospects had dimmed with a series of ill-advised investments. Perhaps it's not always a good thing to outlive one's moment of glory.

The cold, scrub-covered prairie rolled gradually toward the southwest. Vic was restless. I took out my pocket watch, the silver Waltham 57 that Libbie's father had left me. It had stopped, but didn't appear to be broken. I gave the crystal face a tap and it started ticking again. Had I forgotten to rewind it?

Vic and I would need water and shelter by nightfall. A light drizzle began. We traveled for more than an hour without hint of civilization, discouraging me greatly. The sun was setting, the weather turning to a nasty, bone-chilling frost. I had spent many such afternoons on the plains, for General Sheridan often placed me at the forefront of the government's efforts to pacify the West, but this day felt strangely different. This was not the same country I had ridden for so many years.

Then I saw smoke up ahead, just beyond a low hill. Puffy streaks of a campfire made with scrub wood. It could be Indians, or not. Feeling as I did, even enemies would be better than no one. From the top of the next rise, I found a pleasant surprise. Cavalry. Dozens of soldiers camped along a muddy creek huddled around a string of fire pits. A blue and red guidon embroidered with crossed sabers blew from a leafless tree.

I drew my pistol and fired a shot in the air. Two men wearing buckskin jackets jumped on their horses and rode in my direction. It was Tom and Bill Cooke.

"Autie! Autie, thank God you're all right," Tom shouted, his voice higher pitched than usual.

We dismounted and embraced. Somehow it had not occurred to me to worry about the young scallywag, thinking the strange adventure a delusion of my own. That belief had been an egocentric mistake. Sadly, not an unusual one.

"Are you okay?" I asked.

"Strangest damn thing anyone ever heard tell of. One minute we were forming a skirmish line along the ridge. Gunshots coming from every direction. Indians all over the place. Then this fog rose up. The next thing I knew, we were strung out across this plain. No Indians. No village. Nothing. Cold, though. Glad we finally got the fires started," Tom said.

"The command?" I requested.

"Still gathering up stragglers," Cooke reported, his accent as crisp as the chilly air. "We've counted ninety-two enlisted men and six officers. Seven, now that we've found you. And two civilians, Bouyer and Kellogg. Smith and Yates are leading search details. Harrington's trying to find enough brush for some shelters. No sign of Keogh or Calhoun yet. Doctor Lord is by the fire. Not faring so well."

"I'd like to get a feel of that fire myself. Any food?" I asked.

"Caught a couple of fish. Hope you don't mind the bones," Tom said with a grin.

We rode down to the water, a wide stream cutting a flat basin. A thick grove of cottonwoods lined the bank, providing a windbreak. I recognized men from several different companies, all tired and worried. Confounded by our unfathomable situation. The first order of business was a hot meal.

Captain George Yates and Lieutenant Algeron Smith rode in just before sunset with nineteen more men. Second Lieutenant Henry Harrington had made a bonfire on the hill to guide them. Among the newcomers was Captain Myles Keogh, my best officer and a soldier of long experience. Along with a few dazed troopers who had followed our signal, it brought our total to eight officers, the doctor, and a hundred and twenty-six enlisted men. What happened to the other members of my command may never be known. There was no sign of my brother-in-law, Jimmy Calhoun, or my nephew, Autie Reed. Thank God my youngest brother, Boston Custer, had been left behind with the pack train.

We made camp, such as it was, hunched down in a gully using tumbleweeds stuffed between trees to block the wind. Some of the men had shot a few skinny winter rabbits. A dreary quarter moon lit the prairie. The horses were tethered near the creek where they could chew the damp grass. Grain-fed horse weren't likely to thrive on such fodder, but I wanted to parcel out the oats slowly while they made the transition. There was no telling how long it might take to find proper stables.

"Going to be tough on them," Sergeant Major Sharrow said, stroking the neck of his favorite horse, a Morgan-Mustang mix named Sue.

A thirty-one-year-old Englishman from Yorkshire, William Hunter Sharrow was the Seventh's ranking non-commissioned officer, a burly man usually in charge of supply. And unruly men. Or really anything that needed attending to. Everyone knows that an officer without a good top sergeant is bound for failure, so I made sure to acquire the best.

"We only have a few pounds of fodder per animal," I said, for we had not thought it necessary to carry oats into battle.

"Better plan on riding easy for awhile," Sharrow recommended, though it sounded more like an order. "Switching feed on these mounts is gonna cause gastric disruptions. The sort of disruptions you don't wanna think about. Won't catch me riding at the back of the column for awhile."

"Thanks for the warning, sergeant-major," I said.

With our horses cared for and the men settled in, I gathered my officers around a campfire, everyone huddled as close as they dared. Saddle blankets were wrapped around our shivering shoulders.

"Well, Myles, you served with the Papal Guards. What would the Pope think of this?" I asked the tough Irishman.

"Don't know that the Pope thinks much about witchcraft," Keogh answered with a frown.

"Witchcraft?" Tom said, almost with a laugh.

"You got a better explanation?" Keogh asked, his brogue always stronger when he was excited.

"Not yet," Tom said, even less superstitious than I.

"What are we going to do, George?" Cooke asked, holding his hands close to the flames. It struck me as strange. My God, Cooke was a Canadian. Since when do they get cold?

"Rejoin the command, somehow," I said. "Jimmy is still out there, and Reno and Benteen. Terry will be coming up river sometime tomorrow with the Seventh Infantry."

"Don't think so, sir," Bouyer disagreed.

"Why is that, scout?" I asked.

Bouyer gave me that insolent look, again, his long stringy black hair sticking out from under a tall possum hat. He was not a member of the Seventh, having been loaned to me by General Terry. Bouyer and I had been acquainted for several years but were not on familiar terms.

"Cuz we ain't lost. We is goddamned stranded," Bouyer said.

"How's that?" Tom said.

"This ain't Dakota territory, Tommy boy. We're hundreds of miles south. Maybe a thousand," Bouyer said. "Just look at them stars. This here is Comanche country."

"Impossible!" Cooke sputtered.

"Stars don't lie, Canada," Bouyer said, taking a puff on his corncob pipe.

Tom held a cigar. Keogh and Smith had taken to rolling their own cigarettes. Georgie Yates sat quietly back, watching but saying little. Dr. Lord was half asleep, too tired to indulge. For myself, I hadn't had a smoke or hard alcohol since 1862 and wasn't going to start now.

"You're talking fantasy, like those dime novels by that Frenchmen," Lt. Harrington said. Twenty-seven years old, thin and blond-haired, Harrington was only four years out of West Point. Of my surviving officers, only he and 2nd Lt. Reily had not served during the Civil War.

"Jules Verne," Mark Kellogg said, a reporter's notepad in his lap.

"We'll know more when we reach a settlement. Should find something by going downriver," I said. "Saddle up first thing in the morning. Prepare for a hard day."

"Another one?" Doctor Lord unhappily said.

"Sorry, doctor. Not much choice," I replied.

Lord, normally a robust man typical of his native Massasschuetts, had developed a mild case of dysentery on the Yellowstone. The cold weather was making it worse. Chances were he wouldn't last long in the damp air.

As my officers rejoined their men, Yates paused by the fire. We'd first met back in Monroe during the war and served together with General Pleasonton. Four years younger than I, blond and blue-eyed, Yates's good temper never seemed to fail regardless of difficult circumstances. If I had a best friend, I suppose it would be George.

"What do you think the wives would say about this?" Yates asked.

"May be awhile before we find out," I replied.

"I told Annie to take the kids home to Michigan if the campaign went beyond summer. Hope it doesn't come to that."

"Libbie promised to stay at Fort Lincoln until I return. Probably put up those new lace curtains she keeps talking about."

"Any idea how long this will take?" Yates asked.

"Not a clue in the world, Georgie. Not a clue."

That night we slept bunched together for warmth. Most of the command prayed. I didn't.

We were on the move at dawn, following the creek until reaching a minor river. The command rode under a gray sky in column of twos, our horses enjoying a slower pace that the previous few days. The recent rain had swollen the river, making it difficult to cross. Not that any of us had a desire to get wet. The sun came out around noon, and given the short period of time it took to reach its zenith, it was clearly a winter day. Probably late winter. Running short of grain for the horses, we had to stop each time we found a pitiful patch of grass.

Tom and Cooke rode at my side. I envied the protection Cooke's mutton chops gave him from the cold wind. The battalion was divided into four groups, the largest detachments under the command of Yates and Keogh. Smith led a scouting party of twelve men, riding the trail ahead. Young Harrington was ordered to make a final sweep of the area for stragglers and catch up before sunset. Tom and I agreed that Bouyer might be right. After the Rebellion, we'd both had duty on the southern plains. This seemed more like Indian Territory than the Dakotas.

"Buff'lo, Gen'ral. Hundreds of 'em," Bouyer announced from the next rise.

Tough and stringy though it may be, a nice buffalo steak sounded awfully good at that moment. Tom and I went forward with Sergeant Jimmy Butler, we being three of the best shots in the regiment, leaving most back so as not to scare off the herd. Bouyer and Kellogg trailed behind. As civilians, they were only nominally under my authority.

It was a big herd, bigger than I'd seen in years. The shaggy beasts were gradually wandering southwest toward a misty valley in the distance. It's said there were once millions of buffalo, enough to cover an entire state, but hunters had been cutting the herds down to make fur hats. In another hundred years, I feared the buffalo might disappear entirely.

"First kill wins the prize," I said, giving Vic a nudge.

We galloped for a few minutes, then slowed as we approached a wide bend in the river where a stand of trees blocked our view of the valley. The grass was thick here, the soil too loose for hard riding. We climbed a low hill for a better view, and much to my surprise, spotted a small campsite about a thousand yards downstream. And not just any campsite. There were two buffalo hide teepees with half a dozen Paint ponies grazing nearby. Twenty paces from the camp, I saw a heavy freight wagon hitched to four white oxen. Several mules were tethered together. Two horses of the larger Kentucky breed were tied to the tailgate.

"Who the hell are they?" Tom asked.

"Sioux markings on the tents," Cooke said, looking through his field glasses.

"Maybe we're not so far south after all," I surmised.

"There's trouble down there," Kellogg observed, adjusting his wire rim spectacles for a better look.

I raised my Austrian binoculars, observing the scene with surprise and a bit of shame. Several Indians lay on the ground, possibly dead. Four white men in crude hunting leather stood about, three with old-fashioned muskets and one with a large knife. Two squaws and an Indian boy were hovering over the bodies. The man with the knife grabbed one of the squaws, a young woman with a very graceful figure.

"What's going on there?" Tom asked, standing up in his stirrups.

"Looks like those buffalo hunters are plundering the Sioux camp," I speculated.

"More than plundering. The fat one is ripping off the girl's dress," Cooke said.

"That son of a bitch!" Tom shouted.

Before I could stop him, Tom was riding full kilt down the hillside toward the camp, drawing his Colt .45 revolver.

Cooke and I started after him, but Tom's horse, Athena, was said to be Arabian. Fast as lightning. I might have kept close if I'd realized Tom was going to bolt. Vic was my battle horse, a Kentucky thoroughbred, and fearless in a charge. I'd owned him since taking command of the Seventh in 1866 and he'd never let me down. Cooke's horse was a little faster than Vic, but not by much.

"Tom! Tom!" I yelled, but the young gallant's blood was up.

Tom could never stomach abuse of a woman, Indian or not. Libbie had taught him that. He emerged from the war a brave man and decorated hero, but rough in his ways. It was Libbie who patiently molded her poorly educated brother-in-law into a gentleman. Of sorts.

The men in hunting leather turned to see Tom bearing down on them. Two were large, a third not so much, and the fourth short but stocky. All were thickly bearded, dressed warm against the weather. It was the stocky villain who was attacking the young Indian lass, a hand entangled in her long black hair while using a hunting knife to slash her deerskin dress. At first the hunters seemed to feel no danger, but gradually they took alarm as they sensed the approaching rider was not friendly.

Tom raised his Army Colt and fired from fifty yards away, the first shot missing. His second shot hit one of the hunters high on the shoulder, causing the man to howl in surprise. The other three marauders raised their muskets and fired, the reports echoing off the prairie.

I couldn't tell if Tom was hit, but he kept riding right into the camp, shooting another hunter several times at point blank range. The stocky man with the knife pushed the girl backwards and charged at Tom. Tom jumped from Athena and wrestled for the blade. The fourth hunter quickly started to reload, using an antique ramrod to jam a lead ball down the barrel of his rifle. The Indian lass and the older woman took flight for the teepees, dragging a young man with them. The Indian boy stood his ground, watching with curiosity while showing no fear.

The hunter with the knife was putting up a good fight, keeping Tom's attention from his treacherous friend. I pulled Vic to a halt and yanked my Remington .50-caliber from its sheath. It wasn't a long shot, only three hundred yards. Over the years I'd made many a fine kill, a few at five hundred yards or better. More often than not, I'd exaggerated the distance, as sportsmen are prone to do. But I could not afford to miss now. Not with my brother's life at stake.

Tom gave the stocky man a solid left hook, knocking him down, and then pounced. The other man finished reloading and took aim at Tom's back from ten feet away. I drew him in my sight, held my breath, and squeezed off a shot. The hunter's head exploded in a pink cloud, his arms flung out as he fell. Seconds later, Cooke rode up with his revolver ready and shot the wounded man attempting to reload his rifle. The man collapsed against the wagon, made a feeble attempt to lift his weapon, and then toppled over as Cooke shot him two more times. Tom took the knife away from the last remaining hunter and plunged it into his foul heart.

"Damn it, Tom," I chastised, riding in after the fighting ceased.

"No harm, Autie," Tom said, wiping a streak of blood off his forehead.

Two of the Indians lying on the ground stirred, knocked down but not killed. A third was dead, his brains bashed in with rifle butts. All three were young, late teens or early twenties. Of the two women, the graceful beauty seemed about eighteen, the other a crone close to fifty. Ancient by Indian standards. They had dragged an old man into the largest teepee, so old his age was beyond guessing. He had been struck over the head and appeared dazed. The Indian boy I took to be six or seven. A sturdy lad with intelligent black eyes. Bouyer rode up, ready to be our interpreter.

One of the young bucks got up, nursing a wounded arm but determined to be their spokesman. The young woman rushed forward, one hand holding her torn dress together, seeming even more intent on speaking for their party. They argued, silently. The woman won.

"My name is Morning Star," the woman said, her accented English easy to understand. "This is my little brother, Slow, and my cousins, Spotted Eagle and Gray Wolf. Spotted Eagle's mother is called Walking-In-Grass, and my grandfather's name is Jumping Bull. Our lost cousin was Closed Hand. We thank you for saving who you could."

Morning Star bowed gracefully. The other Indians merely watched, apparently unfamiliar with a civilized language.

"You speak well," Tom said.

"I spent two years at the St. Joseph school in St. Louis. You're hurt. Let me wash that cut," Morning Star said.

She found a piece of soft hide and dipped it in a water bag. Tom did not resist her ministrations. I motioned to Cooke and Kellogg to take care of the dead buffalo hunters. Bouyer reluctantly helped. The old Indian emerged from the teepee, wearing a headdress with scores of eagle feathers. He had counted many coup in his day.

"Are we near your village?" I asked.

"No, we have traveled south for many moons on a vision quest," Morning Star said.

"What does your grandfather seek?" Tom asked, taking a second look at the old fellow.

The ancient chief was my height, about five feet, nine inches. His finely cut rawhide outfit indicated a man of great dignity. His deep brown eyes looked tired, not from exertion, but from too many years of a hard life.

"Not my grandfather. It is Slow's vision we seek. Someday he will be a powerful medicine chief," Morning Star explained. "At first I thought we were searching for a white buffalo, for there are legends of such. Or maybe a white wolf. Now I'm not sure."

The boy came forward, first staring at me, then at Tom. I don't think he'd ever seen a white man before. But neither of us was a white buffalo or a white wolf. He wore a deerskin outfit decorated with red and blue beadwork. Rabbit fur mittens were keeping his hands warm. I gave him a smile, being fond of children. Libbie and I had never been blessed.

The explanation made sense. The group was traveling light with just the two teepees and a few horses to drag the lodge poles. An old iron pot hung over their fire, a fine stew offering a pleasant aroma. They had sufficient blankets and some supplies, but not so much as they would have closer to home. Having gone on hunting trips with my Ree scouts many times, I was familiar with the resourcefulness of the plains Indians. Nevertheless, these people were a long way from the Missouri River country.

Bouyer returned from the freight wagon, chewing a piece of jerky, a cured buffalo hide draped over his slim shoulders. It was a large wagon of an older style, like the ones I remembered seeing as a child. It lacked steel springs or a good brake, and the wheels were primitive. My father would never have allowed such a relic to leave his blacksmith shop.

"Buff'lo hunters were doin' good, Gen'ral. 'Bout a hundred or so skins. No horse blanket for me tonight," Bouyer said.

"We also found several sacks of flour, about fifty pounds of jerky, and six tins of coffee," Cooke said. "What should we do with the bodies?"

"Leave the curs for the buzzards," I rashly ordered, though I knew we'd have to bury them eventually.

"And the Indians?" Cooke asked.

"Once we figure where we are, we'll find transport for them back to the reservation," I said.

"Reservation?" Morning Star asked.

"Don't worry, miss. We'll get you home," I promised.

I saw Yates appear on the hill, the rest of the command not far behind. The night wouldn't be so cold with the confiscated hides for warmth, and hopefully there'd be enough coffee to go around. All we needed was to shoot a couple of buffalo and our bellies would be full. There was a canvas tent in the freight wagon for my officers, but I decided one of the teepees would serve better as my headquarters.

"Miss, my name is Tom. Tom Custer. We're going to make camp downstream. Would your family care to join us?" Tom asked. His cheeks were flushed, and not from the recent battle. I'd not seen that dance in his eyes since his fiancée had suddenly died a year before.

"Thank you, Tom. We will come after building a funeral scaffold for Closed Hand," Morning Star agreed.

"Autie?" Tom said.

"Sure, Tom. You and Kellogg give them a hand," I offered, knowing Indian funeral rites were fairly simple compared to Christian burials. And better for it. Maudlin words and empty prayers at tearful gravesides were not to my liking. I'd had enough of that during the war.

Between Cooke, Bouyer and myself, we had no trouble bagging a few buffalo. Sergeant Butler and Corporal Voss came up with some of the men to butcher the meat, cut poles for a travois, and drag carcasses down to the river. Harrington still hadn't caught up with us so I decided to make camp in a tree-lined hollow protected from the freezing wind.

As always, the first order of business was to take care of the horses. The mounts were checked for injuries, brushed down, fed and watered. A cavalryman without a horse is infantry, and we weren't going to get out of this perplexing situation on foot.

I led Vic down to the river myself, scratching him behind the ears and whispering my thanks for many years of loyal service. We'd left my other horse, Dandy, back with the pack train, along with my dogs, so I knew Vic was feeling lonely. A feeling I shared.

Once the horses were settled, campfires were made, the meat roasting on spits. Several jugs of spirits were found in the wagon. I did not indulge, but there was enough to give each man a splash. I kept Dr. Lord nearby while Tom and Cooke interviewed each member of the command, gathering all the information we could. Kellogg was busy making notes for his newspaper.

Harrington rode in just after sunset. There was no sign of Jimmy Calhoun, last seen down near the Little Big Horn River, or of my nephew, who had gone with him. Nor was there any trace of Major Reno or Captain Benteen. Wherever we were, we were on our own.

Our second night on the southern plains was better than our first. Lines were strung between the trees and draped with hides to make shelter for the enlisted men. The tent, teepees and the wagon provided snug quarters for my officers and our guests. There was plenty of driftwood lying along the river bank for our fires.

It seemed a good time to take stock. The battalion had been smartly attired when we'd left Fort Lincoln on May 17th, before toil and sweat had taken its toll. Most of my men wore dark blue campaign jackets, gray flannel shirts, and sky blue pants reinforced in the seat with canvas. A few wore checkered hickory shirts bought from post traders. Our hats varied from the standard black wool caps to store-bought slouches and even a few straw hats. Each man carried a canteen, coffee cup, field knife, a mending kit, and saddlebags with the basic necessities. Having a pack train is fine, but on a rapid march, it's always better to be self-sufficient.

There was one issue that didn't concern me. When we left the Yellowstone before going into battle, each soldier had been issued a hundred rounds of ammunition for their 1873 Springfield carbines and twenty-four rounds of .45 cartridges for their Colt revolvers, but most carried more, afraid the pack train wouldn't keep up. That had worried me, too. As we crossed the divide, I ordered each sergeant and corporal to carry an extra saddlebag. Because Tom and my officers owned repeating rifles, they carried their own supplies. With plenty of ammunition, I wasn't afraid of an Indian attack. We had enough firepower to ride through anything the hostiles might throw at us.

I took a brief stroll through the small camps the men had set up, saying a few words of encouragement. Such a gesture from me was rare, so I'm not sure if my boys were reassured or made more nervous. Most were in their mid-twenties, many from foreign lands.

"Don't worry, fellows. We're in good company," I said. "Bad weather, maybe, but worse at the Washita. Got enough to eat?"

"Still the Seventh, aren't we, sir?" Private Torrey of E Company said, looking brighter with a buffalo steak on his tin plate.

"Got coffee and a fire. Don't need no more," Corporal French added, a fine young lad from Portsmouth.

I could tell that many of my young recruits thought it strange we were camping with Indians, but I'd shared many campfires with Rees, Arikara and Crows. My best scout was Bloody Knife, a half-blood Sioux. Bloody Knife and I had shared many trails over the last eight years. After the Montana campaign, I expected to take him with me to Philadelphia for the Centennial celebration. Maybe even to Washington, if I decided to run for office someday. I wondered how he fared. The last time I saw him, he was riding down the Little Big Horn Valley with Reno.

I returned to my teepee, finding furs laid out near a quiet fire. Though the Indians would be sharing the other teepee, Morning Star and Slow were visiting with Tom. They had been generous with their blankets, a way of saying thank you. Dr. Lord was sleeping in the back, so I kept my voice low.

"Warm in here," I said, dropping my hide covering near the door and sitting cross-legged next to Tom.

"These teepees are amazing. I wish the quartermaster would order some for the regiment," Tom said, handing me a thin metal plate filled with roasted buffalo slices. There was a silver fork in my saddlebags, but I ate with my hands so as not to embarrass our Indian hosts.

"It's a blessing," I agreed, sorry the pack mules had not followed us more closely.

"Hot food has the men feeling better. We should make good progress now," Tom happily said.

"Progress to where?" I asked.

"To wherever you take us, Autie. Hell, we've been in worse spots than this," Tom answered. He was trying to keep my spirits up, which was very annoying.

"I guess we'll muddle through," I said.

"We do not see many white men this far west," Morning Star said, sharing a bowl of rabbit stew.

"You must live in a remote village, miss," I replied, finding the young lady charming. "From what my Indian friends tell me, the plains are swarming with too many white men."

"You have many friends among the People?" Morning Star asked.

"Not among the Sioux. I have been blood brother to the Arikara," I replied.

"There are times I think Autie wants to be an Indian," Tom said with a laugh, almost lighting a cigar before seeing my frown.

"That's not quite true," I disagreed. "I'm proud of the white race, but pride is not an excuse for breaking treaties or cheating the Indians on the reservations. Whenever I reflect on what the Grant Administration is doing, it makes me angry."

"I have not heard of these troubles," Morning Star said, confused.

"Then your village must be *very* remote," I said.

"White men have strange ways. They do not respect the land. They do not revere the spirits," Slow said, his words thoughtfully measured. It was his way of calling us a bunch of barbarians. Until that moment, I hadn't realized the boy even knew English.

"I've known white men who can't be trusted. Known Indians who couldn't be trusted either," I said. "But I think more people value the truth than not. I still remember the oath I took as a plebe back at West Point almost twenty years ago—'A cadet will not lie, cheat, or steal, nor tolerate those who do'. I may have earned more demerits than any other cadet in West Point history, but that is one oath I've never broken."

Slow took a sip of water from a hide bag without further comment. I had the impression he didn't believe me.

I did not understand Wakan Tanka's vision. My mind was suddenly younger, more hopeful, but troubled by a strange journey. My older sister and cousins, long since dead, now lived once more. We were far to the south of our hunting grounds searching for a white buffalo, or a white wolf, but instead we found a white man. A bitter enemy of the People. In what manner could this be a good thing?

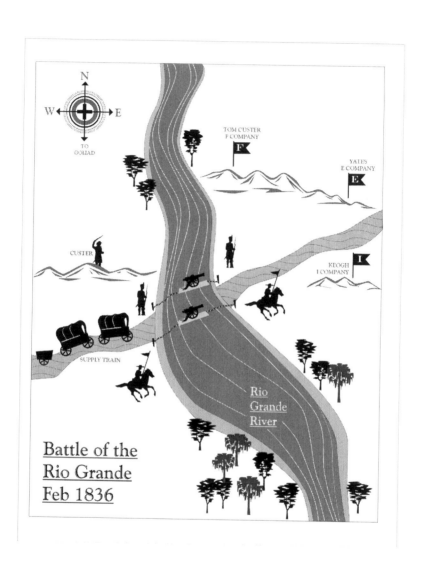

Battle of the
Rio Grande
Feb 1836

CHAPTER TWO

ENCOUNTER ON THE RIO GRANDE

The next morning, I decided it was time to reorganize the command. A company of U.S. cavalry generally holds sixty men and several officers, but we were under strength even before reaching the Little Big Horn. Now we had even fewer. Just after dawn, Corporal Voss trumpeted officer's call.

"Gentlemen, we need to make some adjustments," I announced, standing under a gray leafless tree outside my teepee. Each of my officers held a cup of coffee while Walking-In-Grass served fried trout for breakfast. The young Indian boy sat on a blanket, watching from a distance.

"Finally making me the general, Autie?" Tom asked with a sassy grin. I ignored him.

"We are reducing our five companies to four," I said. "It goes without saying that Cooke and Dr. Lord will remain with my headquarters staff. Company L is disbanded. Myles, as senior captain, you'll retain command of I Company. Harrington will be your executive officer. Draw five more men to bring your troop up to forty. You are the left wing of this regiment."

"Yes, General, thank you, sir," Keogh replied, pleased to be singled out first. But Keogh deserved it. Thirty-six years old, he was closest to me in age. Always reliable, he had fought in Italy before joining the Union army, rode with General Buford at Gettysburg, and held his own against Jeb Stuart in Virginia. By the end of the war, he held the brevet rank of lieutenant colonel.

He was a stout, thick-necked, tough as nails Irishman. A quality we badly needed.

"Fresh, you'll keep command of E Company. I can only spare twenty men for your unit. You'll hold the rear of the column and come forward when needed," I said next, knowing Lieutenant 'Fresh' Smith would be disappointed. "I don't have an executive officer for you, so select a man for temporary appointment. Sergeant Hohmeyer will do if you approve."

"Sure, Autie. Whatever's best for the command," Smith agreed.

A clean-cut thirty-three-year-old New Yorker, Algernon Smith had served honorably in the volunteer infantry during the war, brevetted to the rank of major. He had fought beside me at the Washita, served on the Yellowstone campaign, and again on the Black Hills survey. He was a founding member of the 'Custer Clan,' as Benteen derisively referred to those officers who had served me loyally over the years.

"F Company will be our right wing, thirty-six strong. Reily will be second-in-command," I continued, looking at Tom and Yates.

"And F Company's commander will be?" Yates asked.

A fair question. By rights, F Company belonged to Yates, but there was a complication. My brother had command of C Company for several years, first as a lieutenant and then as its captain, but only fifteen members of his troop had survived. Giving Yates the larger command would leave Tom with nothing but a platoon. I could see the anxiety in his expression.

"Georgie, F Company is yours. I know you won't let me down," I said.

"I never have, Autie," Yates said, giving Tom a consoling pat on the knee.

Tom tried to smile, being a good sport. It wasn't as if I'd given the assignment to one of the junior officers.

"Tom, you'll continue serving as my aide-de-camp. I need you close by to keep me out of trouble," I soon added. "And if something happens to me, I want you to take command of the entire regiment. Under these extraordinary circumstances, I'm giving you a field promotion to major."

Tom was happily surprised. The men clapped, everyone offering congratulations, for Tom had earned their respect many times over. If there was any jealously from Keogh or Yates, they were kind enough not to show it.

"What about Butler?" Smith asked.

"What about him?" I said.

"He's the best shot in the regiment and was assigned to L Company, which no longer exists. Seems to me E Company needs him the most," Smith explained.

"I Company needs him the most. We have the harder march," Lt. Reily protested. Born in Washington D.C. and all of twenty-three years old, William Van Wyck Reily was now low man on the totem pole. Maybe if he's stayed in the Naval Academy at Annapolis, he would have become an admiral instead.

"We can cut cards for him," Yates said, producing a well-used deck from his breast pocket.

"Sounds like a plan," I said, taking the deck away from him.

I cut the cards, cut them again, and then flipped the deck over to pick out the ace of spades.

"Sorry boys, looks like I win," I said, holding the card up for everyone to see. The men groaned.

We continued southwest for several days, hunting, fishing and seeking forage for the horses. There was talk among the men. Some thought we were lost. Some thought we were dead. Some thought to desert, but I ordered my officers to shoot anyone who tried. This was no time for discipline to break down.

I had thought our Sioux companions might make good guides, but they were strangers to the territory. Spotted Eagle and Gray Wolf soon attached themselves to Bouyer, who was fluent in the Lakota language. Bouyer suppressed the anger he felt at all Sioux, who had ostracized him as a boy. Apparently the scout was unwilling to blame these youngsters for the sins of their fathers.

The young braves proved to be good students and eager scouts. Walking-In-Grass and Jumping Bull took up residence in the wagon, Sergeant Bobby Hughes and Corporal Henry French becoming my teamsters. Morning Star and Tom became inseparable, much to my concern. I did not object, in principle, for she was good company and had a lovely laugh, but I remembered my relationship with a young Cheyenne woman several years before. Such affairs never turn out well.

After being held up for two days by persistent rain, we finally reached a river large enough to suggest eventual civilization. I wondered if we might be heading toward the Missouri River, or even the Mississippi, but our course kept turning in the wrong direction. We could not wander forever. There was little forage for the horses, and the buffalo had disappeared. The few game animals we found were not enough to feed the whole command for very long, nor could we depend on the occasional fruit tree and berry bush. Such concerns had me worried, though I did not reveal my thoughts. Right or wrong, a commander in the field must never show doubt.

Finally, seven days after our mysterious encounter with the gray fog, we recognized our location. And discovered an incomprehensible event.

"It's the Rio, Gen'ral, no doubt 'bout it," Bouyer reported.

"The Rio Grande? The Rio Grande River?" I asked again.

"Ain't no lie. We're about half a day from the Old Camino Real. Cross over into Mexico if ya want to," my scout said.

"I have no intention of going into Mexico," I replied in a huff.

"At least we know where we are," Tom said with relief. "If we turn east, we can reach San Antonio in a few days."

"You been there before?" Bouyer asked.

"General Custer and I served in Texas after the war. Mostly stationed in Austin, but we took in a few of the sites," Tom explained.

I remembered those days with fondness. The French government had used a debt crisis as an excuse to conquer Mexico. Our government was afraid the Emperor Maximilian might give aid to unrepentant Rebs, some of who had fled into Mexico hoping to raise a new army. The Fifth U.S. Cavalry was sent south to watch the border and maintain civil authority. Tom Rosser, my old West Point roommate, had come from Texas and bragged about how nice the people were. He'd been right.

"We'll make camp at noon, then start for San Antonio in the morning," I announced.

"We've still got half a day of sunlight, General," Cooke protested.

"We've also got three rivers to cross. Tell Keogh to draw in our flank but keep a sharp eye out for hostiles," I ordered.

"Yes, sir," Cooke said, saluting before riding off.

"Anxious about the horses?" Tom guessed.

"I pressed too hard coming down the divide, exhausting the men and the mounts. By the time we stumbled into the village, we were in no shape to fight. I'm not going to make that mistake again," I explained.

"I'll go forward with Bouyer. Find a campsite," Tom offered.

"I will go, too," Morning Star said, bundled up against the cold on her Indian pony, a white mustang with brown spots and black hooves.

"Are you now scouting for the Seventh Cavalry, young lady?" I asked.

"I will hunt for berries and roots. Thomas and his brother will eat well tonight," Morning Star said with a smile.

My scouting party moved ahead. I lingered behind, waiting for E Company and the wagon while considering looking for some game. I was in no hurry. Even after we reached San Antonio, what then? How would I explain to General Sheridan that four-fifths of my command had disappeared? And how could anyone explain our magical appearance in Texas?

"You must not leave the trail," Slow suddenly said.

The Indian boy was standing up in the wagon, staring at me with disapproval. Jumping Bull sat next to him, nodding agreement.

"What do you mean, youngster?" I asked, using a few hand signals to make my question clearer.

"The birds say you must continue south," Slow explained.

"Nothing but dirt and mud to the south. We've got a fair-sized town to the east," I replied.

"Enemy wait for you," the boy said, pointing down the trail.

"Comanche?" I asked.

"Enemy," Slow said.

His eyes were big and black. Determined. Possessed? Did some dark spirit…? No, I didn't believe such nonsense. Then again, it wouldn't hurt to reach the Camino Real before turning east. Even a dirt road would be easier than going cross-country in such bad weather.

"Okay, boy, we'll hold the trail a few more hours," I agreed.

Slow sat down without responding. Not even a smile of satisfaction.

Just before noon, I saw a messenger riding hard in our direction. We were fairly close to the river, which at this point of the Rio Grande's course, was mostly brown mud churned up by the recent rains. I stayed with Dr. Lord near the wagon, the pace sluggish because of the storm-soaked trail. The messenger was Corporal Voss. He'd thrown off the buffalo hide, riding in his blue tunic, a yellow scarf flapping in the wind.

"General Custer! General Custer! You won't believe it!" the young man yelled. His blue eyes were wide with excitement, the shaggy blond hair spotted with mud. Voss spoke English well despite his German accent.

"Calm down, boy. Are we back in Dakota?" I asked.

"Major Custer says to come on quick. I'm to find Captain Keogh," he said, spurring past me without another word.

It would have been nice to know what the shouting was about, but communication has never been my battalion's strong point. Something to work on. I turned to Harrington, the only officer riding with my group.

"Harry, have Yates draw the command up to escort the wagon. Tell Smith to follow on my trail. C Company, you're with me," I ordered, giving Vic a gentle kick.

We moved at a trot for several miles, sometimes following the course of the river, sometimes cutting over low weed-covered hills. Spotted Eagle and Gray Wolf rode up beside me, agitated by the suspense. Spotted Eagle carried a musket taken from one of the dead hunters, a long ungainly buffalo gun that must have weighed twelve pounds. Gray Wolf not only carried a musket, but he had Tom's spare Colt .45 tucked in his waistband. If Spotted Eagle wanted one of my Webley Bulldog revolvers, he was going to be disappointed. The ivory-handled pistols had been a gift from an admirer and I had no intention of giving them up.

A quarter mile short of the Camino Real, Cooke came out to meet us, holding up a hand for silence. We dismounted and left the horses with Private Engle, creeping up on a long barren ridge. Tom, Bouyer and Morning Star were laying flat on the ground, looking at the river.

"They've got to be crazy," Tom whispered.

I couldn't agree more. Below us, at the ford, was a Mexican army, and they were invading the United States!

"Counted five hundred so far, Gen'ral," Bouyer said. "'Bout fifty cavalry and three hundred infantry."

"The rest appear to be teamsters and camp followers," Cooke said. "We've spotted four freight wagons, two siege cannon, three field pieces, and dozens of carts."

The line of weary soldiers and two-wheel carts spread back along the Camino Real for a mile, but most of them were stopped at the river where the cold choppy water presented an obstacle. The Mexicans' uniforms were largely blue jackets and white slacks, though the dust of the prairie gave everything a brown tint. They looked tired, as if they'd been on the move for several weeks.

"Got to be a hundred draught animals down there. Horses. Mules. Oxen. Few head of cattle. Haulin' lots of supplies for somebody," Bouyer added.

Bouyer was right, and it was the siege guns that had stalled their progress. A pair of 12-pounders were mounted on two rafts, buffeted by the current. Such large cannon are never easy to move. A few cavalry and a squad of infantry had reached our side of the Rio Grande, but only one freight wagon had made it across. It would take them the rest of the day to complete the crossing.

"This isn't the advance guard," Tom said.

"No, it isn't," I agreed, studying the scene through my field glasses.

The invaders had not posted guards. The infantry looked footsore. Their cavalry horses, by all appearances of poor stock, were nearly played out. The column was pushing hard to catch up with their main body. If there were five hundred here, there would be twenty-five hundred ahead of them. If not more. What had possessed the Mexican government to engage in such a foolhardy adventure?

"San Antonio?" Cooke wondered.

"Can't think where else they'd be going. Our closest garrisons are in Austin and Galveston, hundreds of miles away," I guessed.

"What should we do?" Tom asked.

"No question about that. We will attack," I decided.

We crawled back down the ridge. Corporals Brown and French were my acting orderlies. C Company was drawn up behind the low hill, fourteen men clutching their rifles. Within a few minutes, Smith arrived with E Company, giving us about forty troopers. Most of the command was still on the back trail.

"Ten to one odds, Autie," Tom warned.

"You're right, Major Custer, but once the invaders have their big guns across the river, they'll be difficult to assault. Better to throw them into confusion now while Keogh and Yates come forward."

"Algernon and I can hold this ridge," Tom said, studying the ground. And without another word, he walked off and started issuing orders.

"Corporal Brown, my compliments to Captain Keogh," I said. "Tell him to swing his troop east, block the road to San Antonio, and then come on strong toward the river. French, you are to find Captain Yates. Have him come forward at a gallop to support Major Custer. If the firing has already started, he's to pitch into whatever he finds. And get Voss back here on the double. We'll need him to sound the charge."

I was speaking fast. Excited. Cooke took out his notebook and scribbled a few quick instructions for my messengers.

"Sergeant Major, be sure keep the men low. We want the element of surprise. The moment those siege guns reach our side of the river, the entire command is to open fire."

"Yes, General," Sergeant Major Sharrow with a salute.

I looked around, seeing everybody busy, some taking positions on the ridge, others holding our horses to the rear. Tom and Smith were doing a good job of placing the men in skirmish order.

"I need four volunteers," I announced.

"Reckon that's me," Bouyer said.

"And me," Cooke said.

"You need a good shot, General. I'm the best," Sergeant Butler said.

"Second best," I disagreed.

"Sorry, sir, you're wrong about that," Butler insisted.

"Jimmy, I once went shot for shot against Buffalo Bill," I protested.

"Yeah, and I once heard Cody isn't the great shot he pretends to be," Butler replied, patting the heavy Sharps rifle lying across his lap.

Gray Wolf and Spotted Eagle raised their muskets, volunteering to go with us.

"Bouyer, tell the youngsters this is not their fight," I ordered. Bouyer exchanged a few words. He looked surprised.

"Gen'ral, they say Slow told 'em to expect a fight an' stay with you. They ain't going no place you don't go. Is it true? Did the boy know 'bout the Mexicans?" Bouyer said.

"The boy didn't say anything to me about Mexicans," I answered, telling a half-truth. No point in getting everybody spooked by a child mystic. "Come on, boys, let's ride."

With my small detachment, we went back up to the nearest bend and plunged into the cold river. Crossing any river can be difficult, especially one as wide as the Rio Grande. The water buffeted us harshly, and for a moment, I was worried we might be washed downstream. Fortunately, our mounts found footing most of the way, and we were only forced to swim a short distance.

Once we reached the opposite shore, we travelled west a good half mile before turning south, seeking to avoid Mexican patrols. The land here was rolling prairie prone to occasional flooding. Stringy trees and prickly bushes sprang up in pockets. The Comanche Indians were known to roam these badlands before disease and war with the Texas Rangers whittled down their numbers. As far as I was concerned, the Comanche could have it back.

We soon reached a shallow ravine north of the Mexican column, dismounting in a dip fifty yards from the old Spanish road. While Butler and Cooke kept the horses quiet, I went alone to scout the new position. One of the 12-pounders was finally across the river, the raft pulled up on the muddy shore. The long iron cannon must have weighed fourteen hundred pounds, making it hard to manage. Several soldiers were untying the carriage wheels so it could be rolled to higher ground. The other raft was nearly on the embankment.

I noticed a second freight wagon had been floated to the eastern shore. More than fifty smaller wagons, filled with sacks of beans and supplies, were impatiently waiting their turn to cross. The enemy looked exhausted, ready to make camp. A colonel in a smart blue uniform was issuing orders, a plumed gold helmet on his head and a gleaming saber at his side, but most of the Mexicans appeared armed with old-fashioned muskets and lances. Their clothes were soiled, some almost in rags. I assumed many were peasants, not considered worthy of the regular army.

"What are you thinking, General?" Cooke asked, always more respectful of my rank when the shooting was about to start.

"I was recalling that time back in 1866, when President Juarez offered me command of the Mexican cavalry, but Grant refused to let me accept the appointment. He claimed that an American officer serving the Mexican revolution would set a bad precedent."

"Hell, sir, you wouldn't have been the first American officer to accept a foreign appointment. John Paul Jones did," Cooke said, though such accommodations are rare.

"I think Grant was jealous, afraid of the glory I'd win defeating the French. Had he decided differently, I'd have whipped the Mexican army into shape and overthrown Maximilian in three months."

Though I did not reveal my thoughts to Cooke, I have often wondered what might have happened next. Would I have remained in Mexico? Become a general and entered politics? Certainly under my guidance, this army of peasants crossing the river would not be such a rabble.

"What's our plan, sir?" Cooke asked, his Winchester held ready.

Bouyer had his old buffalo gun, Butler carried the Sharps. The Indian lads carried muskets and arrows. Combined with my Remington hunting rifle, we could boast a good punch.

"Tom and Keogh will be the hammer. We are the anvil," I announced, the cold rattling my teeth.

Bouyer looked at me with an expression bordering on insubordination, then looked at Cooke, Butler and the two young braves.

"Gen'ral, we sure is one mighty small anvil," he said, spitting from a chaw of tobacco.

"Be sure to make every shot count," I replied.

It was really only a guess, but I'd used this plan against the Rebs in the Shenandoah. Not with just six soldiers, of course. I was hoping for similar good fortune now.

After digging into our new position, I studied the Mexican army as they boarded rafts and attached logs to help float the remaining wagons. A dozen long ropes were keeping the rafts from floating away as soldiers on the far shore pulled the lines in. All was quiet on the hill beyond the river, which was good. Tom was waiting to strike with maximum advantage, and I expected nothing less from him. Keogh would arrive soon and need no explanations. He had once raided deep behind enemy lines with General Stoneman. Though fond of drink, as are all the Irish, Keogh was not a drunk like Reno.

"Something's happening, Gen'ral," Butler said, having taken a forward position.

I crawled up to the edge of the draw but didn't need my field glasses, for the river was less than a hundred yards to my left.

"The second cannon is finally up on the sand," I observed. "Looks like the officers will make camp once the freight wagons are over."

"There's two hundred soldiers on the other side. Only a hundred left on our side. The rest are just helpers, not even armed," Cooke said, always a good judge of such things.

"I'm surprised they've got so many women traveling in their train. Even old women. This is a small town, not a troop movement," I observed with contempt. Not that wives occupying officers on campaign was unusual. Libbie had often traveled with me during the war. The rank and file were expected to leave their women home.

"Aim for the non-commissioned officers first," I ordered.

"Hey, that's not fair," Sergeant Butler objected.

"War's not fair, Jimmy. Especially this kind of war," I replied.

Hardly a minute later, gunfire opened on the far side of the Rio Grande. I saw an officer in gold braid topple from his horse. Two sergeants went to his aid only to be wounded. Then another uniformed soldier dropped, the commonly dressed peons being ignored.

For just for a moment, the entire enemy army appeared to freeze. Birds had burst from the trees at the first shots, horses had bucked, and startled soldiers were looking in every direction. Then a young *soldado* shouted the alarm, echoed by a dozen others. Sergeants ran to their squads, tightening the chinstraps on their tall shako hats. Infantry reached for their muskets. Officers rushed to issue orders. The sandy riverbank became a mass of confusion.

As a full volley was fired from the low ridge, a troop of dragoons rode forward, drawing pistols. Their striking red jackets were trimmed in blue and highlighted by white cross straps. Most carried long wooden lances and wore silver helmets dressed with black plumes. For light cavalry, they made a marvelous spectacle, but forming as they did was not an effective tactic against rifles fired from a prepared position. The dragoon commander was shot from his saddle. Then the flag bearer was wounded, the banner fluttering to the ground.

"Guess they were surprised," Cooke whispered, kneeling at my side.

"They'll try to rally," I said.

"Tom won't give them time," Cooke replied.

He was right. I watched as a junior officer ordered the bugler to sound recall, but when a second volley tore through their troop, the rest of the dragoons scattered, the majority attempting to regroup downriver.

The sudden withdrawal of the cavalry had the Mexican infantry scrambling, shaking mud off their muskets while looking for their sergeants. Most of the soldiers were dressed in blue tunics with white straps across their chests. Along with the tall shako hats, which appeared to be standard issue, they carried leather ammunition pouches on their wide black belts. Nearly all had long knives and bayonets. A few of the Mexicans knelt to fire at the ridge, the shots sporadic, but a return volley knocked several of them down.

There was just as much confusion on our side of the river. The wagons all came to a halt, the teamsters jumping from their seats. Skittish animals bucked, causing some of the carts to spin around. Women grabbed children, seeking shelter from stray gunfire, while old men desperately tried to pull their mules off the road. There was a great deal of noise and shouting.

The soldiers nearest our position knelt, looking toward the opposite shore, not sure where the shots were coming from as the entire ridge was bathed in gray smoke. Their officers acted more quickly, issuing orders while drawing swords. Slowly, fifty or so men started moving toward the riverbank, but their view of the fight was largely blocked by the dragoons splashing at the water's edge. And there wasn't much to see. Tom was keeping the men so low that even I couldn't tell their numbers.

In the first few minutes of the fight, at least twenty of the enemy lay dead or wounded, but they didn't give up easily. Nearly two hundred soldiers eventually responded to the orders of their officers, loading muskets and forming into units. I expected them to make a bayonet charge up the gentle slope, for Tom's men were only seventy-five yards away. When I saw that Yates had arrived, I knew Tom had the firepower to discourage an attack, but if the Mexicans were determined enough, they just might carry the position with an all-out assault.

But to my amazement, the enemy did not charge. They formed into long ranks, like the Napoleonic armies of 1800, and prepared to return fire while waiting for their field artillery to be unlimbered. As such, they were merely targets.

The firing from the ridge paused. Tom was also surprised, but he only hesitated for a moment. Just as the enemy was about to fire, a fearsome volley was unleashed into the Mexican ranks. Whole groups of men fell where they stood, and before the enemy quite grasped what had happened, another volley cut down even more. Men were sprawled along the shore moaning in pain, torn open by .45 calibur bullets. There was so much blood it couldn't soak into the ground, running down the beach in rivulets.

The Mexicans finally raised their muskets and returned fire, dust kicking up all over the slope, but if they hit anything it was a miracle. It seemed the enemy's weapon of choice was the Brown Bess, a sturdy old smoothbore musket with a limited range of accuracy.

I had not even seen a Brown Bess since visiting the collection of old firearms at the New York Historical Society. To fire the ancient weapon, the Mexicans needed to stand upright, jam a powder charge down the barrel using a ramrod, drop in a lead ball, pack the charge with the ramrod again, and then put a spot of gunpowder in the musket's firing pan before aiming and pulling the trigger. A long and clumsy process, even for a trained professional. Our Springfield 1873 carbine was a completely different creature. All we had to do was open the firing chamber, put in a bullet, close the chamber using the lever, and fire. A raw recruit could easily fire six or seven times for every shot fired by the Brown Bess.

Still another volley erupted from the ridge. Tom had his sergeants controlling the fire, taking their time to hit what they aimed at. The Mexicans began reloading as their non-commissioned officers shouted orders. But before they could raise their muskets and fire again, Tom's next volley tore all along their line. Most of the enemy fire went wild.

At this point I expected the Mexicans to withdraw, spreading toward the flanks while keeping a small holding force behind the supply wagons. As such, they could use their superior numbers effectively. But for the next several minutes, nothing of the kind developed. The enemy stood their ground, reloading as best they could, reforming among the bleeding bodies of their comrades.

Upon the desperate orders of their officers, and Mexicans finally fired a full volley at the ridge, dirt bursting along the crest. And then there was a pause. Beyond the noise of frightened animals and crying children, the battlefield across the river hung in a strange calmness. A calmness that was soon shattered.

My personal guidon appeared atop the ridge, followed by the regimental stars and stripes, the banners flapping in the wind. Then sixty mud-streaked cavalrymen rose to their knees, taking careful aim, and unleashed a storm into the Mexican ranks. Two more explosions followed so quickly that the Mexicans never had time to reload, their formations crumbling. Even the officers realized their position was untenable, but there was no place on the beach for them to entrench. On my side of the river, the hundred or so soldiers who had rushed to the water's edge were waiting for orders to fire. A young officer on horseback was watching but hesitant to act, fearing to hit his own men.

Just as the battered enemy was drawing back toward the ford using the supply wagons for cover, Keogh's command suddenly appeared at the top of the hill with guidon flying. I could only see a few cavalrymen at first, then a dozen, and finally Keogh's whole troop of forty. They looked like a hundred, filling the eastern horizon.

"Now!" I shouted, stepping up and firing at the closest blue uniform. My first shot hit him right between the white cross straps.

Cooke stood up beside me, levering his Winchester repeater and knocking out eight shots in a matter of seconds. Butler took an extra moment to sight his Sharps, killing a captain at eighty yards. Bouyer fired the buffalo gun, the bark so loud it sounded like a small cannon. The surprise flank attack soon caused the enemy to scatter.

"General, watch out!" Cooke shouted, hurrying to reload.

I glanced at Cooke, then saw a brave Mexican corporal kneeling twenty yards away, pointing an old smooth-bore pistol at me. There was no time to reload my rifle, so I reached for one of the Webley Bulldogs, though it appeared I had reacted too late. Suddenly Spotted Eagle jumped in front of me, raised his bow, and sent a shaft through the young corporal's throat. The man's hand jerked up, the shot fired wild, and he rolled backward, legs kicking in his death throes.

"Thanks, youngster," I said, though I still had no intention of giving him one of my pistols. The young brave drew a knife, anxious to claim the corporal's scalp. Bouyer came forward to explain that no trophies could be taken until after the battle.

What had started as an ambush against a superior force now disintegrated into a rout. For whatever reason, the invaders simply had not anticipated an attack at the river. Many of their senior officers were killed in the first few minutes, their sergeants slain as they tried to organize the bewildered troops. The rest began throwing down their arms or fleeing downstream. When Spotted Eagle and Gray Wolf raced forward with fierce Lakota Sioux war cries, the civilians on our side of the river shrieked in terror. Most of the women fled into the desert. Those who didn't dropped to the ground in tears of despair, suspecting an assault by a hoard of wild savages.

"What's that they're saying?" I asked Bouyer.

Though not completely ignorant of Spanish, having studied the romance languages at West Point, my hearing no longer had the clarity of youth. Fifteen years of battlefields will do that.

"They're beggin' us not to unleash our Injuns," Bouyer said with a chuckle. "Get scared enough, two Injuns can look like a thousand."

As the shooting stopped, I cradled my rifle and walked fearlessly into the enemy position, for a confident victor inevitably fares better than a timid one.

Across the river, Keogh and Tom's commands were coming down toward the beach in a steady line, rifles ready for treachery. Neither company had found it necessary to mount a charge, saving men and horses. I heartily approved of their prudence.

"Who's in command here?" I shouted.

Bouyer immediately repeated my words in Spanish, saying it several times. A captain came forward, a bullet hole in his arm.

"*Tengo el honor, señor,*" the young officer said.

He was a tall, handsome fellow, with dark eyes that betrayed a good education. His uniform, even frayed from the battle, was quite elegant, a royal blue jacket, high black boots, and a red sash around the waist. A Toledo sword and steel helmet topped with a feathered plume marked him as a gentleman, probably of Spanish descent.

"You may treat your wounded, sir, if you will promise to give us no trouble," I offered, letting Bouyer translate.

Though I had rarely needed to speak Spanish since my trip to Texas ten years before, much of the conversation seemed clear. Nevertheless, Bouyer's interpretation would prevent unfortunate misunderstandings.

The young officer thought for a moment, now realizing our numbers were small but better armed. The man was no fool.

"*Mi libertad condicional se ha dada, señor,*" he said, offering me his sword. I accepted the blade and passed it over to Cooke.

"Nice," Cooke said, feeling the weapon's weight. The steel blade was finely engraved in Latin. The handle was made of silver and decorated with silk ribbons.

"Myles was unhappy about leaving our pig-stickers back on the Yellowstone," I recounted. "Give him this one, with my compliments."

"And the prisoners?" Cooke asked.

I turned back to the young captain. Though I had many questions, this was not the time or place.

"Stack all arms near the wagons," I ordered. "Take your tents and a day's rations to that clump of trees downriver. We'll discuss your return to Mexico later."

"*Señor, estamos en México,*" the captain rudely responded.

"Not all of you," I answered, believing it at the time.

Cooke and I went to the water's edge where Tom was asking the same questions, though he didn't need an interpreter, having learned the language well enough during our previous assignment. I have no doubt he spoke Spanish with a brothel accent.

"Autie?" Tom called out.

"All's well. Send everyone but the officers back over before it gets dark," I answered. "And have Smith turn those 12-pounders around in case they try invading our country again."

––––––––––

It took several hours to straighten out the aftermath of the skirmish, and by then the sun was setting. We made fires from driftwood found along the river and posted guards every twenty yards from our camp. Two Mexican officers had been kept on our side of the Rio Grande, the rest of the invaders sent back after we had confiscated their best wagons and horses. We expected the rank and file to melt away during the night, for the last thing I needed was three hundred prisoners of war.

"Congratulations, sir," Harrington said, coming in from his post with a shiver. Harrington hadn't shaved since leaving the Yellowstone, giving him a bedraggled appearance. My other officers fared no better; Tom, Cooke and Dr. Lord all looked like steamer tramps. Finding shaving kits for my officers would soon be a priority.

The night had turned cold enough that even a good buffalo hide wasn't always sufficient, though we also had wool coats discovered in the captured wagons. We also found plenty of tents, blankets, lanterns, and most of the necessities left behind at the Little Big Horn. There was even a box of silverware made in Italy, complete with plates and goblets. And several cases of fine wine, not that I would personally indulge.

"Not much of a battle, Harry," I said, eating my fill of tortillas and beans. Which is about all the Mexicans had brought with them out of the desert. It was the most poorly supplied army I'd seen since Lee's retreat from Petersburg. Eventually we would butcher a few of the cattle, but for now we made do.

"But a victory nevertheless," Harrington said. "And on the 4th of July, no less. They'd be singing your praises at the Centennial if they knew."

I hadn't realized the date, but Harrington was right. It was the 100th anniversary of the Declaration of Independence. When the news got back to Philadelphia where the celebrations were being held, I'd be the talk of the country.

"Ready to run for president, Autie?" Tom asked with a grin.

"Smart ass," I replied.

"What's that all about?" Bouyer asked. Having been loaned to us by Colonel Gibbon, the scout wasn't familiar with the joke.

"A few idiots who want to embarrass Grant have suggested I run for president. Some even said this war against the Sioux would be my springboard to the nomination," I explained.

"Lots of generals have become president. Grant and Taylor. Jackson. Even George Washington," Kellogg said, always taking an interest in politics.

"None of them were thirty-six years old, Mark. Will *the Chicago Tribune* support such a campaign? Or *the New York Times*?" I asked.

"I suppose not," Kellogg conceded.

"Maybe I'll run for office someday," I explained. "I even considered running for Congress after the war, but I didn't want to give up my commission. There'll be plenty of time for politics once my military career is over."

"Hell, George, you're a democrat. No one in their right mind would vote for a democrat," Cooke said.

"Last I heard, we weren't letting Canadians vote at all," Tom said, poking fun at his friend.

"Until Reconstruction is over, you're not letting most of the South vote, either. What does that say about your democracy?" Cooke answered.

"If the sons of bitches hadn't started the war, they wouldn't need to worry about their damn voting rights," Harrington objected, expressing what most of the Seventh felt about the Rebellion.

For some, the wounds of the Civil War were still fresh. Nearly every officer and most the troopers had shed blood on battlefields from Bull Run to

Vicksburg. Those who had not served in battle had lost friends and family members. Some, like myself, thought the South needed to be treated more fairly, but mine was a minority opinion.

"We have better things to do than refight the war," I said. "What are we going to do about this invasion? This is only the tail of the beast. Somewhere east of us is the main army, and even though General Sheridan is probably gathering a force to oppose them, it will be several months before he can take the field."

"Do we know who the Mexican commander is?" Kellogg asked.

"Hell, I don't even know who's ruling Mexico these days. They change presidents like soiled underwear," Yates said.

"It's not that bad," I said. "President de Tejada has been in charge since Juárez died. A rebel named Diaz has been trying to overthrow the government, but I don't think he has much chance."

"Is this de Tejada's way of showing he's in charge?" Cooke suggested. "What better way to unite the country than a war?"

"Heard one of them soldiers mention Santa Anna," Bouyer said.

"Santa Anna? Isn't he dead?" Tom wondered in surprise.

"It can't be Santa Anna. He's got to be eighty years old by now," I said, remembering his biography from my West Point days.

Santa Anna, former president of Mexico, had once called himself the Napoleon of the West. I couldn't say if he was a bad general or just unlucky, but he managed to lose Texas in 1836. After that he was overthrown, came back into power, and was overthrown again. During one of his many exiles, he even lived on Staten Island.

"Eighty years old? That would make him their most experienced general," Yates said. Everyone laughed.

Keogh came up to the bonfire with Morning Star and the Indian boy. Morning Star found a place next to Tom, the boy sat between me and Bouyer. Keogh stood for a moment accepting a plate of beans, then squatted close to the fire pit.

"Tents all set up. Finally got the boys settled in. They're all fired up from the fight," Keogh said.

"Causalities?" I asked.

"One dead, four wounded. Looks like the Mexicans lost about forty-five. Hard to tell how many wounded. Most took off back to Mexico," Keogh said.

"Good riddance," Tom said.

"Who died?" I asked.

"Young trumpeter named Martin. F Company. You know, that Italian kid who was acting as your orderly," Keogh said. "Took a musket ball through the head."

"Didn't we send him back to Benteen with a message?" Tom asked.

"He won't be taking any messages now," Keogh answered.

"Strange. We lost thousands of good men during the war. Thousands upon thousands. Out here on the plains, even losing one seems like a lot," Yates said.

"Probably going to lose more, Georgie," I remarked. "Have we gotten any information from those Mexican officers?"

"Naw, they're professionals. Threw their orders in the river," Tom said.

"We got this scrap of paper. Doesn't make any sense, though," Keogh said, pulling a crumpled page from his breast pocket.

I looked the page over. It was in Spanish, the handwriting florid. I recognized the word Béjar and a few harsh lines to the commanding officer. I'd have probably been able to read the whole damn letter if I'd paid more attention in school.

"Scratch orders saying to hurry the artillery along," I surmised, handing the document to Tom.

"Of course, sir. But look at the date. It's from February. Five months ago," Keogh pointed out. He was right. Even though the paper and ink appeared fresh, it was dated February 19th.

"Are their communications that bad? Marching with orders this old?" Tom asked in disbelief.

"Has anyone asked the Mexican captain about this? Or that young lieutenant?" I inquired, for it did seem strange.

"Tried to. None of them will tell us anything," Keogh answered.

"I've seen their faces around the Indians. Take my word for it, Gen'ral, give Gray Wolf a tomahawk and they'll sing like nightingales," Bouyer replied.

"It does not matter," Morning Star said.

"Why is that?" Bouyer asked.

"Slow says you will be going east, regardless of the odds," Morning Star explained.

"Sure, we'll probe toward San Antonio, but . . ." Harrington started to say.

Morning Star raised her hands, her tawny rawhide dress reflecting glowing shadows, and looked to the boy. Slow stood up, his face lit by the campfire. His dark eyes glistened ominously in the flickering light. He studied everyone in the circle before turning his attention on me.

"You will seek the enemy, as you have always done. It is your way," the boy said. Then he sat down and accepted a plate of beans.

The boy was right about that.

It was another freezing cold night. An hour after the command turned in, I walked down to the river. Fires burned on the other side. Most of the invaders had headed back to their homes in Mexico, but not all. I soon learned why.

"General, over here," a trooper called.

It was Corporal French, one of Tom's men. He and four others were manning the cannon at the ford. Each was wearing a Mexican winter coat and draped in a buffalo hide to keep out the killing frost.

"What is it, French?" I asked.

"This fellow here. Says he's a sergeant. Wants a parley," French explained. "Speaks pretty fair English for a foreigner."

I saw three Mexicans dressed in white sackcloth and heavy wool coats. Possibly peasants pressed into service by their government. The sergeant was tall for one of his race, the shoulders straight and head held high. He had come to talk, not beg. He only had sandals and rags for footwear.

"General, sir," he said. "I am Mario Sepulveda of the Zacatecan militia. We rose in revolt against the tyrant, but we were defeated. He burned our homes. Raped our women. Stole our cattle and burned our crops. Then he forced us to come north or face his wrath again."

"I had not heard of these latest troubles," I said, though I recalled reading of such a rebellion many years before. "How may I be of service?"

"It is *we* who would be of service," Sepulveda said.

One of the other Mexicans came forward, hat in hand, and spoke something in Spanish.

"What's that he's saying?" I asked, pretending I had no clue.

"Francisco Sanchez is from Coahuila. He and his three brothers have also been coerced into servitude. They hate the dictator," Sepulveda said.

I heard footsteps. Tom, Morning Star and Slow approached through the gloomy darkness.

"Yes? And so?" I persisted.

"We want to join you, sir, if you will have us," Sepulveda said.

Francisco began speaking again, and then the other one, both agitated. It had taken courage to cross the river on that rickety old raft at night with such a bold proposal, especially as it was difficult to believe. Tom whispered in my ear.

"A few of these boys acting as teamsters would free up our own men," he urged. "We need the wagons. And it wouldn't hurt to keep the three field guns."

"Don't know that I'd trust them," I whispered back, but Tom had good instincts about people. Far better than I.

Tom took Sepulveda by the arm and walked off, asking a few pertinent questions. Tom gestured to the river, then to the east. Sepulveda pointed east as well, then back toward Mexico. They returned a few minutes later. Tom was smiling.

"We've got some teamsters. And a few scouts to check on the locals," Tom said.

"Are you sure he's telling the truth?" I asked.

"Pretty sure," Tom said. "Without help, we'll need to leave most of the supplies. And we already know how much trouble mules are with packs on their backs."

I did know. Mules had been a problem on our march up from the Yellowstone to the Little Big Horn, one hundred and seventy-five stubborn animals tossing about and slowing us at every opportunity. The ornery animals were the main reason I had chosen not to bring the Gatling Guns. Wagons would be even slower, but a lot less trouble. And we weren't on a seven day scout now. There was no telling how long this new war would last.

"They speak the truth," Slow suddenly announced.

Everyone turned to look at the boy, who seemed older in the moonlight. Tom put a hand on Slow's shoulder. Morning Star knelt to wrap his buffalo robe tighter. I felt a chill looking into the youngster's eyes.

"Mister Sepulveda, I am sorry for the many outrages of this tyrant and accept your assistance," I formally invited, bowing my head in respect.

"All of us?" he asked

"How many are you?"

"Forty-two, General. All strong and determined to see the tyrant defeated," he answered.

"Be ready to march at dawn, sir. You will drive the wagons and watch the extra horses. If there's a fight, you'll be welcome to pitch in," I offered.

"*Gracias*, sir. We will be ready," Sepulveda said, taking his comrades back toward the river.

"Tom, assign Sergeant Major Sharrow to keep an eye them," I ordered. "And maybe it would be best if Morning Star and Slow stayed back with our supply train from now on."

"No," the boy said.

"This isn't your decision, lad. Until you've been returned to your people, I'm responsible for your safety," I objected.

"I ride with the White Chief," Slow said with determination.

"So do I, sir. I'm sorry, General Custer. We have not come so far from our hunting lands to ride on a wagon," Morning Star agreed.

She took Slow's hand and they walked back to camp.

"Stubborn woman," I said.

"Yes," Tom said, badly smitten.

I decided to leave a small rearguard at the Rio Grande commanded by Lt. Harrington, whose West Point studies had included the proper use of artillery. As we couldn't take the two big siege guns with us, the 12-pounders were mounted on the ridge overlooking the ford. Any force attempting to cross the river would be badly compromised. As Tom suggested, we did take the three light artillery pieces, sturdy 4-pounders that would add punch to any position we decided to hold.

"Understand your orders?" I asked again, for Harrington had only graduated four years before.

"Yes, sir. Pretty sure, sir. Delay the enemy, watch my flanks. When the position proves untenable, I'm to spike the guns and withdraw east toward Gonzales," he nervously answered.

"Harry, you proved yourself on the Yellowstone, but we're not surveying for the railroads now," I said. "And when Sheridan ordered us into the Black Hills, you were a big help finding the best trails."

"And the gold in that creek," Cooke remembered, a discovery that had riled the Sioux, for greedy treasure seekers had poured into the Black Hills, trespassing on their sacred hunting grounds.

I could tell Harrington was still unsure. When General Stanley led our survey expedition in 1873, there had been a thousand soldiers, engineers, cooks, muleskinners and Indian scouts. And a wagon train that trailed us for twenty miles. We were not, by definition, a military force, but explorers. We had a skirmish or two with the Sioux, but nothing compared to our current situation. A year later, I had led twelve hundred men into the Black Hills, searching for a place to build a fort. Harry had been with me then, too, along with Tom, Algernon, George Yates and Jimmy Calhoun. Bill Illingworth came along to take photographs. There were no major confrontations with the Sioux on that expedition, just two months of hunting, fishing and camping under the stars.

"Harry, we aren't chasing Indians this time," I grimly said. "Unlike the rest of us, you've never fought against a civilized army, but you've got the training. Keep a clear head and everything will be fine."

"Yes, sir. Clear head," Harrington said.

"Good luck, Harry. You'll make a great captain someday," I said, shaking his hand before mounting Vic.

We formed in column of twos, the command moving briskly northeast. Had the road been drier, the air would have choked with dust, so in this respect the damp weather worked to our advantage. The men were trading stories and joking. Some had peeled back their buffalo robes, once again looking like a cavalry unit in their blue jackets. Even the horses seemed to trot with a new spirit, enjoying a brief respite from the rain and cold wind. After cresting a low hill, the land flattened out, the horizon broken only by the occasional grove of trees. I rushed to catch up with Tom, Morning Star and Slow, who were bringing up the rear.

"Autie, why Gonzales? Aren't we headed for San Antonio?" Tom asked.

I had not explained my plan, nor felt a need to. Tom frowned until I relented.

"The invaders have probably reached San Antonio. If they've already captured the garrison, I don't want Harry stumbling into an ambush. We'll skirt south of town, establish a base of operations, and then a few of us will scout the enemy advance. I remember a crossing at Cibolo Creek about twenty miles below San Antonio. From there the command can swing east to Gonzales, south to Goliad, or north to San Antonio as the situation requires."

"I expect you are going to this San Antonio," Morning Star said.

"I'm in command, young lady, and I left my best scouts back on the Little Big Horn. If Bloody Knife or Varnum were here, I could send them for a quick look," I replied.

"I'm going, too," Tom quickly said.

"Spotted Eagle and Gray Wolf will also want to go. And the one called Bouyer," Morning Star said, taking for granted that she and Slow would be members of the party.

As I didn't expect to take on the entire Mexican army with my depleted regiment, there seemed no harm.

"Tell Yates to loan us a few troopers from F Company. Along with C Company and the headquarters staff, we'll have enough. Keogh will escort the supply train to the rendezvous point and hold the position until we rejoin the command," I ordered.

"Splitting our forces again?" Tom said.

"If we run into Mexican cavalry, I don't need a bunch of wagons slowing our retreat," I replied, for I wanted nothing encumbering the scout party should we need to move fast.

"Myles won't like babysitting the bean sacks," Tom warned.

"Are you volunteering to take his place?" I asked.

"No," Tom said, giving Athena a kick to catch up with the column.

Morning Star stirred her mare to follow, leaving me riding at the rear with Slow.

"What say you, youngster? No mystical wisdom?" I said.

The boy's brows were bent in thought. At times, he seemed more sixty than six.

"You face more enemies than you know. Enemies you think of as friends, but this has happened before," Slow answered. Then he hurried to catch up with Tom and Morning Star.

I was dumbfounded. I didn't know what he meant about more enemies, but he was exactly right about the rest. I remembered many friends from West Point who had resigned their commissions to fight for Jefferson Davis. James Parker of Missouri had been my roommate, sharing meals, studies and hardships. I was nearly in tears the night he left for a Southern regiment. Tom Rosser, born in Virginia and raised in Texas, was a classmate who shared the trail with me surveying for the railroad just a few years ago, but we had opposed each other at Trevilian Station in 1864. Such bonds of youth are not easily broken, and though my companions were mistaken to have fought for a cause so unholy as slavery, the essential love of our friendships remained even after the war.

Two days later we reached the Nueces River, primarily keeping to the Camino Real but with scouts well out in front. The Nueces was running fast, but the water was shallow enough not to cause much trouble. We continued on until we were halfway to the San Antonio River, making camp at a small creek among a grove of leafless trees. It was time to divide the command.

The weather had been butt cold and often rainy throughout the march. From time to time we saw a few Comanche Indians following our trail, but they kept their distance. And wisely so. A handful of small farms were deserted, the stock plundered. We formed our four freight wagons in a wide circle with the horses and oxen in the middle. Sentries were set at regular intervals, watching for intruders.

"Our provisions will only last a few weeks. Once you've dug in, send a few of the wagons downriver. Buy whatever food you can. If the farmers won't sell, confiscate it and give them a note for future payment," I told Keogh.

As Tom predicted, Myles was unhappy to be given an assignment watching the wagons.

"I don't know Texas like you do, General," Keogh complained.

"Sergeant Major Sharrow knows the Cibolo Creek area. Plenty of trees for cover and firewood. A ravine will protect and horses and guns. If you haven't heard from us after three days, send a messenger," I instructed. "Myles, we don't know the enemy strength or intentions. You saw what happened when I blundered into the Sioux camp. Let's not make that mistake again."

It was the first time in years I had admitted a mistake to a subordinate. More often than not, I had ducked responsibility for my failures. Blamed bad orders. Blamed the weather. Blamed fellow officers. Had I learned something at the Little Big Horn after all?

Stars started poking out through billowy clouds as we experienced the first dry evening in days. All of my staff officers sat close by, as did our Indian guests. Tom and Morning Star were together, and had also been sharing the same tent, but no more than that. The situation was too dire for such frivolity, and besides, I suspected Tom was beginning to have stronger feelings for her than a quick roll in the hay would allow. Slow sat between Gray Wolf and Spotted Eagle, the lads listening intently. I don't know how much English they'd learned, especially around a crusty half-breed like Bouyer, but I suspected they understood more than they let on.

"How about a song?" Tom said, taking out a Spanish guitar he'd found in one of the wagons.

He played quite well. Keogh produced an Irish flute. Smith used two spoons and a log for a drum. Dr. Lord, whose illness had improved of late, filled three beakers with varying amounts of water, making a pleasant tinkling when tapped with a spoon. I play a pretty mean piano but doubted there was one nearby.

Music at the campfire is as old as soldiering itself. It would not surprise me if the Roman legions had serenaded Caesar.

"*Aura Lea*," Keogh said, starting off with one of his favorites.

After that, we sang *Oh Shenandoah* and *The Girl I Left Behind Me*. Some wanted to sing *Gerry Owen*, the Seventh Cavalry's marching song, but I wasn't ready. Not until I knew where we were marching to.

"Jumping Bull is not faring well. Morning Star and Walking-In-Grass are worried," I said to Dr. Lord as the camp was preparing to turn in.

"I've noticed. He tires easily and has trouble breathing," Lord said.

Born in Maine, Lord had served on frontier outposts most of his professional career, so he had treated Indians before. For such a young doctor, only thirty, he had shown remarkable talent.

"Maybe Morning Star should stay with Keogh," I suggested. "We can't take the old man with us on the scout."

"The Sioux understand death differently than we do. It doesn't mean she won't mourn if her grandfather dies," Lord replied.

Just at that moment, Jumping Bull shuffled close to our fire, pausing next to me as if aware of our conversation. He looked ancient, the long hair slate gray, his face wrinkled into deep crevices.

"I have delivered my grandson. The Great Spirit seeks no more from me," he said, sounding relieved of a great burden.

"I'm concerned your grandchildren will not find you alive when we return," I replied, for losing a loved one is a difficult thing.

"Morning Star has said her goodbyes," Jumping Bull replied. "Slow does not need to. We were destined to follow different paths."

Jumping Bull continued on to his teepee. I let the subject drop, realizing the old man had made his decision.

I did not fear for Walking-In-Grass being left alone with Keogh's detachment. She was an excellent cook and popular with the young troopers. They treated her like the mother they hoped to see again one day, and the old woman enjoyed every moment of it.

My scouting party started east the next morning, thirty-three well-armed soldiers nominally under Tom's command. Joining us were Bouyer, Kellogg, and the four young Indians. Keogh moved southeast toward Cibolo Creek above its junction with the San Antonio River. With Sergeant Sepulveda and our Mexican volunteers, his battalion numbered better than a hundred. I hoped dividing the command wasn't another blunder, but we needed to know what was happening in San Antonio.

Truly, Keogh had no cause for complaint. He had tents, wagons, and cattle for fresh meat. The scout party was traveling light, each trooper bringing only what he needed. Six pack horses carried dried beans and reserve ammunition. We also brought a small tent for Morning Star; everyone else would be using their buffalo hides against the weather.

I chose not to drive directly toward our objective. The main road would be patrolled by cavalry as we got closer, so we moved to a position south of San Antonio but close to the river, using the trees and fields to mask our movement. I knew of a hill that overlooked the flood plain where the old town could be seen.

My unit seemed in good spirits despite the wet winds. Most of the troopers were veterans especially picked by Tom for the mission. Men we had served with for many years and trusted should we find ourselves in a tight spot. And I think having Morning Star with us helped, for having a beautiful woman riding at the head of the column was a delightful break from the otherwise dreary scenery.

I was disappointed that my search for a white wolf or a white buffalo had led me to a white man, but now I realized this was no ordinary man. He had the courage of a Shirt Wearer, rode his horse with the grace of a falling star, and viewed his enemies as the hawk watches the meadow. His friends thought him the greatest living soldier. But I heard there were others who thought him a devil. Reckless, boastful, and arrogant. A man so driven with ambition that he could not be trusted. This would be a bad thing, for above all else a chief must understand his responsibilities. I struggled to know why the Great Spirit had sent me to this strange land, and in what manner could it help my people.

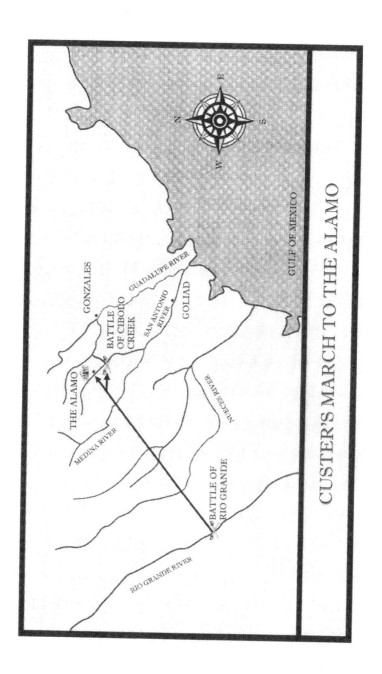

CUSTER'S MARCH TO THE ALAMO

CHAPTER THREE

TROUBLE IN BÉJAR

We approached a small river within a few miles of town, the rolling prairie making it difficult to know what we would find over the next rise. Normally it was a stand of trees or a sudden forest that indicated water. The day was dry, not so cold as the day before. But it was still winter.

"Should be the Medina up ahead, Gen'ral," Bouyer said.

"Or Indians," I drolly replied, for there were several well-armed hostiles near the ford where we intended to cross.

I saw at least seven, all riding brown mustangs. None wore paint, nor were they carrying any special accruements, such as ribboned lances or feathered bonnets. In fact, their thick buffalo jackets and plain hide outfits were rather frayed, reminding me of New Jersey dock workers.

"Comanche," Bouyer instantly knew, drawing his 1861 Navy Colt revolver.

Tom drew his Colt .45, and without a word, the two of them spurred forward. Spotted Eagle and Gray Wolf quickly followed. I stayed behind with the command.

"General, shouldn't we help?" Corporal Voss said, ready to trumpet the charge.

"Nothing Tom and Bouyer can't handle," I said, pretending to yawn.

Morning Star glanced at me with a moment of concern, but I knew the Comanche would flee at the first shot. Then Slow looked at me with a bent brow, as if questioning my judgment. I doubted the six-year-old knew as much about Indian fighting as I did.

Shots rang out, and before my party could get within range, the Comanche scattered. One tried to drag off a captured horse but was unable to handle the startled creature, finally being forced to abandon the effort. I ordered Butler and Voss forward, then signaled the command to remain at a steady pace. Kellogg disobeyed, rushing to meet Tom before the rest of us could catch up.

We found three dead Mexican soldiers at the ford. Two of their horses were gone, but the one that remained was a fine sorrel, fit for an officer, with long legs and a white stripe down the snout.

Tom and Bouyer dismounted, inspecting the bodies. Two were at the edge of the water, laying face down on the rocks. The third had tried to crawl upstream into the brush but hadn't made it more than a few yards. All three had been scalped.

"Dispatch riders," Tom said, holding a courier pouch.

"Must've stopped to water the horses an' got jumped," Bouyer guessed, inspecting the tracks in the mud.

Bouyer took a flintlock pistol and a pocket watch from one of the bodies, a middle-aged man with noble features. The officer wore a blue uniform with white epilates, a red sash around his waist, and a steel helmet crowned with black plumes. At his side was an expensive saber. The other two victims looked like elite cavalry, their crimson jackets trimmed with gold lace. Their high black boots were polished. They had been armed with swords and short-barrel muskets. Arrows in their backs indicated they never knew what hit them.

"I'll have that sword, Mr. Bouyer," I firmly requested.

It was a fine Toledo blade, more ornate than the one I carried during the war. Cavalry has little use for sabers on the plains, as the hostiles never get close enough for hand-to-hand fighting. And sabers also tend to make a lot of rattling noises while on the march, which is why the Seventh left our swords boxed up back on the Yellowstone. I strapped the belt around my waist, enjoying the weight of the steel. Nothing makes a man feel more like a general than a good sword at his side.

"Damn, this is weird," Tom said, handing a dispatch to Cooke.

Fluent in French, Cooke was able to pick out a few words. He whistled and passed the dispatch to Kellogg.

The reporter's eyes went wide with disbelief. His knees wobbled and he fell down in the scrubby grass. I reached for the dispatch.

"Is this some sort of joke?" I asked, angry that anyone would think such a farce amusing.

"If it's a joke, three men have died for it," Cooke said.

I gave the dispatch case to Sergeant Butler, who knew even less Spanish than I did, and wished I'd brought one of the Mexicans with us as an interpreter.

"Okay, this . . . parchment, says it's from General Joaquin Ramierz y Sesma to General Jose Urrea, and it's dated February 27th, 1836," I said. "Gentlemen, I'm not a historian, but even I know Sesma and Urrea were part of Santa Anna's invasion force forty years ago. What the hell is going on here? Were these gentlemen dispatch riders or were they delivering antique documents to their national library?"

I quickly regretted swearing, having promised myself not to, but I was angry. We had enough trouble without the enemy playing absurd pranks on us.

"What should we do, sir?" Butler asked, tucking the dispatch pouch in his blouse.

"No time for a burial detail. Gather their personal effects and drag the bodies into the brush. We'll bury them on the way back if there's an opportunity," I ordered.

Gray Wolf motioned to Bouyer, who turned to me.

"The young braves ask for their knives and hats," Bouyer said. "I don't think we should be leaving their boots or jackets behind, neither. No sense lettin' their kit get scavenged by their killers. And you did take the officer's sword."

Stealing from the dead is an Indian custom, not something white men normally do. Not Christian white men. But Bouyer had a point. We were not in a position to squander resources.

"Take what's needed," I agreed. "But leave them enough for decency. And tell Gray Wolf not to touch what's left of their scalps. He's not here to hang trophies from his lodge pole."

Bouyer and the Indians quickly stripped the bodies almost bare. I gave the extra swords to Tom and Cooke, and armed Morning Star with a short-barreled musket. I had no doubt Tom would enjoy teaching her how to shoot.

After crossing the river we turned north, riding in column of twos. An odd sight, I'm sure, covered as we were in buffalo hides and fur hats. The Indian lads riding ahead of us wore sombreros and carried ribboned lances. Slow rode with them but declined to wear any of the stolen Mexican trinkets. I rode at the head of the column with Sergeant Hughes and Corporal Voss, but my guidon remained furled and there were no trumpet calls. Kellogg came to my side, wanting to talk about the fake dispatches, but I waved him off. Tom and Morning Star fell to the back of the column, joined by Sergeant Butler, where their guns would provide a strong rearguard.

By late afternoon, I was sure we were getting close, perhaps a mile shy of the Gonzales road. The weather remained cold but clear, which was surprising, for we could hear occasional thunder from the west.

"Good cover here," I said, finding a heavily forested bend in the river. "Bill, you'll take command while Tom and I go forward. Keep out of sight. Don't engage the enemy unless you have no choice. If necessary, fall back to Keogh's position and wait for us there."

"And you're going to do what? Ride into San An'tone pretending to be buffalo hunters?" Cooke sarcastically asked.

"Just going for a look, and we're not taking any company. Bouyer, you keep these Indian boys on a leash while I'm gone," I ordered.

"General, please let me go with you," Kellogg begged. "Sorry, Mark, don't need a reporter tagging along," I decided, turning Vic back toward the higher ground.

"Please, sir! General Custer, I have a theory about what's going on. If I come with you, I can prove it," Kellogg said.

"And what theory would that be?" I asked.

"You'll think I'm crazy," he answered.

"I think all you reporters are crazy."

"Let me come and you'll change your mind," Kellogg insisted.

Kellogg had proved himself rugged on the trail, a good shot with his .50 caliber Spencer, and never offered a word of complaint. I relented.

"We'll be back just after sunset. Don't shoot us," I said, tipping my hat to Cooke.

"Keep Tom away from the *cantinas*," Cooke said.

The three of us rode quietly toward the next rise. I intended to find the Gonzales road and approach a tree-lined avenue known as the Alameda. From the top of the hill, and under the protection of the trees, we could survey the town without much chance of being seen. It was important not to be spotted by enemy cavalry that was likely patrolling the area.

"I bet the town has changed a lot in the last ten years," Tom speculated.

It was our experience that most frontier cities had expanded since the end of the war. Thousands of soldiers, unable to settle back down to life on their farms, had headed west for new opportunities. Some became famous, like Wild Bill Hickok, the Kansas City lawman, and Joe McCoy, who created the Abilene stockyards. Many were looking for gold, like the miners in the Black Hills, or starting great cattle ranches in the southwest. Protecting immigrants had become the army's primary purpose in recent years, for the Indians were not well disposed to have their hunting grounds overrun by settlers.

"Rosser told me the Galveston line is being extended to San Antonio next year. Wherever the railroad goes, civilization will follow," I said, a true believer in modern technology.

"You wouldn't say that if you spent a Saturday night in Chicago," Kellogg said, attempting to be funny.

In truth, I preferred New York. A night at the theater and dinner at Delmonico's was my idea of a civilized evening.

A mile farther on, we heard a familiar noise. It wasn't thunder we had heard in the distance- it was cannon fire.

"Field guns. Maybe a howitzer or two," Tom announced.

"Guess we found the Mexican army," I said. The firing was slow and sporadic. Not a hot fight.

"The town must be holding out," Tom said, reaching the same conclusion I had. But they were not heavy cannon. Not like the 12-pounders we had intercepted at the Rio Grande. This was light artillery.

"Maybe we have an army in the field after all," Kellogg guessed.

"Doesn't sound like the guns are dueling. Whichever side is doing the firing seems to have the upper hand," I said.

Tom nodded agreement. From 1861 to 1865, we'd seen plenty of battlefields. After awhile, you know instinctively where the firing is coming from. When Napoleon espoused the soldier's motto, 'ride to the sound of the guns,' the man knew what he was talking about.

"A patrol," Tom said, sighting a group of horsemen off in the distance.

We edged down into a ravine and held our breath. The patrol consisted of ten Mexican lancers on fast horses. Their uniforms, red jackets with white trousers, stood out from the gray landscape. One carried a purple pennant that flapped in the stiff breeze, but I could not make out an insignia. With the firepower at our disposal, we could drive the enemy off, but I didn't wish to be discovered.

The patrol rode south toward Goliad, possibly scouting their next advance. We moved up from the river into thick woods. If I remembered right, there was a low ridge just east of the town called Powder House Hill where the Masonic cemetery was located. I expected such a place to be occupied by the enemy for observation purposes, but it would also help fix our location.

A few minutes later, we reached the Alameda. The long, tree-lined avenue had been paved with stones on my previous visit. Now it was a ruddy track of half-dried mud. The tall, draping trees had grown thicker, and not a single clapboard house stood in the area, which I found very strange.

We dismounted and approached cautiously, pistols drawn should the enemy be laying a trap. We saw no activity in the immediate vicinity, so we tied the horses to branches in the woods and crept up to the road, careful to hide in the brush.

To our right, all I saw was rolling prairie and a few small farms. A dirt trail called the Gonzales Road led due east.

Straight ahead of us was Powder House Hill, but instead of a cemetery, the hill was capped by an old adobe tower that hadn't been there before. Next to the tower was an entrenchment manned by a dozen soldiers, most of them looking bored.

Down and to our left was the town of San Antonio de Béjar.

"By all that's holy," Tom whispered.

"Watch the blasphemy, Thomas," I warned.

But he was right. The bench land from the hill down to the San Antonio River two thousand yards away was a war zone occupied by hundreds of Mexican soldiers. The town on the far side of the river was filled with tents, troops and supply wagons. A blood-red flag flew from the top of the gray stone cathedral. The more immediate activity, however, was on our side of the river around a decrepit old fort.

"What the hell is that?" Tom asked, pointing.

"Thomas," I warned again.

"Sorry, Autie," he apologized.

"Tommy boy, that there is the Alamo," Kellogg said.

"The Alamo doesn't have any walls. It's just an old supply depot," Tom protested.

"It's got walls now," Kellogg replied.

"That makes no sense. If Texas was going to build a new wall around the Alamo, why erect of piece of shit like that?" Tom asked.

"Damn it, Tom, will you quit your goddamn swearing!" I demanded.

"It's not a new wall, Tom," Kellogg gravely said. "It's the original wall. It's the original wall, and that is Santa Anna's army down there. I don't know how, but this isn't 1876 anymore. It's 1836."

"That's your crazy theory?" I asked.

"Have you got a better one?" he said.

I took out my field glasses and hunkered down, studying every facet of the situation. The Mexican cannon were old. Napoleonic vintage. The soldiers were armed with the same Brown Bess muskets we'd seen at the Rio Grande. The fort had a fair number of cannon but not very many defenders. A red, white and green flag with two stars on it flew from the roof of a long two-story building. The south side of the fort, between the main gate and the broken down church, was a timber palisade guarded by a pair of 6-pounders. A crudely built lunette protected the main gate, and mounted on the southwest corner was an 18-pounder aimed toward the town. Thick adobe walls enclosed about three acres of courtyard without a single bastion for defense.

I'd read about the Alamo. Studied the battle, or at least what little we knew of it, for no formal history had ever been written. Without reinforcements, the fort was indefensible, and few if any reinforcements ever arrived. No one with any military experience would get trapped in such a place.

"I'm estimating the enemy at eighteen hundred," Tom said, also studying the battlefield through his binoculars. "Mostly infantry. They've got to have more cavalry, but they're not here. Probably on a scout. Autie, there isn't an American army uniform in sight. The fort isn't flying the stars and stripes."

"Start making notes. Write down everything," I ordered. "You, too, Mark. About time that notebook of yours is finally good for something. I want troop estimates, dispositions, supply locations. Artillery positions. Pin down where their headquarters is located. Let's study the ground. Where can we use cavalry? Where's the best place to fight dismounted?"

"Fight? General, there are thousands of Mexicans down there!" Kellogg protested.

"Maybe we'll fight. Maybe we won't. But I want all my options available," I generously explained.

Tom needed no explanation. He was busy scribbling everything a field commander would need to know. Though I was more charismatic, I still wondered if Tom might not be the better strategist.

"That's got to be the worst looking fort I've ever seen," Tom whispered, making a drawing of the fortifications.

"Strictly speaking, the Alamo was not a fortress," Kellogg said. "It was founded as a mission back in the 1700s. The walls were for protection against Indians. If the Mexicans were armed with bows and arrows, the Texans would be doing fine."

From what I saw, the compound consisted of a roofless old church attached to a tall, rectangular convent. The adobe walls on the west side had rooms for workshops. Two batteries faced the river through holes cut in the wall, a shockingly poor device, for without flanking protection the guns were extremely vulnerable. The east side of the compound had corrals for cattle and horses. A thin wall and two raised batteries shielded that flank, which was also screened by a swampy morass. With a good field of fire, it was almost defensible.

The north wall was a disaster waiting to happen. Though guarded by four cannon mounted on two platforms, it was shored up with logs and dirt. The

Alamo had no ramparts, only wooden ramps that offered the defenders no protection from an attacking force. It would take six hundred men to hold such a place, and history said the Alamo had less than two hundred.

Only a few of those two hundred were visible, most choosing to avoid the cannon balls hitting the old battered walls every few minutes.

In one respect, I had to give the Mexican army credit. They wore impressive uniforms, each unit distinctively its own. The battalions flew their banners proudly and conducted themselves with professional élan. They were gradually surrounding the fort with a series of redoubts, filling in the gaps with small detachments. Though they probably had the strength to take the Alamo by storm, they had chosen a siege instead, possibly waiting for additional reinforcements. Larger cannon would knock down these crumbling walls in a few hours, but if the invaders were waiting for the 12-pounders we captured at the Rio Grande, they were in for a disappointment.

As the sun set, a nearly full moon crawled out from behind the clouds. Enough light to guide us back to our hiding place downriver. We rode in silence most of the way.

"This has got to be a trick," Tom finally said.

"Or a delusion," I suggested.

"It looked like the real thing to me," Kellogg insisted. "I studied the Texas revolution while working for the St. Paul Dispatch. Everything adds up."

"Except traveling back in time forty years. I don't think that adds up," I disagreed.

"You know I'm right," Kellogg persisted.

"I don't know anything yet. I'm certainly not subscribing to this fantasy without more proof."

"What more proof do you need?"

"I don't know. Something. Am I to believe our entire world is gone? Our friends and family no longer exist? That . . . who? Andrew Jackson is President of the United States? I am to believe that I haven't even been born yet? That my wife hasn't been born yet? No, I'll believe I'm dead on some weed-covered battlefield before believing any of that."

"Are we?" Tom asked.

"Are we what?" I said.

"Dead on some weed-covered battlefield. Autie, I . . . I don't know how to say this. I've had these dreams ever since riding through that fog. We were on a hillside. Shot our horses. Hostiles closing in from all directions. I found you on the ground, hit through the chest, barely breathing. I. . . I couldn't let the devils take you alive."

"So you've had a few nightmares. So have I. We had them during the war, and after the Washita. Soldiers have nightmares; it doesn't make us time travelers."

"Who are you trying to convince, General?" Kellogg said.

"I *am* the general. I don't need to convince anyone," I said, giving Vic a kick and riding forward alone. I heard Tom and Kellogg talking but didn't try to listen.

Cooke had pickets guarding the ravine where the command was camped, several small fires discreet enough keep them warm without alerting the enemy. I dismounted from Vic, gave him a scratch behind the ears, and let Voss take him to the makeshift corral. Butler offered a cup of hot coffee when I came close to the largest campfire. After the cold ride, the flames felt like heaven. Tom and Kellogg rode in a few minutes later.

"Well, what happened? Have the Mexicans captured San Antonio?" Cooke asked, growing impatient.

"You could say that," I answered.

"I could, but what would you say? Did you reach the town?" he pressed.

"Yes, Bill, we reached the damn town," I said, backing from the fire to walk down near the river.

Cooke started to follow, but Tom stopped him.

The moon had gradually disappeared behind some clouds, but stars were visible on the eastern horizon. The river babbled and I heard the occasional fish jump from the water. A steady wind rustled through the trees.

I didn't know what to do. What to think. This was new ground, for I had *always* known what to do. Always sized up any situation and acted without hesitation. Usually with great success, for Custer's Luck had never failed me. Until now. Or had it? I had the dreams, too. Knew I had blundered at the Little Big Horn by trying to flank the Indian village without bringing Benteen up first. And then I had waited for him on that cursed hill. Waited for reinforcements that never came. Waited until it was too late to escape.

Texas. 1836. The Alamo. It certainly made no possible sense, but we had something in common, for they had also waited for reinforcements that never came. They had waited until it was too late for anything but a last stand. And none had survived. Was this journey, this hallucination, a sort of redemption? A second chance? A second chance to do what? And how would I explain it to the men? I couldn't even explain it to myself.

Footsteps, soft and unhurried, approached through the woods. I saw the young Indian boy emerge from the trees carrying a blanket. The night was cold.

"For you," he said.

"Thank you, Slow," I gratefully acknowledged, adding the same thought in sign language.

"You are troubled," he observed.

"Yes. Something very strange has happened."

"The world you knew has slipped away."

"Yes, it has. How did you know?"

"Because the world I knew was also slipping away."

"What do you mean?" I asked.

"It is not a thing for words. Wakan Tanka has not made the path clear."

"Son, I don't think your Great Spirit is much of a factor here, though if someone's god was going to intervene, I wish it would be mine."

"Can you be sure the two spirits are not the same?"

"No. At the moment I'm not sure of anything."

"It is possible I am here for a reason. It is possible you are, too," Slow said. Then he pulled his buffalo robe tighter against the night and returned to camp.

The inevitable could no longer be postponed. I stood before the campfire and explained to the men what we had found. At first a few thought I was joking, for I had a history of playing pranks going back to my childhood in Ohio, but Tom and Kellogg added their own grim details.

"Have you got a plan, Autie?" Tom asked.

"Yes. We'll ride into the Alamo and find out what's going on, once and for all. No more fantasies and guessing games," I answered.

"Ride into the Alamo? And what then, sir?" Voss asked. "Are you going to say 'Hello, I'm General Custer. Are you Davy Crockett?'"

"Why not? Do you think Davy Crockett would lie?" I answered.

"Well, no. I don't think he'd lie, sir," Voss said.

"Think Davy can really leap the Mississippi? Or ride a bolt of lightning?" Bouyer asked.

"Maybe he's half alligator and a bit of snapping turtle," Butler added.

"Damn it, Jimmy, do you think this is funny?" Sergeant Mike Kenny said, jumping up with his fists clenched. Kenny was also Irish, a thick-necked brawler with the wit of an ape and the courage of a lion.

Butler stood as well. Sometimes a nice scuffle can ease a troop's tension, but I doubted it would come to that.

"No one thinks this is funny, Mike," Cooke intervened, standing to keep them separated.

"I used to read Crockett's almanac. My pa and his pa read Crockett's almanac. He lived fifty years ago. If this is fifty years ago, everybody we know is dead," Kenny shouted.

"Is that true, General? Is everybody dead?" Sergeant Hughes asked.

"They can't be dead, Bobby. If this is 1836, none of us are even born yet," I guessed, for who could really know for sure.

"And it's only forty years, not fifty," Kellogg added.

"That should make us feel better," a hushed voice said from the back.

I couldn't tell who, which was good for him, as I'd have had the son of a bitch horsewhipped.

"What are we going to do, sir?" Private Engle asked.

"We'll move out before sunrise. At the crack of dawn, we'll attack the Mexican batteries south of the Alamo and ride into the fort," I explained.

"Is it wise to attack such a large force, General?" Cooke asked, surprised.

"We're soldiers in the United States army, and as far as I'm concerned, Texas is still part of the United States. Or will be. We'll hit them hard and fast," I said, anticipating a glorious charge.

"We're riding into the Alamo?" Corporal French asked.

"Coming into the conversation late, Henry?" Cooke said.

"No, no. I was just thinking. Didn't the Alamo lose?" French inquired. "They was massacred, weren't they? Every single one."

"The Alamo didn't have the Springfield Model 1873 carbine. I think we'll see that modern weapons and professional officers will tip the scales," I assured him.

"Hopefully it will tip the scales a lot," Tom said with a nervous laugh.

I let the men get a few hours rest and sat down to write a dispatch for Keogh. I was careful not to give him a blunt appraisal. Such news cannot be transmitted in a letter if it's to be believed, but I did want him ready to move when the time was right.

"Bouyer," I summoned once the orders were ready.

"Yes, Gen'ral," the scout said, still dubious. I could not blame him.

"I need you to deliver a message. Return if it's safe, otherwise stay with Keogh," I instructed.

"Gen'ral, if this is 1836, then I ain't in the army no more," Bouyer whispered.

"Mitch, you're in the army until I say different. We all are. Once this is sorted out, we'll decide what to do next. Can I trust you?"

"Yes, sir, you kin trust me. But I'm gonna ask for a favor when this is all over. A mighty big favor. And I expect you're gonna say yes."

"I will."

"You don't even know what I'm gonna ask," Bouyer said in surprise.

"I need every man, loyal and true. People have said a lot about me, much of it unflattering, but no one has ever said George Custer isn't loyal to his friends. Are you my friend?"

"I reckon so, sir. I reckon so," Bouyer said, taking the dispatch.

Fifteen minutes later he rode off into the darkness.

"Think we'll ever see him again?" Tom asked, standing at my side.

"I reckon so," was my answer.

Just before dawn, we were ready to make our move. Once again I had divided the command, eight troopers with Tom on our right flank with the bulk of our party on the left. I had hoped to keep Kellogg and the Indians from entering the fort, but they would have none of it. They considered themselves part of the unit now, especially Spotted Eagle and Gray Wolf, who intended to lead our charge. I convinced them not to wear the captured sombreros, fearing the Alamo defenders might mistake them for Mexican Lancers.

We came up from the southeast in the first rays of sunrise. Tom's unit split off to the right, riding silently toward Power House Hill where we had observed two cannon the afternoon before. The battery was about twelve hundred yards from the Alamo, far enough that they expected no danger from the garrison. The rest of us rode to the top of the Alameda and waited beneath the trees. The upper portion of the road was screened with tall poplars on both sides as it gradually sloped down toward an old wooden bridge crossing the river. Halfway down the slope, on the right side facing the Alamo, the ground opened into an empty field overrun with tumbleweeds. The left side of the road was thick with woods.

Another enemy battery, better armed, was a thousand yards down the road, just off to the south among a thick grove of cottonwoods. The second battery posed the greatest threat to our reaching the fort, so we would need to neutralize those guns before making the attempt. That would be my job.

From our position atop the hill, I saw no large forces of infantry in the area, most of the troop concentrations being in town or to the north of the fort where a series of encroaching fortifications were being dug.

"Okay, just like we planned, boys. Hit hard and keep moving," I urged, taking the lead.

We moved down the Alameda in column of twos as if we had a right to be there. In the gray light of dawn, we could easily be mistaken for Mexican cavalry returning from a patrol. Just as we approached the nearest battery, commotion was heard from the top of the hill. Gunfire, followed by shouting and the clash of sabers.

I paused the command, looking to see the how the enemy was reacting. The pace of the gunshots indicated Tom's men had caught the small outpost by surprise. I heard Cooke's Winchester, followed quickly by Army Colt .45s, the sounds distinctive over the muffled report of a musket.

A Mexican officer shouted, though we were too far away to make out the orders. An attempt to rally his men, no doubt, but they were soon seen pouring from the entrenchment, retreating north along the ridge. Hardly a minute later, there was an explosion as Tom put a torch to the battery's powder barrels. A fireball erupted that lit the eastern horizon.

Anxious to see what had happened, twenty or so Mexicans ran out on the road in front of us, their questions muttered in Spanish. Some pointed in our direction, others toward the flames on the hill. An officer came forward issuing orders, but I couldn't make out what he was saying.

"Okay, boys, have at them!" I shouted, spurring Vic forward with one of my Bulldogs drawn.

I fired the first shot. Hughes and Butler opened fire with their Colts, and then the whole command began shooting. In seconds we were on them, chasing the surprised soldiers back into the entrenchment. Yelling and cursing surrounded us, the enemy startled by the sudden assault. A few tried to organize a defense only to be cut down. A brave officer in a silver helmet lunged at me with his sword. I shot him through the forehead. Then the Sioux lads let out a blood-curdling Indian war cry. Voss blew the recall on his trumpet, letting Tom know it was time to rejoin the command.

Another group of soldiers came up through the trees, bayonets on their muskets, but none of them fired. It seemed none of their rifles were loaded. I turned Vic sideways, firing until my Bulldog was empty, and then drew the other. I could see the astonishment on the young soldiers' faces, for they had never seen a pistol fire so rapidly, nor with such devastating force. At close range, the Bulldog's .44 Short Rimfire bullets tore through flesh far more harshly than any musket ball.

Several of the Mexicans paused, unsure what to do, until a few brave lads pointed their bayonets and rushed forward. I shot three of them in rapid succession. At a distance of fifteen feet, it was impossible to miss. Kellogg killed a fourth, the Spencer's .50 calibur round tearing the young man's head nearly in half. Butler shot two more. Of the small band that had rushed toward us with bayonets fixed, not one was left standing.

The enemy, never more than fifty to begin with, finally gave up the fight and fled into the woods. I wanted to take their field artillery, a nice pair of brass 4-pounders, but there wasn't an opportunity. In ten minute's time, hundreds of Mexican troops could be charging over the bridge from town and cutting off our approach to the fort. If I had the tools, I would have driven spikes through the cannon touchholes, rendering them useless.

"Quick boys, give me a hand," I said, dismounting near one of the field pieces.

We dragged several barrels of powder up, packed them underneath the gun mount, and prepared to light a fuse. Butler cut open a powder sack, pouring a trail back to the ammunition wagon. Six frightened horses were tethered to a line. We cut them loose and managed to catch two of them.

Tom rode up, excited and out of breath. His squad seemed to have suffered no casualties.

"Get going, I'll be right behind," I ordered, waving a torch made of dry grass.

Only Butler stayed behind, holding Vic's reins, as the rest of the command moved out. Cooke took the lead, followed by Morning Star, Kellogg, and the two young braves. Hughes and Voss were keeping an eye on Slow. Tom shifted his unit to a flanking position, letting others pass. The south gate of the Alamo was three hundred yards away.

Now there was more shooting. The battery near the town had fired at the fort. Fifty or sixty Mexicans soldiers were emerging from the trees across the river, coming up at the double-quick. Perhaps they thought some of the Alamo defenders were attempting to break out. A ragged volley of musket fire came from the fort, though they probably didn't know who to shoot at.

"Okay, Jimmy, let's get this done," I said, setting the torch to our powder trails.

I jumped on Vic, wheeled around, and followed Butler out on the open ground, leaving the Alameda behind us.

Firing was now general between the fort and the Mexicans attempting to cross the bridge. More cannon fire came from across the river, though none aimed at us. From such a distance, they may still have believed us Mexican cavalry rather than intruders. The battery behind us exploded in three large blasts, the last shaking the ground.

I looked toward the fort. Men were standing on the gatehouse roof, firing muskets. The chapel was to the right, quiet as there were no enemies in that area. At the end of the wall to my left, where the 18-pounder was mounted, a group of buckskin clad men were shooting toward the river, giving us what cover they could. Most of the enemy appeared to be beyond the river, well-entrenched but caught off-guard. A string of broken-down shacks lined the side of the dirt road, helping to cover our approach.

Cooke had moved to the front of our column, shouting in English to the garrison so they would know we were friends. Seeing the enemy gathering at the river's edge, Tom dismounted his wing into skirmishers, six men kneeling four yards apart while two men held their horses. They fired a volley, ejected the spent shells, and fired another volley within seconds. When a third volley was fired only seconds after that, the Mexicans retreated back toward their entrenchments.

Suddenly another enemy force appeared from the rear, dozens of soldiers coming along our side the river in a quick but undisciplined rush. I saw that, deep in the trees to the south, another battery had been established among a group of slovenly adobes. I had not been able to see the camp from the top of the Alameda, and now they were charging Tom's exposed flank.

"Butler, the left!" I shouted, pointing at the new threat. It was hard for him to hear me. The battlefield was raging with gunfire and artillery shot. Dust rose from the Alamo walls when the cannonballs struck, and occasional bursts of dirt showed where shots were landing short.

"Yes, sir," Butler said, taking aim at the advancing enemy column.

An officer in an elegant white uniform was waving his sword, hurrying his men on. The soldiers, all outfitted in dark blue jackets and light blue trousers, were hastily dressed, their tall shako hats barely strapped on. They carried muskets, but not the clumsy Brown Bess we had encountered on the Rio Grande. These men were armed with English Baker rifles, a much deadlier weapon. I guessed their numbers at forty, all on foot.

Tom mounted his horse, Sergeant Hughes at his side, and they opened fire with their repeating rifles, hitting four or five of the enemy. Then Hughes took careful aim and killed the Mexican officer with a shot through the heart.

"*Andale!*" one of their sergeants yelled, ordering his men into a firing formation.

A dozen of them formed a long line, taking shot from their pouches to load their guns. Butler saw the sergeant who was giving directions, a burly man in a haggard blue uniform, and with a great deal of regret, he shot the man dead. Knowing Jimmy as I did, he would have rather killed an officer.

Another volley from Tom's skirmish line broke the center of the Mexican formation, four soldiers falling with grievous wounds. The rest beat a hasty retreat.

Butler and I caught up to the command, providing cover for the skirmishers as they remounted.

"Voss! Sound recall!" I shouted.

Corporal Voss sounded the signal to withdraw, the bugle crisp in the cold morning air. Cooke paused before the rough log stockade shielding the south gate, waving the men forward as the defenders dropped a heavy plank over the ditch protecting their position.

"Come on, boys," I shouted, waving my hat jubilantly.

The operation had gone just as I envisioned. Tom and his men followed Cooke while Butler and I brought up the rear. We charged over the stockade's wooden ramp and into the Alamo no worse for wear. A hundred beleaguered frontiersmen sent up a cheer at our arrival.

I had never known such excitement. The iron guns of the Mexicans were large and loud, the soldiers opposing our charge anxious to shoot us. Bullets flew like summer hailstones, but Custer was fearless in battle, everywhere at once, taking the biggest risks to win the greatest glory. His brother said the white general secretly yearned to be an Indian. Though I do not think this is true, without doubt he would have made Crazy Horse jealous. But Crazy Horse knew from his vision quest that he could not be killed in battle. The white general had only his luck.

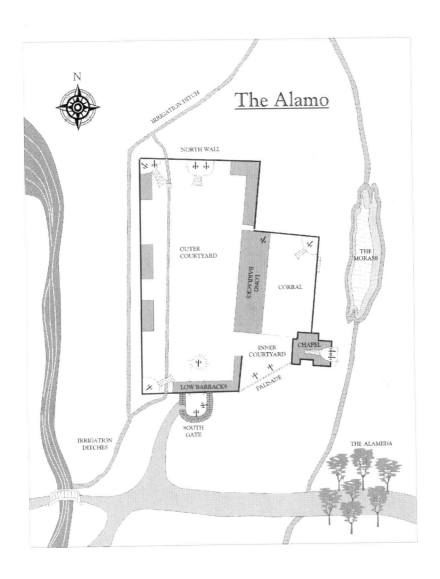

The Alamo

CHAPTER FOUR

COMMANDING THE ALAMO

We dismounted in the courtyard just inside the south gate, the mounts breathing hard from the sudden sprint across the prairie grass. Dozens of men in dirty brown leather rushed to greet us. Even the better dressed amongst them looked a bit ragged. One tall man wearing fringed buckskin looked familiar. I had seen his portrait while in Washington.

"Guess this answers our question," Cooke said, shoulders slumping.

I was disappointed, too, for I dearly hoped until the last moment that this was all some sort of huge mistake. But it wasn't. Our families were really gone, the world we knew not yet created. We were lost in every way one can be lost from one's home and roots, except one. I still had my command, or part of it, and that would sustain me until the world started to make sense again.

"Crockett. David Crockett. Sure glad to see you boys," the tall man said in a classic Tennessee drawl.

Crockett was about fifty years old with good features, an aquiline nose, and a week-old salt-and-pepper beard that contrasted with his otherwise dark brown hair. He wore a gray broad brim hat rather than a coonskin cap, and an aura of electricity was felt from his smile. The man had been a congressman.

"George Custer," I introduced. "This is my adjutant, Lieutenant William Cooke. My non-commissioned officers are Sergeant James Butler, Sergeant Bobby Hughes, and Corporal Henry Voss."

"Mark Kellogg, late of the Bismarck Tribune. Pleased to meet you, sir," Kellogg gushed, pushing forward to shake Crockett's hand.

"Bismarck? Don't believe I've heard of a Bismarck Tribune," Crockett said.

"It's in North Dakota, sir," Kellogg explained.

"Odd, I didn't know any white men lived in the Dakotas," Crockett said, trying to be nice.

A fellow standing next to Crockett reached to shake my hand. He was tall and lean like Crockett, in his early forties, and had the gleam of a good education in his cool blue eyes. His clothes had been mended in several places, indicating he'd seen hard times.

"This is my friend, Micajah Autry, also from Tennessee. We came out from Nacogdoches together," Crockett introduced.

"Proud to meet you, sir," I said, returning the handshake.

"Glad to see so many friends, especially on horseback. Not many good horses to be had hereabouts," Autry said, which explained the dreadful condition of his worn leather boots.

Another man came forward, this one nattily dressed in what was supposed to be a navy blue cavalry uniform. He wore a dress sword and a broad white sash around his waist. His black boots were polished.

"I'm Colonel William Travis, commanding the Alamo," the young man said with an Alabama accent.

I took Travis to be no more than twenty-five or twenty-six years old. He had light brown hair, dark brown eyes, and a clear complexion. I could tell that he had recently shaved, smelling of lilac water.

"General George Custer, commanding a battalion of the Seventh Cavalry," I responded, making it clear who the ranking officer was.

"United States cavalry? Here?" Travis said, looking at my men with doubt. Though roughly in the same uniforms, the long march from Fort Lincoln and more recent travails had taken a toll. And none of us had shaved in two weeks. What stood out most were the buffalo hides we used to stay warm.

"I suppose you can't say were officially *United States* cavalry. At the moment. But we're here to stop this invasion," I replied.

Tom finished giving Butler instructions for billeting our horses, then approached with Morning Star and Slow. They raised many eyebrows.

"Gentlemen, my brother, Lieutenant Colonel Thomas Custer," I said, using Tom's brevet rank from the Civil War. "And my guests, Morning Star and Slow of the Great Sioux Nation. My scouts are Gray Wolf and Spotted Eagle."

"You're traveling with Indians?" a gruff pioneer said with a sneer of disapproval.

"I travel with whom I please. Do you have a problem with that?" I answered, focusing on the boorish ruffian and several of his friends.

Tom stepped forward with his fists clenched, but I put out an arm to keep him back. We hadn't come to fight with a bunch of illiterate bumpkins.

"I guess not," the rude frontiersman said, wisely backing off.

"Where are the rest of your men?" Travis asked, making a quick count. "From the licking you gave the Mexicans, we guessed your strength at a hundred."

"Or two hundred," a voice said from the watching crowd. I took a quick look at the Alamo defenders, seeing brave men with frayed nerves.

"Only thirty for now. Maybe a few more later," I said.

Travis stepped up to take a closer look at my Remington hunting rifle. He saw the Winchesters carried by Tom and Cooke. A closer glance at my troopers revealed their Springfield carbines.

"Sir, I think we should talk. Mr. Dickenson, officer's call. The barracks in ten minutes," Travis suddenly said.

And with that he walked away without another word.

"Young Travis can be a bit abrupt," Crockett said.

"Me, too," I responded.

I did not rush to the young lawyer's officer call. My men were tired and needed food. The horses needed care. Suddenly artillery was heard from the river. Everybody but me ducked as a cannon ball sailed over the west wall and bounced into the courtyard. Another shot struck the east wall, dust flying up from the impact. The fort's defenders hurried to find cover.

"They're at it again," Crockett said. "Every few minutes, all day long. All night long. And when they're not shootin' at us, their brass band plays those damn marches. We ain't slept in a week."

I went to the southeast corner of the fort and up a sloping ramp where the 18-pounder was mounted. It was the largest cannon I'd seen in years and must have weighed two thousand pounds. The main gate was to my left, a low adobe structure with several small rooms attached. To my right was a long straight wall protected by a shallow ditch. I saw a battery across the river about three hundred yards away. Trees and brush grew thickly along the San Antonio riverbank. The other enemy battery, on our side of the river, was three hundred and fifty yards south hidden among the shanties. A squad of cavalry and a hundred infantry had rushed to the positions we attacked on our way in. The woods were still smoldering where we had blown up their ammunition wagon, and atop Powder House Hill, the old observation tower had caught fire, raging like a red torch in the morning sky.

Crockett and another Alamo officer joined me on the firing platform.

"Just a bit out of range," Crockett said.

"We'll see about that," I replied.

"If you sortie out, they'll have two hundred rifles on you," Crockett warned.

Tom and Cooke came up the ramp just as the cannon across the river fired. The ball fell short, striking the wall below us without effect.

"To hell with that. Let me get a Springfield and give those bastards a lesson in manners," Tom said, starting back down the ramp. I stopped him.

"No hurry. The batteries don't warrant my attention yet. Better to let the enemy think themselves safe," I ordered, for it would not be prudent to warn the enemy they were within range of our carbines.

"We didn't expect the Mexicans until the middle of March, if they came this far north at all. I needed a few more weeks to get our defenses ready," the other officer said, explaining and apologizing. He didn't look like a soldier, being slightly overweight and casually dressed in a gray woolen suit.

"Even a few more months would have made no difference. This rat hole would still be indefensible," Tom said.

"Sir, this is a strong position. We have more cannon than any post west of the Mississippi," the insulted man answered.

"Your name, sir?" I asked.

"Green Jameson. Chief engineer of the Alamo," he said, not offering to shake hands.

"What is your real profession? When not patching adobe with mud?" I inquired.

"I have a law practice in San Felipe," he admitted.

"Mr. Jameson," I said. "Let me suggest that you stick to robbing widows of their pensions, and leave military engineering to those who understand such things."

The cannon across the river roared again. Apparently the enemy felt insulted that we stood on the wall without bothering to duck. We returned to the courtyard where my men were beginning to assemble in front of the dilapidated church. Many held tin plates of hot beans and cornbread.

"General! General!" Kellogg shouted, running to meet us. "General, it's February 28th. They've been besieged since the 23rd."

"The battle was when? March 8th?" I asked.

"March 6th. Seven days from now every man in this fort will be—" Kellogg blabbered from excitement.

"That's not much time to whip these boys into shape," I interrupted, for the garrison seemed to have more courage than discipline. The guards stood casually at their posts. The clothes of the rank and file were unkempt. Most of the men appeared to be huddled in small groups with nothing to do.

From a door on the ground floor of the two-story barracks, I saw Travis emerge, scowling. I had completely forgotten about his officers' call, and still felt no particular need for one.

"Maybe we should hear what the youngster has to say," Crockett gently suggested, sensing my disapproval.

It's easy to forget that in any situation, be it a war council, business meeting, or a ballroom dance, there is always an element of politics. Many in Lincoln's administration tried to block my promotion to major general, calling me a McClellan democrat. The accusation was true, but it didn't stop me from endorsing Lincoln's policies to win my star. I resigned myself to indulging Travis, at least for the time being.

"My apologies, sir. We've had many a long march these last few weeks," I said, following Travis, Crockett, Jameson and several others into the long adobe building. It seemed the lower floor was being used as a billet and storehouse. I guessed part of the upper floor was the Alamo hospital.

We found an empty room off the south entrance, taking seats around an old oak table. The sparse quarters were dimly lit with two oil lamps and a small fireplace in the corner. The room had a foul, overcrowded smell to it. After so many weeks on the open plains, it was an odd way to reacquaint myself with civilization.

One of the men slumped in his chair, a deathly pallor haunting his face. I took him to be the famous Jim Bowie, though now he looked like a broken-down drunk. He was a big man, probably six feet, with broad shoulders and shaggy, dirt blond hair. He had shaved recently, possibly within the last few days. His high cheek bones were red with years of too much drink.

I decided to bring Cooke and Kellogg to the meeting, letting Tom find quarters for our men. Slow entered the room and stood in the corner, much to everyone's surprise. But no one told him to leave.

"Have you word for us? Fannin? Houston? Has the convention responded to our appeals for help?" Travis asked.

"I'm afraid you won't receive reinforcements in time, Mr. Travis," Kellogg said. "Fannin feels his three hundred men aren't enough to be of assistance. Houston is off speaking with his Cherokee friends."

"But Houston sent you?" Bowie asked, his voice raspy.

"No one sent us. We are an independent command," I answered.

"Where did you get them fancy guns? I was in Washington only ten months ago. War department's got nothin' like them," Crockett said.

"We're not here to discuss our weapons. The first order of business is how to stop this invasion of Texas," I said, weary of questions for which we could not give satisfactory answers. Answers that would only make us sound like lunatics. Even Kellogg came to realize that time travel wasn't something these hard-pressed men were likely to swallow.

"We can certainly use your help," Travis said. "I intend to post your men on our north wall. It's our weakest flank. If the Mexicans get their artillery close enough, they'll have no trouble knocking it down."

"Your north wall is hopelessly compromised. And you won't be posting my men anywhere," I quickly replied. "I'm a professional officer with fifteen years experience. You can't expect me to take orders from a militia colonel."

"I'm regular army, sir!" Travis protested.

"An army of what?" I asked. "A hundred and fifty amateurs?"

"Santa Anna will eat you for breakfast and piss on your bones," Cooke added, doing a poor job of hiding his disdain.

I didn't approve of the language, but Cooke was right. Right down to the pissing part. This rabble had no chance against a trained army.

"I've earned this command. I didn't ask for it. Even tried to resign it. But the provisional government assigned me this post, and I will hold it to the death," Travis argued, a proud young upstart.

"Travis don't command *my* boys," Bowie insisted with a trace of resentment. "All volunteers. Come and go as we please. But Travis is right about one thing. Béjar is the gateway to Texas. If we lose the Alamo, Santa Anna rides roughshod over the colonies. No one to stop him."

"Santa Anna *will* ride roughshod over the colonies. You can't stop him," Kellogg said.

I hoped Kellogg wouldn't start talking about San Jacinto, Houston's surprise victory over an overconfident Mexican army six weeks after the Alamo's fall. If time had been altered in some inexplicable way, how could we know if San Jacinto would ever happen? In addition to being time travelers, would we now be soothsayers?

"With all due respect, gentlemen, this position will not stand with its present defenses. The walls are not strong enough, and you lack the firepower to hold them," I said, calmly and with conviction. "If we begin now, it might be possible to . . ."

"Mr. Custer. General, if you are a general, we are not turning command over to a stranger who rides in from nowhere," Travis adamantly said. "For all we know, you're one of those English mercenaries hired by Santa Anna, sent here to trick us."

"I was born in Ohio," I said, struggling to hold my temper.

"Gentlemen, gentlemen . . ." Crockett attempted to intervene.

"Ohio? That explains much," Travis said.

"What's that supposed to mean?" I replied.

"You Yankees have no idea what we're fighting for. This is a free land, not a factory run by your rich banker friends," Travis answered.

"You preening popinjay," I responded, a hand on the hilt of my sword. "From what I've seen, there's not a whorehouse in all of Texas that isn't being managed better than the Alamo."

"You, sir, are no gentleman, and we of the South know well how to deal with your kind," Travis smugly declared.

"Care to back that up?" I said, rising from my seat.

"At your pleasure. Just name your second," the peacock agreed, standing with a hand on his sword.

The man was a damn lawyer. I had spent four years on the back of a horse with my saber killing Rebs just like him. The duel would be short and sweet. Probably too short.

"Gentlemen! This is no time for personal quarrels!" Crockett shouted, pounding on the table.

"Hell, let'em fight," Bowie said, evidently no fan of Travis.

"We will not," Crockett insisted. "I believe we can find one or two more important challenges than a clash of egos."

"You have no command here, Crockett. When offered responsibility, you declared yourself a high private," Travis said.

"Buck, there are a lot of high privates in this fort, and most of us prefer to live long enough to claim our lands and raise our children," Crockett answered with profound truth.

Dickenson and Jameson, both reported to be family men, nodded that they agreed. Travis shut his damn mouth.

"I would like to inspect your fortifications. Perhaps I can make some suggestions based on my experience of such things," I offered.

"Mr. Jameson will see to it," Travis said, abruptly leaving the room.

The moment he was gone, everyone relaxed.

"Sorry about that. Travis may be an ass, but he gets things done. These days, Texas has a lot of leaders but very little leadership," Captain Dickenson said.

I remembered reading about Dickenson who, like my father, had once been a blacksmith. He seemed a grounded young man now in his late twenties. Six feet tall, short black hair with snowflake white skin, his blue-gray eyes gazed with the experience of an ex-soldier. Like Crockett, he was from Tennessee, come to Texas for free land and a new life.

"What kind of leader gets you boxed up in a place like this?" Cooke asked.

"Mexicans caught us with our pants down," Bowie said, coughing into a bloody rag. "No clue they was so close. Night before, we was celebratin' Washington's birthday. Next mornin', their army was movin' into town. Barely had time to reach the Alamo."

"Why didn't you burn the town as you retreated?" I asked.

"Burn the town?" another officer asked.

"Your name, sir?" Kellogg asked.

"Captain John Baugh, adjutant for Travis. Came to Texas with the New Orleans Grays."

I guessed Baugh in his early thirties, slightly pudgy, and by his accent, from Virginia rather than Louisiana. The young man appeared intelligent and good-natured, which explained his popularity with the volunteers.

"Standard tactic," Cooke explained, seeing nothing but blank faces.

"Guess none of us thought of it," Bowie admitted.

"My wife and my daughter are here with me. So is the family of Gregorio Esparza," Dickenson explained. "We would have sent them to Gonzales if there'd been time. Santa Anna is known to kill the families of rebels, so we're in a tough spot. Travis has sent riders for help."

"It isn't coming," Kellogg said. "Not enough, anyway."

"How do you know?" Jameson asked.

"We have a small force south of here. If help was coming, we'd have seen it," I said, stretching the truth. And wishing Kellogg would quit being such an expert.

"Sir, we would like your help, but Travis is the legal commander of the garrison until relieved," Dickenson regretfully said.

"Gentlemen, some think bad leadership is better than no leadership. I am not one of them. When outnumbered ten-to-one, you can't afford anything but the best. From what I've seen, Crockett is a natural leader. Far better than that wet-nosed kid," I said.

"Thank you for that, but Colonel Travis and Colonel Bowie have been in command since I arrived. And Colonel Neil before them. I have never led anything larger than a scout against the Creeks, and that was twenty-five years ago," Crockett said.

Bowie coughed again. The man was barely able to sit the table. I guessed a fever, possibly malaria, though it could also be a sickness of the lungs. Dr. Lord would know more, but I had left him behind with Keogh.

"Not much anyone can do anyhow," Bowie said. "We got a hundred and fifty men, only twenty horses. Can't leave, and stayin' don't seem like such a good idea, neither. Tried gettin' honorable terms, but all we gots is that red flag flying from the church. It means no quarter. Least Travis writes a good letter. Should bring us some help."

Kellogg shook his head. "Travis writes a great letter, but only the men from—"

"Mark, these gentlemen have pressing duties," I interjected. "So do we. Let's get to work."

I nodded to Cooke and we hustled Kellogg out into the dreary courtyard, preventing him from saying anything more than necessary.

"General, what the devil?" Kellogg protested.

"Mr. Kellogg, we can't pretend omnipotent knowledge of every event. There's enough distrust already," I lectured, angry with him. "For now, let them think what they want. It doesn't matter. What matters is bringing Keogh up and whipping this garrison into shape. I'm going to inspect the defenses. I want you to talk to the Texans. Get a feel for their morale. Will they fight? What are they fighting for?"

"Yes, sir," Kellogg said, saluting.

He marched off, notebook in hand.

"Bill, look for the best place to position our sharpshooters."

"We have some good shots in the regiment, George, but not enough to turn back an all-out assault," Cooke said.

It was true. Many of the troopers were good with their Springfields, but not experts. And we didn't have enough spare ammunition for target practice.

"Dickenson says this post has twenty-one cannon. Not much powder and shot, maybe, but concentrated fire can discourage even the most determined attack. Let's see what the possibilities are," I said, studying the various positions where the guns had been posted.

"There's a lot more cannon than men to handle them," Cooke said, doing the math. "And probably not more than a handful of experienced gunners. Hell, George, our best artillery man is Harrington, and we left him on the Rio Grande."

"Bill, at the range we'll be firing these guns, we aren't likely to miss," I replied.

We were busy throughout the morning. Morning Star made me eat breakfast, a tortilla stuffed with steamed beef and rice. She and the other Sioux had attracted a good deal of attention, the local Texans more accustomed to Comanche or Apache. Many, such as Crockett, had fought the Creeks. Within a few years, the Cherokee Nation would be forced off their lands, driven into Oklahoma by Andrew Jackson's unjust policies. Much as the government was trying to do to the Plains Indians in my own time. I did not approve of such practices, convinced that civilization would find the Indians in God's own time, without bullets or a bayonet. And with a little help from the railroads.

Morning Star, in particular, was an object of interest. Even in a buffalo robe, she drew every eye as she walked about the compound. Her obvious affinity for Tom did not stop several of the frontiersmen from seeking her attention. She smiled and put them off with polite remarks, indicating her education in St. Louis had prepared her well for dealing with wolves.

There were several Tejano children among the garrison's families, so Slow was less conspicuous. Other than his mysterious gaze and tendency to ask unusual questions. Spotted Eagle and Gray Wolf soon blended in, eager to learn about the strange fortifications and the men who hid behind stone walls. When the Mexican artillery fired on us, which they did every ten or fifteen minutes, the young Sioux would climb up on a rampart and fire their muskets in response, often getting a cheer from the men. The Alamo garrison, worn down by six days of siege, found encouragement from their enthusiasm.

I discovered that, as engineers go, Jameson was not a complete fool. With limited resources, he had set firing positions to cover the most likely approaches. I pulled him aside, walking through the compound as he pointed to the fort's strong points.

"The south gate is well protected by that stockade you entered," Jameson explained. "Armed with two cannon and screened by a ditch. Our high firing platform at the back of the church guards the east flank, and another battery is stationed above the corral. The west wall is close enough to the river that a direct assault would be difficult. But, as you said, our problem is the north wall. Patched it as best we could, but all it's held together with is mud and a few skinny logs."

The Alamo was not a fort. Before the siege, the sturdy abode buildings surrounding the courtyard had housed workshops and homes for the workers. Like most 18th century missions established by the Catholic Church, its function had been to convert Indians to Christianity, not hold off a force of several thousand soldiers.

Jameson seemed to recognize the situation clearly; he just didn't have a good solution. Initially, I didn't see a solution, either. But I would. The Mexican army may have had the upper hand for the moment, but they weren't the Seventh Cavalry, and they weren't led by George Armstrong Custer.

During the day, I noticed my men spreading throughout the fort, talking with the Texans, checking on our horses, and looking for a dry bunk in the long barracks, for the weather remained wet and cold. We had more in common with the defenders than I originally thought. Though the majority were Southerners from states like South Carolina and Georgia, there were also some from the North and others born overseas, much like the composition of the Seventh. We found immigrants from England and Ireland, Scotland and France. There was even a Dane and a German. Since the earliest days of the Civil War, the ranks of the U.S. Army had been filled with men from Europe come to fight for freedom and a better life. Thousands had fallen on battlefields from Virginia to Mississippi, but those who survived had become Americans.

"Is that why you're here, David? Have you come from Tennessee to start a new life?" I asked Crockett.

Calling him David was a sign of respect, for he didn't like to be called Davy. A better life appeared to be the primary motivation for the Alamo's garrison, though everyone's experience is different.

"Provisional government of Texas promised 640 acres of land for six months service. Got a few troubles with my creditors back home, so that land would come in mighty handy. Though saying Texas has a government is a bit of an exaggeration," Crockett said

"How so?" I asked, for Kellogg had been vague on the details.

Crockett leaned against one of the 6-pounders guarding the south palisade and offered me a chaw of tobacco. I declined.

"Well, seems these Texans got fed up with Santa Anna and besieged General Cos here in San Antonio. Cos surrendered in December, just before I rode in. Cos is Santa Anna's brother-in-law, so you know the family honor's at stake. Santa Anna swore he'd crush Texas, whatever it takes. You'd think that would unite everybody, but it ain't so. Colonel Frank Grant decided to invade Matamoros and took most of the volunteers with him. Stripped the Alamo bare of supplies. Governor Smith had himself a fit and ordered Grant back. The governing council, friends of Grant, decided to impeach Smith and appoint Robinson governor, but Smith refused to quit.

"So now we got two Texan governments. Worse, some folks say Sam Houston is commander of the army. Others say Grant is commander of the army. Jim Fannin's got a few hundred men down at La Bahia, and since that's the biggest army in Texas, they say he's the commander. And here in the Alamo, Travis and Bowie have been a right testy, too."

"And this conglomeration of schoolyard bullies expect to defeat Santa Anna?" I said, disgusted by the bickering. Though having attended several sessions of congress, I should have known better.

"They beat the Mexicans at Gonzales, and at the Grass Fight, and here in Béjar. These Texans don't think much of the Mexican army," Crockett said, his personal thoughts on the subject hidden.

"They haven't fought the Mexican army, David. Just a poorly trained frontier force."

"I reckon Santa Anna will be a surprise to them," Crockett admitted.

"A fatal one," I said.

Pending a declaration of independence, Texas was still a province of Mexico. The governor was fighting with his council. Leaders of the different militias were fighting with each other. Travis had issued a call to arms, warning Texas that Santa Anna was about to march through their colonies with fire and sword. From what Kellogg said, few had answered. Had the nation responded to Lincoln's call in 1861 in a like fashion, the United States would now be three or four different countries.

My tour with Jameson ended on the north wall where a battery of two 6-pounders overlooked approaches from the San Antonio River. To my right, the weed-covered prairie was cut by irrigation ditches. In days past, it would have been farmland. The Mexican army had stationed several hundred infantry just beyond musket range and were busy digging siege works, gradually moving their light cannon closer and closer. The crumbling wall was shored up with timber beams.

I leaned against the makeshift rampart, studying the enemy positions through my field glasses. They were well-entrenched.

"We needed another month to fix this wall," Jameson said with sigh. "After we took Béjar from General Cos, the army started to disband. Then Grant took most of our ammunition and horses, leaving the garrison half-naked. It's a miracle the men have stuck it out this long."

"I must agree with you, there," I said. "In the army, if a soldier tries to walk away, we shoot him. Militia is a constant discipline problem."

"It doesn't mean we won't fight," Jameson said.

"With that red flag flying over there, I don't see that you have much choice. The question is, *how* will you fight?"

"I guess we just wait for the Mexicans to make their move, then hurt them so bad they back off. If we hold on long enough, eventually our friends and neighbors will come to our support. Or maybe the Mexicans will starve. Food can get scarce this time of year."

"That army out there is fifteen hundred strong. In another week, it will grow to two or three thousand. How many friends and neighbors are you expecting?" I asked, attempting not to sound sarcastic.

"Not that many," Jameson conceded. "Why? What's your plan?"

"I would not wait in this fort for extinction," I immediately replied. "I would attack. Burn the enemy's supplies. Capture their guns. Harass their patrols. Cut their communications. I would locate their commanders and drive down on them in the pre-dawn hours. But I'm a cavalry officer, and that's what cavalry officers do. I've never been good at waiting for the enemy to seize the initiative."

Crockett came up with Tom and Morning Star, standing beside us on the platform. Another cannon shot sailed over the south wall, landing in a ditch that supplied water for the fort. Apparently a necessary source of water until they finished digging a new well. I noticed two Negroes, slaves of Bowie and Travis, busy with their shovels. The work would go faster if their masters pitched in.

"That's getting very annoying," Tom said when a second cannon fired, this one from the north side. We saw the Mexicans had pushed a gun within five hundred yards of the northeast corner.

"We should wait until all their guns are in range," I decided.

"We've been fired on since the moment we rode in, and the Alamo is so low on ammunition, they rarely return fire. It won't hurt to slow those siege works down a little," Tom suggested.

"Okay. Just enough to make them duck," I reluctantly agreed.

Tom waved to Cooke. He and Butler came running with their rifles and my Remington.

"That's a long shot," Crockett warned. "My Tennessee boys have wounded a few across the river. That battery is only three hundred or so yards off. These rascals are a lot farther."

"We'll see," I answered.

Butler returned first with his modified Sharps carbine, rubbing dust off the sight. Tom had borrowed a Springfield, his Winchester better suited to shorter ranges. My Remington hunting rifle was the only one in the command with an octagonal barrel, giving a distinctive appearance. I had used it while hunting elk on the Black Hills Expedition.

"One shot each, gentlemen. Best hit wins," I announced.

Crockett and Jameson thought we were crazy. Seeing the attention on the wall, Travis came up to join us. John Baugh and Almaron Dickenson quickly followed. Had the Mexican artillery been fortunate at this moment, they could have wiped out most of the Alamo's commanders. When Spotted Eagle and Gray Wolf joined us, the packed dirt firing platform grew crowded.

"Other than presenting targets for the enemy, what nonsense is this?" Travis demanded.

"A shooting contest," Crockett said, loading his Kentucky long rifle.

I saw it wasn't the famous Old Betsy we boys had read about in grade school, but still a good weapon in capable hands. He took out a powder horn, tapped in a bit of powder, added a piece of wadding, and dropped a round lead ball down the barrel before packing it down with a ramrod. A spot of priming powder in the flash pan and a flint would ignite the gun powder. Such muzzle loaders were used early in the Civil War until paper cartridges came into regular use.

Crockett knelt at the wall, took careful aim, and squeezed the trigger. A delayed half second later, the rifle fired with a puff of black smoke. A speck of dirt kicked up about a hundred yards short of the Mexican entrenchment. Several soldiers digging a new ditch looked up without much concern. One laughed.

"Just a touch far off," Crockett concluded.

Tom did not bother to kneel down. He opened the trap door on the Springfield, loaded a copper cased 45-55 bullet in the breech, and snapped it shut with the lever. He then sighted the most likely target, a sergeant standing above his men giving orders. When Tom fired, the sergeant keeled over, shot through the shoulder. Several men rushed to his aid.

"Howdy do, boy!" Crockett shouted.

"Good Lord," Jameson added, taking the Springfield from Tom to look it over. Travis took the gun from Jameson, opening the trap door and staring at the firing mechanism.

It seemed everyone in the fort was suddenly watching our game. Men on the adjoining gun platform, and on the roof of the long barracks, were waving to their fellows who could not get a view. They had wondered what our strange weapons could do.

"My turn," Butler said, kneeling where Crockett had and gazing down his sights.

Butler was using a customized falling block Sharps carbine. Though a single shot weapon, it had great range. I had never faced off against Jimmy in a contest, but everyone knew he was a crack shot. He took his time, watching a group of peasants as they crowded around the wounded sergeant. But one man was better dressed, possibly an officer. Butler held his breath for a moment, then squeezed off a shot, hitting the man through the forehead. The blood spray was visible even from such a distance.

Most of the peasants dropped their shovels and ran. Those who remained ducked behind their partially dug earthwork.

"You didn't leave me much to shoot at, Jimmy," I complained, taking his place on the wall and kneeling to steady my aim.

"General, you couldn't beat my shot even if you had something to shoot at," Butler bragged, which certainly was not true.

I saw an officer come forward yelling at the workers to pick up their shovels. A few obeyed. The man's uniform was not elaborate enough to be a colonel, or even a captain, though I was not an expert on such things. I guessed him to be a lieutenant. Three soldiers in white were following, two carrying cannon shot, the third a small powder barrel.

I noticed Slow had made his way up on the platform, standing at my elbow. He seemed intrigued with the proceedings.

"A warrior's game," I whispered, happy to see the quiet boy so excited. "Would you like a shot?"

"I have come to see the sunrise," Slow said.

"That was hours ago," I replied.

"There will be another," the youngster insisted. How he had guessed my plan is something I'll never know.

"Gentlemen, it saddens me that we did not place a wager on this contest," I said.

"Get on with it, Autie. We'd all have aimed twice as good if money had been involved," Tom said. As usual, he was probably right.

I didn't need to think twice about my target, taking aim at the unlucky private carrying the powder barrel and squeezing the trigger. The powder barrel exploded, a brief fireball lighting the gray day. A second sunrise. The man carrying it was killed instantly, his companions burned. When I last saw the junior officer, he was crawling for the trench with his arm on fire.

"Jesus Christ Almighty," Captain Baugh whispered.

The men watching from the walls and the roof of the long barracks sent up a cheer. Travis returned the Springfield to Tom and walked away without comment.

"Looks like I've won, gentlemen," I casually said, ejecting the spent shell.

"Lots more targets," Butler glumly said, studying the entrenchment.

"No, Jimmy. It might slow them down a little, but the siege works will still get closer. Better an overconfident enemy than a cautious one."

Tom nodded that he agreed. Cooke made a note in his memo pad.

"My cousins think we should steal the iron guns," Morning Star said. "Spotted Eagle says we could come on them under the moon while they sleep." I turned to look at Gray Wolf and Spotted Eagle, liking their aggressive attitude. But in this situation, it wasn't very practical.

"Good thinking, lads, but they'll have pickets guarding the batteries," I said, using my hands to emphasize some of the words. "If we attack, it will be at dawn."

I wrapped an arm around Spotted Eagle's shoulders and walked my party down from the firing platform, receiving another cheer from the garrison. I tipped my hat with a smile. Then a cannon shot flew over the fort, whistling as it cut the air and almost hit the corral. Tom was right about it being annoying.

The bombardment continued throughout the day, sometimes several guns in rapid succession, followed by a lull.

I met with Jameson and Crockett inside Bowie's quarters next to the south gate. The room was small, warmed by a wood-burning stove, and decorated with colorful painted tiles. The dirt floor had a small woven carpet and rushes. The plank table was surrounded by three rickety benches. A Mexican woman, the cousin of Bowie's late wife, hovered nearby with broth and a pitcher of brown ale.

The officers were divided on how to proceed, none of them experienced in siege warfare. Having lived through the siege of Petersburg at the end of the Rebellion, I knew there would be but one outcome. Even Robert E. Lee had not been able to fend off the inevitable. After my inspection of the fort, I'd spent some time thinking of a plan that might achieve victory—or at least a stalemate.

"What do you think?" I asked, pushing a hand-drawn map of the Alamo out for Jameson to study.

There was just enough light given by the candles for him to see. He dwelt on it for several minutes, tracing lines with his finger.

"It's a lot of work. And fatal if the enemy doesn't respond as you think," Jameson finally said.

He gave the drawing to Bowie, who lay bedridden on a cot. He was useless in a fight, but as leader of the volunteers, he held the most sway over the garrison. I hoped. Travis had gained a great deal of respect for his stubborn resistance.

"Didn't like defendin' these walls to begin with. This here is even crazier," Bowie said, making to put the map in a candle flame. The paper had almost caught fire when Crockett snatched it back, tapping out the glowing embers on the table.

"It's sneaky. Maybe what we need, but an awful risk. I thought you wanted out in the open? Smack the enemy on their own ground," Crockett said.

"Travis may be a pompous amateur, but he's right about the odds," I reluctantly said. "The thirty extra guns my command brings aren't enough to drive off an assault by three thousand trained troops. Even after bringing up the rest of my men, there are only a hundred of us. Once the ammunition gives out, the fight's over."

"So this is your plan? Give up the strength of our position?" Jameson said, taking the map from Crockett and rolling it up. "I'm sorry, sir. You mean well, but Travis knows our situation better. Once Houston and Fannin arrive, we'll push the Mexicans back across the Nueces just like we did before."

Jameson got up and left the room. Bowie pulled up his thick wool blanket and went back to sleep, his late wife's cousin quietly parked on a stool next to the bed. A Catholic crucifix hung on the wall above him.

Crockett and I entered the small quadrangle in front of the church. An offshoot of the main compound, the area was guarded by the rough timber palisade and two cannon. With the long barracks on my left and the lower barracks behind me, the position formed a fort within a fort. Crockett and his Tennessee boys, many of whom were not really from Tennessee, had been assigned the area's defense.

I walked back toward the main compound, shaking my head. According to Cooke, the Alamo encompassed three acres. Too many walls, too few men. The fort was quiet at the moment. It had rained again, keeping everybody indoors except for the sentries.

"We can present your idea to the men. Take a vote," Crockett recommended.

"You're a good man. I see why the people of Tennessee sent you to Congress. But an army can't be led by voting. If you rely on these beaten down old walls to keep out the enemy, you're all going to die. It won't be a matter of weeks, but a matter of days."

"You can't be sure of that. When Fannin . . ."

"David, Fannin isn't coming. You know it, so does Travis. How many of your men would stay if *they* knew?" I asked.

"We've got to hope, George. What else is there?"

"If you see a chance for victory, you take it. You don't stop to think. You don't wait for advice. You don't call for a vote. You charge with everything you have and batter the enemy until they break."

"Is this a military strategy or your philosophy of life?" Crockett asked with a grin, for he was good at reading people. Like most politicians.

"It's worked for me so far," I answered.

"Care to explain where you've come from?" he questioned after hinting all afternoon. "The weapons. Your uniforms. Even the saddles on your horses. Not like anything I've seen before."

"You wouldn't believe me. I hardly believe it myself."

"Does it have anything to do with that Indian boy?" Crockett asked.

"Why would you say that?" I replied in surprise.

"Had a talk with him. Odd sort. I've known plenty of Indians. Known their families. Sat in their sweat lodges smoking the pipe. They see the world different than we do, but it don't mean their vision is any worse."

"I really don't have an answer for you. We helped Slow and his family while riding south, and they just sort of fell in with us."

"Riding south from where?"

"That's where the story gets complicated," I said, unwilling to say more until it started to make sense.

There was a thick oak gate between the long barracks and the church leading to the corrals. I passed through into the rear of the fort, where the walls were lower and our horses were bunched together against the cold wind. A sturdy lean-to was used as a livery and blacksmith shop. From there it was a short walk to the corral holding sixty horses, most belonging to the Seventh. In the enclosure beyond, I counted about thirty head of cattle. Voss was not watching our mounts. Or Sergeant Hughes. Or even Corporal Foley.

Suddenly I realized that none of my men were around, as if they'd just disappeared. My heart beat faster, wondering if another strange occurrence was taking place.

A moment later, Kellogg appeared with Morning Star. I didn't see Tom.

"In the chapel," Kellogg said, seeing my concern.

"General Custer, your people have much spirit," Morning Star said rather elusively. She took my hands, giving them a squeeze, and gazed at me with an uncomfortable admiration.

The Alamo church was not the hump-shaped building I had visited in 1865. The hump was a feature added by the Army Corp of Engineers several years after the battle, while they were converting the ruin into a warehouse. Several of Crockett's men watched me from the palisade as I went to enter, apparently expecting trouble.

The inside of the old church was also different from my previous visit. The roof was gone, replaced by a partial skeleton of beams where the roof should be. The wide floor area, that had held supplies for troops, was now filled by a long dirt ramp leading to a battery at the rear of the structure. At the top of the ramp, three large cannon were perched ten feet above the ground. It was a strong position, allowing the artillery to guard the approaches from the swampy prairie to the east and the Alameda to the southeast. The only sheltered rooms were to the left and right of the door where several families had taken residence. The church walls were the thickest in the entire compound.

The men of the Seventh Cavalry were assembled at the bottom of the dirt ramp, some sitting on the ground and others on tree stumps. Tom and Cooke were standing. Two of the Alamo defenders were manning the battery, watching but remaining quiet. Wrapped in blankets against the damp air, Slow and his two older cousins were halfway up the ramp, interested in the proceedings. The boy was particularly attentive, his black eyes searching for nuance as well as meaning.

"What's this all about?" I asked, seeing many guilty expressions.

"We've got a problem, Autie," Tom said, coming down the ramp to intercept me.

"That's obvious. How does hiding in this old church help?" I replied.

"We're not hiding, George. We needed time to talk," Cooke said.

Outrageously so, for in ten years of serving together, he had never used my first name in front of the rank and file.

"Bill and I had lunch with Kellogg. He is a fount of information," Tom said. "Discovering ourselves here, in this strange place and time, is hard enough. Our families are gone. Our wives and girlfriends. From how I figure it, Pa is a year younger than I am now, still living with his first wife in New Rumley. You and I haven't even been born yet. Or Libbie. Each of us is trying to decide what it means. But when Kellogg reminded us about the history of Texas, that was really the last straw. We called the men together for a talk."

"I don't see the point. We are where we are. Let's get back to work and cry in our soup later," I ordered. "I've conferred with Crockett and Jameson. With a little persuasion . . ."

"We're not getting back work. Not here," Cooke said.

"Autie, in a day or two, Texas will declare independence. And then they're going to write a constitution. A *slave* constitution," Tom explained. "Ten years from now, they'll join the Union as a *slave state*, and fifteen years after that, they're going to join the Confederacy."

"If we help these Texans, we're helping the goddamn slavers. Helping that goddamn traitor Jeff Davis and his plantation overseers. I didn't join the army for that," Butler said, a hand fixed on his Colt.

"Me either, sir," Voss added. "I left Germany for freedom in America. Freedom for all, like Mr. Lincoln wanted."

"What happens in the future is for the government to decide. It can't be our concern," I said, pointing Voss and Butler toward the door with a frown.

"It *is* our concern," Tom said, holding Voss back. "We're pretty close to a decision here, and I've got a hunch our decision is to leave."

"Leave? You can't be serious. Don't you understand? This is the Alamo for God's sake!" I shouted. "The Thermopylae of modern times. A victory here will be immortal. It will dwarf our victories in the Rebellion."

The men looked down, some grumbling. Many were cold, impatient, and unhappy. I could not understand their reluctance. Tom motioned for Cooke and Butler to step back, revealing himself as the conspiracy's leader.

"Autie, maybe it is Thermopylae. Maybe you're Leonidas reborn. But we aren't three hundred Spartans," Tom said, looking at me with disapproval. "We're thirty ordinary Americans who think slavery is a dirty business. And certainly not something worth dying for."

"I was too young to serve in the war, sir, but my father and uncles did," Corporal Foley said, standing at Tom's side clutching his rifle. "28th Massaschuetts. Uncle Daniel lost a leg at Cold Harbor."

"Sir, I lost a brother at Shiloh," a young private added, red-faced with emotion.

"General, sir, we spent four years fighting the Rebs. Lost family and friends. A lot of them Rebs were from Texas. I just don't see how helpin' now makes any sense," Sergeant Butler growled.

"I was in Washington the night they shot President Lincoln. So was Tom," Cooke said, his voice firm as a glacier. "We stood vigil outside Petersen's boarding house as he lay dying. Lincoln was a great man. He died to make this land free. Free from the Atlantic to the Pacific."

"I know you and Pa are democrats," Tom added. "You thought slavery would fade away on its own, given enough time. But it didn't. Slavery died in a bloodbath like this world has never seen, and Texas was on the wrong side."

"We can't let that affect our decisions now," I urgently protested. "Whatever might happen, this is the United States, and it's been invaded by a foreign enemy. It's our duty to resist."

"No, Autie, this isn't the United States. It's 1836, and this is Mexico. Texas hasn't even declared independence yet. We're the foreigners here," Tom replied.

"These are still Americans, fighting for the American way of life. We can't turn our backs on them," I insisted.

"They're not fighting for *our* way of life," Private Engle said, spitting on the floor.

"I'm sorry, sir. Engle is right. I call for the question. All in favor or riding out, raise your hand," Cooke said.

Every enlisted man raised his hand except two, who hesitated. Frowns from their comrades soon caused them to join the majority. Tom and Cooke put their hands up last, showing they agreed.

"Have your equipment ready. We leave at sunset," Tom said.

The men jumped up and filed out of the church, none daring to look me in the face. Gray Wolf and Spotted Eagle followed, leaving only Tom, Cooke and Slow. The Alamo gunners on the rear platform had heard most of the meeting. One went to tell Captain Dickenson and Travis.

"Sorry, George. A man's got to do what's right," Cooke said, offering to shake hands before leaving.

I turned my back on him until he was gone, angry and speechless. If Tom had dared smile, I'd have wrung his neck, but there was nothing lighthearted in his visage.

"Autie, I don't know who or what sent us here. Maybe it's God's doing. Maybe something else," Tom said. "But whatever is it, we weren't sent here to protect slavery. I shed blood to fight it once. I'll shed blood to fight it again."

"You could have talked to me first. Found another way than mutiny. If you're going to command, you must command. All you've done is set loose thirty men armed for chaos. Where will they go? What will they do?"

"We'll figure that out after rejoining Myles," Tom said.

"Tom, call the men back. Let me convince them to stay," I begged.

"We ride at sunset, Autie. You can ride with us or not," he answered.

Tom left the church to organize the men. Nothing I could say would change his mind. A cold wind blew through the open roof, chilling to the bone. I stepped into one of the small side rooms, the space lit with candles, the walls decorated with pictures of Catholic saints. Idolatry of this sort is not permitted in Christian churches, but during the war soldiers of all religions grew to respect each other's faith. Well, maybe not all soldiers, but a good number of us.

I sat down on a bench, watching a candle flicker before the altar. Slow entered, sitting next to me.

"Colonel Tom is leaving. They are all leaving," he said.

"I know."

"Are you going to leave with them?" Slow asked.

"Don't know that I have a choice."

"You have traveled far from your home. Is it your destiny to die in this place of stone?"

"I had no intention of dying, youngster. These Texans are fighting for freedom. The freedom to speak their minds. To worship as they please. The freedom to decide what laws they'll live by. I wanted to be part of that."

"And you wanted glory," Slow observed, the candlelight dancing in his black eyes.

"Is that such a bad thing? What soldier doesn't want glory?"

"My people are warriors, too," Slow said. "We fight for our families."

He slid off the bench, looked up at the pictures of the saints adorning the walls, and quietly left the room. A cannon shot echoed in the distance.

Glancing to my right, I noticed a small portrait in a dark corner. It was Saint Jude, the patron saint of lost causes

---

I had always thought that white men fought only for themselves. The white hunters who came to our land slaughtered the buffalo to sell the hides, leaving the People hungry. The miners came only for gold rocks, their hearts infested with greed. Everywhere the white men built their roads, the game would disappear. The treaties they made quickly flew away on the next wind. But I was wrong to think all white men the same. Many of my own people killed game to sell for whiskey and rifles. Some raided settlers to steal their horses and women. Among all people, one can find good and bad. These soldiers were not cowards, but they would not fight to enslave the black men, though there was profit in such a thing. The white chief Custer was angry his men would not follow him to glory.

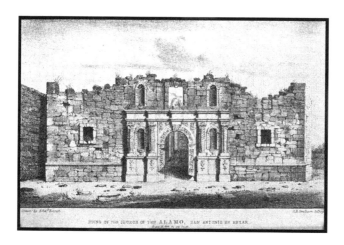

RUINS OF THE CHURCH OF THE ALAMO, SAN ANTONIO DE BEXAR.

CHAPTER FIVE

IGNOMINIOUS RETREAT

"Custer! Custer! What is this?" Travis shouted, running across the court-yard with Crockett and Captain Baugh. I stopped outside the gate between the church and the long barracks. Cooke and my troopers were saddling their horses in the corral.

"We've decided not to stay," I said, feeling as dreary as the weather.

"Why is that? Because I won't give you command?" Travis asked. His face was red with anger. And a trace of desperation.

"You don't need to give what I can take," I defiantly replied.

"Not turning yellow, are you?" Travis said.

I took off one of my white leather riding gloves and slapped him across the face, familiar with the custom. Travis put a hand on his saber, a fine piece of Spanish steel.

"Captain Baugh will act as my second. Pistols or swords?" Travis said.

"Why wait?" I answered, reaching for the sword taken from the dead Mexican courier.

Tom and Butler came running. Crockett grabbed Travis. Cooke grabbed me. A cannonball flew overheard, striking the long barracks with an adobe splintering thud.

"This isn't the time," Crockett said.

"Autie, get a hold of yourself," Tom demanded.

I stepped back, sheathing the sword.

"Too bad the Mexicans will kill you first, you damn fool," I said, turning my back on Travis.

Crockett followed as I started toward the corral. We passed underneath the arch into the stable. The rough plank walls were hung with tack and harnesses. An old wagon sat to one side next to a blacksmith's forge. To my left, several doors led into the rear of the long barracks.

"George, why are you leaving so suddenly?" Crockett asked. "Green and I have been discussing your plan. We think—"

"David, my men and I come from a free land. We've heard Texas is getting ready to pass a slave constitution. They won't fight for that. Now that I've had time to think, I won't fight for it either," I answered.

"Hell, I don't own any slaves. Hardly a man here owns a slave," Crockett said. "My wife had a few slaves once, inherited from her father, but the lazy bastards were eating us out of house and home, so I sold them off to a Quaker family. They're sharecroppers now."

"Not everybody in the South is so generous, David. And most are a lot worse," I said, knowing well from experience.

"I've seen Northern workers in Philadelphia, and the slums in New York City," Crockett defended, an old and tired argument.

I pointed toward the new well where the two slaves were throwing up a mound of dirt. Most of the garrison stayed near the walls to avoid the cannon fire while the black men were largely in the open. Crockett read my expression.

"There are more important things at stake," Crockett said.

"No, I don't think so. I think John and Sam over there say it all," I disagreed.

The sun had set, the night dark because heavy clouds were covering the nearly full moon. It hadn't rained since early morning, so the prairie would be reasonably dry. Good for fast movement.

"Give us a chance to change your mind," Crockett asked.

"It's not my mind you need to change, David. It's your slave holding friends. If riding out of here wasn't so dangerous, I'd be taking those two men with me. I've heard Santa Anna protects slaves. Joe and Sam might be the only ones still standing when this is all over."

I went into the corral where the men were ready to mount. Voss already had a saddle on Vic. Everyone was tightening their cinch straps and adjusting their stirrups. The corral was divided into two sections by a rough wooden fence. The north and east walls were formed by eight foot high stone walls. A cannon mounted on the northeast corner protected the fort from attack.

"Autie, I figure we'll go out this gate, skirt along the morass, then go over the hill between their north battery and the powder house," Tom said, having studied the ground.

"Just a minute, I have something to say first," I interrupted.

I got up on a barrel, the stable behind me. A dozen of the fort's defenders were also gathered around, more watching from the roof and walls. My men paused in their preparations, afraid I was going to berate them for their rebellious behavior. Even Tom seemed apprehensive.

"Gentlemen, I want to apologize," I said, speaking loud enough for everyone to hear. "I want to apologize to all of you. I've been a solider my whole life. Sometimes it's hard to remember what we fight for. It's not just to oppose an enemy, or capture a piece of land. It's to defend an ideal. To uphold our principles. And to earn the respect of our families. I won't forget again. That's a promise."

I jumped down from the barrel to shake Cooke's hand, giving Slow a grateful nod. The boy almost smiled.

"Thank you, General," Cooke said.

"Thank me after we get out of here," I answered.

I held Vic by the reins and walked toward the northeast corner of the corral to a heavy wooden gate. The adobe walls here were not as high or as thick as courtyard, but subject to good covering fire from two directions. Crockett came to open the gate, which creaked as it swung in.

"Good luck, David," I sincerely said, for I genuinely liked him.

"Hope we meet again, George," Crockett said, reaching to shake hands.

I gave him a firm grip. Too bad Texas would never know the wisdom of this remarkable man.

"Okay, boys, keep it quiet. Use your Colts if we run into a patrol. Tom, have your men watch our flank. Cooke, bring up the rear. Jimmy, you're with

Cooke. Voss, stay at my side and keep the bugle ready," I rapidly ordered. "Slow, where are you?"

"We're over here, General," Morning Star said, the four Indians bunched with Kellogg.

"Walk close to me at the head of the column. Everybody stay together. Once we're clear of the swamp, we'll mount up and ride over the ridge beyond their lines. If we get separated, listen for Voss to sound recall. Are there any questions?" I asked.

There were no questions. Most of us had ridden together for several years, and some longer. Each knew what to do.

I led the way, though Spotted Eagle and Gray Wolf quickly moved out in front, scouting the path. I don't believe Indians can see in the dark better than white men, but the Indians believe it. I wasn't going to argue.

Slow came up on his young mare, the only one of us mounted. Tom and his six skirmishers were ten yards to the left. Campfires of the besieging army were visible several hundred yards away. A small fire burned on the hill to our right where Tom had attacked the battery that morning. Troops had reoccupied the hill, but we'd seen no cannon.

Suddenly there was a loud boom. The Alamo's 18-pounder had roared to life, firing on the town. The echo reverberated though the entire valley. Rifle fire erupted from the lunette protecting the south gate.

"Is the fort under attack?" Voss asked.

"No. They're providing a diversion. Giving us a chance to slip away. Those are good men back there," I said.

We had just cleared the last of the irrigation ditches, the morass falling away to dry ground as we skirted to the left. The burned-out mill on Powder House Hill was off to the right. I heard Tom's men mounting up.

"Okay, boys, let's get going," I whispered, jumping on Vic and giving him a nudge.

A musket fired from our left. Then two more. Both were from too great a distance. We did not return fire for it would have given away our position. A few minutes later, we reached the top of the ridge. A guard fifty yards to the right stirred with curiosity but no apparent alarm. Gray Wolf and Spotted

Eagle were waiting for us, carrying lances and once again wearing their sombreros. They were terribly proud of themselves, convinced the enemy had mistaken us for Mexican cavalry. And they were probably right. On a dark night, in such cold weather, no one was looking for a fight.

We moved on another half mile before Voss blew his trumpet. I wasn't worried about the sound now. We had passed through their siege works and beyond range of the guns. If a mounted patrol sought to challenge us, they'd find more trouble than they could handle.

"The lines around the Alamo aren't so tight," Tom said, rejoining the march as we moved east through rolling hills. Kellogg and Morning Star rode with him.

"Half of Santa Anna's army isn't drawn up yet," Kellogg said. "Another thousand infantry won't arrive until the 3rd. Colonel Almonte is on the Goliad Road with most of the cavalry. On March 4th, Santa Anna will draw his divisions together and decide on an assault. They'll use the 5th getting into position, and attack before dawn on the 6th."

"I feel bad for them. They are very brave," Morning Star said.

"They are on a journey. Not all will see the new day," Slow grimly announced. He seemed very preoccupied.

"What about us? How many of us will see the new day?" I playfully asked.

"More than would have survived on the grass-covered hill," Slow said, seeming to speak from a long forgotten memory. He booted his mare to catch up with his cousins.

I glanced around, saw we were making good time over the strange terrain, and ordered the command to turn right. We would cross the Gonzales Road and continue south until reaching the San Antonio River. The moon helped, peeking out from behind the clouds.

"Morning Star, tell me why you came on this adventure," I requested.

I was riding at the head of the column with Morning Star and Tom, Cooke and Voss close behind. The night was cold but not windy.

"I do not remember all. I recall much of my youth, and my schooling in St. Louis. Not long after returning to my people, there was alarm in my village. People ran back and forth screaming. I think there was a raid. Spotted Eagle came to help me. I thought . . . It is all a very strange dream. I thought someone had shot Spotted Eagle. Women were crying. A teepee was on fire. I turned to see a man standing behind me. He was a Crow, a bitter enemy of my people. He held a war club. I usually carry a knife, but it had been left near our campfire. I found a branch instead and hit the Crow. He . . . I thought . . . It is hard to remember.

"Then there was a fog. A deep, disturbing fog, and I thought myself lost forever on a long trail. Praise the Great Spirit, a star came to light my path, and soon I was traveling on the plains with my cousins."

I reined Vic in, an icy grip on my heart. The command was coming up behind me, not one of whom hadn't been plagued with strange dreams. Tom stopped next to me.

"What's wrong, Autie? We've got a clear trail and plenty of moonlight," he said, a happy dance in his eyes as he glanced at Morning Star.

What had I done back on the Little Big Horn? Had I sacrificed my brother to ambition? And Bill Cooke? Georgie Yates? How many others? Had I now been given a second chance? To do what? And what did the strange Indian boy have to do with it?

We rode in silence for several hours before dismounting to give the horses a rest. The weather gradually worsened, forcing us to find shelter in a tree-lined ravine. Somewhere in the area the Mexican cavalry was patrolling. At midnight we started out again, walking our horses carefully in the black night as Tom and the Indian boys found our path. Kellogg stayed close, having tried to talk since we'd left the Alamo, but I kept waving him off.

"A few reinforcements will make it in," Kellogg said when I finally allowed him to broach the subject. "History says thirty-two men from Gonzales will enter the Alamo before dawn on March 1st. They still think Fannin is coming to help."

"March 1st? That's tomorrow," I said.

"It will give the garrison a bit of hope, but on March 3rd, a courier will arrive confirming that no help is coming. I'm sure Travis already knows, he just isn't being honest with his men."

"Being honest with your men can be difficult. A commander needs to judge their commitment. And their character. Most of the time, troops don't want the truth, they just want good leadership."

"Travis seemed like a good leader to me," Kellogg said.

"Yes, right up to the point that he got his entire command massacred," I replied. "Travis is an amateur. I'm a professional military officer with a long record of success."

"Until the Little Big Horn," Kellogg dared to say.

"You can't judge an entire career by one mistake," I replied with some irritation, for I've found that many civilians find it convenient to criticize battlefield decisions from the safety of their easy chairs.

Cooke approached, walking side-by-side with Morning Star. Cooke and Tom were best friends. With Tom having taken such an interest in the young maiden, it was no surprise Bill wanted to discover the attraction. I recalled the winter I'd spent with Monahseetah, who was not only beautiful, but delightful company. Such attractions are easy to understand.

"Once we find Keogh, what will we do next?" Cooke asked.

It was an awfully good question.

"I don't know. We're still soldiers in the United States army. I guess we'll ride east and report for duty," I said.

"Report to Andy Jackson? After what he did to the Cherokee?" Cooke protested.

A protest I agreed with, at heart. I had met quite a few Cherokee over the years and admired their tenacity. And unlike most Indians, they are as civilized as any white man.

"I have not heard of the Cherokee," Morning Star said.

"They are a proud people who once lived in the east, mostly Georgia and Tennessee. They owned farms and ranches. Some even owned slaves," Cooke said. "Though they were friends of the United States and signed many treaties, the Southerners decided to steal their land. President Andrew Jackson helped."

"When the Cherokee protested their eviction in Federal court and won, Jackson ignored the judges and ordered the Indians removed by force. Thousands died," Kellogg added.

I knew this to be true, for my father had spoken of it. Not just the Cherokee, but many peaceful tribes had been robbed of their land, forced west beyond the Mississippi.

"Maybe we'll go lend the Cherokee a hand, Bill," I light-heartedly suggested. "If Jackson can march them out of Tennessee, we can probably march them back in. Until our ammunition runs out."

"You would do such a thing?" Morning Star said.

"I might *like* to do such a thing, young lady. There's not much chance we'd be successful," I answered. "There aren't many white men on the plains in this time, but that's going to change. In the East, it's already changed. There's no turning back the clock."

"But we *have* turned back the clock," Cooke said.

"I'm still not sure what's happened," I disagreed.

"General, what do you mean, *in this time*?" Morning Star asked.

"When you attended school in St. Louis, what year was it?" I replied.

"The missionaries told us it was the year of our Lord 1834," she said.

"You were, what, sixteen years old? Born in 1818?" I guessed.

"Father Duncan thought I was born in 1817, but mother said I was born the year the fox fell under the moon," she said.

"I was born in 1839. Tom was born in 1845. Bill was born in 1846," I recounted.

Morning Star remained quiet for a moment, her thin eyebrows bent in thought.

"General, that cannot be true. The numbering of years do not go backward, unless Father Duncan misled me about your ways," she concluded.

"He did not mislead you, and yes, it is impossible. But here we are, in the year 1836 when we should be in the year 1876. You wouldn't know how we got here, would you?" I asked.

"I have not heard of such a thing," Morning Star said. And I believed her. She was not a person who felt a need to lie.

"Would Slow know the answer?" I pressed.

"You would need to ask him," she said.

The nearly full moon poked out from behind the clouds, then disappeared again.

"Bill, tell the boys we're making camp. We'll start again after sunrise," I decided.

We found a bend in the river that provided a defense on three sides. Posting a sentry near the trail, I went down toward the water where I could see the western plain, thinking for a moment of Libbie, my dogs, and our home at Fort Lincoln. Except for a wind rustling through the thick trees, the camp was quiet. Far better than the noisy Alamo, where Santa Anna's marching band was harassing the garrison one sleepless night after another.

After three days of near constant activity, we were tired, too. When Voss blew taps on his trumpet, it sounded like home.

Because of the inclement weather, we waited until mid-morning before moving south, taking time to catch some fish and hunt a few rabbits. The horses were groomed, gratefully by their reaction, and allowed to graze on the tall grass growing along the riverbank. Slow and I tracked a deer for almost an hour but never got a clear shot. The boy had grown quiet since leaving the Alamo. I caught him looking at me several times, seemingly waiting for some great revelation. I had none to give him.

By nine o'clock we were once again out on the rugged plains riding in column of twos, four scouts in the lead and four flankers on the left. We had the San Antonio River on the right. From what I remembered, Goliad was seventy miles to the southeast, but that wasn't our destination. Fannin could fend for himself, dithering over his summons by Travis until it was too late.

"You're not going to warn him?" Kellogg asked, thinking it a simple thing. Which it wasn't.

"Mark, even I know about the Goliad Massacre," I said. "James Fannin attended West Point but washed out, eventually immigrating to Texas. In command of the garrison at Goliad, he promised to relieve the Alamo, but changed his mind. After the Alamo fell, he delayed his retreat east and eventually surrendered his entire command to the mercy of Santa Anna. And on Palm Sunday, his unarmed men were marched out into the Texas wilderness and shot to death. Four hundred of them."

"Fannin was being cautious," Kellogg explained.

"Fannin forgot the first rule of leadership. A commander may play Henry V, shouting 'Once more into the breach, dear friends, once more into the breach.' Or he may play Richard III. 'A horse, a horse, my kingdom for a horse.' But if nothing else, Fannin proved there is no room on a battlefield for Hamlet."

"I didn't know you had such an affinity for Shakespeare," Kellogg said, laughing with surprise.

"Have you heard of Lawrence Barrett?"

"The actor? Of course."

"Larry is one of my best friends. While in New York, I saw him perform as Cassius in Julius Caesar a dozen times. The theater is a wondrous place. I've seen many a performance in Washington, including Edwin Booth. And his accursed brother. I've been to McVicker's in Chicago. But nothing beats the theaters in New York. The Winter Garden is a cathedral."

"Hamlet aside, shouldn't we go down to Goliad and tell Fannin what's coming? It could avoid a lot of useless bloodshed," Kellogg pressed.

"Travis and Bowie didn't take my advice. Why would Fannin? Maybe we aren't here to change history," I said.

"We shouldn't stand aside and do nothing," he disagreed.

"Maybe we can join the Mexican army? Have you considered that?"

"No, that never even crossed my mind," Kellogg sputtered.

"I turned down an appointment to the Mexican army ten years ago. In this time, the country is in chaos. Providences in rebellion. Santa Anna is a dictator leading his army from one uprising to the next, and eventually, his regime will collapse. Our intervention could give Mexico the stability it needs."

"You wouldn't really join the Mexican army, would you?" he asked.

"I suppose not. But it's a thought," I replied.

Just after noon, we saw two riders coming in our direction. I quickly recognized Lieutenant Smith and Mitch Bouyer. They were moving quickly with a single pack horse carrying their supplies.

"News, Gen'ral. Big news," Bouyer said. "Guess what day it is?"

"How about February 29th, 1836?" I answered.

"Goddamn, maybe not such big news after all," Bouyer said, his shoulders drooping.

"Mr. Smith, a report?" I asked.

"Captain Keogh reached Cibolo Creek like you ordered. He's dug in about twenty miles south of the Gonzales Road," Smith said with a salute. "All the wagons are drawn up and the artillery deployed. Later in the day, about thirty frontiersmen entered our camp, planning to join the Alamo once Colonel Fannin arrives."

Tom rode up and shook hands with Smith. Like Cooke, they were fast friends. All three were in their early 30s, veterans and heroes of the Civil War. Those who called the tight group of officers who dominated the Seventh Cavalry 'the Custer Clan' usually blamed me, but they were wrong. Tom was the linchpin of that brotherhood. Most of my time was spent with Libbie or writing my latest article for *Galaxy Magazine*.

"So you've heard?" Tom asked.

"Yeah. 1836. Isn't that a hell of a thing?" Smith said.

"We were just in the Alamo," Tom said.

"Naw. The Alamo? Did you meet Davy Crockett?" Smith asked, his blue eyes dancing with envy.

"In the flesh. The old bear killer himself. Saw Jim Bowie, too," Tom bragged.

"Bowie really seven foot tall?" Bouyer asked.

"Bowie's a six foot tall drunk and dying of black lung," Tom replied. "He led his men into the Alamo and now he's too sick to lead them out."

"Are we going back?" Smith asked.

"Don't think so. Let's take a ride," Tom said, taking Smith off where they could talk privately.

I had no doubt Smith would accept Tom's point of view. Algernon was from a New York abolitionist family. And even if he wasn't, Tom could talk the fur off an Eskimo.

"Captain Keogh sent us to find you," Bouyer said, quite unnecessarily, for it was obvious why they'd come. "Any orders?"

"We'll reunite the command. You can ride scout with the Indian lads or hang back with us," I casually said, for I was no longer in a hurry. Not until I had someplace to go.

"Guess I'll grab some grub and ride up front," Bouyer said, heading for our pack horses. "Oh, bad news for the young lady. The old Indian died last night."

I was not surprised. The old man was frail, our journey strenuous. But such a loss is always difficult. Then it suddenly occurred to me that I had suffered a similar loss. I would not see my father again, for he was just a struggling young farmer back in Ohio. I would not see my mother, who was still married to her first husband. Libbie would not even be born for another six years. By the time she was old enough to marry, I'd be an old man of fifty-five. Tears crept into my eyes that I was forced to wipe with my sleeve.

"Something wrong, Autie?" Tom asked, riding up.

"All's well, Tommy. How is Algernon taking the news?"

"As well as anybody, I guess. Knows he won't be seeing Nettie again," Tom answered. "I'll always miss Lucia, but it makes me glad we never got married."

Tom had been thinking about the loss, too, but declined to burden me with his feelings. I told him about Jumping Bull so he could tell Morning Star and her cousins, being better at such things.

We left the San Antonio River behind, cutting southeast at an angle toward Cibolo Creek. The land was dry and swept with icy winds. Away from the river, there was scant water or forage for the horses. What few trees we found provided little protection, but we did locate a deep gully for our campsite with plenty of firewood nearby.

Smith had been generous enough to bring two small pup tents on their packhorse. I let him and Bouyer keep one, not wanting to be unfair, while I shared the second with Cooke and Slow. Tom would be sharing Morning Star's tent, but respectfully so. Sergeant Butler was left to stand guard. In such a wilderness, I suspected our only enemies would be the Comanche.

"It's getting colder," Cooke complained, crawling under the buffalo robes keeping Slow and I warm.

"Queen's Own whining about the cold? That's a laugh," I teased.

"A Canadian who knows something about the weather, George. Bouyer says there's a ranch half a day's ride from here. We're going to need the shelter," Cooke said.

"The Cibolo is well-sheltered by the woods," I said.

"If we get there by tomorrow night," Cooke pressed.

"We should," I supposed.

"But you won't," Slow suddenly said.

"And why is that, youngster?" I asked, waiting for a mysterious pronouncement. He did not disappoint.

"Friends await you at the ranch. And enemies," Slow said.

"Slow, you need to be a little more specific," I protested. "We can't keep riding this way and that, forty years out of our time, merely to chase phantoms."

"I think you can," Slow answered.

"And why would that be?" I said.

"Because you have nothing else to do," he defiantly answered.

Damn if the youngster hadn't hit the nail on the head.

"Bill, tell Tom and Bouyer we're going south in the morning," I said.

Cooke poked his head from under the buffalo robe.

"Damn it, George, I just got into bed!" he pleaded.

I rolled over and went to sleep. When and how Bill carried out my order was up to him.

We were off the next morning after a cup of coffee and a bit of dried beef. Bouyer was dispatched with letters for Keogh, informing him of the situation in San Antonio. He was to remain on station while I would join him in two days following a scout to the south. Yates was to cover Harrington's withdrawal from the Rio Grande, reuniting that portion of the command.

I did not tell Keogh about our reasons for abandoning the Alamo. As an Irishman, he had never been very sympathetic to the abolitionist's cause, but most of the command would be. Better to tell the men myself about our decision. Or let Tom do it.

We turned south, back toward the San Antonio River, reaching it in a few hours. From time to time, we saw small farms, but much of the land lay fallow. The houses were mostly adobe, though we noticed the occasional straw shack. Nothing was especially noteworthy until late in the day, some thirty miles from San Antonio, when we approached a lovely valley nestled among wooded hills.

Coming over a shallow pass, we stopped at the crest. The flatlands along a tributary creek were rich with farmland. Sheep and cattle herds lay in the gullies sheltering from the wind. Tom and Morning Star dismounted to stretch their legs. I remained seated on Vic, distracted by many memories.

"This must be it," Cooke said, recognizing Bouyer's description of our destination.

"Nice," I absently observed.

Much of the green valley was fenced to contain animals. Several sturdy buildings were surrounded by low adobe walls. A two-story hacienda sat on a rise back from an irrigated field. The red tile roof was slanted to drain off rain and a second-story porch ran around all four sides. Some of the windows were tinted in blue and green. Near the hacienda stood a long two-story bunkhouse, many smaller adobe houses, and half a dozen barns of all sizes.

Though Spanish in style, this remote ranch reminded me of my child-hood back on the farm in New Rumley. Chasing chickens. Playing pranks on my brothers. Being lectured by my father. Making my mother laugh. When money became scarce, I was sent to live with my older sister in Monroe. My days on the farm were over.

We paused at the top of the pass, the command trailed out behind me. The Sioux lads formed up on my flanks, impatiently awaiting orders. And I soon saw why. Twenty or so Comanche Indians occupied the main road just before the main gate of the ranch, half mounted and the others armed for combat.

The mounted warriors were carrying lances with iron spear points. Those on foot had bows and arrows. Most wore fur jackets, hide pants and mocca-sins. Some of the outfits were decorated with colorful beadwork and feathers, but most were rather plain. I did not see any war paint or elaborate headgear.

The Comanche were opposed by three or four defenders in a dugout below the hacienda. A musket shot rang out.

"From the house. It's a signal they need help," Tom said, pointing to the besieged ranchers.

"We will attack. Voss, sound the charge," I ordered, giving Vic a boot.

I drew one of my bulldogs and galloped down the dirt road toward the hostiles, feeling the cold wind in my face as Vic grunted beneath me. I felt the excitement again, the sudden flush of fear and anger. Future worries faded in the face of imminent combat. The past became a fond memory, a source of strength. The present crystallized with the certain knowledge of living from one second to the next.

The Comanche turned at our approach, mostly in surprise. They neither retreated nor appeared alarmed, though all held tightly to their weapons. For all I knew, the rest of my command was still on the hill and I was charging alone like a crazy lunatic. But I was not alone.

Spotted Eagle and Gray Wolf appeared at my side, their eyes shining with a warrior's quest for glory. Their horses were snorting at a near run, anxious to best each other. I let loose a Sioux war cry and spurred Vic on. The lads managed to keep up, but barely. We were but three against twenty, and it was glorious.

By now the Comanche must have thought us completely insane, and no one, especially Indians, wants to fight mad men. They mounted in a hurry and started into the woods toward the river. We closed so fast they were finally forced to hurry their escape, ignominiously fleeing like cowardly rabbits. It was a bloodless triumph for George Custer.

I reined Vic in before the rough wooden gate, seeing no point in chasing the hostiles through endless thickets. When Spotted Eagle and Gray Wolf stopped beside me, I hollered a victory cheer, which they joined in. Fifty yards behind us were Tom, Cooke and Jimmy Butler, their Colt .45s ready for action. Morning Star and Slow soon caught up as well. The entire command was pouring down the road, looking like a hundred instead of a ragged thirty.

"Good work, lads," I congratulated.

"Yellow Hair! Yellow Hair!" Gray Wolf shouted, waving his sombrero.

"Hell, Autie, you could have given us a minute," Tom complained, holstering his Colt.

His horse was breathing hard, and Athena was the fastest horse in the Seventh. I had given them a good run.

"Cooke, reform the command. Butler, throw out a picket," I quickly ordered. "Lads, wait here. These folks have had one good scare already."

With Tom at my side, we rode up the gravel road toward the hacienda, taking our time so the defenders would not think us enemies. The sheep pens were to the left, away from the house. A tilled field lay on the right. The defenders emerged from the stone bunker below the main building. I saw three men, all somewhat gray-haired, a young woman, and an older woman. The young woman was especially graceful, having a good figure, large dark eyes, and long black hair.

"*Gracias, señor, gracias.* We thank you," the oldest gentleman said, a slender *Don* in his mid-fifties. He wore a colorfully woven suit of wool, a black sash around his waist, and carried a double-barreled shotgun. His gray-bearded face showed great relief.

"I'm George Custer," I said, reluctant to claim a rank that might no longer be valid. "This is my brother, Tom, and supporting us is the Seventh Cavalry."

The Spanish gentleman looked at the four Sioux riding in our party and smiled. Friendly Indians were not outside his experience.

"My name is Erasmo Seguin, master of Casa Blanca. I was once *Alcade* of Béjar and postmaster of all Texas. You are welcome to shelter here from the coming storm," he said, his broken English spoken with a strong accent.

One of his assistants ran forward, equal in age to Señor Seguin and just as gray-haired.

"*Aqui, señors,*" he said, pointing toward the bunkhouse.

Señor Seguin mumbled a few words. His man nodded, taking our horses into the stables.

The Seventh came forward, riding in column of twos, and dismounted in the courtyard. Most were directed toward the bunkhouse, but Tom, Morning Star, Slow and I were guided toward the hacienda. The attractive young woman fell in beside us. Her eyes were a vivid brown. I guessed her at no more than twenty-five years. She was dressed in a white cotton blouse with long silk sleeves in pink and a calico skirt. She wore women's riding boots, much as Libbie always had, and a bright red scarf around her neck.

"We cannot thank you enough," she said, her accent educated. "My name is Isabella Juanita Seguin, daughter of the *Alcade*. You will find our home comfortable against this harsh wind."

Isabella took Morning Star by the elbow and hurried her to the hacienda. Slow rushed to follow, pulling his buffalo robe tight.

"Good luck for these folks that we showed up," Tom said.

Luck, of course, had nothing to do with it. The move south had been Slow's idea, but I chose not to let on about my suspicions. Tom might think me addled.

"Good luck for us. We needed some hot food and a warm place to spend the night," I added.

"I guess this is our first breath of civilization in several months, isn't it? Not since we left Ft. Lincoln," Tom said.

"And maybe our last for quite some time," I grimly surmised.

The house was richly furnished with padded furniture, lush tapestries and thick carpets. Much of it was locally made, but some was imported from Europe. A middle-aged woman emerged from the kitchen, dressed in brown woolens. She was startled at first, but when Isabella whispered something, the old woman smiled and took our Sioux friends into the kitchen. Tom and I shook out our coats before a massive stone fireplace.

"My father would greet you in the drawing room, if you are not too weary," Isabella said.

"We are not too weary," I agreed.

Isabella curtsied and went to make the arrangements.

"Señor Seguin has quite a few accomplishments," Tom said, looking at documents decorating the walls. "I can't make out all of this, but it looks like Señor Seguin helped write the Mexican Constitution in 1824. Until recently, he was quartermaster of San Antonio. Autie, he may be loyal to Santa Anna."

"I am not loyal to the dictator, sir. I am a patriot," Señor Seguin said, entering the room suddenly. Tom looked embarrassed, as was fitting.

"I'm sorry, sir," Tom apologized.

Now changed into a black suit with gold sequined trim, Sequin was carrying a bottle of fine white wine and several elegant glasses on a silver tray.

"All of northern Mexico has opposed Santa Anna since he abolished our constitution and gathered power under this centralized rule. His methods have been cruel and vengeful. Many American settlers have come to oppose him, as well. I take it that is your purpose?" Señor Seguin asked.

"No, sir. We are not here to oppose Santa Anna, though I sympathize with those who do," I responded, glancing at Tom. He looked a little uncomfortable, but it did not alter his resolve.

"Am I to understand that a United States cavalry unit is merely traveling through Texas, saving ranchers from the Comanche?" he asked, the sarcasm gentle.

"It's a little more complicated than that. A long story," I answered.

"The sun is setting. A north wind blows through tonight, chilling the bones of those not so fortunate as ourselves. We will have plenty of time for long stories."

Señor Seguin led us into the ornate drawing room filled with family portraits, silver candlesticks, and a collection of antique swords. Truly this was a successful man of great experience. And the more we spoke, the more I was impressed.

"So, let me understand this," Señor Seguin asked an hour later. "You were spirited off a battlefield to be abandoned forty years in the past. You believe Texas will win independence, but at an unacceptable cost to the future. You may not oppose Santa Anna, but cannot bring yourselves to support him, either."

"That's about the size of it, sir," Tom said, working on his fifth glass of wine. Out of courtesy, I had accepted a small glass, sipping it slowly. It was the first wine I had tasted in many years.

"This battlefield you were on, were you winning?" Señor Seguin asked.

"No, we were pretty bad off," Tom said.

"That is unfortunate. You are not only soldiers lost in time, but not very good soldiers," Señor Seguin said.

I straightened up in my chair, fists clenched, but Señor Seguin was only teasing. He flashed a smile, gold showing in his dental work. I let out my breath and sat back, brows bent in humility.

"The Seventh Cavalry was the finest fighting unit in the world, Señor Seguin," Tom said. "Until our last battle."

"This is not an ordinary thing," Señor Seguin remarked. "I have not heard of anything like it, except from the Apache, who believe in black magic. Were you fighting the Apache when this transformation occurred?"

"No, we were up north in Montana. Fighting the Sioux and Cheyenne," Tom said.

"I know of the Cheyenne. Good with their horses. Aren't the Indians traveling with you Sioux? Are they the ones you were fighting?" the old gentleman asked.

"No, they are from your time. We think. Even they aren't sure," I explained, shifting closer to the fireplace.

In the past, I was always indifferent to heat or cold, comfort or discomfort, but now I felt older. The heat was heavenly. I noticed a distinguished oak bookcase filled with leather volumes. A stuffed owl looked down on us from the corner. The artwork was distinctly provincial, but of good quality. Señor Sequin donned a fine linen jacket embroidered with white and silver threads.

"Is there anything you would ask of me?" he inquired.

"No, sir. You have given us a temporary refuge from our troubles. We will always be grateful," I assured him.

"It is I who must be grateful," Señor Seguin said. "My son has led our *vaqueros* to Béjar, there to hold the town against the dictator. The Comanche have sought to take advantage. I am friends with the local villages, but there are so many Comanche bands, it is hard to be friends with them all."

"They better be friends with us, if they know what's good for them," Tom said, finishing his drink and holding out his glass for another.

"Are you so formidable?" Señor Seguin said with a smile, filling Tom's glass.

Tom went back into the main room and retrieved his Winchester Model 1873. One of the best weapons ever made. He withdrew fifteen live rounds, set them on the table, and handed Señor Seguin the rifle with the chamber open.

"Tell me that's not formidable," Tom dared.

A man of much knowledge, Señor Seguin quickly sensed the power in his hands.

"This hammer allows you repeated fire," Seguin guessed, playing with the level. "And there is a space underneath here for ammunition. Are these powder charges self-contained?"

"We call them bullets. No ramrods. No dropping a lead pellet down the barrel. Just pull the trigger, cock the lever to eject the spent shell, and fire again as a new round is pushed into the chamber," Tom said. "A full magazine can be fired in less than a minute."

"And what happens when you run out of bullets?" Señor Seguin asked.

"You know, Autie, I've been wondering about that, too," Tom said, trying to make joke of it. But neither of us thought it was funny.

"Maybe we can talk," Señor Seguin said, suddenly sounding like a merchant.

"Father, may we join you now?" Isabella asked, poking her head through the doorway.

He waved his hand, causing Isabella, Morning Star and Slow to enter and take seats. The old woman followed with hot soup and fresh baked bread. Slow's eyes lit up at the wonderful aroma, convincing me he was partially human after all.

"What have you gentlemen decided?" Isabella asked, pouring everybody a round of excellent port.

"About what?" I asked.

"About defeating Santa Anna," she explained. "Morning Star has spoken of your feats. Certainly soldiers of such remarkable valor can ride the dictator down?"

I was not sure if Isabella was serious. The intelligent gleam in her eyes indicated a joke, but she was also seeking information.

"We have not taken sides in this rebellion, Señorita Seguin," I said, accepting her challenge. "But if we do, being soldiers of valor, we will put up a good fight."

"Not all are good fights," Slow said, the first time he had spoken all evening.

"That depends on who you're fighting," I said.

"And what you're fighting for," Tom said, just as earnestly.

The others in the room felt our tension. Was I still angry about the mutiny at the Alamo? Was Tom feeling distrustful? I had given him cause.

"The fights will be better," Slow said, finishing his soup.

Then Slow jumped from his chair, going into the next room and sitting before the great fireplace. Perhaps he was seeking another vision.

"That's a strange boy," Isabella said, though not unkindly.

"Is he a seer?" Señor Seguin asked.

"I don't think he sees the future," I said.

I did not say what I was really thinking—that Slow didn't see the future so much as he seemed to remember it.

After dinner, Tom and Señor Seguin adjourned to an upstairs balcony for cigars. Morning Star and Slow left, too, leaving Isabella and I alone. We went out on the front porch, looking at the bunkhouse across the courtyard. Most of the lights were out, the men exhausted.

"You never smoke?" Isabella asked, taking my arm.

"No. And I rarely drink. Tonight was my first glass of wine in a very long time."

"And Thomas says you object to swearing."

"That is true, too. Swearing shows a lack of character."

"You must be a perfect human being," she laughed.

I laughed, too. It was very funny.

"There was a time I believed in perfectibility. If not for others, at least for myself. But though I gave up drink and smoking and swearing, I still gambled at cards and horses. Not always wisely. And I was not the perfect husband I should have been."

"Not all men are honest enough to admit such things," she said.

"Dishonesty has never been one of my failings, though I exaggerate on occasion."

"This journey of yours. From another time. It is not a story many would believe."

"I haven't decided to believe it myself. For all I know, this may be a delusion," I said.

"And if you were going to have a delusion, why Texas? And why would I be in it?" Isabella asked, fluttering her long eyelashes.

Awfully good questions. If I was going to have a delusion, riding into the Alamo and dying gloriously might make some sense. But riding out again? Finding this lovely ranch, and this beautiful girl? These events tended to exceed my imagination.

"How does an insightful young woman, such as yourself, become stranded so far from civilization?" I asked, squeezing closer to her on the bench. "Is your husband with Juan Seguin at San Antonio?"

"I am a widow, señor, but we do not talk of such intimate matters with new acquaintances. Perhaps when I know you better," Isabella replied. And charmingly so.

At midnight, the vicious wind miraculously began to die down. I checked on the men, a few smelling of rum, and went to visit the horses. Vic was tucked in a cozy barn with plenty of feed. Corporal Voss was on guard duty, alert for trouble.

"Goodnight, Henry," I said, going back to the house.

"Goodnight, sir. God bless you," Voss said, a rare and inappropriate outburst. I let it pass.

The wind soon picked up again, howling like all the banshees of hell descending on the prairie. The Texans called it a norther. Trees bent halfway to the ground. Ice flurries flew sideways, pounding against the glass of my bedroom window. It would not surprise me if birds dropped from the sky, frozen solid. I huddled for warmth under a thick quilt, glad for once to have taken someone's advice. Cooke had been right about the need to find shelter.

A new day began with grim clouds. I decided to hold up at Casa Blanca, giving the horses a chance to rest. After breakfast, I played three games of chess with Señor Seguin. He won the first two with little trouble, but was surprised when I won the third with a daringly aggressive opening. At lunch time, I summoned an officers' call.

The dining room on the hacienda's ground floor was large but still warm. It was paneled in oak and rosewood, the floors made of colorful clay tiles. In addition to Tom, Cooke, and Smith, I had also invited Morning Star and Slow. And our host, Señor Seguin. Sergeant Butler and Sergeant Hughes acted as my orderlies, letting Voss get some well-earned sleep. I even let Kellogg in the room, much as I was annoyed with him.

After a fine meal of broiled steak and rice, we cleared the table and rolled out a map Señor Seguin was kind enough to loan me. As a campaign map, it left much to be desired.

"Captain Keogh is here, about fifteen miles northeast of Casa Blanca through these low hills," I said, drawing a line with my finger. "Harrington should be up by tomorrow. If we leave in the morning, we should be there by late afternoon."

"And then what? Our previous lives are gone. Our families don't exist anymore," Butler said, speaking for the rank and file.

"For a few of us, the command *is* family. We still have that in common," Tom said.

"But most of the men don't," Smith said.

I did not doubt Smith's observation. I trusted him almost as much as I trusted Tom, for we had been close for many years. Brothers on the campaign trail. Companions in the dining parlor while our wives knitted socks in the next room. A young man of sound judgment.

I briefly reflected on Jimmy Calhoun, the brother-in-law I would never see again. And my little brother, Boston. In fact, all of my family were now gone, and Tom's as well. We hadn't spoken of it. I doubted we ever would.

"The command must not be allowed to break up, no matter what," I insisted.

"We should have a talk with the men. Soon," Smith said.

"And tell them what?" I objected.

"Give them a choice, General. We're not the only ones whose lives have been turned upside down," Smith said.

"Algernon is right," Tom agreed. "There are a hundred men without homes or loved ones. Many can't read or write English. A third weren't even born in this country. It needs to be their decision."

"That is not going to happen, little brother. Not ever," I swore. "We are not letting a mob of Springfield-toting homesick men roam the Wild West. I don't know why we're here. Hell, it looks like Slow doesn't know why we're here. But we came here as the Seventh Cavalry, and whatever lies in store of us, we'll meet it *as* the Seventh Cavalry."

"I hope you're right, Autie," Tom said, doubting my chances.

"Once the command is reunited, we'll huddle with Georgie and Myles. Something will work out," I confidently said.

But I was not confident. Under the circumstances, it would not surprise me if some of the men deserted. I hate deserters, but that doesn't mean I didn't know how they feel.

The door opened. Señor Seguin looked surprised by the interruption. It was one of the older servants, his expression horrified. The servant spoke quickly in Spanish and shut the door. Señor Seguin looked stricken.

"It is my daughter, Isabella. She was in the field harvesting winter tomatoes. The Comanche have taken her," Señor Seguin said, slowly rising from his chair.

Everyone was stunned by the news, Morning Star in particular. She and Isabella had struck up quite a friendship, as women will on the frontier. Señor Seguin looked to me with the obvious request. His four ranch hands, three of them fifty or older, could not take on a band of Comanche by themselves.

"Bill, inform the command about what's happened. Ask for volunteers," I ordered. "Señor Seguin, have you any hunting dogs?"

"Excellent dogs," he bragged.

Not so excellent as my dogs, I thought. But I would never see Maida and Brutus again.

"Have them ready. We will find your daughter no matter what it takes," I assured him.

"The Comanche often steal women. Usually as wives, or slaves. Only a few are ransomed back to their families," Señor Seguin said, thinking me too optimistic.

"Sir, I have been recovering women from hostile Indians for the last ten years. It's an aspect of my profession," I instantly said. Perhaps with some exaggeration, but it was not an empty boast.

General Custer would not let me ride against the Comanche, who are bitter enemies of our cousins, the Cheyenne. The General said I was too young. He said if the enemy proved too strong, the white soldiers may be forced to flee. This was a lie. I knew the General would not abandon the woman who made him smile.

Nor was it his nature to flee in the face of danger. Morning Star said the General followed a code that his own people thought foolish. A code once lived in ages past by men who wore iron suits, fought dragons, and saved beautiful women from ogres. I did not understand anything Morning Star said, but if someone was going to fight a dragon, I wanted to see it. Minutes after the soldiers left, Morning Star and I saddled our horses to follow.

CHAPTER SIX

NEGOTIATING WITH AN ENEMY

"The men are saddling their horses," Smith reported as I stepped out into the cold afternoon air. I wore the Spanish sword, the two Bulldogs, and carried my hunting rifle. My red scarf was tied carefully around my neck. Smith was dressed in the same buckskins he'd worn at the Little Big Horn.

"How many volunteered?" I asked.

"All of them," Smith said with a salute.

"There's no point trying to follow the hostiles with the entire company," I decided. "Tom will take half the men and search near the river. Bill, you take the other half and explore the bench land to our left. I will accompany Señor Seguin and his *vaqueros*, along with the Indian lads. Send me Butler, Voss, French and Engle."

The command was quickly mounted, initially moving southeast along the river before splitting up. My group followed the trail of the hunting dogs. Knowing close quarters might become necessary, I traded my Remington for Tom's Winchester. When we spotted the kidnappers, I would alert the company to our position and the three units would converge.

We pressed our horses for the first hour, turning east along a rushing tributary that fed the San Antonio River. The dogs indicated the Indians had crossed at a ford just below some heavy woods. We stopped while I surveyed the area with my field glasses.

"What do you see, sir?" Sergeant Butler asked.

"A deer trail leads from the creek to a high pasture. Up there, screened by those cottonwoods. I can't see the village, but there's a faint gray haze rising above the trees."

"They must be on the west slope. Among the old grove of walnut trees," Seguin said, pointing to a forest about a mile away.

"How big is a Comanche village?" I asked, more familiar with the plains Indians farther north.

"Forty warriors. Perhaps two hundred in all, counting the women and children," he answered. "Sad we could not stop the villains before reaching their stronghold. I hope they will accept ransom."

"We'll see who accepts what. Señor Seguin, please send a *vaquero* back to alert the command. Have him take the dogs. We will proceed to the village," I ordered, not wanting to lose time.

Though surprised, there were no objections. We plunged into the creek, the horses swimming part of the way as we struggled to stay dry. Once up on the opposite bank, we dismounted to check our equipment and reload the weapons. Everyone brushed down their horses as best they could.

"Let me go first," Seguin said. "I know some of these Comanche. It's my daughter we seek."

Two of his *vaqueros* rode to his side, both of Seguin's age. I gathered they had ridden the trail together for thirty years and would not be divided now. Good friends to have, and their loyalty spoke well of Seguin's character.

"Sergeant Butler, unfurl our colors. Arms at the ready, gentlemen, but no firing unless I give the command," I said. "Especially you, young warriors. We are here to rescue someone, not to fight."

"Yes, Yellow Hair," Spotted Eagle and Gray Wolf said.

But they did not seem disappointed, expecting a fight one way or the other. Comanche scalps hanging from their lodge poles would be quite a prize.

We rode casually up from the river through some low-lying flatlands, heading toward the grove of walnut trees while doing nothing to mask our approach. Between my Winchester, Butler's Sharps, and the three Springfields, I figured us for enough firepower should a retreat prove necessary. Once back across the river, with Tom and Smith coming to our support, there would be little danger except for the stray arrow or lucky musket ball.

A shallow brook ran on our right, a thick wood off to the left as we followed the deer trail. The winter scrub was too sparse to attract game, but we did see some meadowlarks. The woods closed in on the trail, then opened again to a large pasture just below the foothills. On the far side of the pasture, I saw three dozen teepees nestled together at the edge of the trees.

Some of the Comanche boys had been fishing in a pond until we emerged from the woods. Women were cooking a late lunch. In many places, buffalo hides had been stretched on wood frames for curing. The warriors were mounting their horses. They were armed with bows and arrows, a few lances, and one musket. At fifty yards distance, I halted my small force.

"Sergeant Butler, you will form a skirmish line here," I decided. "Señor Seguin and I will go forward alone."

"General, I don't think that's too smart," Butler protested.

"Jimmy, no one has ever accused George Armstrong Custer of being smart," I answered.

I looked to Seguin, wondering if he had the courage. He looked back with a gleam of admiration. We understood each other.

"Into the lion's den, Señor," I said, giving Vic a nudge.

Seguin's horse was also a superior specimen, a white Spanish stallion with brown spots and black leggings. A much finer breed than the mustangs running wild on the plains.

"I hear the Comanche like to steal horses," I mentioned, having read some interesting articles in *Harper's Weekly*.

"They are brazen horse thieves," Seguin said. "It is a game with them. The young men vie with each other for the most daring exploits. Alas, the Comanche steal people, too. Women and children. This is harder to forgive."

I heard the bitterness in the old gentleman's voice, but I also sensed he sympathized with the Indians. He suspected what I already knew, that the Comanche culture was doomed. By 1876 they would be pushed onto reservations, poor and without hope. But first there would be bloody days, for the Comanche would not give up their way of life without a fight.

"I think they are a band of Quahadie. I do not know much about them. They usually range north of here," Seguin said.

"The Comanche drove the Apaches off this land, didn't they?"

"Yes, many years ago. And they waged war on the Jumano, who were virtually wiped out. The Comanche are the best fighters in the world, especially on horseback."

"You've never seen the Northern Cheyenne, my friend. Or the Seventh Cavalry with a good head of steam," I said, filled with sudden confidence.

When the warriors saw only two of us coming forward, they fell back into their village and dismounted.

A path of curious Indians opened before us. Most were women and children, including some very old grandmothers and grandfathers, which surprised me, for old age in the West is not common. Deer hide seemed the most popular outfit, but I noticed a few fabrics and lots of fur trimmings. Many of the faces glaring up at us were amused, as if delighting in some great joke. I dropped off my buffalo hide blanket, revealing my fringed buckskin jacket and red scarf. The bulldogs in my holsters were cleared for action. The Winchester lay across my lap. I threw the buffalo hide to a pretty young squaw and winked. Her face flushed.

We reached a large bonfire pit, embers still smoking, but some of the tree branches were only charred, dampened by last night's rain. Three chiefs, garbed in traditional rawhide coats, stood to one side of the fire pit. Twenty feet behind them, I saw Isabella and four other young women. Two were white and two Tejano. Isabella straightened up when she saw us, squaring her shoulders and looking proud. The other captives were terrified, thinking their would-be saviors a pair of fools.

Seguin dismounted and began to make introductions in Spanish, motioning to his daughter. The chiefs nodded without betraying their thoughts. Good poker faces.

"Señor, I need you to translate for me. Who is in charge?" I suddenly insisted.

"Soars Aloft is the senior chief, but he cannot speak for the others. Chiefs have no such authority among the Comanche, only influential opinions," he explained.

The plains Indians were not much different. Among the Sioux and Cheyenne, a warrior generally did as he pleased. They would listen to the chiefs, and follow a strong leader, but they would not be bound by another man's will. In this I envied them.

I looked around the village, studying the mass of people watching for my reaction. My love of the theatre served me well, for I took a dramatic pause that made them hold their breath. Seguin then translated what I said, his pace rapid as he sought to keep up.

"Honored leaders, I am General George Custer of the Seventh Cavalry. I have fought many battles. I was leader of the Wolverines in the Great War of the North against the South."

To emphasize my point, I let out a wolf howl that caused everyone to jump back. Even the chiefs. Vic stirred at the sudden movement, but I held him in check.

"Now I am commander of a regiment raised by the spirits," I continued. "A regiment returned from beyond the setting sun with secrets of days that have not yet happened. You are brave. Masters of your world. But a new world comes. A world that is not friendly to the Comanche. I would speak to you of this new world."

The chiefs did not react, at first. Each appeared dumbfounded. Then Soars Aloft stepped forward.

"We have seen the white men who fight among their own. And the Mexicans, who also fight each other," Soars Aloft said, letting Seguin translate. I noticed that Soars Aloft's Spanish was excellently spoken. "Now the Mexicans and white men are fighting. Each seeks to claim the land, but this is our land. Comanche land. We take what we need, as we have always done."

"One day the white men will rule all the lands north of the Rio Grande, and the Mexicans will rule all to the south," I replied, pointing in both directions. "On that day, the white men and the Mexicans will remember the Comanche who stole their women and children. That will be a bad day for the Comanche."

"I am not afraid of the white man. Or the Mexican," Soars Aloft said, brows bent.

"A chief who leads such brave warriors could never be afraid, but a wise chief is cautious. May I show your people a reason to be cautious?"

The village was quiet except for a dog barking in the background. Soars Aloft gave me a careful inspection. I leaned forward in my saddle, returning the gaze, and giving Vic a scratch behind the ears. This was not my first negotiation with an Indian tribe, and I knew that a degree of mutual respect was needed. I would not embarrass Soars Aloft before his people, nor would I show weakness. The chief was puzzled by my confidence, sitting calmly amidst so many enemies.

"If you have such magic, let it be shown," one of the lesser chiefs finally said, growing impatient. He held a steel knife in his hand, probably stolen from a dead settler.

"Our people will be insulted if you disappoint them," the third chief warned.

"Expect there to be a price," Soars Aloft added.

"I have not ridden so far on a cold day to insult the Comanche," I replied, looking back toward the edge of the village.

There was a spot I had scouted on the ride in, a barren patch of dirt not far from the pond, but first I gazed about as if contemplating my options.

"I agree there should be a price. A price my new friends the Comanche will need to pay, if you have the courage," I said.

"We have the courage, white man," Soars Aloft replied.

My challenge did not sit well with many, especially the young men, who sensed a lack of respect. I wanted them stirred up. Anxious. But I needed to strike a balance between their curiosity and desire to take my hair.

"We need to gather nine pots," I requested.

"Few women will give up their pots," Soars Aloft objected.

"They can be old pots that no one wants."

"We have some old pots," Soars Aloft agreed.

I rode Vic back to the clearing, eagerly followed by the entire village. After dismounting, I handed the reins to a smart-looking teenager and took off my riding gloves. Four women ran up carrying old clay cooking pots, the decorations nearly worn off except for one, which had a large crack in it.

Several poles ringed the edge of the village, each about eight feet tall. I assumed they were used for drying meat. I set one pot high up on a pole to my left. Fifty yards away, Butler and my intrepid army were in the meadow watching our every move. I motioned to the pot and twirled my finger, then moved right and placed a pot on another pole ten paces away.

"Seven volunteers, please. Seven brave young men willing to face death," I announced.

As I spoke, the remaining seven pots were placed on the ground in a semicircle next to the pond, each two yards apart. I backed up about ten yards while seven young Comanche walked to the line of pots. They ranged in age from fourteen to eighteen. A good selection. I placed the oldest challenger at the far left end of the line, moving chronologically to the youngest at the far right. I looked toward Butler and raised my Winchester, letting him know all was well.

"We will only play this game if everyone agrees," I said.

"What is this game?" the third chief asked, his weather-beaten face crinkling when looking at the youngest volunteer.

"Your name, honored sir?" I asked.

"His name is Dark Cloud," Seguin translated after a brief discussion. "The youngster is his son, Buffalo Hoof."

"Tell Dark Cloud this is a simple game. When Soars Aloft gives word, I will raise my weapon. The young Comanche will raise their weapons. I will seek to destroy the pots at each young warrior's feet. If successful, that warrior will drop his weapons."

"And once our warriors have weapons in hand, what are they to shoot at? You have no pot," Soars Aloft asked.

"Your warriors will shoot at me," I answered, pounding my chest. "But if their pot has been destroyed, they cannot shoot at me. Is this a good game?"

"This is a good game," Soars Aloft said, pleasantly surprised.

He went to explain the rules to his warriors. I suspected they would be good as their word, but looked over to Señor Seguin for assurance. He nodded. Except for a few scoundrels like Crazy Horse, I've found that most Indians keep their promises.

The sun broke briefly through the gray clouds, a blue blaze in a dark sky. I stood before my seven opponents like Wild Bill Hickok in the dime novels. The oldest brave to my left had a hatchet tucked in his belt. The youngest to my right held a bow with a quiver of arrows. That's all I needed to remember.

"Custer, we would be fair with you," Soars Aloft said, disturbed by the seven-to-one odds.

"Soars Aloft, let the Great Spirit decide the fairness of it," I said.

He nodded and stepped back. The chief seemed to understand the dramatic pause as well as I, raising a hand to begin the contest. The people crowded closer, mindful that arrows would be flying but wanting to see. Isabella had pushed to the front, getting an excellent view. She seemed in good spirits, her dark brown eyes dancing with excitement. I smiled and doffed my hat. Soars Aloft dropped his hand.

I whipped the Winchester up, took a slight crouch, and blasted the first pot on the left before the oldest youngster had raised his hatchet. He looked up in shock, for the muskets they had seen could never be fired so quickly. They also knew it took thirty to sixty seconds to reload a musket. The other six lads slowly raised their weapons, amazed that I hadn't even drawn my pistols. Then I suddenly cocked the Winchester's lever and fired again, hitting the second pot. Had the targets been elevated or at a longer range, they might have proved more difficult. On the ground, just a few yards away, they looked like giant pumpkins.

The Indian boys began to react as I fired a third and fourth time, moving steadily to the right, each warrior jumping as the shattering shards pelted their legs. The crowd behind me murmured in marvel, for they had never seen such a thing. Some pulled back in fear.

Shots five and six followed in rapid order, the pots bursting. The youngsters looked to their chiefs, saw Soars Aloft frown, and tossed their weapons down in disgust. They were true to the rules of the game, which was good for their sake. My Winchester held fifteen rounds. I could easily have killed all of them, and the three chiefs as well.

Only one opponent remained, the fourteen-year-old at the end of the line. He'd nocked an arrow but hadn't had time take aim. I pointed the

Winchester at his chest. The circle was deadly quiet as I stood ready to fire. Dark Cloud looked concerned for his son, but honor would not let him interfere. The boy lowered his bow, acknowledging defeat. I could not blame him for being scared.

Exploiting the moment, I slowly walked forward, patted the plucky lad on the shoulder, and broke the pot with a stomp of my foot. The village let out a cheer. I raised my hand and twirled my finger. Like a summer thunderstorm, the two pots I had placed on tall the poles suddenly exploded, shards raining down on the three chiefs.

"There," I said, pointing at Butler and Voss. Both crack shots at a range of fifty yards.

The village elders were impressed. The warriors were amazed, and a little worried. The women did not look afraid. Had the Great Spirit sent a demon into their village, the demon would not look handsome and dashing like me.

I heard a bugle in the distance. Many of the young men were startled, and the oldest boy who had accepted my challenge reached for his hatchet, raising it as if to throw. For a moment, I was afraid I might have to shoot him after all, but Soars Aloft intervened, giving his warriors a stern look.

"You have played a good game, white general," Soars Aloft said, his translated word betraying Seguin's relief. "The Comanche would be your friend if it is a good thing."

"Being my friend is a good thing," I said, reaching to shake his hand. "See now, how good a thing it is."

My timing was flawless. A blue-gray mass emerged from the woods to the west, hooves thundering and company guidons flying. Tom took his men to the left, forming up on Butler's skirmish line. Smith moved his men to the right. Cooke took position in the center. In the time it takes to steal a pie off a windowsill, the nine men who arrived with Señor Seguin and I had become an army of forty, all carrying strange looking rifles.

"I have given the Comanche the gift of this game. I think you should give me a gift," I requested, trying to be diplomatic.

"Would you have one of the captives?" Soars Aloft guessed.

"I must have *all* the captives," I quietly demanded.

"All might be too many," Dark Cloud said, his face furrowed with frustration.

"I am General George Custer. I must return with all the captives, for that is what my people expect of me."

"Sometimes people expect too much," Soars Aloft said, though it seemed more of a comment than an argument.

"That is true, but I still must have all the captives," I insisted.

"Let us sit and talk. We will smoke a pipe," Soars Aloft suggested.

"I will be honored to smoke a pipe with Soars Aloft," I answered.

Mark Kellogg could be a pain, but on this occasion he proved useful, supporting Seguin's assessment of the Comanche. They were inveterate thieves. Horses, cattle, people, it made no difference. The years ahead would not be easy for them, for they did not perceive the wrong the way a civilized culture does.

"We will be friends," Soars Aloft finally said after an hour of bartering, holding out his hands in the gesture of acceptance.

"Yes," I said, shaking his hand. As was *my* custom.

The teepee was not crowded. Soars Aloft, his two sub-chiefs, and a few women sat on one side of a small fire. Tom, Señor Seguin and I sat on the other.

"We will tell our people. In the spring, we will meet again to speak of a new treaty," Soars Aloft said.

"I hope we will meet again," I agreed, for I had started to like the old chief, thieving rascal though he may be. Soars Aloft did not fool me, and I don't think I fooled him.

The command had moved into the village for lunch where they accepted hot soup and rested under the trees. The men were friendly but watchful, having visited many similar villages over the years. I allowed Sergeant Butler to fire his Sharps at a few ducks, much to the delight of the Indians, but he was careful to conserve ammunition. Spotted Eagle and Gray Wolf were more guarded, having no special love for enemies of the Cheyenne.

It was late in the day as we prepared to return to Casa Blanca. There had been no rain, though dark clouds threatened.

"You are quite the cavalier," Isabella said, holding my arm as we walked from the camp. "Do you always rescue damsels in distress with such flamboyance?"

"No. Sometimes lobbing an artillery shell does just as well," I said, captured by the glint in her exquisite eyes.

The other freed captives trailed behind us, preparing to ride double once we cleared the woods.

"You remind me of someone I loved," she said.

"A lost love?" I asked, jesting in the accepted style. Isabella grew serious.

"My husband, Joaquin. He was a captain in Santa Anna's cavalry, and a hero of our revolution against Spain," she solemnly explained. "But Joaquin spoke against the tactics used by Santa Anna to crush his enemies, believing them harsh. In revenge, the dictator ordered my husband to his death in a pointless skirmish. We had no children, so I left our beautiful hacienda in Mexico City, having no further interests there. I returned home last year. And now the revolutions have followed me."

I looked again at this beautiful woman, the wife of a cavalry officer, and wondered what my Libbie would do without her beau. We were in debt when I left for the Dakotas, my career wrecked by Washington politicians. The press was no longer interested in Indian fighters. The newspapers wanted to hear about the latest inventions by Thomas Edison and Alexander Graham Bell. *Harper's Weekly* wrote of Cornelius Vanderbilt's great wealth and the depravations of Boss Tweed. Americans no longer cared about the soldiers they sent to fight their wars, flocking instead to Wild West shows and boardwalk carnivals.

"Have you travelled somewhere else, General Custer?" Isabella teasingly asked, noticing I had become distracted.

"A great distance, but I'm returned now."

"Very good. A woman does not like to be ignored."

"Rest assured, señorita, I could never ignore you."

"Thank you, sir," she said, fluttering her eyelashes.

It must be admitted that having such a beautiful woman nearby was confusing. Though I could not imagine marrying outside my race, or faith, there could be no doubt about Isabella's attractions. She was charming, intelligent, and wealthy. And I was now a bachelor, whether I felt like one or not.

The hostiles, or rather, our new friends, followed us from the camp until we reached the tree line, waving and shouting. I noticed a few of the privates wearing beaded Indian jackets and long-legged moccasins. I don't know what they traded for these comforts and didn't ask, provided they were still carrying their Springfields and Colts.

Once we were through the woods and ready to ford the creek, we mounted the horses and let out our breaths. Though successful this time, no one believed that every encounter with the Comanche would end as well.

"You know that is only one band. One of dozens. They have no central authority," Seguin said.

"Word will spread of our meeting. The other bands will want to know more about the Seventh Cavalry before starting trouble," I said, for that's usually how things work.

"War is their way of life," Kellogg said.

"Mine, too," I replied, spurring Vic to the front of the column.

Two of Seguin's *vaqueros* were leading the ride back to Casa Blanca. Spotted Eagle and Gray Wolf were riding flank. Tom and Morning Star rode just behind Butler and Cooke. The men waved as I passed, their spirits high.

"Don't know how you did it, Autie. And without firing a shot," Tom said.

"Fired nine shots," I corrected.

"Yeah, and where did you learn that trick? Buffalo Bill?" Tom asked.

"It could have been Wild Bill Hickok," I answered.

"Or P.T. Barnum?" Tom said.

"Yes, I suppose P.T. Barnum," I agreed, grinning.

"Are these medicine chiefs you speak of?" Morning Star asked.

Tom and I laughed.

"No, my flower," Tom said. "Hickok is a lawman turned actor. He goes before an audience to do tricks with guns. Buffalo Bill was an army scout who has started a traveling rodeo for Easterners. And P.T. Barnum is the world's greatest showman, regularly pulling the wool over people's eyes and calling them suckers."

"They sound frivolous. How can they compare with what General Custer has done?" Morning Star said, shocked by our lack of reverence.

"My cousin speaks truly, Yellow Hair," Gray Wolf said. "Tell us where to find this Barnum. His scalp will hang from your lodge pole."

"I am sorry you and Spotted Eagle did not get to fight your enemies," I apologized, for they were eager young men.

"You will find us more enemies," Gray Wolf said.

"Did Slow tell you that?" I asked.

"He did not need to," Gray Wolf answered, waving his new feathered lance and giving a hardy cheer. The men behind us cheered, too.

Their good morale pleased me, but I wondered what they could be cheering for. We were still on a mysterious journey.

"Casa Blanca, then on to Cibolo Creek. Then what?" Tom asked, reading my thoughts.

"We can't go back East," I said. "Andy Jackson would lock us away as imbeciles, swindlers, or maybe Frenchmen. I don't see how we can stay here, either. I was thinking of California. I happen to know a nice little creek next to Sutter's Mill that might be nice."

"You're not the only one who's had that thought," Tom mentioned. "But not everyone agrees. At some point, the men will want to break off. Go their own way."

"Not going to worry about that today, Tom," I said, giving Vic a kick.

Gray Wolf and I caught up to Spotted Eagle, racing him along the flat river road. I let out a whoop and waved my hat, urging them on. The lads laughed, struggling to keep up.

"Your brother is like a child sometimes," Morning Star told Tom.

"Autie was known as the Boy General during our Civil War. He wasn't much older than Gray Wolf, yet he achieved great glory and fame. And now eleven years have passed, and he's no longer a boy."

"Except in spirit," Morning Star said.

I rejoined the column near sunset, Slow riding to my side as I fell in behind Voss and Butler.

"You did not slay your enemies," Slow said.

"Which enemies?" I asked, egging him on.

"The Comanche who stole your woman. Though they had greater numbers, your guns could have swept them aside. You did not need to make peace with them. They had many good horses you could have captured."

"Superior firepower does not win every battle. In the great war of the whites in the East, the Union army often had superior firepower, but they only won half the battles. Warriors on both sides sold their lives dearly for causes they believed in. The Comanche are a brave people. It's better not to fight unless we must."

"You win all your battles. You always expect to win," he pressed.

"I don't win all my battles, but I've been luckier than most. I figured that luck would reward me today. It's wet, it's cold, and food is scarce. And it's still winter. The Comanche did not want to fight. I just needed to give them a good excuse."

"So they could keep their pride?"

"Something like that."

"You could have been killed. An angry warrior might have defied his chief. Or Tom's gun might have jammed."

"I've walked into hostile villages before. It looks more dangerous than it is."

"But never into a Comanche village. My grandfather said they are a people without honor," Slow declared with conviction.

"All people have some sort of honor. Even Comanche. You just have to look for it."

"Would you still have saved the women captives if Isabella wasn't one of them?" the impertinent son of a gun asked. And it was a good question. I wasn't sure of the answer.

Near the last stretch of road before Casa Blanca, Señor Seguin summoned me to the rear of the column for a private conversation.

"No thanks are too great for your service, George," he started.

"None needed, sir."

"You must call me Erasmo, because we are going to be friends. And business partners."

"Business partners? Sir, I don't want a reward for saving your daughter," I said, almost insulted.

"Isabella can do her own rewarding, I am speaking of arms," he said, taking no offense.

"I'm not inclined to sell our guns."

"But you are going to need ammunition," Seguin said.

He took several .45-calibur copper cased cartridges from his breast pocket, holding them up in the waning sunlight. "The bullets you carry are not an ordinary thing in 1836. You are going to need more."

"Do you know where I can get more?"

"I was quartermaster of San Antonio, responsible for purchasing supplies for the garrison. I have many friends. Jewelers. Blacksmiths. Machinists. They will make your bullets. And someday, make your guns, too. I think great riches may be had by manufacturing such weapons."

"It's good to have friends," I said, making a quick decision, for the ammunition supply had me worried.

"Erasmo, instead of copper, can we make the bullet casings in brass?"

"That should not be difficult," he said.

"If the opportunity arose, would you be quartermaster for Texas?" I asked, for he seemed a logical choice.

"Texas has no government, only squabbling land grabbers devoted to self-interest. And even if Texas had a government, there is no money for a quartermaster to spend. Why do you ask?"

"Just a thought," I answered.

We spent a final night at Casa Blanca. Ten of the *vaqueros* had returned from rounding up cattle. A few had been in San Antonio but left when Santa Anna's army grew into the thousands. Señor Seguin was worried about his son, but I had not remembered seeing Juan while we were there. Kellogg mentioned Juan had probably been sent to find Sam Houston, but a dozen of his neighbors had been left behind in the Alamo.

I had not smoked a cigar since the night before my wedding in Monroe, but Seguin coaxed me into relaxing on the upstairs veranda. It had been a fine meal of roast beef and creamed corn, with all of my staff invited. We even sang a few songs before most went off to bed.

The night was cold but pleasant. Isabella sat to my right, Seguin to my left. Tom and Morning Star cuddled together at the far end of the balcony, in a world of their own. I had seen Tom with scores of girls over the years: tavern wenches, seamstresses, nurses, and even a congressman's daughter. Morning Star seemed different. She certainly had a charming smile, deep enticing brown eyes, and a perfectly shaped figure, all of which ranked high on Tom's necessary list, but the couple also had something very important in common—they were both ghosts.

"What troubles you tonight, George? Not enough victories for one day?" Isabella asked.

"Señor Seguin, you have a very insolent daughter," I remarked, puffing cautiously on my Cuban cigar.

The outline of the ranch was vaguely visible in the moonlight, and it was a comforting sight. The farmland below us was tilled and ready for spring planting. Nearby, a herd of sheep lay bunched in their pens. In the darkness beyond, I heard the river despite the rowdy noise coming from the bunkhouse. The boys were celebrating, making me glad I'd put Cooke in charge.

"My daughter is of age to have her own mind," Seguin said. "And her question is well asked. Though, as you say, insolent."

"Young woman, I have been a soldier since I was seventeen years old," I said, taking a good puff while suppressing a need to cough. "I fought in my country's greatest war. Then I fought the Cheyenne and the Kiowa. And I fought the Klu Klux Klan. Now I've fought the Mexican army, and I almost had to fight the Comanche. So your answer is no, one victory a day is not enough for George Custer. I expect more."

"And how often do you get more, Señor Custer?" she asked.

"More often than people think, señorita," I relied in a whisper.

Señor Seguin stood up, his shoulders a bit stiff, and snubbed out his cigar.

"The hour is late for an old man. I will let you young people have the beauty of it," he said, quickly retiring to his rooms.

He had barely left the balcony when Isabella was in my arms. We didn't speak, for there seemed no need to. We understood each other perfectly.

The next morning, after a leisurely breakfast of eggs and ham, I went out to the corral to saddle Vic. We could delay our departure no longer, finally starting out at seven o'clock. Vic seemed rested, ready for the trail. I gave him a carrot I'd found in the kitchen.

"Thank you, George," Seguin said, holding an envelope of signed documents we had drawn up.

The papers signified our partnership, for a new thought was lingering in the back of my mind. Something strange and unlikely, yet so intriguing that I couldn't let it go.

I have rarely known fear. After four years of leading daring cavalry charges into hails of bullets and cannon fire, one learns to separate desire and fear. Desire for victory can make one fearless. Anything less on a battlefield is not helpful. But I was sensing fear now. Not a physical sense of fear, but just as troubling. A fear of gambling with people's lives in a way that could end badly.

The command fell into formation, a steady column of twos ready for a full day's march. Tom led the men out, followed by Cooke, Morning Star, and my sergeants. Only Slow and Kellogg lingered back with me.

"Thank you for such hospitality, Erasmo," I said, doffing my weather-beaten campaign hat.

"You are always welcome at Casa Blanca," the great gentleman said.

"But next time, don't bring so many friends," Isabella added, offering a short curtsey.

"Madam, it will be as you say," I lustily agreed, giving Vic a boot.

Kellogg, Slow and I followed the column out to the road and turned south. The road east that we needed was only two miles away.

"Sad, isn't it?" Kellogg said, announcing that he was going to be an ass again.

"Yes, Mr. Kellogg. What is sad this time?" I routinely asked, looking aside to Slow and rolling my eyes. The boy smiled.

"After Houston wins independence for Texas at the battle of San Jacinto, white men will flood into Texas. Southern white men, and they'll bring their slaves with them. Tejanos like Erasmo Seguin will be pushed aside, often treated no better than the Negros. Their rights will be trampled, and in time, their lands will be stolen."

"Just like the Cherokee were pillaged by Andy Jackson. And just like the Sioux will have their land stolen by a succession of corrupt congresses," I interrupted.

"You already know?" Kellogg said, dumbfounded.

"Lord Almighty, you must think me a dunce," I said.

"So what are you going to do about it?" he demanded, as if I were omnipotent.

"Ask Slow," I said, tired of hearing the reporter's preaching.

In school, I had learned of Rome conquering Gaul. Genghis Khan conquering China. England conquering India. Peoples get their lands stolen all the time—it's just the way of things. Better to stick your finger in a dike than try to stop history.

I looked at Slow, riding quietly to my left. The boy was not on a pony now but a golden Spanish mare loaned by Señor Seguin. The saddle was fine leather with full-length stirrups, the rings stitched higher to accommodate Slow's short legs.

"What does Slow know of such things?" Kellogg asked.

"My God, Mark!" I shouted. "How long have you been a reporter?"

"Well, I've been bumping around here and there the last ten years. Council Bluffs. Brainerd. St. Paul. A little of this, some of that."

"If this story with the Seventh worked out, what was your next career going to be?"

"Thought I might run for mayor of Bismarck."

"And we wonder why the world is in such a state," I said.

"I think you're trying to insult me," Kellogg suddenly realized.

"What do you think, Slow? Am I trying to insult Mark?" I asked.

"You merely think faster," the boy said.

"And you know what I'm thinking?" I responded with a grin.

"Not always. In some ways, you think faster than me," he solemnly answered. "But in other ways, you have not thought at all. I think it is your way not to see too great a future, for it frightens you."

"Maybe you can see a greater future for me?"

"That would be a grave a responsibility," Slow said, disturbed by my teasing.

We pushed toward the rising sun, leaving the San Antonio River behind. Low hills and badlands became our world, for this portion of Texas is more prairie than the lush counties farther east. The wind kicked up, forcing us to buddle against the cold.

"California?" Bill Cooke said, riding to my side.

"No gold in Canada," I said.

"No slaves, either."

"No slaves in California. Isn't that what you and Tom want? Take the battalion to a place where slavery isn't permitted?"

"I'm not sure what Tom and I want, we just don't want to fight for the Confederacy. Not now or twenty-five years from now."

I sensed Cooke was nervous, scratching his famously long brown sideburns more than usual. We'd served side by side for ten years, but he had never made a point of pressing his opinions. Especially opinions opposed to mine. Maybe that's why we got along so well.

"Bill, you're family. Like Tom and Algernon. Georgie and Jimmy Butler. We've been through a lot together. I'm not just your commanding officer; I'm your big brother. And as your big brother, I expect you to do what you're told."

"Thanks for clearing that up," he said, smiling. "What about. . ?"

"Ask me again tomorrow night," I abruptly said.

"Tomorrow? You're sure? Do I have your word on it?"

"Tomorrow," I repeated, riding to the head of the column.

Slow had lagged behind us, but as I moved forward, he rushed up beside me as if he'd been waiting his turn.

"The white soldiers ask many questions that you won't answer."

"I don't know all the answers. Not yet," I patiently explained.

"They think you do."

"It's important that they think that."

"Can you hope to fool so many?" he asked.

"My young warrior friend, command isn't about fooling your men. It's about not fooling yourself."

After leaving the place called Alamo, we fought the Comanche and saved the land of Casa Blanca. Many were in good spirits, but I felt lost. The past that I could not quite remember was now the future. The future, that should have been the past, had not yet happened. I sought insight from General Custer, but he was a disturbed man, struggling with strong emotions. The white soldiers had equally strong emotions, but they were less disturbed. They followed their leader as moths flock to a flame.

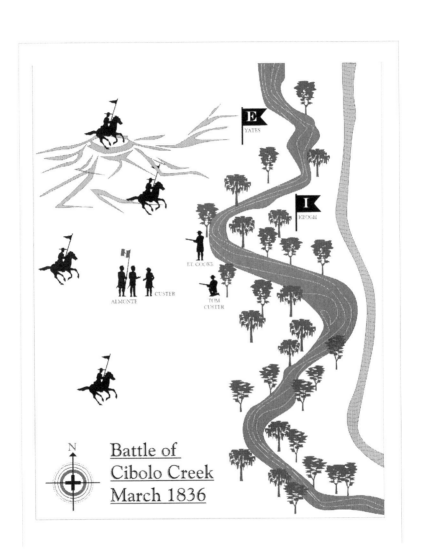

E YATES

I KEOGH

LT. COOKE

ALMONTE CUSTER

TOM CUSTER

N

Battle of
Cibolo Creek
March 1836

147

CHAPTER SEVEN

THE BATTLE OF CIBOLO CREEK

Late in the afternoon, a few miles short of Cibolo Creek, Bouyer rode out to meet us, falling in at the head of the column. Sergeant Bobby Hughes was with him. It was butt cold with a light drizzle, the sky a mass of angry gray clouds. There had been rain to the north, but so far, we had been spared another soaking. Our pace was slower than usual to save the horses.

"Took your time, Gen'ral," Bouyer complained.

"Army business, Mitch," I said.

"Is this still an army?" Bouyer daringly questioned. I placed a hand on a Bulldog pistol, glaring defiantly.

"Damn right it's still an army, and I'll shoot the first man who forgets it. Bobby, how's morale?" I asked.

"The battalion is sitting in a wet forest, eating beans and dry buffalo meat. How good can morale be?" Hughes said. "It's all Captain Keogh can do to keep them together."

"That won't be a problem much longer," I announced.

We had reached open flatland when, well off to our left, I spied a Mexican cavalry patrol. They were just a few, at first, watching us from a distance. Our company was stronger, so I expected no trouble unless the enemy achieved equal numbers.

"Keep a steady pace, men," I ordered. "Tom, bring Slow and Morning Star to the front. Voss, keep your bugle ready. Bill, fall back with Bobby and keep the line moving."

"Not going to need much prodding today," Cooke said, wheeling his horse around and waving for Sergeant Hughes to follow.

"Bouyer, how far to the command?" I asked.

"I'd say 'bout three miles as the crow flies, but they're camped on the far side of the creek. Only a few places to cross without getting tangled up in the woods."

"Ride ahead. Tell Keogh we might need help," I said, seeing enemy cavalry appearing at our rear.

"Better I should lead you there," Bouyer objected.

"You don't need to tell me where Keogh is. One glance at the creek and I'll know," I stubbornly replied, for Myles and I prided ourselves on picking the best camping ground.

Bouyer knew better than to argue, spurring forward on the eastern trail. I looked again to my left. The shadowing cavalry had grown from twenty to thirty, and finally to fifty. A signal from their captain caused them to move in closer. The officers wore silver helmets plumed in red. The rank and file wore black sombreros and carried long lances with tapered purple banners that fluttered in the breeze. Most had white shoulder straps over red jackets, though the officers wore ivory jackets trimmed in gold. Their horses looked thin, worn from a long trail.

"Flankers," I ordered, three men on each side spreading out to give our column a buffer.

I took a special interest in our right flank, for no enemies had been seen there as yet.

The Mexican cavalry went from a walk to a trot, beginning a diagonal shift in our direction. They would not do that unless they expected to intercept us in the next few minutes.

"Voss, sound the gallop," I said. "Tom, take the lead. Throw out skirmishers to cover our crossing at the creek."

I drew Vic out of line, pulling my Remington rifle from its sheath as the command rode past me. Then the bugle sounded clear in the moist air and the horses began to move faster. Our guidon flew proudly in the cold wind.

Cooke and Hughes brought up the rear, their repeating rifles drawn. Spotted Eagle and Gray Wolf had joined them.

"We'll deal with them at the crossing," I said, riding Vic hard as it became a race.

It was not the first time I'd discovered myself in such a situation. In 1873, during the Yellowstone Expedition, I had chased a small band of hostile Sioux down a long green valley, only to realize there were five hundred more Indians waiting at the far end. The same trick Crazy Horse had used on Fetterman in 1868. But Fetterman had eighty men while I was far out in front of my battalion, alone. I turned around and rode for my life. Had I been riding a horse other than Dandy, they'd have caught me for sure.

We crested a low, scrub-covered ridge, seeing Cibolo Creek half a mile down a long sloping plain cut by a few dry creek beds. Tom's unit had almost reached a pasture near the woods. Beyond the Cibolo was a faint trace of dust from the north, perhaps two miles off, though the source was unknown. The Mexicans closed in from the left, and as expected, another unit of thirty lancers was now visible to our right. By the time we reached the creek the enemy would have us outnumbered four to one.

"Let's pick it up, gentlemen," I recommended, kicking Vic to a full run as the Mexican cavalry finally began the chase in earnest.

For a moment, I thought it was going to be close, but our mounts were in better condition, having thrived in Casa Blanca's stables.

Tom had dismounted the command at the wood's edge, setting a skirmish line while every fourth man led the horses into the trees. Twenty-four men were spaced eight feet apart, giving us a broad front. As the horses were tied to trees and logs at the water's edge, several more troopers came back, standing behind the line as a mobile reserve. I rode through the position, jumped from Vic's back, and knelt next to Tom at the center of our line, my rifle pointed.

Our pursuers slowed, a few dozen spreading out toward our flanks while the main body came to a halt two hundred yards away. I noticed several well-appointed officers conferring with their staff. Groups of sergeants and corporals awaited orders, loitering under a red, green and white Mexican flag emblazoned with a golden eagle.

"If we're forced to fight, target the noncommissioned officers first," I said.

"To hell with that. The officers. Kill the officers," Butler insisted.

I started to object, then reconsidered. The cavalry bearing down on us showed no fear. In a typical volley of musket fire, they could expect nine or ten casualties before overrunning our position. Our speed of fire could triple those casualties, but they would still be on us in large numbers. Unless . . .

"Tom, have the men hold their fire unless fired upon. If the Mexicans cut loose, return two volleys and fall back into the trees. Smith, you have the right flank. Cooke, command our left. Hughes, Voss, you're with me," I decided, running back for Vic.

The woods behind our position were thick enough for cover, but the creek was running high. Difficult to cross under fire. If Keogh came up in time, we'd have an easy escape, but I couldn't count on it. And after all we'd been through, I had no intention of getting killed next to some stupid river.

"Off with the buffalo robes. Uniforms only. Straighten up and look professional," I ordered Hughes and Voss, tugging down my weather beaten campaign hat and clearing my Bulldogs for a quick draw. "Voss, carry my guidon. Bobby, you've got the colors."

Just as the three of us were riding up from the creek bed, I saw Private Gustav and motioned for him to follow. Gustav had emigrated from Italy a few years before and spoke fairly good Spanish. I let him carry my silk guidon and had Voss hold his bugle ready to sound a call. Spotted Eagle and Gray Wolf were quickly mounted at our side, determined to participate. I tried to wave them off. Gray Wolf raised his lance and grinned.

"Autie, what are you doing?" Tom asked.

"Negotiating," I replied. "But if they start shooting, you all start shooting back. Kill the officers first."

"Yes! Thank you, general," Jimmy Butler said.

Butler let out a shout, joined by the rest of the command. For men outnumbered by such steep odds, they sounded awfully optimistic.

I rode directly toward the Mexican officers, moving slowly and without a white flag of truce. Such would have defeated my purpose. When the Mexicans saw the six of us casually coming forward, they paused their preparations to attack. No doubt the battle flag of the United States had aroused their curiosity.

"Señor, what is the meaning of this hostility?" I boldly asked the commander. He was a junior officer riding a thoroughbred Spanish charger and wearing an expensive sword. His finely tailored uniform was soiled from hard riding.

"Is it not the responsibility of the army to intercept invaders?" the young officer said, his well-spoken English tinged with a Southern accent.

"May I ask who I am addressing?" I inquired.

"I am Juan Neponmuceno Almonte, secretary and aide-de-camp to His Excellency, General Antonio López de Santa Anna," the man said. "My father was General Jose Maria Morelos. I was educated in New Orleans and have traveled as far as London. Why have you traveled so far? To steal Texas for America?"

To say the least, I was surprised. I had never traveled to Europe. My father was a blacksmith. Almonte made me feel like a country bumpkin. I guessed him in his early thirties, about my height, and stately in appearance, with blue eyes and curly black hair. He spoke with the confidence of born leader. If he was not a Spanish aristocrat, he could easily have passed for one.

"We are not here to steal Texas for the United States," I said.

"Then explain yourself," Almonte demanded.

"I am Lt. Colonel George Custer, commander of the Seventh Cavalry. We visited the garrison surrounded in the Alamo, and when we learned they are trying to impose slavery upon the people of this region, we rode away. We do not serve President Jackson or the politicians attempting to annex Texas to the United States."

"That does not explain your presence in Mexico," Almonte said.

"There is no easy explanation, sir, but it is not a deliberate incursion on our part."

"Deliberate or not, I must require you lay down your arms and ride with me to San Antonio. General Santa Anna will decide your fate."

"I'm afraid that is unacceptable," I responded.

"You have no choice," Almonte said.

I glanced back toward the creek. As I suspected, the dust cloud coming from the north was getting closer, made by dozens of cavalry horses. They would be here in fifteen minutes, at the most. If it was another Mexican patrol, we were certainly doomed, but I had already determined it to be Keogh and Yates. Almonte read my thoughts.

"Another hundred rebels will not help you. Lt. Manchara and I have three hundred dragoons close by, and they are on *this* side of the Cibolo," he said with a confident gleam.

As if on cue, two more companies of Mexican cavalry appeared on the northern ridge a quarter mile away, their ranks forming a long battle line with banners fluttering in the cold breeze. A rumble of the earth and dust on the horizon hinted that more were on the way, but I did not believe they could muster three hundred dragoons in such a short period of time. I doubted Santa Anna's entire cavalry amounted to more than four hundred, with many of those still back at the Alamo.

Within minutes, another officer and several sergeants rode down the hill to Almonte's side. Their horses were tired, the tongues dry. They had come cross-country with little water or fodder. A closer look at the soldiers showed frayed uniforms. A few held short-barreled muskets but most were armed with long wooden lances and swords.

"You are just in time, Manuel," Almonte said.

"We were almost to the Seguin ranch when your messenger arrived," Lt. Manchara said. "You have captured a nice batch of pirates."

"They say they are not pirates. And they say they are not captured. Perhaps they intend to fight," Almonte reported.

The young lieutenant looked surprised. Like Almonte, he appeared well-educated, possibly the son of an aristocrat, as were many officers in the Mexican army. He was dressed in a blue tunic with white trousers now stained with mud, tall black riding boots, and a pair of fancy brass pistols. His staff was equally well-dressed, indicating a formal cavalry unit rather than the militia we had fought on the Rio Grande.

"The entire 2nd company of Tamaulipas will be drawn up in the next few minutes. If the pirates do not surrender, there will be no quarter," Manchara announced, his tone reeking with arrogance.

The young fool must have thought himself a god of war. Or maybe Ulysses S. Grant.

"Well, sir, your decision?" Almonte asked.

Almonte thought he had me, but I no longer felt my earlier insecurity. The enemy had halted their advance and it would take time to reform an effective charge. Fighting from the trees, and with Keogh in support, we'd give a good accounting of ourselves. I was not alone in these thoughts.

"What do you think, Bobby? Should we surrender?" I asked.

"Take 'em in the arse, sir," Sergeant Hughes said.

"Voss?" I summoned.

"Let us shoot the sons of bitches, sir. The day is getting late," Voss said, a hand ready to draw his Colt.

I looked back at Private Gustav, who had a Springfield lying across his lap. Almonte noticed the weapon with a raised eyebrow. My subordinate was not carrying a Kentucky long rifle or Brown Bess, but a gun he'd never seen before. Almonte was not an ignorant savage. Even in 1836, there had been efforts to invent a breech loading rifle. He noticed Voss also carried a Springfield, and then Hughes slowly revealed his Henry repeating rifle.

"Spotted Eagle, what do you think? Should we fight?" I asked.

The youngster nudged his horse forward, one hand holding the reins, the other holding the Colt .45 Tom had given him. Again, Almonte took note of the strange weapon. A pistol of this era, like the ones Manchara was carrying, would fire once before requiring reloading. A cumbersome process, especially on horseback. A few pistols might have double barrels, but those were uncommon. Almonte motioned to Manchara, pointing at the Colt.

"Let us have many scalps, General," Spotted Eagle said, his accent similar to Bouyer's.

Gray Wolf shouted a fierce Indian war cry that startled the officers surrounding Almonte, though Almonte himself remained calm.

"The boy called you General," Almonte questioned.

"An honorary title, sir," I answered.

"Your unit appears filled with mysteries," Almonte said.

"Let me be frank, sir," I said, speaking with quiet firmness. "My men have not decided if we will stay in Texas. If we do, we are not yet sure who we might fight, if anyone. It may be that we will need to fight you, but I would rather not fight you today."

"A bold speech, sir, for one facing certain defeat," Manchara said.

"Señor Manchara, if there's anything I've learned this last month, it's that nothing is certain," I responded.

Suddenly a shot rang out. I couldn't tell where it came from, for the sound echoed off the hills, but it seemed to come from my right. Another shot answered, followed by the barest pause. Almonte seemed as confused as I, for neither of us had given an order.

"General! General!" Sergeant Hughes alerted.

Lieutenant Manchara had drawn one of his pistols, a flintlock with a large bore, and pointed it at my chest. Hughes swung his Henry around and shot the arrogant fool through the forehead, the silver helmet flying off in a spray of blood. The report sounded like a cannon, causing some of the horses to buck. Vic remained steady under my grip, but Almonte's mount threw him hard into the damp scrub grass.

The quiet pasture now exploded in general gunfire, my command firing a full volley, the Mexicans returning fire with scattered shots. Officers were shouting orders. Flag bearers sought to catch the attention of their units. Horses not trained to such commotion grew skittish.

There was no point in continuing the negotiations. I drew a revolver and fired five quick shots, hitting three of Almonte's men at point blank range. Voss and Gustav fired their Springfields, smart enough to hit soldiers presenting the most immediate threat. A Mexican corporal brought up his lance and tried to spear Spotted Eagle, but the youngster shot him between the eyes with his Colt.

The first rank of Mexican cavalry, fifty strong, raised lances before kicking their horses in the flanks, urging the steeds toward our skirmish line. Another fifty were right behind them, colorful lines of fierce horses and noble men, waving banners and glistening steel. A beautiful sight to every cavalryman's heart. Such pageantry reminded me of our brave battles during the Rebellion.

Jeb Stewart's daring ride around the Army of the Potomac. Tom Rosser's bold attack at Trevilian Station. The 5th Michigan at Gettysburg.

The enemy advance was hesitant at first, the horses needing a good prodding, but then the charge was on, the dragoons yelling encouragement to their comrades above the thundering of the hooves pounding the weed-covered plain. Behind me, I heard Tom give the order and thirty rifles barked as one, emptying a dozen Mexican saddles. Ten seconds later, the skirmish line fired again, killing both men and horses. A third volley brought the charge to a calamitous halt, falling soldiers and screaming animals caught in a mass of panic and blood.

All sense of organization around me dissolved, for my small band was caught in the middle of the battlefield. Horses bucked and neighed, many hit by errant bullets, while ten dragoons surged forward to cut us down with their sabers. It seemed like gunfire was coming from every direction, some from muskets carried by the Mexicans, others from my men down near the creek. A rapid series of shots I knew to be Tom's Winchester.

"Let's get the hell out of here!" I shouted, drawing my other Webley and firing at the approaching dragoons.

Two went down right away, a third slowly dropped off his horse into the path of his fellows, who drew off rather than ride over him.

Private Gustav reeled in his saddle, a hand clutching his gut. Voss toppled over with a grunt, blood on his hands, and fell from his mount. I could not see where he'd been hit. Gray Wolf raised the fine Kentucky rifle Señor Seguin had given him and shot Almonte's flag bearer, then fell backward to the ground, lying still with a wound to the head.

"Bobby, retreat!" I ordered.

Hughes took the reins of Gustav's horse and rode back toward the creek, ducking under the heavy fire. I dismounted, grabbed Voss by his blouse, and shoved him over Vic's back. After yanking my rifle free of the saddle boot, I gave Vic a slap and sent him running toward our line.

Spotted Eagle had ridden within a few feet of his cousin, firing at any enemy who dared approach, but the Colt was soon out of ammunition. I pulled the youngster off his horse, taking him out of the line of fire, and knelt next to Gray Wolf, firing my rifle with careful deliberation.

Mexican soldiers were dropping all around us. Cooke and Smith were directing the fire from the skirmish line, keeping the men steady. The companies of enemy cavalry on the ridge were too far away for immediate support, and those closest to our position had been thrown into confusion, their crazed horses untrained for the terrifying noise of battle.

Then, for a moment, the scene grew quiet. Two hundred yards back on the ridge, the Mexicans were trying to reform. Some were pulling wounded from the field, others giving orders for a counterattack. Horses with empty saddles ran to and fro, frothing at the bit and eyes wild. The skirmish line ceased firing, the best targets having retreated, but only momentarily. By the yelling and gesturing, I guessed the Mexicans would be on us again in a few minutes, only this time they'd have a better idea what to expect.

Kneeling on the ground, I experienced a disturbing sensation. Similar to my dreams of the Little Big Horn and the weed-covered hill, for I was in the middle of the exposed battlefield fighting for my life. Though, ironically, I now had two Sioux warriors at my side rather than my own men. As a group of three dozen lancers prepared to overwhelm our position, it looked to me as if George Custer had made his last stand.

Then a bugle sounded in the distance. It was Keogh crossing the creek, riding to our aid at a full gallop, forty heavily armed troopers of the Seventh Cavalry. With him were a score of roughly clad frontiersmen, not so well-armed but just as determined. Cheered by the reinforcements, Tom ordered the skirmish line to stand up, firing methodically at the disorganized enemy. Few of the Mexicans were stupid enough to resist the sudden tide, falling back in ragged groups.

Even as Keogh was riding through the trees, I heard renewed fighting break out on the right. The Mexicans were being stuck in flank, probably by Yates. Many of the better armed lancers dismounted, forming a defensive line at the crest of the hill. The firing grew intense, but it was soon clear the Mexicans lacked the firepower to hold their ground. Cooke sent a platoon of dismounted troopers to Yates's support while Keogh veered in that direction as well. Before long, we had control of the field.

"Autie! Autie, thank God," Tom said, coming to my side.

"Thank somebody. Who started the shooting?" I asked.

"Don't know. The sons of bitches were coming for us anyway."

"It would have been nice to wait until I finished speaking with Almonte," I complained.

"General, are you well?" Morning Star asked, riding up on her painted mare. Slow and Kellogg were with her. I wiped a streak of blood from my forehead, but I'd only been grazed.

"Custer's luck again, young lady," I said.

"Perhaps you have the magic of Crazy Horse," Slow suggested.

"I'll settle for my own luck, youngster, but thanks all the same."

I saw Cooke directing our men back toward the creek. Keogh pressed the enemy to the top of the hill, then retreated in good order. Our wounded were being carried to a gully near the ford. Most of the men were still in skirmish formation, rifles ready but with no one to shoot at. Which was for the best. I had not wanted a battle here, nor did I want to waste ammunition.

Suddenly the grass-covered plain seemed calm. A few horses wandered aimlessly. Thirty to forty Mexican cavalrymen lay dead or wounded. I saw Almonte struggling to sit up, his arm bent in pain from the fall. It would not take long for the enemy to regroup and consider charging down on us, for that's what I would do.

A howl of anguish rose beside me. It was Spotted Eagle, who had discovered Gray Wolf's wound had proved fatal. There was no time for a death song.

I looked back toward the Cibolo where I Company was dismounting. Keogh saluted and pointed to his new recruits, the ragamuffin frontiersmen who had ridden in his wake. It was a motley group. Rawhide jackets and store bought coats. Cloth shirts and linen cravats. Coonskin caps and silk hats. They were trappers and storekeepers, ranchers and lawyers. Family men and adventurers. I assumed Keogh had stumbled across a group of local militia. Farther down the line, I saw F Company regrouping after their flanking attack.

"Voss! Voss, where are you? Are you still alive?" I called.

"Yes, General. Got me through the arm," Voss said. He was sitting under a tree where Dr. Lord was dressing the wound.

"Corporal French, sound recall," I ordered.

The men began withdrawing, watchful for trouble. Horse holders let the mounts drink from the creek. More of the wounded gathered under the tree where Dr. Lord had setup a makeshift field hospital.

"General, what the hell happened?" Cooke asked, walking to my side through the carnage.

"Guess we've made more enemies," I answered, gazing at the Mexican bodies lying all around us.

Tom and Morning Star were kneeling next to Gray Wolf trying to console Spotted Eagle. Without needing orders, Keogh had extended a skirmish line into the meadow should he need to cover our withdrawal.

"We can't stay here," Cooke said. "It's just a matter of time before they come back."

"Get the command ready to move. Priority to the wounded," I ordered.

"And the bodies of the dead?" Cooke asked.

"Have we so many?"

"Not many, but enough."

"Let's not leave anyone behind," I decided.

Cooke went back to the creek, ordering poles cut for litters. I had other business.

"Señor, how do you fair? Is the arm broken?" I asked, kneeling next to Colonel Almonte. He had fallen hard, his fine uniform soiled.

"I hope not," he said, sitting on his butt while fashioning a sling with his red sash. "Have I become your prisoner?"

"I have no need of prisoners. If one of your men fired the first shot, you've gotten what you deserve. If it was one of my men, you have my apology."

"Gallantly spoken, General Custer."

"*Colonel* Custer," I corrected.

"I know a general when I hear one, damn you all," Almonte said.

Gray Wolf's body had been laid over the back of Almonte's horse and led away by Spotted Eagle, followed by Morning Star and Tom. We would mourn the brave lad once we were safely beyond reach of the enemy. Slow remained behind, coming to stand next to me.

"And who is this Indian boy? A Comanche ally?" Almonte asked in painful jest.

"Lakota," I said, offering Almonte a handkerchief. His cheek was scratched, a trickle of blood seeping into his three-day-old beard.

"I have not heard of Lakota," Almonte said, wiping his face and keeping my handkerchief.

"You will. One day you will know all the nations," Slow said, staring at the young man with great interest.

"Will I live so long?" Almonte said.

"Longer than most," Slow said.

"So the mysterious Seventh Cavalry travels with a boy medicine chief. Thus is your victory easily explained," Almonte said with a sigh.

I liked the man. A cheerful, if ironic sense of humor. I helped him to his feet and waved Dr. Lord forward.

"Not bad. Sprain, no break," Lord said, wrapping the arm well.

We had captured a few medical supplies on the Rio Grande. If Almonte noticed the source of the doctor's bandages, he was discreet enough to keep it to himself.

"Thank you, sir," Almonte said.

"An honor, señor," Lord said.

"May I ask your plans, General Custer?" Almonte asked.

"I'm not in a position to make plans at the moment. But when I do, your Santa Anna will be the first to know," I said. "Advise him to think well on his thirst for conquest. I do not fight for the United States, but I am an American. We take a dim view of tyranny."

"We seek to preserve our country," Almonte answered, a grim look in his pained eyes.

"I understand, sir. And I wish you well," I said, shaking his hand.

I did not leave Almonte a horse. Spotted Eagle had stolen his fine mount, as Indians are wont to do, and I saw no reason to interfere.

A few minutes later, the command was mounted and crossing the Cibolo, riding north toward the Gonzales Road. We plundered some of the enemy for weapons, especially their swords and gunpowder. Their horses weren't the best quality, but we rounded up a group of them for pack animals. A handful of Mexican dragoons watched us from the ridge but refused to engage. I don't know where the rest went and didn't especially care so long as they weren't following us.

As we moved north in column of fours, Keogh fell in next to me.

"Five dead, nine wounded," he said, knowing that would be my first question. "And some bad news, I'm afraid. George Yates. And young Reily, too."

"Georgie and Little Billy?" I said, scarcely able to believe it. After all we'd been through, how could Yates die in a pointless skirmish?

"What happened?" I asked.

"George got shot through the thigh. Cut the artery. Reily stopped to help and took a musket ball through the spine. George bled out before anyone could stop it," Keogh said, handing me Yates's watch and wallet. "Said to tell Annie and the kids that he loves them. If we ever get back to where we belong."

I took out the photo of Annie Yates that Georgie always carried. We had served together during the Civil War. I had been at their wedding in Monroe. Helped George get his commission with the Seventh Cavalry. If not for me, he might have become an insurance salesman in Ohio and lived to be a grandfather. I hadn't known William Van Wyck Reily all that well, but it seemed to me he'd have been better off staying in the Navy.

"We weren't looking for trouble," I said, putting the photo in my pocket.

"Plenty are. There's a camp upriver of militia volunteers looking for a way into the Alamo. Call themselves Texians," Keogh said.

"Not our job to stop them."

"How many men are in the Alamo?" Keogh asked, pleasantly ignorant of Kellogg's lectures.

"A hundred and fifty amateurs surrounded by eighteen hundred Mexican troops, and another two thousand on the way."

"Our little band won't make much of a difference there. What are we going to do?" Keogh said.

Having survived Stoneman's raids into Georgia, Keogh was in no hurry to get himself killed.

"I've been giving it some thought."

"And?"

"Still thinking," I said.

———

We rode north along Cibolo Creek toward the Gonzales Road, the main trail between San Antonio and the Texan colonies to the east. It was an exaggeration in this part of Texas to call anything a road, for most were nothing more than worn paths through the wilderness. The creek on our left was heavily wooded. Bench land rose to the right leading to the occasional hill sparsely occupied by red oaks. The weather turned from damp to frosty.

Bouyer was scouting ahead, knowing the best route. Tom, Cooke and I rode at the head of the column with Keogh. Hughes and Butler brought up the rear, keeping the men in good order. The bodies of our lost comrades were tied over their horses, awaiting a proper funeral. I had been worried about desertion, but now we had several victories under our belt. No one likes to quit a winning team.

"Harrington?" I asked, seeking a report from Keogh. I had already guessed the answer but wanted Tom and Cooke briefed on the situation.

"Up from the Rio Grande in good order. Spiked the siege guns and rolled them in the mud," Keogh said with an Irish grin, for the people the Emerald Isles enjoy such destruction.

"What about this encampment?" Tom asked, pressing Athena so close to Keogh's horse, called Comanche, that their stirrups were bumping together.

"A rabble," Keogh said. "Scattered militia bands and groups of volunteers. There's sixty or seventy of them, including this bunch that rode with us."

"Slavers?" Bill asked.

"What?" Keogh said.

"These militia bands, are they fighting for slavery?" Cooke said.

"Never asked them, though I had the impression they're fighting for liberty," Keogh said, seemingly mystified.

"Jefferson Davis's form of liberty. Are you forgetting which side Texas fought for during the war?" Cooke pressed, almost angry.

"Guess I hadn't thought about it that way," Keogh said, scratching his shaggy, month-old beard.

Though Keogh was a year younger than me, he was already showing gray. I promised myself to shave off my beard if I ever started looking like an old grizzly bear.

"If these guys are Rebs, reckon we should shoot them?" Keogh asked.

"This isn't funny," Tom protested.

"That doesn't mean we can't shoot them," Keogh answered with an impish wink in my direction.

It was good to see Myles in such high spirits. After Tom and Bill, and with Georgie gone, there was no one I trusted more.

"What is the Seventh's position in this manful gathering of eager patriots?" I inquired.

"We're camped in a river bend ten miles below the main road," Keogh said. "Harry has the Mexican volunteers guarding our wagons. Sharrow has a scout probing west of here. The Rebs didn't even bring wagons, only what they could carry in their saddlebags."

"Myles, they aren't Rebs. Not even in fun," I felt required to say. "And they're not soldiers, either. They're just a mob of husbands, fathers and brothers banded together as our grandfathers did in 1776. As for the rest of it, we'll just have to see."

"What are you trying to say, Autie?" Tom asked.

"I'm still the general," I insisted.

It was close to sunset when we rode into camp. Five different circles had been arranged around Harrington's position near the river. Bouyer led us past the curious companies, each with its own name and elected captain. They were suitably dressed for the weather, armed with good rifles, and each had a horse.

"Shouldn't we stop and talk?" Tom whispered as I ignored the curious pioneers gathering along our trail.

"The militia leaders will be coming to me before long," I said. "It's better that way. The command needs rest."

There were many smiles as the three segments of the Seventh Cavalry finally reunited. Stories were quickly exchanged of Indian battles, fights with the Mexicans, and how nice it was to have a campfire. No one spoke of the bigger questions, for most weren't ready to admit that our former way of life had come to an end.

With the compliments of the Mexican army, I had a large canvas campaign tent and a small Franklin stove. Two lanterns hung from the crossbeam. Private Engle chopped up a few logs, and before the sun set, had built a crude desk. Tree stumps were used for chairs. Spare buffalo robes passed for fur carpeting. As the teepees were being used for the wounded, Slow, Morning Star and Walking-In-Grass would bunk with me.

A welcome dinner of roast duck and turnips was almost ready when the first militia captains came to talk, passing through alert sentries with a sense of fear and resentment.

"John Chenoweth of the United States Invincibles," the first said, a tall, lean roughneck with ten years of frontier life written on his face. "This is George Kimball of the Gonzales Rangers, and Edwin Mitchell, personal representative of Colonel James Fannin."

Neither Kimball nor Mitchell appeared particularly remarkable. Brave enough, I supposed, or they wouldn't have responded to Travis's call for help. But they looked like storekeepers to me, average in features and modestly dressed.

"I am General George Custer, commanding the Seventh Cavalry operating in this region. How may I help you?"

I had stood as the men entered, waited for them to remove their hats, and then sat down. During my years in Washington, and visits to New York, I had noted how men of power entertain those who come seeking favors. John Astor III had treated me with great respect, but never as an equal.

"We assume you are fighting Santa Anna. He has invaded Texas," Chenoweth said, clenching his fists.

"I am aware of that. Three days ago, I was in the Alamo conferring with Colonel Crockett. But the Seventh Cavalry is not at war with Mexico," I explained, being very matter-of-fact. And convincingly so.

"You cannot mean to say such a thing?" Mitchell said.

"Santa Anna will massacre women and children from here to the Sabine," Chenoweth said, "just as he massacred the people of Coahuila and Zacatecas. He is not just a tyrant. He is a butcher."

I stood up slowly, my expression grave, hands clasped behind my back. Slow and Morning Star watched from a blanket in the corner, Tom and Cooke from the mouth of the tent.

"Gentlemen, though I sympathize with your dilemma, there is a problem," I explained. "Most of the men of the Seventh Cavalry are from the Northern states. Some are from countries overseas where there is no slavery. We think slavery is wrong. Your congress in Washington-on-the-Brazos is preparing to write slavery into your constitution. We cannot fight for you. Thank you for visiting. We can spare some beans and rice if you need them."

I sat down and started to write a report on our recent activities, dismissing the captains from my mind.

"That's it?" Kimball said, bewildered.

"This way, sirs," Tom said, ushering the men out. He glanced at me, then nodded to Bill. They disappeared into the dark.

"The white men think you are not being honest," Morning Star said as we sat down to eat. "Certainly you will fight this Santa Anna who kills children?"

"If Santa Anna wins, there will be no slavery in Texas," I responded. "If the rebels win, Texas will have one of the most brutal slave systems in the entire South. When I was stationed here after the war, I saw what the slaves had gone through before Lincoln set them free. My men have seen it, too. There are no easy choices."

"But there *are* choices," Slow observed.

"Yes, there are always choices," I acknowledged.

The duck was very good. The turnips a bit hard.

Two more delegations of frontiersmen came to call, each more cautious than the last. The first called themselves the New Orleans Grays and claimed to have friends besieged in the Alamo. They had entered Texas as a company but split up after the first few months.

The second delegation said they were Tumlinson's Rangers, a local militia band, but none of them knew where Captain John J. Tumlinson was. Some thought their leader had gone back to Gonzales for more reinforcements.

Through the evening, Tom and Cooke were busy interceding on behalf of the militias, or so they claimed, but I kept dismissing each delegation with respectful regrets. After a final appeal, I finally agreed to visit their camps.

The delay gave Corporal French time to wash my clothes, shine my boots, and repair a tear in my shirt. The Spanish steel sword hung at my side. My twin bulldog revolvers were holstered on either hip, the ivory handles showing. My party included Tom, Bill and Kellogg, though I ordered Mark not to give any history lessons. Slow tagged along without my permission.

The first camp we visited were the so-called Invincibles, a group up from Goliad numbering about twenty-five. They seemed to have two captains, Chenoweth and Francis De Sauque, a gruff, black-eyed storekeeper with a slave named John. I shook hands with Chenoweth, then the storekeeper, and then with John, much to the shock of the group. But none were more surprised than the slave, who drew back in fear of his master's angry gaze. Their camp was made up of a few fires, some canvas tarps and bedrolls.

"We could sure use your help, General Custer," De Sauque said, saying 'General' with some hesitation. He did not have a Southern accent. More Eastern. Possibly Pennsylvania.

"I am leading a professional force, sir. I have no use for militia who can't obey orders," I responded.

"We don't need to follow you. We don't need to follow no one we don't elect," a rebel sergeant said, arms crossed angrily over his chest. His long hair was coal black, the bushy beard full enough to sweep the floor with. Just like a thousand I'd seen on the battlefields of Virginia.

"Quite right. Have a pleasant evening," I said, turning to leave.

Chenoweth caught me by the arm, turning me around. I could have knocked him down, but didn't.

"Sergeant Dijon doesn't speak for all of us," Chenoweth said, giving the subordinate a disapproving stare. "Look, Custer. Most of us were sent by Fannin. We're just a few now, but more are on the way. We've got friends in Béjar who need our help."

"I'm sure you know by now that Fannin isn't coming. Houston isn't coming, either. You Texians are proud, but pride won't turn back the three thousand troops surrounding the Alamo. Not with the handful of volunteers you've managed to gather."

"Fannin may be a coward. I don't doubt Sam Houston *is* a coward. Just like he's a drunk. But I ain't no coward. Either are my men. How yellow are you?" Chenoweth said.

"Brave enough to fight for what we believe in," Tom said, getting in Chenoweth's face.

I noticed the frontiersman was bigger than Tom, and ruggedly built, but I'd seen my little brother in more than one scrap. If Chenoweth wanted a brawl, he'd found the right man.

"We believe in Texas," Dijon said, rolling up his shirtsleeves.

"A Texas where slaves do your work," Tom answered. "A Texas where an honest day's work is paid off with a whip."

"Ain't that the natural order of things?" Dijon replied.

"Not natural to the Seventh Cavalry. To us, the natural order of things is freedom," Tom said, both fists clenched.

"You're nothing but a damned abolitionist," Dijon said, spitting on Tom's boots.

Tom reared back to belt the man in the mouth. Cooke and I pulled him off. Chenoweth's men were grumbling, some with hands on their knives. I wasn't worried. A Colt .45 would cut half of them down before they could blink their eyes.

"We need your help, Custer. Is there anything we can say?" Chenoweth asked, pushing Dijon away.

"Maybe, but I will require a gesture of good faith," I offered.

"Name it," Chenoweth said.

"Give me the slave," I said.

The Texans were surprised, if not shocked. I noticed Tom smile.

"John is *my* slave," De Sauque protested.

"Give him the slave, Frank," Chenoweth said.

"No. No, he's mine. Bought him fair and square," De Sauque replied.

"Damn your money-grubbing soul, the lives of our friends and neighbors are at stake. That's more important than your damn Negro," Chenoweth hissed. Most of his men nodded agreement, though not all.

I watched them with great interest. From what Kellogg had said, many of these men would probably survive the Texas Revolution, but not those who managed to reach the Alamo. Or those who returned to Goliad, for they were doomed as well.

"Goddamn it. Goddamn you all," De Sauque said. "John, you go with this arrogant bastard. You belong to him now."

"No. No, this 'ere ain't right. Sell him to me," Dijon said, pushing his way in. I detected a deep accent, likely from Mississippi. The man's face was red with outrage.

"René, if you can get John back from these slave stealers, you can keep him," De Sauque said, marching off. Dijon looked around, gave me a look fit to kill, and soon followed. The rest of Chenoweth's men stayed to listen.

"I will speak with you again at midnight," I said, addressing the entire group. "At that time, I will ask your Invincibles a question. Each of you will need to answer for himself. I will only ask once, and the answer must be yes or no. Know that if George Armstrong Custer decides to fight Santa Anna, I will be victorious. I am always victorious."

We left the camp of the United States Invincibles, a ridiculous name for a group of would-be soldiers. John rushed to catch up.

"I will serve you all well, master. I kin cook good, and clean, too," John said, using the exaggerated Southern accent common to slaves when addressing white men. There was a time I would have thought nothing of it, but I was no longer so naïve.

"John, you're a free man now. Serve who you want, or no one at all. It's up to you."

"Can I stay with you, sir? Until better times?" he asked.

"Are you really a good cook?"

"Yes, sir. Really good."

"Then you're hired."

John's face lit up with a smile. He had good teeth.

I visited two more camps, each time declaring my conditions. And my ability to defeat Santa Anna, though for the moment, I had no way of supporting such a boast. After each visit, I left Tom, Cooke and Kellogg behind to gauge the mood of the frontiersmen. They had seen our weapons, and some told stories of our victory at Cibolo Creek over a force ten times our strength. These were brave men, willing to challenge the army invading their country, but they knew the odds were against them.

"You are going to fight," Slow said, walking at my side as we returned to our camp.

"That choice isn't up to me, but I would like to fight."

"It is your way."

"It's a good way if you know what you're fighting for," I said.

We had just passed the first row of sentries when a shout went up from the edge of our position. Seconds later, two men riding exhausted horses appeared on the dark trail. One of them was David Crockett.

General Custer was not a liar, but being a leader of men, he could not always tell the truth. I sensed wisdom in this, though in what manner the two thoughts could be honorably reconciled eluded me. I knew the General had a plan, still unfocused, but clear enough that he would not disclose his thoughts even to his closest friends. Perhaps this is as it must be, I decided, for I had once been a leader, too. A leader who had lived longer than Custer, but given the ultimate results, perhaps no better.

CHAPTER EIGHT

CROCKETT'S SECRET MISSION

The camps sent up a cheer as Crockett dismounted on the main trail and waved his hat, standing tall and broad-shouldered in the moonlight. He was riding a good mount, stronger than any I'd seen while in the Alamo. Likely he had slipped free of the fort and found a better horse along the way. With him was a young Hispanic man, slim and agile, with familiar features. I was no less excited than everybody else, running from my tent with Slow right behind me.

"David! Damn, it's good to see you," I shouted with a rare burst of swearing.

"George! Just the gentleman I was looking for. And it seems you've gathered a few friends," Crockett answered, his face lit with a winning smile. Though only a portion of our encampment was visible, dozens of campfires could be seen through the trees.

"Not sure how many friends, but plenty of brave men," I said. "What are you doing here? Did the garrison decide to escape?"

Crockett looked around. Fifty militia volunteers and most of the Seventh had already gathered. More were coming, some carrying torches. The former congressman from Tennessee seemed reluctant to speak of military secrets before such a crowd.

"Give me a moment to address these stout fellows and we'll talk," Crockett said, giving me a confidential wink.

"Crockett! Crockett!" the men were chanting.

The dreary evening had grown brighter, the air felt warmer, and our small numbers suddenly seemed larger. Such is the impact of a truly charismatic leader. Crockett waved a coonskin cap, something I had not seen him wear at the fort, and climbed up on a log.

"Friends, fellow countrymen, thanks to ya all," Crockett said, holding up his hands for attention. "I've come from the Alamo where a band of your neighbors are holding Santa Anna at bay. We've whooped him sound so far, but there's thousands of them and only a few score of us. We sure could use your help. I've got to speak with General Custer now, but later I'd like to come by on a visit. I'll answer any questions you got. If ya got any cider, I'd sure be glad to share."

Watching Crockett in the torch light give me the final bit of inspiration I needed. It was as if God had read my thoughts and responded in a manner that none could doubt. Though I would not claim my relations with God had been all that close in recent years. Not since the final days of the Rebellion, when everyone was praying the war would be over soon.

"It is a sign," Slow said, tugging my sleeve.

"You think so?"

"We both think so," Slow replied.

"Lad, I need you to fetch Tom and Kellogg for me. Tell Tom to bring one of the extra rifles," I said. "John, prepare my tent for guests. See about hustling up some coffee."

Slow backed up, going around the edge of the mob where Tom and Morning Star were standing with Cooke and Smith. John headed for the wagons, speaking good Spanish with our Mexican teamsters for the requested supplies. Crockett jumped down from the log, shook hands, slapped a few backs, and came up with his Hispanic companion.

"George, this is Captain Juan Seguin. The Mexicans shot my horse while I was riding out of the Alamo, but the old girl got me far enough to find some friends. Juan's got ten men gathered from the local ranches, and I've got to say, I was mighty scared to find myself surrounded by a bunch of Mexicans out in the dark."

"We are not Mexicans. We are Tejanos, and more Texan than many who claim such a right," Seguin said, his English rough but readily understood.

I saw the resemblance clearly now. Juan was taller than his father, but the face was rounded the same. The smile, with its white teeth, looked just like Erasmo's. The searching brown eyes looked more like Isabella, as did the tousled black hair.

"*Conocí a tu papa y a tu hermana en tu rancho, señor,*" I said, responding in my rudimentary Spanish, for I still needed much practice. "There was some trouble with the Comanche, but all was well when we left there yesterday."

"So I have been told. I thank you for your gallantry, sir. My father sends word to trust your judgment," Seguin said.

"Enough to put your men at risk?" I asked.

"We are at war with a great tyrant. Everything we hold dear is at risk," Seguin said. "Will we ride to the Alamo? I left many friends there when Travis ordered me to find Houston."

"And did you find Houston?" I inquired.

"In a whisky bottle. He will come, but I fear he will come too late," Seguin said, spitting on the ground. "He sits in Washington-on-the-Brazos making a government that will benefit the United States more than it will help Texas."

I noticed Crockett frown. He was not surprised by the bad news.

"Where are your men now?" I asked.

"On the Gonzales Road. They will be here within the hour."

"Sergeant Sharrow, find provisions for Señor Seguin and his men," I ordered. "David, care for a cup of coffee?"

"Right gladly, George," he said, following me back to my tent.

Though the night was dark, the moon often covered by clouds, the campfires cast a decent glow. And a legendary woodsman like Crockett would not even need that much light. John was already brewing a pot of fresh coffee when we arrived. I pulled the flap shut and offered Crockett a seat on a rough wooden stool.

"You are a man on a mission," I said, letting John serve.

Crockett gave John a look, wondering why the commander of the Seventh Cavalry who had ridden out of the Alamo to protest slavery now had a black servant. I had to smile at the irony.

"A desperate mission, I fear," Crockett said. "Bonham returned from Fannin. We won't get any help there, and now Seguin says Houston is dallying

173

on the Brazos, neck deep in the saloons. He doesn't even believe Santa Anna's in Texas. Travis tried to cut a deal with Santa Anna, but all the tyrant wants is blood. George, if you don't help us, the entire garrison will be put to the sword."

"I want to help. You know why I can't."

"Funny you should mention that. Me and the boys, we had us a talk about this slavery thing. Mind you, not all are happy 'bout it, 'specially Travis. But most of the men are willing to go along with you. Hardly any of them even own slaves. You know I sold the few I had years ago, being too poor to feed them. Even Bowie said he doesn't give a damn. He set Sam free on the spot, for all the good it will do."

"Did Travis free Joe?"

"No."

"Is Travis ready to abolish slavery?" I asked.

"One fight at a time, George," Crockett replied, giving me a subtle nod to speak of it later.

I heard rustling outside my tent. Slow had brought Tom and Kellogg, as requested, but I wasn't ready for them yet. I sent John out to keep everybody away for a few more minutes.

"David, when you first arrived at San Antonio and the people called you Colonel Crockett, you humbly declared yourself a high private. I would like to help you, but a humble private is no good to me. I understand why you want to play down your celebrity. You're a stranger to Texas, just like I am. You're afraid of offending those who have already set down roots here. I'm not happy about that, either. But we play the cards we're dealt."

"What are you asking?"

"I'm asking you to take on a more important role. One I can't fill. I don't know how you or I individually can succeed, but together, we just may well make history."

"Are you really from the future, George?"

"I guess that depends on what future we're talking about."

I went to the tent flap and looked out. Most of my officers were nearby. I waved to Kellogg. When I saw Slow, I waved him in, too. Tom started to follow but I sent him back, much to his displeasure. Seguin had found my troop of Mexican teamsters and was deep in conversation, his eyebrows raised by the stories they were telling.

"David, you remember Mark and Slow. Mark is our expert on the Texas Revolution. Slow is a sort of mascot."

"A guide," Slow said.

"A guide and a mascot," I replied, letting him sit next to me. "David, at the Alamo you asked me why we were leaving. I couldn't tell you then, but I will now. When you know our story, maybe this will all make sense to you. I'm still trying to figure it out."

I refreshed Crockett's coffee, took a cup for myself, and settled down. Kellogg was looking at me curiously, for I'd generally ignored him the last few days.

"I was born December 5th, 1839, in New Rumley, Ohio. Oldest of four brothers and a sister," I started to explain. "After teaching school in Cadiz, I won an appointment to West Point. From 1861 to 1865, I was a soldier in the United States army fighting a great Civil War. So was my brother Tom. Bill Cooke came down from Canada to sign up. Most of the officers you've seen riding with me are veterans of that war. We were fighting eleven southern states that had seceded from the Union, including Tennessee, Virginia, Arkansas, and Texas. David, by the time the Rebellion was defeated, half a million men had died."

"Half a what?" he said.

"Half a million," I repeated, looking him in the eye.

Crockett leaned back with a low whistle. It wasn't that he didn't believe me, but it was still hard to comprehend.

"The Union was led by a great president named Lincoln," I continued. "For much of the war, most of the people didn't think too highly of him, myself included, but in time we saw his wisdom. Slavery had been the cause of the war, and by ending slavery, he guaranteed that our country would never be divided again.

"Now we find ourselves forty years in the past, by what means is a mystery. For us, it's twenty-five years before the Civil War. America is once again divided. The plague of slavery exists once more. There's nothing we can do about slavery in the Southern states, and maybe we can't stop the Civil War from happening, but I think there's a chance we can keep Texas from being part of it. Maybe that's why we're here."

"It is not the only reason," Slow gravely said, his brows bent.

"And there's more," Kellogg said. "Mr. Crockett, as you know, many of the Cherokee have migrated to northern Texas, their native land stolen by Andrew Jackson. In the next few years, the remaining Cherokee will be forcibly removed from Tennessee. Thousands will die in a forced march known as the Trail of Tears."

"I fought tooth and nail against that damned Indian Removal Bill," Crockett said, getting his dander up. "Some say it's why I lost my seat in Congress. We had a treaty with the Cherokee. Good neighbors. Good friends. Every bit as civilized as us whites. Maybe more civilized than some I could mention."

"As we speak, the Cherokee are trying to build new lives. Sam Houston has promised them their lands if they stay out of the war with Mexico," Kellogg said, recounting facts of which I was unaware. "But Houston is making promises he can't keep. In 1839, President Mirabeau B. Lamar will renounce Houston's treaty and order the Texas Rangers to attack the Cherokee settlements. Women and children will be slaughtered, their land seized. The survivors will be driven into the Indian Territory where they'll starve on barren reservations."

"That ain't right. That just ain't right after all those folks have gone through," Crockett said, genuinely appalled. As was I. In my own time, the Cherokee were barely an afterthought, but injustice to the Indians was an ongoing outrage.

"Would you have it otherwise?" Slow asked.

"Of course I would," Crockett said, surprised by the question.

"This Houston you speak of makes false promises. Such is the way of the white man. Is Crockett or Custer any better?" Slow asked.

"I always keep my word, boy," Crockett said. "Everybody knows my motto. *Be sure you're right, then go ahead.* How about you, George? Do you keep your word?"

"Most of the time," I said.

The tent flap opened. It was Tom.

"We're ready, Autie. Got a nice spot down next to the river," he said. "Morning Star says their gods won't be mad that we're burying Gray Wolf at night."

"Yates and Reily?" I asked.

"Figured we'd bury them in San Antonio. In a proper Christian grave-yard," Tom said.

"It's a damn shame we've got to bury them at all," I replied.

Thinking of George Yates was still too painful. I fondly remembered our days in Monroe, and serving with Sheridan. Our nights at Fort Lincoln playing whist with Libbie and Annie. I needed to remove him from my thoughts or lose composure.

As for Gray Wolf, he had reminded me of my young nephew, Autie Reed, lost on the Little Big Horn. I hoped my little brother, Boston, had the good sense to stay with the pack train. It would be a bad day for my mother if three of her sons had died on that godforsaken hill.

"Lost some men fightin' the Mexicans?" Crockett asked.

"Family members," I glumly answered.

Crockett followed Tom and I down to the river where several members of the Seventh were watching. Morning Star and Walking-In-Grass were kneeling in wet weeds next to the body. Spotted Eagle stood a little farther on among the willow reeds, gazing at the dark prairie to the west. Torches had been lit, held by Bouyer and Voss.

"We have little to offer the Great Spirit," Morning Star said.

I saw from the forlorn expression on Walking-In-Grass's face that she was equally disturbed, for they had traveled down from Dakota Territory with the barest of supplies. Sioux funerals were no mystery to me, however, for I have witnessed many during my years on the plains, as well as those of the Arikara, Crow and Cheyenne. Each tribe performed the ceremonies differently, yet they all had things in common.

Had we a teepee to spare, Gray Wolf might have made use of it. We had discovered a dead warrior in just such a teepee only an hour before reaching the Sioux village on the Little Big Horn, the body wrapped in fur and surrounded by weapons and food. But here, in the wilderness, a tall tree with sturdy branches would suffice.

The men had found a buffalo robe to wrap the body, but it wasn't long enough, leaving Gray Wolf's feet sticking out. I motioned to Butler.

"Jimmy, fetch a tarp from the wagons. And some rope," I ordered. "Bring the musket Señor Seguin gave him. John, find some coffee and jerky from our stores. Ask Captain Keogh if he can spare some tobacco."

Tom took the hint, going back to camp with Butler to gather a few articles for Gray Wolf's journey to the next world. The women began to moan, clawing at the ground and pulling at their hair. I thought their form of grief primitive, but could not help wondering if my Libbie would do the same for me. I like to think she would. Before long, groups of frontiersmen were gathering around the unusual sight.

Gray Wolf's body had been washed in the creek. He wore his leather breeches and moccasins, but the shirt had been a bloody mess, the bullet that killed him having gone through his jaw. Tom returned with a long sleeve cotton shirt from the Buffalo hunter's wagon. Butler came back with the tarp. We laid the musket next to Gray Wolf, added some food and tobacco, and began to wrap him, starting at the feet. It was important to make the covering watertight. At the last moment, I took off my red scarf and knotted it around Gray Wolf's neck. A good luck charm the lad might need.

The wailing of the women grew louder. Walking-In-Grass took locks of her torn out hair to weave into Gray Wolf's long black tresses. Morning Star wiped tears from her face to moisten the boy's cheeks. Spotted Eagle had found a white, chalky rock that he used to mark Gray Wolf's arms. We had no war paint, but a little soap and alcohol helped bleed some red dye from an old shirt, enough to make a few streaks.

At last the body was properly bundled. Six of us, with Crockett helping, lifted him to a tree branch eight feet above the ground, where it was secured with additional rope. The scaffold would keep Gray Wolf closer to the stars and safe from roving wolves.

"The father must speak," Slow said.

"You're the medicine man," I answered, unwilling to extend myself so far. Even at funerals for Christians, I rarely had words to say. Death touches some too closely, especially me. What could I say about a young heathen that the gods would want to hear?

"I am not a man. In another life, some may have called be a medicine man, but it was not true," Slow said, drawing deeply from dim memories. "To know the spirits is not to know the arts of healing. The white man may not know the difference, but the People do."

"The boy is right, General. One of us should say the words," Cooke said.

"Then you say them," I replied, miffed at his presumption.

"I am not the father," Cooke said, just to be an ass.

"Autie, it will mean more coming from you," Tom said. "Gray Wolf looked to you as a father."

"Just like the men do," Cooke added.

I was startled by this, and shaken, but it made sense. And Bill was always, above all else, a sensible man. In such strange circumstances, it should be no surprise that the rank and file would invest their hopes in me.

Slow took my hand, walking to the base of the tree. The women stopped their wailing. It was not unusual for Indians to cut and mutilate themselves during mourning, but this I had forbidden. Doctor Lord was pressed enough already by our recent skirmish.

The night had turned frosty, causing us to bundle up against the breeze rustling through the trees. The burning campfires along the rough dirt road looked like dim stars among the woods. The men, unafraid of the Mexican cavalry now that we were gathered in sufficient strength, chatted boisterously in small groups.

Nevertheless, our three artillery pieces were posted on the north trail against an unexpected incursion. Bringing the cannon had slowed Keogh's march, but worth the effort. Once again, I thought back on the Gatling guns that Terry had offered me on the Yellowstone, wishing now I had taken them.

"Great Father of us all," I prayed. "We knew this boy as Gray Wolf, no older than many who fell on the battlefields of Virginia and Pennsylvania. He was brave and loyal. A good companion. Have mercy on him for his sins, praise him for his devotion, and protect him in the world to come, as I hope you will protect us, your servants, in life everlasting. Amen."

"Amen," a dozen soldiers chanted.

"Lot of trouble for a damn Indian, if you ask me," a shaggy-bearded frontiersman said from the crowd. He was tall, lanky, with big fists that were clenched. A red and black checkered scarf covered his head.

"Waste of a good rifle, too. Let's climb up there and take it back," his burly friend agreed, pushing forward. Like the other, he was dressed in buckskins but wore a beaver hat. Trappers, most likely. His bright red hair hung down to his shoulders.

"Leave my cousin alone," Morning Star protested, standing in the man's path. She looked like a stick compared to the two men coming at her, but stood her ground.

"Out of my way, squaw," the tall trapper warned.

"And you squaw men better back off, too," the burly one said, pointing a finger in our direction. "Don't know why you even buried this red devil. Nothing but raping, murdering scum. Better left to the scavengers."

"Goddamn Indian lovers," a third frontiersman said, short but thick at the shoulders, his head so covered in matted hair that he looked like a small black bear. The coverings on his feet weren't even boots, just furs wrapped by leather twine.

"That's far enough," Cooke said, standing at Morning Star's side.

Tom was already there, his brows bent. The long scar on his jaw was beginning to bulge. Smith and Butler were with them. Even Voss came up despite his wounded arm, passing the torch to Walking-In-Grass so he could grip the hilt of his sword.

"No fighting," I demanded, this being neither the time or place.

"Cowards," one of the trappers said.

It looked like he was going to push Morning Star out of his way. A glance over his shoulder found fifty or so militia members standing behind him in a group. Men he expected to support his intrusion. Crocket went to intervene. I put a hand on his shoulder.

"George?" Crockett whispered.

"Let's give them a moment," I said.

The Custer Clan closed ranks, Tom and Cooke taking charge. A dozen of their friends were ready to join in, including Smith, Harrington, Butler and Hughes. Not all were particularly fond of Indians, nor had most of them known Gray Wolf, but that didn't matter. It was one for all and all for one, regardless of the cause.

"We got you blue boys two-to-one," the little bear-man said.

"Make it ten-to-one and see if we care," Tom dared, taking off his heavy coat and dropping it in the damp grass.

Keogh walked down from the camp, saw the trouble, and hurried to prevent an altercation. He put one hand out to stop Tom, the other to ward off the frontiersmen. With a buffalo robe over his uniform, he looked bigger than any of them, and the month-old beard gave him a formidable look.

"That's enough, boys. We're all in this kettle together," Keogh said, his Irish accent thick. I knew he'd been drinking.

"Orders from the Pope?" someone said from the back, alluding to the Irishman's religion.

Even though settlers immigrating to Texas were compelled by Mexican law to convert to Catholicism, most were confirmed Protestants. It seemed that even here, in this godforsaken backwater, prejudices from the East ran deep.

"No reason for insult, friend. We are all equal in the eyes of God," Keogh replied.

"Equal my ass," the stocky trapper said. "No idolater ever stood eye-to-eye with me."

"Nor with me, you damned Friday fish-eater," the bear-man said, forced to look up at Keogh.

"The saints have their place, boys. Let's not fight over it," Keogh said, offering to shake hands.

"You're nothing but a damn abolitionist," the red-haired man said.

"A damn what?" Keogh asked, the smile disappearing.

"Abolitionist, darkie lover," the trapper answered.

"That's what I thought you said," Keogh said.

When Keogh reared back and punched the trapper in the face, the man went down hard, his nose spurting blood.

The tallest of the frontiersmen jumped forward, swinging at Keogh, but Cooke blocked the blow and returned a kidney punch. Tom leaped into the fray and soon the fight was on, ten or fifteen men jabbing, kicking and sprawling on the ground. A hundred others came to watch, cheering friend and foe alike.

There was a good deal of yelling, most of it good-natured, though a few seemed determined on blood. Sergeant Hughes was standing next to me, his Henry rifle cocked should anyone draw a knife or pistol, but so far fists appeared the weapons of choice. A brawny fellow knocked Keogh to the ground. Cooke, watching Tom's back, launched a solid round-house punch followed by two left hooks. Queen's Own must have had boxing lessons during his busy career.

Let them have a fair fight, I remembered saying during my cadet days. Those words had cost me a court-martial. But I wasn't the sergeant-at-arms anymore. Now I was the general.

Voss had run to Keogh's assistance, helping the big Irishman up. A blow from behind sent Voss reeling, but the corporal was tough as German leather, turning to kick the dastardly attacker where it hurt the most.

Two of Chenoweth's men decided to gang up on Tom, which was a mistake. Tom was already a wild lad when he lied about his age to join the army. They caught him, kicked him out, and he turned right around to rejoin. Libbie had struggled for years to curb Tom's drinking, swearing and fighting, but she had only managed to curb the drinking. Tom hit one man with a strong right-hand punch, threw him against the other, and then pummeled them both until they retreated.

"George, don't you think we should stop this?" Crockett asked.

"What?" I said, lost in thought.

"Maybe they've had enough," Crockett said.

"I suppose you're right, David," I agreed.

We waded into the battle, pushing the two groups apart with little difficulty, for the bitter cold was not conducive to a good brawl.

"That was a mighty fine scrap, fellers," Crockett announced. "Now let's get cleaned up and have some vittles."

"We have a cask of Santa Anna's Portuguese bourbon in our wagon," I added. "Some of you may need a sip after such a good fight. Come by our camp. No hard feelings."

I saw Chenoweth and Dijon in the crowd but didn't know if they'd thrown any punches. Chenoweth seemed lighthearted about the incident, but Dijon was still harboring a grudge.

"Myles, is that how you stop a fight?" I asked, wrapping an arm around Keogh's shoulders.

"Damn ignoramuses," Keogh said, rubbing his jaw.

"Tommy would have started the fight for you."

"Don't need no snot-nosed kids to start my fights, thank you. Or any damn generals stopping them," Keogh said, going back to his troop with a limp. I saw the flask in his back pocket.

"Satisfied with yourselves?" I asked Tom and Cooke.

"Hell yes," Tom said, holding Morning Star close.

Morning Star looked up at him like the hero he was, her big brown eyes filled with admiration.

"Whooped them Rebs good, didn't we?" Butler bragged, shaking mud out of his overcoat.

"Return to your units, gentlemen. Officer's call in half an hour," I said, declining any encouragement. "John, see that Morning Star and Walking-In-Grass eat some supper. No nonsense. They need to be strong for the days ahead."

I gave the women a firm look. Squaws can take their mourning rituals to an extreme if not kept in check.

"We will eat," Morning Star said, leading Walking-In-Grass away.

"Spotted Eagle and Slow, you may remain here with Gray Wolf until the moon sets, then you must take food and rest. We have enemies to fight," I said.

"Yes, General," Spotted Eagle gratefully said, for he feared to be ordered back to the tents with the women. I would not shame him so fearfully. Slow had no such apprehension, secure in his own path.

"You've got unusual problems," Crockett said, joining me on the walk through the dark woods.

"Your problems are just as bad."

"How's that?"

"I need your help, David. There might also be a few rewards involved, if you're not shy."

"Don't know that anyone has ever accused David Crockett of being shy. Need me to lead one of your troops? It's been awhile since I led the Tennessee militia under Andy Jackson against the Creeks, but I reckon there's enough spunk left for another campaign."

"The campaign I've got in mind is bigger than that. Maybe the biggest fight we've seen since George Washington whipped the British. Are you ready for a scrap that big?"

"You're a corker, George, that's for sure," Crockett said. "Just tell me where to march."

"I'll tell you where *we're* going to march," I happily replied.

———————————

I had made my decision, now it was time to talk with the men. For obvious reasons, this was not a conversation to have in front of the Texan volunteers. I ordered my immediate command and some of our friends into the lower pasture beyond a thick growth of trees. We took food, blankets to sit on, and I allowed them to bring the captured spirits, for a bit of cheer often makes hard choices easier.

"What's going on, Autie?" Tom asked, rushing to my side.

"Taking your advice, Tom. Giving the men a choice," I replied.

"Are you sure? Now?"

"You were right. They should know what they're fighting for."

"What *are* they fighting for?" he asked.

"What we all fight for, little brother. Now take a seat and listen," I said, going to the edge of the clearing.

The command was drawn out in a semicircle, most sitting on boulders or tree branches. Some had heavy jackets, others buffalo robes. It was cold enough to see the frost on their breath. The wind had died down and stars crept out through the clouds. The moon was close to full. We had scared off the game, but there were plenty of birds chirping in the trees and the occasional fish leaping from the stream. Butler and Hughes had gotten to the pasture first, lighting a bonfire. The flames climbed ten feet into the dark sky.

I stood near the fire, leaning against a fallen tree trunk, the Cibolo flowing behind me in the darkness.

"Fellas, I've asked Colonel Crockett to join this meeting," I said, taking an informal approach. "He knows more than he probably should. We probably know than we should, too, because we've gotten ourselves into quite a situation."

Crockett took off his hat, grinned, and waved the Springfield Model 1873 I had given him. The rifle that had belonged to Corporal Martin. A bandolier with fifty rounds of ammunition hung over his shoulder. The men cheered. Everybody cheered Davy Crockett.

"Other than the loss of our family, and our friends, I know you're all wondering about three things: what is the command going to do? What am I going to do? And what are you going to do?" I continued. "All are fine questions. First, let me tell you what you're going to do."

The men glanced about, the expressions mixed. Most looked encouraged to have leadership, a few frowned with resentment.

"As far as I'm concerned, this is still the Seventh Cavalry. 1876 or 1836, it makes no difference. Our duty is to serve the people of the United States. And I believe we're in an historic position to do that. A position that can save half a million lives. Some of those lives are your fathers, brothers and uncles. Because of this great responsibility, I expect each of you to continue following orders."

I walked back and forth before the group, hands behind my back, staring at a few who clearly disagreed. I stopped to look Tom in the face. He was completely mystified. Good. Cooke and Keogh were clueless as well. Even Slow showed an unusual curiosity.

"Gentlemen, Texas must be free of Santa Anna's tyranny," I announced. "But a free Texas must never join the Confederacy. A free Texas must encompass true American values. A free Texas must never own slaves."

I felt a wave of sudden energy as they began to suspect the scope of my ambitions. Tom sat down on a log, his mouth open. Cooke was scratching his whiskers.

"I think we can create a free Texas," I said, taking a confidential tone. "One that will hang back from the quarrels of the North and South, and when the day comes that the Union has reconciled itself, we can join that Union with a clear conscience. Proud to have upheld our ideals, and secure in the knowledge that we will emerge a better nation. The kind of nation that President Lincoln wanted us to be."

I stopped again near the fallen tree trunk, leaning back just a touch, arms crossed before me. Every man in the command was leaning forward, hanging on my next words.

"It's also true that, as the core the Texas army, there will be benefits. Generous benefits," I confided. "Each member of this battalion who survives the coming trials will achieve wealth beyond your grandest expectations. That is my promise to you."

The men sat quietly. Despite my reputation as a blustering braggart, and sometime exaggerator, none doubted my sincerity.

"Before I continue, each of you has a decision to make," I suddenly announced, hearing a few murmurs.

I began pacing again to keep their attention. To create a moment of drama, I sat down on a bent branch of cottonwood and I fiddled with my sword, laying it across my lap. The blade bounced softly on my knee. Lawrence Barrett would have been proud of me.

"Anyone who wants to forgo this obligation, to leave the Seventh Cavalry, may do so now," I finally continued. "But if you do, you will leave completely and forever. You will not be taking your Springfield or Colt; those belong to the army. Your horses, saddles and equipment also belong to the army. Sergeant Major Sharrow will help you find a musket and a powder horn. Bill Cooke will see you have food and warm clothes. You can walk away from this army and never look back. But if you *are* going to walk away, you must do it now. Get up and leave, because the business of this army is no longer your business."

I stood up and waited for the first deserter, my fists clenching. I hated the thought of letting any of them go, but there was really no choice. Better to weed out the cowards now. Tom came to stand at my side, then Cooke, Keogh, Smith and Harrington. Each was so proud they could burst. I noticed Kellogg, Dr. Lord and Bouyer standing in a group off to the side. They seemed pleased. Morning Star, Walking-In-Grass and Spotted Eagle sat on a blanket near the bonfire, interested but not absorbed by the problems of white men.

Private Daniels slowly rose to his feet, then Privates Cooper and Schmidt. Daniels waved to a few friends and left the circle. Corporal George Brown got up and followed. They were tactful, thankful enough to escape that they didn't gloat. Daniels and Brown were soon joined by Private Nathan Short, one of Tom's men.

"Sorry, fellers, I already got kilt once," Short apologized before disappearing into the dark. I nodded for Sergeant Major Sharrow to make the arrangements. When it looked like no one else was leaving, Cooper and Schmidt glanced at each other and discreetly sat back down. The meadow fell quiet.

I expected more men to rise up. At least twenty or thirty, if not half the command. Perhaps a few wanted to, but brothers- in-arms are loath to turn on their own. Even more had no desire to wear buckskins and carry a squirrel rifle the rest of their lives. I held my shoulders erect, a hand gripping my sword.

"Let me be clear about this," I said. "If you stay, there is no changing your mind later. You will be members of a new army. A grand and noble army. And a prosperous one. But you will not be allowed to back out of your obligations. I will track deserters down, even to hell itself if necessary. I've done it before, so you know I'm telling the truth."

"And if my brother doesn't catch you, I will," Tom said, cocking his Winchester.

"We all will," Harrington added.

The men remained quiet. None made an effort to leave, much to my amazement. Perhaps being lost in this strange time had created a greater bond than I realized.

"Okay then. Raise your hands and swear," I instructed.

Again I had caught them by surprise. I remembered how the oath I'd taken on the parade ground at West Point in 1857 had bound the class together. I hoped it would again. And I hoped I was doing the right thing, for I'd reached unfamiliar ground.

Once everyone was standing with their hands up, I glanced at the moon, caught my breath, and began the ritual.

"I solemnly give oath, by the Grace of God, to serve as a dedicated soldier of the Seventh Cavalry. I will fight for the constitution of a free Texas, uphold its honors, and obey my officers. So help me God."

"So help me God," the men concluded, having repeated every word.

"I think that deserves a cheer," Tom said, raising his fist. "Hip, hip, hurrah! Hip, hip, hurrah! Hip, hip, hurrah!"

The men smiled and seemed to relax. Bottles were passed around. Some threw off their fur hoods to proudly don their cavalry hats.

"Okay, now that we've settled what you're going to do, I'm going to tell you what the command is going to do. I'm even going to tell what I'm going to do," I said, once again sitting on the log. "At sunrise, I'm dividing the regiment."

"Jesus, Autie. Again?" Tom whispered none too softy. It made the men laugh.

"It's finally your chance at an independent command, Tom. Time to prove who the better general is," I said. "And when this is over, we'll see who has the most medals."

"I've always won all the medals. You're just a general," Tom said, the men laughing again.

"And being a general allows me to say something else. Now that those gutless quitters have left, I want to speak about something you've all been thinking about. Something you've earned with your loyalty. This is 1836, not 1848, and no one but us knows how much gold there is in California. Some of you might want to ride out right now and go look for it. Hell, boys, I'd like to do that, too. I love gold as much as the next man. But there's a few good reasons why we can't.

"You've got to keep in mind, John Sutter hasn't built his mill on the American River yet. There's nothing out there but wilderness and Indians. And California still belongs to Mexico. Even if you did find gold, the Mexican government would confiscate it. And they'd probably hang you. After that, they'd send in an army to enslave the Indians and keep the gold for themselves. That's how the Spaniards have done it since the days of Cortez, and they aren't going to change now."

"Have you got a plan, General?" Private Torrey of E Company asked, a timid lad barely out of his teens, but excited by the possibilities.

"Yes, Billy, I do. Maybe I wasn't always the best student, but that doesn't mean I didn't learn anything. Rome was just a small Italian city, but with good weapons and martial discipline, they created an empire. Napoleon had a ragged army short of supply, but blessed with high spirits and a vision. They conquered all of Europe.

"Now we're a small band. A band of brothers, like Henry V said before the Battle of Agincourt. We're outnumbered and fighting in a strange land, but we've got the best weapons in the world. And we're a trained force, unlike the rabble on both sides of this Texan Revolution. Through the Civil War and our years on the plains, we've seen more blood and suffered more trials than all of our adversaries combined. What we lack in numbers, we make up with experience. And guts."

I paused to catch my breath. Much of this hadn't even occurred to me before I began speaking, though the ideas had been building up for days. Now they were bursting forth spontaneously. I walked among the men, then sat down on a rock, feeling them wait for my explanation. Like the Bard at Niblo's Garden, I could feel the power over my audience.

"So you see, my plan is to win freedom for Texas. And California. For all of the American Southwest, and even those provinces of Mexico who want to join us. Then we'll go to the gold fields of California, and the silver mines of Nevada. We'll build ranches in Texas, mansions in San Francisco, and travel on railroads that we're going to build from the Caribbean to the Pacific. And if any one of us dies old and poor, it will be because of too much gambling, too much drinking, and too many women. Does that suit you, Billy?"

"General, that suits me just fine," Private Torrey said.

"How about the rest of you boys?" I asked, walking to the bonfire and standing near the warmth of the flames. "Do you want to create an empire, or become squirrel hunters like those deserters?"

"Can I build my mansion in Monterey, sir?" Corporal Briody asked.

"Johnny, you can build your mansion any damn place you please," I replied.

It was already late by the time our conference ended. The men spent the rest of the evening preparing their equipment for a fast march the next morning. The officer call lasted a little longer. Having assembled in my command tent, I huddled with Tom, Cooke and Keogh, joined by Crockett, Bouyer and Dr. Lord. Captain Seguin was busy organizing his Tejanos. At the last minute, Slow and Morning Star entered to sit quietly in the corner. Mark Kellogg nestled on a stool near the door, wearing his spectacles in the dim light and taking notes.

"That was quite a speech, Autie. How'd you ever think of it?" Tom asked.

"Actually recalled a little bit of history. During the English Civil War, when everything was going to hell, Oliver Cromwell created the New Model Army. It was an independent command. Independent of the politicians. They brought order out of chaos. And it didn't hurt to remember that Cromwell was a cavalry commander."

"You're comparing yourself to Oliver Cromwell?" Kellogg asked, his sarcasm uninvited.

"No, Mark, I'm not comparing myself to Cromwell. Cromwell was a Puritan. I'm a Methodist," I responded.

The men laughed. Kellogg looked embarrassed.

"So what do we do now, George? Attack?" Bill Cooke asked.

The men laughed again, and so did I.

"With the militia companies and Seguin's men, we've got nearly two hundred and fifty reinforcements," Crockett said, not getting the joke. "That should hold Santa Anna off until Houston arrives."

"Colonel Crockett, let's not fool ourselves. How many men can Houston bring? Three or four hundred?" I answered.

"Not enough. Not nearly enough," Tom said.

"We still need Fannin," Crockett admitted.

"And you're the one who has to get him," I replied.

"I've got to get back to the Alamo. I made a promise," Crockett protested.

"I will apologize for you," I said.

"George, we both know why that won't work," Crockett respectfully disagreed. "If I don't go back, everyone will know I broke my word. Even if we survive, no one will give me any respect. And I wouldn't deserve none."

"It's true, Autie," Tom said, nodding his head.

They made a good point. I noticed Slow watching from the corner, his black eyes searching my thoughts.

"David, I suppose you're right, so this is what we'll do. Tom, you're going to take C Company to Goliad. Bill and Kellogg will go with you. Bouyer will scout. Take command of the garrison there and return to San Antonio at a full march. No wagons, no cannon. Travel light and fast."

"And the rest of us?" Keogh asked.

"Myles, you'll be taking I Company west of the San Antonio River," I said. "Your mission is to harass the Mexican line of supply. All Santa Anna is thinking about now is reducing the Alamo and moving east. A blow from behind will shake his confidence. Can you do that?"

"Hell, sir, it will be just like me and Stoneman done in Georgia. Good times," Keogh replied.

"Am I guarding the rear, George? Again?" Smith asked.

"Fresh, E Company will patrol east of San Antonio. Keep the Mexican cavalry off us as long as you can. Harry, you'll move to the Gonzales Road with our wagons and artillery. Establish a strong position to protect our line of supply. You'll have Dr. Lord and our Mexican allies."

"What will you be doing, sir?" Harrington asked.

"I'm taking the rest of the command into the Alamo."

"What if the men at Goliad don't come?" Crockett asked.

"Tom and Bill can be pretty persuasive," I assured him.

"We should hope so, but what if Fannin still refuses?" Tom asked, worried by such a responsibility.

A heard a snort of derision from the corner where Mitch Bouyer was sitting. The scout was bundled in rawhide and a thick fur cap. His cheeks were flushed from too much drink. Bouyer glanced in my direction without apology.

"Hell, Tommy boy, you're going to take command away from the craven bastard whether he likes it or not," Bouyer said, echoing my thoughts. He looked around for a place to spit before wiping his mouth with his sleeve.

"Mitch is right. If Fannin objects, you'll just have to blow his brains out and assume command," I said.

Tom was shocked, and so were my officers, but I was completely serious. Mostly.

"Mark?" I summoned.

Kellogg emerged into the lamplight, taking a place next to me. I had asked him in advance to provide an explanation, but he'd grown so smug that I immediately regretted it. Nevertheless . . .

"Some of you know about the Alamo, but most of you don't know what happened to Colonel Fannin," Kellogg said, adopting a professorial air. "After receiving a plea for help from Travis, Fannin waited several days before starting out with three hundred volunteers. Fannin went a few hundred yards, had one of his wagons break down, and decided to turn back."

"Coward," someone whispered.

"Fannin's three hundred were probably not enough to help the Alamo, but that's not the point," I said, knowing the rest of the story.

"After the Alamo fell, Houston ordered Fannin to retreat, but he delayed again," Kellogg continued. "By the time he finally left Goliad, it was too late. His entire garrison was surrounded by General Urrea out on the open plains.

"When he surrendered, Fannin thought it was on honorable terms, but Santa Anna overruled Urrea. Seven days later, on Palm Sunday, over three hundred unarmed men were marched out into the prairie and massacred by Mexican troops. Fannin was the last man to be executed—sitting in a chair, blindfolded."

My officers gasped. To die in battle is one thing. To surrender and then be murdered is quite another. It was good for them to realize what sort of enemy we were fighting.

"So you see," Kellogg concluded, "Fannin and his men have nothing to lose. If they don't come to help the Alamo, they're going to die anyway. They won't even die as soldiers, just victims of a cruel tyrant."

I let everyone dwell on that for a moment. I saw Crockett was thoughtful, too. Only the Seventh Cavalry stood between the Alamo and a similar fate.

"I should stay with the command. I'm still your adjutant," Cooke said.

"Bill, I need you to go with Tom. You make a good team," I said, ready to issue unpopular orders.

I knew Cooke's spirit enough that he'd rather join me in the place of greatest danger. He was young, strong and brave. One of the best men I'd ever served with. Even if he was a Canadian.

"I must not leave Custer's side," Slow announced.

"You *will* be at Custer's side, my young chief. *Thomas* Custer's side. You are not the only one who may have a vision," I answered. "In my vision, you grow up to be a great leader. You will have a voice in the government of Texas. In the Alamo, I will merely be fighting. I'm just a soldier, hopefully a better soldier than I was a few weeks ago. But Thomas and Bill have a more difficult mission. They must draw men together, meet arguments, balance needs, and use force where argument fails. These are the lessons of leadership."

"Perhaps you are wiser than you appear," Slow observed.

Custer had denied an ambition to become president of his people, but now he schemed to become an emperor. Or was it Crockett who would be the emperor? The ways of white men often make no sense, for in the end, there is only the land and the spirits. I had asked Wakan Tanka for a new path that my people might live better lives. How could this place called Texas, several moons from the home of the Lakota, offer such a gift? I would travel south with Thomas Custer, for he had a good heart, and learn of leadership among the wasichu. But I did not want to leave the white general, who had determined for himself either death or glory. In some manner, a great destiny was to be decided at the Alamo. It was there I wished to be.

CHAPTER NINE

RETURN TO BÉJAR

Crockett and I visited the militia camps before getting a few hours sleep. There was no talk of a free Texas or gold fields, for these rough and tumble pioneers were not ready for such ideas. We simply explained that the Alamo needed help, and any who wished to join the garrison could ride in with us. About fifty agreed, mostly from the New Orleans Grays and Chenoweth's volunteers from Goliad.

Chenoweth himself announced he would go in search of additional reinforcements. A convenient excuse, but I made no protest. Dijon announced that he would go to the Alamo. I did not like the man but could not fault his courage.

One volunteer who wanted to go with us was persuaded not to. Fannin's courier, Edwin Mitchell, would serve better as an emissary for Tom, and he knew the trails. Not that I doubted Bouyer's skills, but Goliad was ninety miles from San Antonio. An extra guide would improve Tom's chances.

"The Tejanos are ready to serve, sir. What would you have of us?" Captain Seguin asked. Though his command was small, their knowledge of the area was important.

"I am dividing my command. If you could assign a few of your men to each detachment, their service would be invaluable," I requested.

"That is easily done. But what of me? I have friends in the Alamo," Seguin said.

"Not so many as you think," Crockett remarked, and though reluctant to insult Seguin, there was an edge to his voice.

"What do you mean, Colonel Crockett?" Seguin asked.

"By the time I left, most of your men had slipped away. Hardly more than a handful left," Crockett said.

"You call them cowards?" Seguin angrily shot back.

"Ain't discussin' nobody's character, just sayin' most of your boys decided not to stay with Bowie like you thought," Crockett explained.

"They must have good reasons," Seguin slowly said, not quite apologizing. "Most of the garrison is Anglo. Perhaps . . ."

"Captain Seguin, that's really not important now," I interrupted. "We're all fighting against this dictator. If you could ride the countryside and rally your people, it could make a great difference. Tell them the Seventh Cavalry is an army like no other, and if they are loyal, we will protect them from Santa Anna."

"I shall do as you ask. You will see. The Tejano people will flock to the cause of liberty," he promised.

And with that, he returned to his men, issued orders, and rode out of the camp. He was an angry man, but I wasn't quite sure who he was angry with.

"It wasn't good, his men running out like that," Crockett said, recalling what the men in the Alamo thought. "Made some of the boys think all the Mexicans are traitors. Poisons the well, if you know what I mean."

I considered Crockett's words, wondering if the bad blood I'd seen in Texas in 1865 between the whites and the Hispanics had anything to do with the rebellion of 1836.

As was my habit, I inspected the horses before returning to my tent. They had been tethered among the deep grass near the creek where they could feed and find water. The exertions had been hard on them this last month, for they were accustomed to better food and regular attention from our veterinary.

I went to Vic, scratching behind his ears and giving him a small turnip. He shook his head in appreciation, though I could tell he missed Dandy and our dogs. I missed them, too. Other than my trips to Washington and New York, I could not remember the last time I'd slept without a dog at the foot of my bed.

A habit that had taken Libbie a few years to accept. Crockett knew how I felt, for the old bear hunter was famous for his tracking hounds.

Dr. Lord found me coming back to camp. George had been posted to the Seventh Cavalry about eighteen months before the Dakota campaign, after being promoted to first lieutenant. He was a Massachusetts man, a graduate of Bowdoin College, and just a few months over thirty years old. I had some affection for Bowdoin alumni. My good friend, General Joshua Chamberlain, was president there. Josh had not only won the Medal of Honor at Gettysburg, but served as Governor of Maine after the war.

"General, we need to talk," Lord said.

Lord had gradually recovered from the fever that had laid him low, but he was still thin, his uniform hanging loose on his wide shoulders. He had not shaved in several weeks, giving him a ragged appearance.

"Your advice is always welcome, Doctor," I said, for he was not prone to extreme opinions.

"I should not be left behind with the wagons. Take me into the Alamo. That's where the wounded will be. I can keep men on the walls that will otherwise fill the hospital."

"There's going to be plenty of wounded, that's for sure," I agreed. "But Crockett tells me the Alamo has two doctors already."

"Witch doctors," Lord said with a huff. "Do you know what kind of medicine they practice out here? They'd be better off with an Indian medicine man."

"Too bad I'm leaving Slow behind," I said.

"This isn't a joke, General. You're keeping me from where I'm needed most."

"No, I'm not. George, you're not merely a good physician, but in 1836, you're the most educated doctor in the entire world. When the war is over, we'll be building you a clinic. You'll be writing books, or rewriting them, depending on how you look at it. You know techniques and cures that haven't even been imagined yet. The fifty men you might save in the Alamo are nothing compared to the thousands your knowledge will save in the years ahead."

"One of the lives I save in the Alamo might be yours."

"Don't you think I haven't considered that?"

"I'm a member of the Seventh. I should share its dangers."

"Familiar words. That's exactly what I wrote to President Grant while begging him to let me ride with the command to Montana."

"There wouldn't have been a problem if you hadn't called his brother a liar and a thief," Lord said, quite correctly.

"I was called to testify before a congressional committee about larceny at the frontier trading posts. It's not my fault one of the crooks was Orvil Grant."

"And President Grant suspended you from command."

"He changed his mind."

"Just like you should change your mind and let me go."

I wrapped a friendly armed around Dr. Lord's shoulders, taking him back toward camp with a frosty smile on my lips.

"Hell, Doc, regardless of where you're stationed, you still have an excellent chance of being killed," I said.

"Promise?" he asked.

"You have my word."

———————

We broke camp at dawn, ready to march. Only a stern speech had convinced Tom to leave my side, and I would miss him.

"Autie, how long can you hold the Alamo? The odds are still twenty-to-one," he asked.

"Kellogg says the Alamo fell on March 6th. A Sunday. Even though our ammunition won't last, I'm guessing we can hold Santa Anna off until you get back with reinforcements. Captain Seguin says the colonies to the east are mustering their militias. Houston won't be able to stay behind, drunk or not. The Alamo will hold Santa Anna in check as long as possible."

"I'll bring an army back, Autie, and kill any man who tries to stop me," Tom swore, reaching to shake my hand.

I took it firmly, not sure if I would ever see him again. If he sensed my feelings, he didn't show it. I did not offer advice on what to do if the Alamo fell. He would need to figure that problem out for himself.

"Morning Star is a good woman," I said, stepping back.

C Company was mounted, Bouyer in the lead. Cooke rode with Tom while Voss carried the colors. They were twenty strong, all armed with Colts and Springfields. I made Tom give me his Winchester, as I expected to need the extra firepower.

"Be careful, Thomas," Morning Star said, rubbing her nose against his. She was not happy at the separation, but C Company needed to travel fast. Without distractions.

"I'll be back soon," Tom promised. "Have Walking-In-Grass keep a warm lodge, and tell Spotted Eagle to stay out of trouble."

He took her in his arms, kissing her fully. Then, to my astonishment, he took off the red scarf I had given him on his promotion to captain and knotted it around her neck. After the significance the Indians attached to the scarf I had bequeathed Gray Wolf, the implication was unmistakable. I looked at Tom, seeking an explanation, but he only smiled in that devilish way of his.

As Tom's unit prepared to move out, Slow came up to me. He was dressed in cut buckskins and a black headband. His long hair was tied back and ducked into his collar. The black eyes searched for something: an explanation, perhaps, or some profound wisdom. I had neither to give him. I was making it up as I went along, hoping that Custer's Luck would see me through.

"You always seek the greatest danger," Slow observed.

"That is where glory is found," I replied.

"Is there no more to life than glory?"

"There is home, and family, and country. There are happy days. But in the end, only glory lasts forever."

"Nothing lasts forever but the earth and sky," Slow said.

"History will need to judge that, my boy. I have a favor to ask."

I waved to Corporal French, acting as my orderly now that Voss was leaving with Tom. French brought Vic forward, saddled and ready to ride.

"Slow, you have a long journey and need a good horse. Will you take care of Vic until our enemies are defeated?" I requested.

The boy's eyes went wide with surprise, for Vic was one of the best horses in the regiment. Possibly the very best, after Tom's Athena. Like Athena, Vic was a Kentucky thoroughbred, a brown sorrel with four white socks and a blaze on the forehead. He was my most dependable mount, having served well in many campaigns.

"Is death at the Alamo so certain?" Slow asked, for among the Indians, a warrior does not give away his warhorse.

"Death is never certain, but I won't be leading a cavalry charge from inside those adobe walls. Vic is better off out in the open, free to run and graze. I would not see him blown up by an artillery shell while trapped in that rat-infested corral."

I lifted Slow into the saddle, keeping a hold on the reins until he was settled. Vic could be skittish with an unfamiliar rider.

"Take care of my young friend, old boy," I whispered, giving Vic a kiss on the snout. He returned a soft whinny. I would miss him almost as much as Tom.

"I will honor this gift," Slow said.

"This is a loan, youngster. I want Vic back hale and healthy."

Slow smiled, showing white teeth. He did not smile often. I gave Vic a slap on the rump and he ambled over to C Company's assembly point.

"Boots and saddles, Mr. Voss," I ordered.

Voss sounded the signal on his bugle, and a few minutes later, Tom and Slow disappeared into the southern mist. Their equipment clattered as the horses reached a steady gait, and the last thing I heard was the rattling of the sabers we'd captured on the Rio Grande.

Not long after, our wagons were moving north along the creek road. I had put young Harrington in charge. With our forty Mexican teamsters and a unit of ten men, I had no doubt he would establish a strong position astride the Gonzales Road. From there he could communicate with relief forces coming west. Should Santa Anna's cavalry challenge our control of the road, Harry had the three artillery pieces. What the enemy wouldn't know was that Harry was short on ammunition.

"Hell of an idea, George," Crockett said as we prepared to follow the wagons.

"You said the Alamo is short of powder. It seems the best solution."

"Gun powder in bean sacks?"

"To defeat Santa Anna, we're going to need powder a lot more than beans," I answered. "The supply train we captured had plenty, but there's no way we can drive those heavy freight wagons down the Alameda and through the Alamo's front gate. Now each man is carrying two plump sacks on the back of his horse."

"Along with a couple of cannon balls," Crockett said.

We rode north for several miles before it was time for Keogh to split off. He had the assignment I desperately wanted, to cross over the San Antonio River and drive the Mexican army crazy with hit and run attacks on their rear. An exciting task for any cavalry officer, but especially for an Irishman.

"Good luck, Myles," I offered, shaking his hand.

A gray fog was rising from the creek, the frogs making quite a racket with their croaking. The command was spread out on the trail behind us, most of it not even visible.

"Remember, we'll fire the Alamo's 18-pounder every morning at sunrise," I said. "It's probably the biggest cannon west of St. Louis, so you'll be able to hear it for miles. We'll fire again at sunset as long as the Alamo still holds out. If you don't hear the cannon, reunite the battalion and move east."

"And when you fire the gun twice?" he asked with a grin.

"When we fire twice, it means I'll be launching an offensive operation. Give us the best diversion you can."

"If we took everyone into the fort, you'd have a stronger force."

"But we'd still be badly outnumbered. I'm sure Santa Anna would love to find his enemies all boxed up and ready for slaughter. No, Myles, the Seventh is a cavalry unit. We'll play to our strength."

"Santa Anna's strong point is his infantry, but they won't stay strong without a line of supply," Myles emphasized.

He knew his job, and he'd do it well.

"Remember to use your muskets!" I shouted as Keogh rode back to his troop.

We had found a hundred Baker rifles in the ordnance wagons. A musket may be no match for an 1873 Springfield, but a Springfield is worthless without ammunition. Every soldier in the command now carried both.

I Company broke off to the left, heading for a ford on the San Antonio River. With Keogh went Sergeant Major Sharrow, thirty troopers, five of Juan Seguin's Tejanos, and fifteen of the Gonzales Rangers. Fifty-two in all. Unless Santa Anna could mass his cavalry against them, they'd be hard to catch. And I had no intention of giving Santa Anna such free reign.

The dirt trail led up from the creek bed to a stretch of bench land. Smith's E Company, assigned twenty troopers, was in the lead. Harrington and his teamster's were holding the center, the wagons moving faster on the dry trail.

Bringing up the rear was my immediate command, mostly F Company and a few of the hardier boys who volunteered to ride with me. The Texian militia took up the trail on my right, riding in small groups.

Calling them all Texian volunteers was not precisely accurate. From what I'd learned, Stephen Austin had started bringing colonists into Texas fifteen years before, three hundred families in all, living on land grants from the Mexican government who needed a buffer between their northern providences and the Comanche Indians. Over the next decade, several thousand more colonists immigrated to Texas, most illegally, seeking refuge from sheriffs, nagging wives and debtor's prisons back in the states. The Gonzales volunteers, and those from Mina, were local militia gathered to fight for hearth and home. These were the true Texians, as they liked to call themselves.

Most of the men riding to my right were not Texians. Chenoweth's United States Invincibles and the New Orleans Grays had come to Texas in the last few months seeking fame and fortune. Just as Crockett had done. They wanted land, or spoils, or just a chance to fight someone. Most of these mercenary bands broke up and went back home before getting near a battle, but a few were tough enough to stay the course. I could not agree with their politics, but they were prepared to serve.

I had watched our new companions for a good part of the morning when a nervous delegation rode over. Crockett and I were curious, for they seemed intent on having a discussion. Their leader called himself Major Cyrus Johnson, though I doubt he held a real commission. Leadership in most militia units is by election. He was better dressed than the average frontiersman, wearing a nicely cut blue frock coat and a cherry red cravat under his shaggy black beard. I guessed him at twenty-five years old, formally well-to-do, now seeking a new start.

"General Custer, we would have a word," Johnson said, the accent Southern and educated. Possibly another lawyer.

"It's a free country, Mr. Johnson. Or will be, once this is over," I answered, finding myself in an impish mood.

Crockett smiled, too. We had been discussing the volunteers since the night before, pondering whether or not we should hold them in high regard. Crockett thought more of them than I did, which was to be expected.

"General, are you really from the future?" Johnson asked.

"That is a strange question," I said.

In fact, it was not strange at all. Though I had not spoken of such things in my meetings with Chenoweth and Mitchell, rumors notoriously spread though a camp like the pox. They had seen our weapons, our command structure, and no doubt heard stories from my men. And I had no doubt that, the more of Santa Anna's wine they drank, the better the stories got. Still, it took nerve to ask such a fantastical question. A glance toward the volunteers revealed dozens of men watching our conversation. Had Johnson been chosen as their representative?

"What if Custer and his troopers *are* from another time?" Crockett asked.

"Some of us might want to join up," Johnson said.

"Do we need so much help?" I asked.

"General, we all know you don't like slavery. Well, to tell the truth, most of us don't have no problem with it. Seems like a natural thing. But we don't much care, neither. None of us is rich enough to own no slaves. But we do like gold, and we heard there'll be plenty for those willing to fight for you."

"What if there is no gold? What if someone made that story up?" I asked, leaning from my saddle as if to speak confidentially.

"We don't figure it to be a yarn, sir. No sir, we see what we see," Johnson replied. "We came to fight, and get some land, and maybe become rich. But this war ain't likely to make no one rich, the way these Texians are fightin' it. So much arguin', and comin' an' goin'. This council says this, that governor says that. Bad as a bunch of old crones fightin' over a Christmas ham. We figure it be better to fight under a real general. One who knows where the goose squats."

I laughed. It was the best assessment of the situation I'd heard in days. Crockett was grinning, too.

"Being a soldier isn't the same as being a volunteer, son. Any of my men tell you what I do to deserters?

"You shoot 'em," he said with awe.

"Only if I don't have time to hang them," I said. "Mr. Johnson, go back to your friends. Tell them I may take on a few good men, but only if they know how to obey orders. If they're still interested, we'll speak again."

"Yes, sir. Thank you, sir," Johnson said, saluting before he rode off.

"And so it begins," Crockett said.

"And so what begins?"

"Word's going to spread about you ghost riders from the future. Some will say you're sent by God to free Texas. Others will say you're sent by the devil to stir up mischief. Either way, people are going to be talking."

"I'll come up with some sort of explanation. Maybe say we're from Canada."

"George, with so many of your men knowin' about the future, ain't it gonna gum up the works?" Crockett asked.

Tom and Bill Cooke had hinted about this, too. Were we living history or changing it? If I went back to Ohio right now and killed my father, how would I ever be born? These might be good questions, but I didn't much care to dwell on them. Philosophy has always been my worst subject.

"What future would that be, David?" I answered. "The one that was, or the one that's going to be?

———————

We made good time, reaching the Gonzales Road in the late afternoon. The wagons were formed against the creek in a wide half circle north of the road. Close enough to reach water if besieged, with cottonwood trees for cover. The horses and oxen were moved to a nearby pasture.

"What do you think, Harry?" I asked.

"A cannon can watch the ford. Another pointed north should hold off an attack from the prairie. We can station the third to cover the road," Harrington said. A textbook analysis.

"Señor Sepulveda, will your Zacatecos militia find this a suitable position?" I inquired.

Sergeant Sepulveda's corporal frowned, for Francisco Sanchez was from Coahuila and wanted recognition for his province. But only seven of our forty teamsters hailed from Coahuila. Most had followed Sepulveda to this desolate spot.

"Yes, General, but we would rather fight with you," Sepulveda said.

"That time will come, but now I need you to support Harrington. My division is spread thin. Too thin to harass Santa Anna and protect our supplies. And to be frank, sir, I'm afraid the Alamo may fire upon you on approach. I'll feel better knowing there are loyal friends keeping this road open."

"We will not disappoint you, sir. But this war will not end in Béjar. Promise us a chance to pull the tyrant down," Sepulveda requested, humbly holding his old white hat before him.

"You have my word, sir," I said, reaching to shake his hand.

The Mexican's weather-beaten face lit up with a smile and returned my grip. Had Santa Anna burned my towns and murdered by people, I would want revenge, too, but I sensed more in Sepulveda. A common man with much potential.

"Mr. Harrington, you have command of this position. And don't worry, you'll do fine," I said with a salute.

"Thank you, sir," Harrington answered.

I paused, giving the situation some thought.

"Harry, off-duty, why don't you call me George from now on," I offered. The youngster burst with a grin bigger than Crockett's.

"Yes, sir. Thank you, sir," Harrington said, pumping my hand with gratitude.

I made an inspection of our relief station, finding it adequate. The men were setting up a teepee for Walking-In-Grass and Morning Star. The second teepee would be used as the headquarters. My command tent became

Dr. Lord's hospital and was surrounded by two dozen pup tents, courtesy of Santa Anna's commissary.

John was acting as Lord's assistant, for I didn't need a stolen slave complicating my relations in the Alamo. The surrounding meadows were filled with horses, mules, oxen and cattle. Spotted Eagle was unhappy to be left behind, but I suggested he might be needed as a courier, which softened the blow.

I did not want to delay, for San Antonio was still twenty miles away and I needed time to reconnoiter before fighting our way into the fort. But I had made that mistake before, pushing the men and mounts too hard. With the greatest reluctance, I ordered the men to get some rest. A good thing, too, because the moonlight I was counting on never materialized. It started raining just after sunset.

I reclaimed the second teepee for the night, shared with Crockett, though Morning Star served us a meal and kept company with us most of the evening. Crockett was perfectly comfortable with her, telling tales of the Cherokee and life in west Tennessee. Morning Star laughed at many of his jokes.

"It is still hard to understand," Morning Star said after one of David's stories. "How can you be two people?"

"I ain't exactly two people, young lady. You see, there's me, and then there's this other fella who plays a character based on me. On a stage, in front of folks who buy tickets," Crockett tried to explain again. "But because so many people see this fella, this actor, they think he's playing me and not a character."

"But who is the real David Crockett?" Morning Star asked.

"Hope I am. But then again, I've spent six years in Congress, so it's kinda hard to tell," Crockett said.

We rode out the next morning just after dawn, Crockett and I at the head of the column. I was still pondering how our entry to the Alamo was best accomplished. Smith and his troopers would not be going in with us, nor ten of the Gonzales Rangers. They would move north to harass Santa Anna's flank while staying in position to fall back on Harrington's position. He had the same instructions I'd given Keogh, and Smith had the same objections.

"Algernon, I'm not getting the entire Seventh trapped in that decrepit old fort," I patiently explained. Again. "Even I have no special desire to go back, but it's necessary."

"Then you have a plan to defeat Santa Anna?" Smith asked.

I saw Crockett's ears perk up.

"Yes, I have a plan," I said. "Most of a plan. Well, to tell the truth, it's more of an idea. If it doesn't work, I'll let Davy grin the Mexicans down."

"Or escape on a bolt of lightning?" Smith joked.

"Mighty touchy things, them bolts of lightning. Better to let George here snuff the rascals out the old-fashioned way," Crockett said.

"We'll have some time before riding into the fort," I decided. "Mr. Smith, while I'm scouting the position, have the men practice their musket drills. Crockett can show the boys how it's done."

"I bet he can," Smith said, breaking off to join his troop.

We rode in silence for a few minutes, Crockett wondering what I was thinking. Few of my thoughts had been revealed, even to him.

"We can hold up for a few hours. Ride in after sunset," Crockett finally said, looking back along our line.

Crockett saw fifty troopers of the Seventh Cavalry, thirty under my command and twenty with Smith. Following were fifty American militia volunteers. We brought no wagons and only twelve pack horses. If we were forced to make a quick dash through the Mexican lines, I wasn't sure how many animals we could control.

"Sunset might be the smartest time, but easier for their cavalry to surprise us. We could get scattered on this plain," I said, studying the countryside.

The terrain started out flat before turning into rolling hills. The yellow grass was scrubby. Good ground for a cavalry action, but I doubted Santa Anna would let me draw him off his prey.

His prey. It occurred to me to wonder why Santa Anna had allowed his invasion of Texas to be stalled in San Antonio for almost two weeks. Held up by an undermanned fort that could easily be stormed at any time.

"You said Bowie tried to negotiate with Santa Anna?" I asked.

"Sure did. Offered to lay down our guns and walk away. The dictator would have none of it," Crockett said.

"Fannin's men were allowed to honorably surrender by General Urrea, but then Santa Anna gave the order to murder them. Why wouldn't he do the same to the Alamo? Why not let them surrender and then kill them anyway? The man clearly has no scruples about such things."

"Can't say. Does seem a right strange thing," Crockett admitted. "Unless he's using the Alamo as bait. He might want to draw Houston in. Cut up the army of Texas piecemeal."

"You're a clever man, Crockett. Good with strategy," I said, realizing he was right. "How'd you ever manage to lose your seat in congress?"

"Lost the first time I ran," he recalled. "Then won a couple, lost one, then won again. Might have kept winning after that, but I got Old Andy's dander up by opposing most everything he did. Presents himself as a man of the people, but plantation owners are the only folks Andrew Jackson cares about. Plantations and land speculators. That's why he robbed the Indians despite our treaties. And he's robbed thousands of whites who settled the west only to be kicked off their land by crooked lawyers."

"We won't let that happen here," I said, for my own family had similar stories. Hell, I didn't know of a family in all of Ohio who didn't have similar stories.

"George, how'd you ever wind up at West Point? That school's a fine place for rich spoiled brats playing at soldier. No place for a blacksmith's son."

"Davy Crockett's disdain for West Point is famous even in my day," I said, grinning, for Crockett had tried to abolish West Point while a member of Congress. To say the least, Crockett's memory was not revered among the older officers. Especially Winfield Scott, who was said to spit every time Crockett's name was mentioned.

"The academy has changed since the 1830s," I said. "Most of my classmates were from families of modest means. In the North, the wealthy sort sent their boys to Harvard or Yale."

"Bet you was top of your class," Crockett jovially said.

"34th in a class of 34, David. It was a miracle I graduated at all."

"Ya ain't dumb, George. Believe me, I'd know if ya was."

"No one thought I was dumb. Seems some folks thought my discipline was lacking."

"Still got more schoolin' than I did. Hardly spent more than a few months getting taught how to read and write. The woods was my teacher. My rifle was my tutor."

"I may have learned to read in a classroom, but my teachers were the battlefields at Bull Run and Gettysburg. My tutor was a strong sword and thousands of dead countrymen."

"Maybe this time around, it don't have to be that way," Crockett said, quieted by my bitterness. "Sometimes fightin' is necessary, but more often than not, we can get what we what without fightin'. Just takes a little extra thinkin' on is all."

"I suppose. There was a time with this Cheyenne chief that I. . ."

My thoughts trailed off, struck by something Crockett had said. I swear, there were times the former congressman from Tennessee could be a genius.

"Bobby, up here on the double," I ordered.

"Yes, sir," Sergeant Hughes said with a crisp salute.

He had taken off his heavy overcoat, riding in a regular cavalry uniform. Two cartridge belts were crisscrossed over his shoulders, a third wrapped around his waist. Many of the men had done the same, carrying as much ammunition as they could. Hughes' slouch hat had been washed and decorated with a sprig of sagebrush. I glanced back and saw most of the command had given up their trapper's clothing for our traditional dress, showing a nice *esprit de corps*.

"We left something behind in the wagons captured from Santa Anna," I said. "Take three men and ride like hell. We'll wait on the outskirts of town until you rejoin the command."

"What am I looking for, sir? More muskets?" he asked in puzzlement, for we had plenty.

"Musical instruments," I said.

Late in the afternoon, the first Mexican cavalry patrol appeared just a few miles short of San Antonio. We could not see the Alamo or Santa Anna's army, but we could hear the sound of cannon firing every few minutes. The small unit of ten lancers kept a safe distance, or so they thought. Dressed in red dragoon uniforms, they made excellent targets even on a gray day like this one.

Our road was reasonably straight, and though wooded on occasion, generally open ground. Recent rains kept the countryside moist, but the trail had dried out just enough to be free of mud. The command continued in column of twos, four of Seguin's scouts out in front, the Texans in the center, and Smith bringing up the rear. The Mexican cavalry gradually increased to thirty but made no effort to engage.

"We've got the numbers, sir. Should we take a run at them?" Butler asked, his Sharps lying across his lap.

The enemy had gotten within two hundred yards, riding parallel to our march. Some were gesturing and smiling, not taking our small force seriously.

"We'll keep the mounts fresh, Sergeant. If the Mexicans get too close, throw out some skirmishers."

"They won't be gettin' close," Crockett said. "They is just a watchin', wondering what the hell we're doin'. George, what are we doin'? Shouldn't be we waitin' for dark?"

"That was my original plan, but I grew bored with the idea."

"Riding into the Alamo with a thousand Mexicans shootin' at you sounds too dull?" Crockett asked.

"A friend suggested something different."

I halted the command a mile from Powder House Hill. The Mexicans had reestablished a guard on the ridge, but through my field glasses, I was unable to see a battery. Tom had done a thorough job of destroying the first one; apparently Santa Anna hadn't bothered to post a new one. East of the ridge, the landscape was rolling prairie and a few small farms. We had passed several adobe houses, but the livestock was gone, driven away by their owners or stolen by Santa Anna. A campsite, now abandoned, had been used by the Mexican cavalry watching the Gonzales Road. Our horses helped themselves to the leftover grain.

"I half expect the Mexican army to pour down that hill," Nathaniel Brister said, acting captain of the New Orleans Grays.

I had learned that Brister was a Virginian. A tall man, about Tom's age, with a strong physique. His brown hair was short, the curly beard trimmed. Since arriving in Texas, he had already been in several battles, including the siege of Béjar the previous December.

"Not too likely," I said. "To come over the hill, Santa Anna's right flank would have to leave their siege positions and march up the Alameda. His left flank would need to leave their trenches and cross that swampy morass underneath the Alamo's cannon stationed in the church. Do you think Travis's garrison would sit quietly and watch?"

"No, I reckon not. They'd be shootin' like crazy," Brister said.

"And if the Alamo was shootin' like crazy, we'd hear it," I concluded. "Tell your men not to worry, Captain. We'll have plenty of warning if there's going to be trouble."

"You don't think there's going to be trouble?" Crockett asked.

"I have no desire to expend our ammunition so near my goal, but I doubt the enemy can reach us in sufficient strength out here on the road. Not against fifty .45 caliber Springfield rifles. No, David, they're going to watch. Wait for my next move."

A boom echoed off the hills, the Alamo's 18-pounder. There was just the one shot. A signal?

"At least we know Travis and the boys are still there," Crockett said. "Bet Texas can hear that cannon thirty miles around."

I doubted it could be heard so far away, but it was certainly loud.

A few minutes later, Sergeant Hughes returned with my musical instruments. Spotted Eagle was with him, grinning like he killed a buffalo single-handed. And worse, John was riding with him, two flintlock pistols tucked in his belt. In Texas, in 1836, a black man rarely carried sidearms. It was not common in 1876, either. But there was no time to worry over such prejudices.

"We got a bunch of 'em, sir. Drums, horns. Even a fiddle," Hughes said, waving some sort of flute.

"A fiddle? I'll take that," Crockett eagerly said, reaching for a finely made violin.

"Gather some of the boys who know how to play these things," I ordered. "Butler, prepare the command to move out. Smith, ride with me."

I was not worried about finding enough musicians. Frontier life is not the constant din of Indian battles and gunfights that the dime novels like to portray. Most of the time is spent at the post waiting for new assignments, allowing plenty of time for reading, music, and even a few of the scientific arts. And excessive drinking, which is typically the army's greatest challenge.

With Lieutenant Smith, Crockett and Spotted Eagle, I rode west where the road made its final gradual climb to the top of the Alameda. Brister and John soon joined us, Brister giving my new servant a wary glance. John handed me a canteen of cool river water and I drank thirstily before speaking.

"Algernon, you've got the hardest part of this operation," I began. "E Company is going to cover our movement toward the fort. Take a position on the ridge, skirmishers ready. Have your scouts hold the mounts back of the line. I'm not taking all the horses into the Alamo. The garrison is short on feed, so we'll only take the horses needed to carry the supplies."

"You're going in on foot? In broad daylight?" Smith asked, incredulous. "How do you expect to fight your way in?"

"I don't. Colonel Crockett says it's better not to fight."

"*Sometimes* it's better not to fight. I never said this is one of those times!" Crockett protested.

"Where's your sense of adventure?" I asked.

"General, you're beginning to scare me a little," Smith said.

"It's okay, Algernon. This gamble is most likely a stacked deck. One way or the other, we'll know soon enough."

We rode slowly up the long sloping hill. I noticed the cannon fire had stopped, almost as if in anticipation of some new event. At the crest of the hill, I dismounted the command.

"Santa Anna has been busy," Crockett remarked.

It was true. The size of the Mexican army had doubled since our previous foray, from fifteen hundred to three thousand. The town across the river was filled with tents and wagons. With the army were several hundred camp followers who cooked the meals, washed the clothing, and supplied various other services. A large house off the main square flew Santa Anna's personal banner.

To the north of the Alamo, an entire camp had grown among the cottonwood trees just beyond an entrenched battery. South of the Alamo, among the shanties referred to by the locals as La Villita, a smaller camp had been expanded, supporting two batteries near the main road. To my right, near the fire-damaged Powder House, a tiny garrison had pulled back along the ridge. The wreckage of two destroyed cannon lay behind a crude rock wall.

"Officer's call," I ordered.

Corporal French's bugle sounded sharp and clear in the crisp air, audible all the way down the hill to the Alamo.

Smith, Brister, and nearly everyone else who thought themselves important came running, all curious about my strategy. The bustle of activity around the Alamo had quieted. On the walls, and from the gun platform at the back of the chapel, I saw dozens of men looking in our direction. One appeared to be Travis, another Jameson. I did not see Bowie. The Mexican army was equally interested, many coming out of their fortifications to see the strange battalion on the hill.

"Sergeant Hughes, unfurl my guidon," I instructed.

My blue and red silk banner soon fluttered in a light breeze. The red and white company flags of E Troop and F Troop appeared beside it. Our regimental flags had been left behind with the supply train, for we were no longer fighting as a division of the United States.

"Gentlemen, we are going to march down the Alameda and enter the Alamo," I announced. "Corporal French, you will lead the band. Eight men should be sufficient, drums and horns. Butler, you'll have three skirmishes forward. Hughes, three skirmishers to the left. No one is to fire unless fired upon, and only then under extreme pressure. The rest of the command will march in formation behind the band. Brister, your men will follow mine. All will be on foot. Select twelve men to lead the pack horses. The rest will bring up the rear, rifles on their shoulders, four abreast, three paces between your ranks. When my command stops a hundred yards short of the bridge, make a right oblique and take your men into the fort."

"General, if the Mexicans attack . . . ?" Brister started to ask.

"Let me worry about that," I answered.

"But sir . . .?" he persisted.

"Nathaniel, can your men follow orders or not?" I snapped.

"By God, sir, you'll see our worth," Brister agreed.

Brister went to issue the orders, no doubt wondering how to explain the situation.

"Crockett, Spotted Eagle and I will remain mounted, leading the procession," I continued. "Most of the Mexican army is out of range with those antique muskets, so we'll keep an eye on their artillery. If you see a man about to touch off a cannon, kill him. Otherwise, I don't want any shooting. None. Gentlemen, is that clear?"

"Yes, sir," several quickly repeated.

They were starting to understand, and though there was the normal amount of fear in such a precarious situation, I noted a bit of amusement, too.

"Mr. Smith, you'll hold this position until the command has entered the Alamo. Appear as if you're waiting for additional reinforcements," I said. "Once we're inside, withdraw as quickly as you deem prudent. Return the extra horses to Harrington, then move north against Santa Anna's left flank. Questions?"

"No, General," Smith said. "Good luck, sir."

As with Keogh, I envied Smith's assignment. Riding free on the open plain, striking behind the enemy lines. Creating havoc. And I was headed into a decrepit fort. Trapped behind those adobe walls. I could only hope that Custer's Luck would see me through.

I rode forward with Crockett and Spotted Eagle. The youngster didn't care a whit about all the fuss, he just wanted excitement. He had stripped off his heavy robes, riding in a gold vest stolen from a dead Mexican officer. His rawhide pants had fringes down the sides. He carried a fine Kentucky long rifle and one of Tom's Colts. Two eagle feathers were stuck in his beaded headband.

"Spotted Eagle, I think you will find more scalps with Algernon. Would you not ride with him?" I asked, for the Alamo seemed no place for an Indian.

"Slow said I will count many coup at your side," Spotted Eagle said, raising a knotted war club.

He had painted red and black stripes on his cheeks, his brown eyes dancing with anticipation. Striking an enemy, whether with club or lance, was a revered Sioux custom. A mark of high prestige. But not very helpful if the enemy responds with a bullet.

"Take scalps instead, youngster. You'll live longer," I advised.

Crockett sat on his horse gazing at the battlefield. I heard a low whistle.

"Not a one of them is shootin'," Crockett said.

"Surprised?" I asked.

"Damned surprised."

"There's always a hush before the curtain rises," I said, my heart pounding. I had often ridden into battle with sabers flashing, but this was quite different.

"Command, take your positions!" I yelled. "Band, strike up the Gerry Owen! Forward march!"

And so the Seventh Cavalry marched down the Alameda in good order, rifles on their shoulders with heads held high. Hughes had picked his musicians well, performing a rousing version of the old Irish drinking ballad. And then, suddenly, the men started singing. I could not help but join in, knowing that the enemy, and our allies, must think us crazed.

As the trees along the Alameda receded, I took my boys straight ahead toward the old wooden bridge crossing the San Antonio River. With a nod, Crockett peeled off with the Texian volunteers, heading for the lunette guarding the south gate. They were not marching with military precision, but doing their best.

My skirmishers were watching the Mexican artillery on the left, for they were closest to our position. The faces of our enemies were bemused, if not awed, by my audacity. None made an effort to fire on us, perhaps because they had no orders to cover such an unusual occurrence.

The Alamo on our right grew near enough to recognize the defenders on the walls. They were equally startled. Though their rifles were ready should a fight break out, it did not look like they expected trouble. There was a wide, stone-paved plaza where the roads between the Alamo, the Alameda, and the bridge to San Antonio all intersected. Toward the Alamo eighty yards away, several burned-out hovels showed there had been a skirmish. Crockett had told me he helped burn the shacks to deny the Mexicans cover so close to their walls.

"Command, halt," I ordered, forming the troops in two squares with the band in front. "Present, arms!"

The men stood in a steady line as if on parade. Though I pretended nonchalance, my Remington lay across my lap ready to shoot the first artillery officer who dared fire on us. Butler and Hughes were similarly disposed, but it soon became clear that Crockett had been right. Santa Anna wanted more victims *in* the Alamo. More fodder for his bloodbath. And even if he decided to open fire, giving the order would take more time than I would give him.

"Gentlemen, *Marching Though Georgia*, if you please," I ordered.

The band struck up a favorite tune of General Sherman's, and though I had not the honor to serve on that glorious campaign in 1864, I knew the song well. We stood at attention until the stirring ballad was finished. I sat erect on my mount, an old mare named Daisy, staring across the river as if I didn't have a care in the world.

Crockett and his men reached the south gate, scrambling through a portal of the lunette into the fort, followed closely by the supply horses. I looked to my left where there was a Mexican battery hardly more than forty yards away. The lieutenant in charge was standing near his cannon but showing no sign of hostility. I even detected a hint of admiration in his eyes. The Mexicans were no slouches when it came to marching and drilling, and in this we shared a common bond.

"Right shoulder, arms!" I shouted. "Right wheel, march!"

Formed in column of twos, the battalion turned toward the Alamo, skirmishers at the rear, and made a steady drive toward the south gate. The burned-out adobes sheltered us on the left. The Mexicans on Powder House Hill were more than a thousand yards away. I lingered behind, being the last to leave, then drew my saber while waiting for the command to reach the fort. Across the river, among the trees lining the bank, I saw a dozen Mexican officers dressed in silver and gold trim. One of them, I supposed, was General Antonio López de Santa Anna. I saluted him and rode into the Alamo. Not a single shot had been fired.

Damn it felt good.

Among the People, it is not unusual for a warrior to give away their possessions when death in battle is certain. Custer had given me his horse, but I did not know if he expected to die. White men do not dwell among the spirits. Then

I remembered the legend of a great warrior who saw many enemies coming, but rather than retreat, he pounded a stake into the ground and tied it to his ankle, promising never to run. The warrior was killed in that place, counting many coup, and winning great honor. I wondered if Custer now sought similar glory. I wondered if the Alamo was to be his stake in the ground from which he could not run.

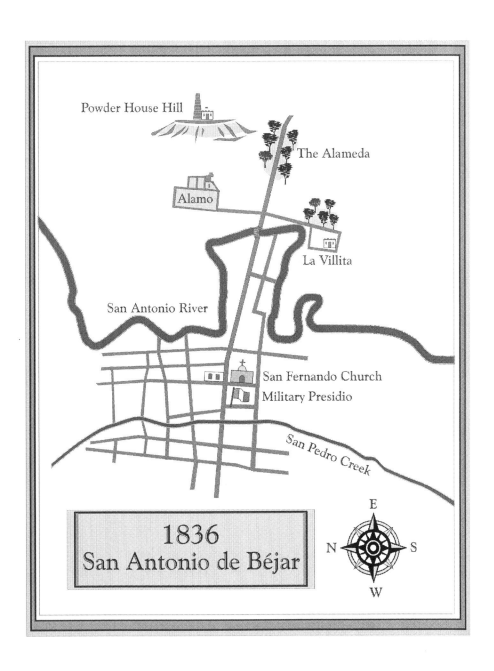

Powder House Hill

The Alameda

Alamo

La Villita

San Antonio River

San Fernando Church
Military Presidio

San Pedro Creek

1836
San Antonio de Béjar

CHAPTER TEN

A LINE IN THE SAND

"What the hell was that all about?" Crockett asked as I led my horse across a rough plank bridge into the lunette.

The Alamo was not a castle. It did not have high towers and a drawbridge to protect its gate. The long gatehouse, generally called the low barracks, did not even offer a crenellated wall, forcing the rifleman to expose themselves to enemy fire when standing on the roof. This is why the defenders had built the lunette before the south entrance, hoping to supply some flanking protection.

"I don't know what you mean, Colonel?" I said, feigning innocence.

Ten of the Alamo defenders stood at their stations within the grimy lunette, their frayed clothes stained with splotches. They were tired, lean in both body and spirit. Santa Anna's prolonged siege was having the desired effect. Through the gate, I saw that Hughes and Butler were keeping my men in line awaiting orders. My newfound mercenaries were formed up as well, seeking favor by appearing professional. To an extent, it was working.

"You know what I mean!" Crockett protested. "Is that what you learned at West Point? March under the enemy guns in broad daylight, playing at parade?"

"It was your idea."

"The hell is was."

"You said that sometimes we can get what we want without fighting, we just need to think about it. Well, I did think about it. And it worked."

"You're very proud of yourself, aren't you?"

"Yes."

I nodded to the small group of men around us, who were yet to utter a word, and walked with Crockett through the crude gate, the heavy oak doors left open. Twenty or so men were at their posts in the sprawling compound. About forty had rushed to greet us, including William Travis and Green Jameson. They looked thin. Unshaved, except for Travis. One would think that eighty reinforcements would lift their spirits, but this was hardly the case. Santa Anna's army had pressed them hard since the Seventh Cavalry had ridden out nearly a week before.

"Davy, thank God," Travis said, rushing to shake Crockett's hand. "Where's Houston? Will he be here this afternoon?"

"Houston?" Crockett said, surprised.

"You're the advance guard, ain't you?" a burly sergeant asked. "Got to have a thousand men behind you, a comin' in brass balls like ya did."

"I don't know where Houston is. Still back on the Brazos, probably," Crockett admitted.

"But the rest of the men? Our relief?" Jameson asked.

The Kentucky lawyer turned engineer was more haggard than the rest, exhausted by rebuilding the fortifications that Santa Anna's artillery kept knocking down. His fine blue coat was tattered.

"General Custer here is the only relief I found. Custer and these volunteers up from Goliad," Crockett explained.

Travis gazed at the men standing in the courtyard, frowning at the count.

"Fannin has four hundred men, I only see fifty," Travis said.

"The rest were coming, sir, but they must've turned back," Brister said. "Colonel Fannin believes Urrea is coming up from the south. Maybe he thought he couldn't spare no more."

"No one else is coming?" Jameson asked.

"Nothing from Houston. A handful from Fannin. Goddamn them! Goddamn Texas if this is all they'll send," Travis said, his fists clenched in frustration.

How the young attorney expected all of Texas to rally in the space of ten days was a mystery to me, for the territory was vast and the eastern colonies hundreds of miles away. I sensed the man's idealism had gotten the better of him, only to be confronted by a grim reality.

"If that's the way you feel about it, I reckon we can march back out," Brister angrily said. "Can't we, General? Can't you march us right back out?"

All eyes turned towards me. I had not interjected myself in their conversation, gauging their reactions. The situation was not favorable, and nothing I could say would change that. But I was not without resources.

"Captain Brister, billet your men. Sergeant Hughes, find quarters for ours. Keep everyone to the south side of the fortress," I calmly instructed. "Mr. Jameson, I'll need you to gut those workshops on the north side. Strip out all the timber and metals. Then . . ."

"Sir, what the hell do you think you're doing?" Travis asked. "This is *my* command. I give the orders here."

"Where is Colonel Bowie?" I asked, causing the young man's face to turn red with resentment.

"Sick. Most likely dying," Captain Baugh said, pointing to one of the small rooms in the low barracks.

"Mr. Travis, your commission is from the regular army of Texas, a government I don't recognize," I said. "The rest of these men are Bowie's volunteers, my troopers, and the militia who came in with me. How many in this garrison are actually under your direct authority? Ten or twelve?"

"Eighteen," Travis reluctantly admitted. "But Bowie and I agreed to share command when Colonel Neill left."

"And what orders are you going to issue? How are you going to save these men's lives?" I asked.

"Are you sure no one else is coming?" Travis said, turning to Crockett.

Crockett looked down at the ground. He knew I'd sent Tom and Seguin off to find more help, but nothing could be promised.

"Sorry, Bill. For now, we is all thar is," Crockett answered.

Travis looked around the Alamo with a momentary flash of despair. He had two hundred and fifty men to defend three acres of broken down fort. A few good cannon, but short on powder and shot. Kentucky long rifles were generally accurate up to two hundred yards, but slow to reload and worthless in hand-to-hand fighting. Travis turned to a scrawny youngster holding a French horn.

"Jimmy, call the men together," he ordered.

Private James Allen, barely twenty years old, blew a call on his trumpet that I didn't recognize, more gibberish than a military summons, but the garrison responded just the same.

As the defenders of the Alamo began to gather, I noticed an unusually large number of corporals, sergeants, lieutenants and captains. Perhaps because communications were so poor, extra leaders were needed. Or maybe it was just a way to make the volunteers feel more important.

Most of my men had followed Sergeant Hughes towards the long two-story barracks looking for a place to sleep, but now they surged back into the courtyard. The famous Alamo church was behind them. Extending from the church to the low barracks was a log stockade guarded by two cannon overlooking the prairie we had crossed coming in. I stood with Crockett and Jameson, closer to the south gate. In the middle of the Alamo's southern courtyard, a redoubt had been built for a 6-pounder, and it was near the foot of this low dirt mound that Travis took his position. All but a handful of men gathered around, a few left on the walls to watch for enemy treachery.

The day was growing late, not half an hour left before sunset. As the sun faded, the frosty cold returned, for it had been a gray day marked by stubborn clouds. The firing from Santa Anna's cannon had paused, and in the distance, I heard a band playing Mexican music. Not the famous *El Degüello,* but just as annoying.

The men were mumbling, wondering what had caused Travis to call them together. James Bonham, the courageous twenty-nine-year-old dispatch rider born in South Carolina, came to Travis's side with a leather pouch. Kellogg had told me of Bonham. Of all the messengers sent from the Alamo to find help, only Bonham and one other had returned. Like Travis, he was tall and lean with blue eyes and a clear complexion. A popular officer with a winning smile. His loyalty to Travis had brought him back to this place of certain death, just like Tom's loyalty to me had led him to the Little Big Horn.

"Friends, I bear tragic news," Travis announced, loud but not quite shouting. He took a letter from the leather pouch, waving with one hand while gripping his sword hilt with the other.

"Yesterday, Major Bonham brought good news from Three-legged Willie, urging us to hold out. My good friend thought help was near at hand. My friend was wrong. It is now clear that no help will arrive in time."

Travis stepped back up the dirt hill for a better view of the men, letting his words sink in. It could not have been startling news, for in the eleven days of the siege, only a handful of men from Gonzales had answered the many letters Travis sent out.

"Mr. Custer and his men have returned, and a few friends from Goliad, but we are still only ten dozen against Santa Anna's army of thousands. The dictator has promised us no quarter. When he attacks, be it tomorrow or the next day, every patriot in the Alamo will fall. You have bought Texas precious time. Time that will allow our country to arm and organize. Though this will come too late for us, our sacrifice will bequeath a rich heritage of freedom for our children."

Travis walked down from the hill, unsheathed his long Spanish saber, and drew a line in the cold sand extending from the gatehouse toward the long barracks. I turned to look back at the church, seeing Mrs. Dickenson and some of the Tejano wives watching the proceedings from the doorway. Mrs. Dickenson had a baby clutched to her breast, staring from hollowed cheeks. Her blond hair was gray with dust. I also noticed John standing with Travis's slave, Joe, and Bowie's servant, Sam.

"You've done all you can. All that can be expected," Travis continued. "If any of you wish to surrender, or take your chances going over the wall, you may do so with honor. None here will doubt your courage. But if you stay, I believe we can bleed Santa Anna's army. Make his victory so costly, it will be a defeat. It's even possible that once the tyrant realizes our determination, he may relent his harsh terms. I can promise nothing. Nothing but that our names will be remembered by posterity."

Sheathing the sword, Travis walked back up the mound, going halfway to the top before turning to face his troops. His hands trembled, not for fear, for he was a brave man, but with nervousness. This was not a backwoods court-room. Rarely does a lawyer tell his jury they are doomed.

"Major Bonham and I are determined to sustain ourselves to the last. If you will join us, cross over the line to stand at our side," Travis concluded.

He straightened his shoulders, head held high. An artillery shell from the battery across the river sailed over the west wall and struck at the northern edge of the long barracks, but Travis didn't flinch.

"Guess there ain't much choice," a middle-aged frontiersman said, clad in worn buckskins.

The man hefted his Pennsylvania long rifle and crossed the line, turning to see what his fellows would do. With sighs of resignation, more surged forward. It appeared the entire garrison that had endured the siege under Travis would answer his final call, except for one. An old Frenchman with a gold earring was hanging back, clinging to his shotgun. I did not catch his name. By the fuzzy black beard and red bandanna wrapped around his head, I would have taken the grizzled old veteran for a pirate.

"I am sorry, my friends. I did not survive Waterloo to die 'ere," the Frenchman said.

With most of the original garrison joining Travis, my own men looked to me for direction. Crockett was yet to cross the line, but it was clear he would. Noise from the low barracks caught our attention.

"Don't leave me back!" Bowie shouted, his voice was weak.

Crockett and three others rushed to Bowie's room, carrying him out on his cot. The famous knife-fighter was bone white, racked with fever. I doubted he had more than days to live.

Crockett crossed the line as he carried Bowie to the foot of the mound, looking for my reaction. Dijon waved to his boys and crossed over, then Brister as well. The New Orleans Grays followed. Only my command remained.

"What do you think, sir?" Sergeant Hughes asked.

"We're in a tight spot, Bobby. The men should make their own decision," I replied, though of course, I had no intention of giving command to Travis. The drama needed to play itself out.

"I'm with you, general, whatever happens," Sergeant Butler quickly stated, holding his Sharps ready.

"Me, too," Hughes said, cocking the Henry.

"And me," Spotted Eagle added, drawing his borrowed Colt.

"We all are, sir," Corporal French said, the thirty of us banded together.

As if it were an old dream, I recalled our final minutes on the sun-baked hillside in Montana, the smoke of gunfire obscuring thousands of hostiles swarming at us from all directions. There had been no choice then. No place to run.

John came forward, the muzzle-loading pistols still tucked in his belt. Sergeant Dijon frowned, a promise of revenge in the bent eyebrows. I felt like shooting the son of a bitch right then and there, but it wouldn't have been prudent.

"Well, General Custer, what have you to say now? Are you a coward?" Travis said, frowning with scorn.

"Coward? You goddamned . . ." Butler started to protest, but I put out my arm. Hughes quieted the others.

Truth is, I now wanted to shoot Travis even more than I wanted to shoot Dijon, but I kept my temper. None of this was unexpected, and during our ride up from the Cibolo, I'd given much thought on what needed to be done. My plan was not perfect, nor detailed, but during the Rebellion it had often been necessary to size up the situation and act. Today would be no different.

"Gentlemen, let me congratulate you on your courage," I said, stepping forward with hands clasped behind my back. "You have held Santa Anna at bay for nearly two weeks, even though you were taken by surprise and forced to flee into this fort without adequate supplies. It's unfortunate your leaders underestimated Santa Anna's resolve and were not prepared for his arrival."

Many of the men murmured agreement. The night before Santa Anna's arrival, the San Antonio garrison had been celebrating George Washington's birthday with a drunken all-night party. The average soldier had no reason to know the town was about to be overrun, but good commanders are not so careless. I walked up to the line in the sand, stopped to study it for a moment, then paced back and forth along its edge without stepping over.

"Even though you were not expecting to be trapped in this noble fortress, you have fought well," I graciously complimented. "You have cost the enemy time and blood. And now you're ready to die for liberty. Ready to be put to the sword. Your corpses will be mutilated by an angry foe and then burned on a giant funeral pyre, cast into gray smoke for all time. Most of your names will be lost to history, but I have no doubt that Mr. Travis, Colonel Bowie, and Colonel Crockett will be remembered. Your sacrifice will make *their* names immortal."

I thought it unlikely the Alamo defenders wanted to die just to make their leaders immortal, anymore than my men would sacrifice their lives merely to be footnotes in a book about Custer's Last Stand. Such things read better in the history texts.

I paced a bit more before stopping in the middle of the courtyard, gazing steadily at the men. I stood erect. Confident. A soldier's solider, as General Phil Sheridan had often described me.

"Even though you have chosen to die with Travis, I would suggest another possibility," I said, finally getting to point. "He has done a sufficient job of leading you, for a lawyer and amateur soldier, but he has no vision for victory. I am a professional officer, a graduate of West Point. Santa Anna is a great general when he's attacking an unarmed village, torturing helpless victims, and raping young girls. These are effective instruments of terror, and those in his path have reason to be afraid. But the Alamo is not an unarmed village. We are not helpless victims. And you are not young girls."

The men laughed. None guessed I had a sense of humor.

"My men and I did not come here to die, and Mr. Travis is wrong to assume the Alamo must fall. No battle is decided until one side or the other concedes defeat, and that I will never do. I am General George Armstrong Custer of the Seventh Cavalry, and where I ride, victory rides with me.

"Holding the Alamo will be difficult. It will take hard work, discipline, and steady nerve, but if you have the guts to meet the challenge, Santa Anna will find far more trouble than he's bargained for. So I'm asking you boys to give up on this idea of martyrdom. Join me. Join my brave troopers. Give me a chance, and I will lead you to glory."

My men cheered, raising their rifles and pumping their fists. Crockett was the first to cross back over the line, smiling like he just killed a bear. Brister and the New Orleans Grays quickly followed.

"Well, boys, ya got a choice," Crockett said, standing at my side. "We all talked about this before I went to find help. What are ya gonna do?"

The men looked back at Travis, turned to look at me, and finally seemed to focus on Crockett. Micajah Autry crossed the line, then Green Jameson. There were a few whispers, and suddenly the garrison surged forward en masse. Handshakes and backslaps were exchanged, many of the men smiling.

Soon only Travis, James Bonham, Renee Dijon, and a score of hardcore followers remained. Even Almaron Dickenson had crossed the line. I turned to see Mrs. Dickenson smiling with relief. It was the first time since the siege began that she'd felt a glimmer of hope.

"Mr. Travis, it appears the votes are in," I said, finding several hundred on my side of the line and only twenty-two on his.

"You have command of the volunteers, sir. Only the volunteers," Travis bitterly conceded.

"No, this ain't right," Dijon shouted, coming forward with a hand poised on his hunting knife. "Don't you boys understand? This Custer fella is a Northerner. A slave stealer. He stole John from Mr. De Sauque, and he'll steal your slaves, too. He ain't fit to lead this fight."

"That's true. We heard you don't take with our Southern way of life," Bonham said.

"The Seventh Cavalry doesn't tolerate slavery. There's no secret about that," I answered. "We're fighting to make a free Texas. Free for everyone."

"And if any of you Carolina scum don't like that, crawl your yellowbellies over the wall," Sergeant Butler said. "Once we've dealt with the Mexicans, we'll deal with you next."

I had preferred that Butler not say that, even if it was the inevitable conclusion to our disagreement. Dijon drew his knife, a twelve-inch steel blade with a guard at the handle. A man-killer, much like the famous Bowie knife. Sergeant Hughes drew his Colt and pointed at the man's forehead from a range of ten feet. I raised my hands to halt the confrontation even as Bonham and Travis were grabbing Dijon.

"Boys, I suggest we stop this here arguing among ourselves until we've whooped Santa Anna," Crockett said, playing the peacemaker.

"I am calling you to account, sir," Dijon said, pointing an angry finger at me. "You will face me on the field of honor, unless you are a coward."

"Mr. Travis has first call on my services, as I recall," I replied, glancing at Travis for his reaction. "But rest assured, Mr. Dijon, I look forward to the contest."

I wondered how well the arrogant mercenary could handle a saber. As the challenged, the *Code Duello* dictated that I have the choice of weapons, and I've always enjoyed a good tussle with a long blade. Travis struck me as the type who would favor a dueling pistol, the great equalizer for those of modest skill. Too bad for him.

"Enough of this nonsense. Don't make me act as Mr. Custer's second," Crockett warned. "I've only done this a few times and never lost a man yet. Or a friend."

"Thanks, David," I said, putting a hand on his shoulder. "Colonel Crockett is right, this has gone too far. I take responsibility, and if I've given offense, I apologize."

"You'll give me the slave?" Dijon asked.

"No, sir. But I'll ask Spotted Eagle not to hang your scalp from his lodge pole," I answered.

Dijon huffed and walked away. Spotted Eagle smiled, though I doubt he had any idea what all the fuss was about.

"General Custer, sir. Now that you've taken command of the volunteers, what are your intentions?" Travis asked.

Except for another enemy cannon shot, one far to my right that struck the rubble strewn north wall, the courtyard fell into silence. I let the moment linger, enjoying being the center of attention. As General McClellan had shown me, this is what ranking officers do to maintain their authority. Then I drew my sword and walked to Travis's line in the sand.

"Here, sirs, is the Alamo," I said, drawing a square in the damp ground. "I believe Santa Anna intends to launch his assault on the morning of March 6th, thirty-six hours from now. To do this, he must move his troops to the north where our defenses are weakest."

The men made a wide circle around my sketch, everyone trying to see. I gave them a moment to settle down. Bobby Hughes was grinning. I suspected he already knew what I was going to say.

"Every general knows you must mask the movement of your army to take an enemy by surprise," I explained. "To do this, Santa Anna will need to pull his infantry from their present positions under the cloak of darkness, cross the San Antonio upriver beyond the trees, and assume new positions behind his entrenched batteries."

I indicated where Santa Anna would concentrate his forces to the north and northeast. Then I showed how he would move his cannon forward to supporting positions.

"To the southeast, along Powder House Hill, he'll station his cavalry to block an attempt by the garrison to break out," I said, almost done with my presentation. "A nice snug trap, but so much maneuvering takes time. And for the next twenty-four hours, Santa Anna will leave his siege lines thin."

"Are you suggesting we try to escape?" Jameson asked. "What of our wounded? What of the women and children?"

"No, Mr. Jameson, I am not suggesting we try to escape," I quickly said. "My plan is far bolder than that. We will attack."

I held an officer call on the second floor of the long barracks, a musty room lit by candles now that the sun had set. A few Texian wounded lay in the far corner on straw mats, mostly quiet and minding their own business. A small coal-burning stove kept the room warm.

"Who are they?" I asked, pointing at the old oil paintings hanging on the bleached stone walls.

"That one is Ferdinand VII, the last Spanish King of Mexico," Green Jameson said. "Most of these others are Catholic saints. The Franciscan monks used this room as a library before General Cos turned it into the infirmary."

I guessed as much, but was still impressed by Jameson's breadth of knowledge. Of medium height and a bit round in the middle, he looked more like a bookkeeper than a soldier. He wore his brown hair cut short, and his blue eyes squinted as if he needed spectacles. Crockett told me Jameson hailed from Kentucky, though I had not noticed an interest in slave owning. He became the first member of the garrison that I invited to join my personal staff, and he agreed without hesitation.

Also included in the war council were Travis and his adjutant, Captain John Baugh. Crockett sat at my right, Sergeant Hughes on my left. Dickenson, Brister and Sergeant Butler filled out our roster. Bowie was too ill to attend. I recalled Dr. Lord's words, that his presence in the Alamo might save lives, and wondered if Bowie might have been one of them.

The meeting was not long, for there was much to do. And unlike most war councils held during the Texas Revolution, this would not be a debating society. I entertained no democratic resolutions. In fact, the only counsel I valued was from Crockett, whose wits I respected.

"Does everyone understand?" I asked after presenting my plan.

"It's madness, General," Sergeant Butler remarked.

"It should work," I calmly said.

"Oh, hell, I'm sure it will work. Just the kind of lunacy those Mexicans will never expect. Right out of Longstreet's handbook," Butler agreed.

"Actually, I got the idea from Stonewall Jackson," I said. "No one knew how to press a flank better than old Stonewall."

"You always were too fond of those Rebs," Hughes complained, for the rank and file had not shared the camaraderie of the officer corps.

"Jameson, you've got a long night ahead of you. Keep your workers busy," I concluded. "Travis, the north wall is yours. Hold it to the last. Everyone else, clean your weapons and grab an hour's sleep. We sortie at dawn."

My officers trudged down the stairs and out the lower door into the gloomy night. Santa Anna's artillery fire had slackened, replaced by a brass band playing loudly enough to keep the Alamo's defenders awake. Apparently this had been a pattern since the beginning of the siege. For those of us accustomed to noisy camps, restless horses, howling wolves and clumsy orderlies, a few musical instruments hardly cost us a wink.

"Even if this does work, I don't see what you expect to accomplish," Crockett said, rocking back in his chair.

Someone had found him a keg of corn whiskey, which he was sipping gingerly. I was drinking brown water from the well.

"I doubt Tom can get here with Fannin's men before the 7th. Reinforcements from Gonzales may take longer. Captain Seguin might provide some help, but I'm not counting on it. By hitting Santa Anna before he hits us, we just might buy some time. In the war I fought, there was a rebel general named Lee who kept a larger army at bay for four years with his aggressive tactics."

"George, I don't give a damn how smart you are, I ain't stayin' in this Alamo for four years," Crockett said.

I laughed. And knew exactly how he felt.

On the morning of Saturday, March 5th, an hour before dawn, I walked up the long sloping dirt ramp to the 18-pounder guarding the southwest corner of the fort. A few night lamps from the town were visible across the river. The enemy camp to the south was asleep. A dim haze to the north showed where Santa Anna's army was marching by torchlight. The man thought himself clever.

"Good morning, gentlemen," I said to the gun crew.

The Alamo had nineteen working cannon, but most were antiques, some better than fifty years old. A few looked like they'd been stolen from Blackbeard's pirate ship. But not the 18-pounder. It had been brought all the way from New Orleans just a few months before. Properly handled, it was a formidable weapon.

"Morning, General," Dickenson said, offering a salute.

"Would you please fire the gun, Captain?" I requested.

"At what, sir?" Dickenson asked.

"Doesn't really matter. How about that battery near the bridge? No, better yet, fire on the cathedral. Let's see if we can knock down that blood red flag."

"That's a long shot," Dickenson said with a whistle.

"Good practice," I answered.

The crew of six set to loading the gun. One swabbed the barrel with a wet sponge to clean out the dirt. Another used a ramrod to jam a power charge down the barrel, then wadding made of hay to trap the charge. A fuse was inserted into the touch hole at the rear of the barrel to set the powder off. Last came an eighteen-pound cannon ball wrapped in paper for a tight fit.

"Let's try the maximum elevation," Dickenson said, his gunner turning a screw on the gun carriage to incline the barrel.

"Permission to fire, sir," Dickenson said.

"Permission granted."

The gunner lit the fuse and the cannon roared to life, almost jumping back off the platform as a blast of crimson fire and black smoke streaked through the dark sky. By the sound, the shot hit something, but we couldn't see what. The echo could be heard throughout the river valley.

"Reload and fire again," I instructed.

"Sir?" he asked.

"See if you can drop this one on the Presidio."

"Yes, sir," Dickenson said.

The crew reloaded the cannon, taking only two minutes, and fired another shot. Again, no clue what the ball hit, if anything.

"Thank you, gentlemen. We launch our assault at dawn. Get some rest, but be ready," I advised, walking back down the ramp to my new quarters next to Bowie's room in the low barracks.

I've always had the ability to grab some sleep, even a few minutes worth, in any situation. It was one of the things that allowed my inexhaustible energy to be inexhaustible, but this time I couldn't close my eyes. It wasn't the battle that bothered me—war had been my life since I was a teenager. It was the politics, by far my weakest quality. I'd turned down a chance to run for congress in 1866, afraid my temper was not up to the task. I'd even flirted with the governorship of Michigan. I wished Tom was here. He'd know how to handle these squabbling frontiersmen.

As dawn approached, I got up to get dressed. One of the Tejano ladies had washed my uniform, including my gray campaign hat. A colorful scarf of red silk was tied around my neck, a gift from Jim Bowie's cousin-in-law. The twin bulldogs were holstered on my hips.

I had decided not to take my Remington hunting rifle on the raid. When General Cos had abandoned San Antonio, he left several hundred Brown Bess muskets behind, along with a bayonet for each. One of these muskets was now gripped before me, the bayonet locked on the muzzle. This undertaking would not be about long range sniping, but close range combat. We would be meeting the enemy with cold steel. With Tom's Winchester slung over my shoulder, I was ready.

"Should I sound assembly, sir?" Corporal French asked, waiting outside my door.

A New Hampshire lad now twenty-six years old, French stood five and half feet tall. Average for a cavalryman. He had hazel eyes and a complexion bronzed by the sun. Promoted to corporal just a year before, he was not a great bugler but capable enough to sound a charge.

"Henry, this is a surprise attack. We don't sound assembly for a surprise attack."

"Yes, sir. Of course, sir," French said with a dumb grin.

The command was forming near the south gate, a hundred in all, divided into four sections. Hughes had the first company of twenty men, Butler the second, Crockett the third, and I would lead the forty man vanguard.

"Good morning, gentlemen. Any questions?" I asked.

They stood quietly. This was not a complex operation, and anyone who had ever fought Indians knew what was needed, but it was best to nip confusion in the bud.

"Very good. Let's move," I ordered, being the first through the gate.

The men guarding the lunette opened the portal and ran several sturdy planks across the muddy ditch. We filed out as quietly as possible, creeping toward the dirt road leading to the Alameda. I could hear the river to our right and saw a few enemy campfires through the trees.

The dozen burned-out adobe shacks lined our path to the main road. Sergeant Butler started positioning his company among the rubble, guns facing the river. The ground to the left was open except for a shallow irrigation channel that Santa Anna had tried to dam. Sergeant Hughes deployed his men along the ditch, guns facing Power House Hill where the enemy cavalry was stationed.

"So far, so good," I whispered to Crockett as we continued to extend our line. "Remember, you asked for the toughest assignment."

"You took the toughest assignment, but I got me a good one," Crockett whispered back.

Brister and Johnson were at his side, most of their detachment being the mercenary volunteers. I had promised them that if they served well, they would be accepted as recruits into the Seventh Cavalry. I had also decided they were best placed in the middle of the battle line where they couldn't flee at the first shot.

We reached the old wooden bridge crossing the San Antonio River, the enemy no wiser to our movement. Like so many rivers, the San Antonio made a crazy square-shaped loop at this juncture. Generally the river ran north to south, but at this point it bulged out toward the Alamo, straightened for a hundred yards, and then turned back west. The low-lying bulge, probably susceptible to chronic flooding, was mostly filled with quaint houses and animal pens.

The town center was a thousand yards back of the bridge. I suspected Santa Anna still had several hundred men quartered there, for San Antonio de Béjar was built around two large plazas designed for occupation by a garrison. The nearest plaza was a public square, and, behind that, a walled enclosure for the military. Between the two squares was the Cathedral of San Fernando, the tallest structure for miles around.

Several fine haciendas and a number of warehouses lined the downtown streets, all laid out in a rough grid pattern. It had been through these streets that the Texan's had defeated Cos the previous December, fighting from house to house. If necessary, I would do it again. But not on this day.

Santa Anna's western battery, consisting of two 4-pounders, was the nearest danger, lying a few dozen yards from the bridge among thick trees. I had given Crockett an important assignment.

"Hold the bridge, David," I said, waving his boys into the rocks and shrubs near the river.

"We can burn the damn thing if you like," Crockett quietly replied.

"Maybe tomorrow," I said, thinking the bridge might be useful if I decided to storm the town.

I took my command past the bridge and stopped only ten yards from the trees where the first Mexican entrenchment was dug in. We heard no challenge. If they had a sentry, he was asleep. An adobe warehouse, battered by errant artillery shots but still intact, stood on our side of the road. With a gesture, I put three sharpshooters on the roof where they would dominate the approaches from every direction.

Several hundred yards beyond the road were the shanties and saloons of La Villita. If we were looking for tequila and whores, we were on the right track. La Villita also sheltered two 6-pounders, the largest entrenchment south of the Alamo on our side of the river.

Several cooking fires showed through the trees where I estimated their camp at two hundred strong. The road south, and it wasn't much of a road, was still too dark to see, though the first glimmer of sunrise was appearing on our left. Before long, the enemy would be stirring.

"Okay boys, here we go. Shoot anything that moves. Burn everything. No looting until the enemy is routed," I said.

There was no specific order to move, I just crept forward toward the first enemy entrenchment with the Brown Bess ready for action. Mumbling could be heard up ahead, and crickets in the pasture beyond the trees. An icy wind rose from the river.

"*Quién es?*" a voice asked.

"*Es el Diablo*," I replied, jumping over the earthen barrier and running the man through with the bayonet. The sentry moaned and fell backward as I pulled the blade free. A startled corporal came toward me, so surprised he had not drawn a weapon. I jabbed the bayonet into his heart.

A heavy mist shrouded the woods as dawn broke over Powder House Hill. The half-dozen men holding the night watch in the trench soon found themselves overrun with swords and bayonets, but not before shouting for help.

"That's it, lads! Have at them!" I yelled as gunfire echoed off the hills. And then the Alamo cannon opened fire, the guns along the north wall shelling the Mexican positions. Scattered rifle fire erupted throughout the valley, friend and foe aiming blindly at shadows.

I fired the musket, then tossed it aside and drew my Bulldogs, running toward the battery while we all screamed like banshees. The gun crews jumped to their posts to load the cannon, and one managed to ram a ball down, but didn't have time to fire. I shot the commanding officer, a young lieutenant, who bravely went down still calling out orders. The rest of the Mexicans fell in a storm of hot lead, our forty sweeping over fifteen startled defenders. But more enemies were on the way. Fifty or so soldiers were on the road, arriving for their morning posting. The yelling and firing had them confused. They began running toward us to see what the uproar was all about.

"Swing the gun around!" I shouted, jumping to the 6-pounder that was already loaded.

Four men quickly had the cannon turned. I picked up a match from a dead Mexican gunner.

"Watch out!" I warned, touching the fuse.

The gun roared, sweeping a red path of death down the road through the enemy ranks. The cannon jerked back from the force, the wheel hitting me above the ankle, for I had neglected to get myself clear. I would have cursed myself for a fool, but there wasn't time.

"Are you all right, sir?" someone asked, helping me to my feet.

"Yes, private. French! French, where are you?"

"Here, sir!" French said, climbing over the sandbag barrier.

"Sound the charge!" I ordered, half running and half stumbling toward the enemy camp.

I was not in the lead, nor even close. The moment the 6-pounder had cut loose, men were driving on our objective. No more instructions were needed. No urging on. Our blood was up.

Thick trees and a rail fence screened us on one side, heavy brush along the river on the other. The road was strewn with dead and wounded men. Those who moved too much were instantly bayoneted. We had no time for the others.

The hovels of La Villita appeared on the right, the village in chaos. Not just soldiers, but women and camp followers were fleeing in every direction. A few of the Mexicans stood their ground, raising their muskets and firing. A man went down next to me, one of the buckskinned volunteers. Then I saw one of my own boys take a hit, Private Tim Donnelly of F Company. I holstered the Bulldogs and pulled out Tom's Winchester, cocking and firing as I advanced steadily on the village. The closer I got, the better my aim.

The small group of Mexicans defending their camp tried to resist the onslaught, but all it brought them was destruction. Those who fell under our gunfire were rapidly finished off with swords and knives. No one was taking prisoners.

Suddenly Spotted Eagle was at my side. He had been told to stay behind with Crockett, but disobeyed. It reminded me of Tom at Sayler's Creek. Though shot through the face and bleeding like a Virginia ham, Tom seized a Confederate battle flag, rode back to our lines in triumph, and then returned to the fight against orders.

Spotted Eagle was stripped to the waist, streaked in war paint, and wielding a bloody hatchet. When he let out a Sioux war cry, some of our terrified enemies froze. Others merely ran that much faster.

"Do not get yourself killed," I told him.

"I cannot die at the General's side," he answered.

"Gray Wolf died at my side."

"I am not my cousin. Today, I live forever!"

He saw a group of Mexicans heading for the river and went after them, thirsty for more coup.

A musket ball whistled past my head. I reloaded the Winchester and looked for the miscreant, but no one seemed to be giving me special attention. I shot a sergeant trying to reload his gun, then a private fumbling with his bayonet. Turning, I spotted an officer in a white uniform waving a lance, but he disappeared behind a shack before I could take aim.

Amid the fighting, I saw women grabbing babies, fleeing into the woods. An old woman rocked on the ground, an old man lying dead in her arms. A boy emerged from an adobe shack waving a cooking knife, only to be shot down.

"Sir, is something wrong?" French asked, coming to my side.

"For a moment, this reminded me of our attack on Black Kettle's village. Warn the men to avoid shooting at the women and children."

After a few hectic minutes, firing in our portion of the field gradually ceased. Skirmishes continued on the flanks, but we mounted no pursuit when the broken enemy ran for the west ford.

"Sir, we found some wagons. Ammunition wagons," a breathless youngster said. He'd lost his leather hat, his wild red hair a mass of curls. Smoke streaked his pink face. It was Jimmy Allen. I'd seen him in the fort but didn't realize he'd been assigned to my troop.

"Hitch some horses and take them home," I ordered, breathless myself, for my shin ached.

"Already being done, sir. Ready in a few minutes," Allen said, running back to wherever he had come from.

"Fire the shacks. Burn it all," I said, finding a torch and setting it to a haystack.

Some of the men followed my lead, others were grabbing sacks of grain and tying them to the backs of burros, for the Alamo's food supply was growing thin. I regretted not thinking of it myself.

Within minutes the ramshackle village was in flames, and we hardly needed to make an effort. The place had been a firetrap to begin with.

"French, sound recall," I said, leaning against a rail fence.

The bugle call summoned our force back along the narrow road. We returned toward the Alamo, picking up equipment, retrieving our wounded, and cutting enemy throats along the way. From time to time, we came across an adversary who was so young that murdering them seemed a crime. Some died anyway, but a few were spared. All was random chance.

Among the fallen soldiers, I noticed a battle flag and picked it up. The red, white and green banner decorated with an eagle was a worthy souvenir of our effort.

We emerged into the open space where the roads came together. Crockett's men were keeping a hot fire on the bridge where a hundred soldiers in blue uniforms were attempting to cross. Some of the enemy fired their muskets, but most were trying to press the bridge armed with bayonets. A dozen had already fallen.

I was relieved to see Crockett still alive, kneeling in the center of the line, firing his Springfield. Micajah knelt next to him, handing the former congressman ammunition as fast as he could reload. The smoke of the Texan muskets was thicker than the river fog.

Up Powder House Hill to the east, a cavalry charge of fifty dragoons was being forestalled by Sergeant Hughes, his skirmishers taking a heavy toll of officers. His favorite targets. The first rush was stopped with a volley. As the cavalry tried to reform, the flag bearers were shot from their saddles. Cannon from the rear of the Alamo chapel struck the enemy right flank. After a few minutes of frustration, the cavalry slowly withdrew, waving their short barrel carbines. None had even gotten within range.

The wagons we'd captured were rushed toward the gate, followed by several burros. Suddenly the artillery pieces in the woods across the river opened fire. The first wagon exploded, blowing fragments and splinters in every direction. Both horses were killed and several men went down. Bits of flaming wreckage lit the gray trail.

Like many, I was momentarily stunned by the bright flash, catching my balance against a broken adobe wall. My leg still hurt. I aimed a revolver only to find the gun empty. Our retreat had stalled.

"Let's go! Let's go! Come on, boys," I shouted, my voice high-pitched with excitement. I grabbed a soldier and pushed him toward the fort, and then another, waving the tattered Mexican flag.

The men began to move again. The surviving wagons were hurried on. Wounded men were helped to their feet, using their muskets as crutches. Two needed to be carried. I saw a burro rush by with a dead Texan thrown over its back.

As my men reached the approach to the lunette, Crockett's men fell back in good order, then Hughes and Butler, collapsing the line we had extended fifteen minutes before. The Alamo walls were filled with riflemen protecting our retreat. The 18-pounder roared, then several of the 6-pounders. I could not see who or what they were firing on, for the confusion of battle was all around me. This is why cavalry commanders are so fond of their horses. It not only makes us look important to sit astride a noble steed, but it helps us see above the fray.

The men in the lunette hauled the wagons over the ditch into the fort. The burros were not so cooperative. A few were led across the creaking planks, the others unloaded and cut free. My men, having been exposed to the greatest danger, were the first to reach safety, followed by Crockett and Hughes.

Butler's troop brought up the rear, bringing the last of four dead and nine wounded. Not a bloodless foray.

It was the best breakfast I'd eaten in months. Pan-fried bacon, fresh flour biscuits, and a scrambled egg. I sat on a stool, a cracker barrel for my table, just outside my headquarters near the south gate. Crockett and Jameson were with me as I discussed a reorganization of the Alamo's defenses. Kellogg had told me how the Alamo fell, in its original history, and I was determined not to make the same mistakes.

"Trouble in the town, general," Captain Dickenson reported.

We ran up the gun platform next to the 18-pounder and looked west. Columns of black smoke swirled in the morning light, for it was barely after seven o'clock. The commotion was coming from the far side of San Antonio where we supposed Santa Anna's supply wagons were parked. Travis joined us on the platform.

"What the living hell?" he said, looking through a spyglass.

I held my binoculars, but didn't need them to answer the young lawyer's question.

"It's Captain Keogh. I gave him fifty men with orders to harass the enemy supply," I explained. "Firing the 18-pounder this morning was a signal for him to attack. It's just a raid, however. He'll burn some wagons and then withdraw. Or he might burn a lot of wagons. The Irish like that sort of thing."

"That's not all, general. Take a look," Jameson said, pointing toward the bridge.

What I saw was a surprise. Two Mexican officers were waving a white flag. It seemed that General Antonio López de Santa Anna, the Napoleon of the West, was requesting a parley with the commander of the Alamo.

Custer had sent me south with his brother to learn of leadership, but it was a trick. He thought me too young to be a warrior. What the white general did not understand is that a warrior's heart is not measured in years, and the farther I rode away on Custer's horse, the more I thought about Wakan Tanka's gift. Was it to seek more learning? Or was it to share the wisdom I already had? There were birds in the trees and I listened to their song, for the birds are not bound by that which can be seen from the earth. They told me of a great battle, with much blood and death. I gave my reasons to Thomas Custer, for I would not have him worry, and turned back, riding Custer's horse as hard as I dared.

CHAPTER ELEVEN

PICKS, SHOVELS AND BOWIE KNIVES

I went back to finish breakfast, asking Jameson and Crockett to join me. Travis was unhappy not to be included, but he had duties on the north wall that required his attention. And from what I'd heard, Travis's negotiating skills weren't the best. Early in the siege, he had fired a cannon shot at Santa Anna's messengers.

"The first day, I rode out to the bridge and met with Santa Anna's adjutant," Jameson recalled, sitting next to me outside the low barracks. "Bowie was still in command at the time. Or so I thought. We hoped to withdraw from San Antonio without a fight. The dictator's minion said His Excellency would never negotiate with pirates."

"Good I left my peg leg at home," I said, dabbing my chin with a clean napkin. Quite the luxury in this godforsaken land.

"What do you think Santa Anna wants?" Crockett asked. "He's not givin' up the siege. His name would be shit in Mexico."

"Does he think we'll surrender after kicking his butt this morning?" Jameson asked. He ate another biscuit, knowing we might not have time later.

"We didn't exactly kick his butt, Green. Just ruffled a few feathers," I said, looking around to see if Juana might have another egg for me.

It was a greedy thought, though not an unusual one. Generals expect such things. Juana smiled but shook her head.

Having Juana Alsbury serve me was quite a privilege. She was the cousin of Bowie's late wife and the daughter of a prominent San Antonio family. Her uncle had once been governor of Texas.

"Call it what you want, General. The men are stirred up like I've never seen them. After today, they'll walk into hell if you give the order," Jameson said.

"Let's not make the same mistake twice," I said, standing up and straightening my buckskin jacket. "Is the messenger still on the bridge?"

"Yes, sir. Waiting for our reply," Dickenson said.

"Let's not keep him waiting," I decided.

We started toward the south gate. Bobby Hughes and Jimmy Butler were quickly at my side as word spread. Corporal French and Spotted Eagle caught up as we entered the lunette. And then Travis arrived.

"No negotiations unless I'm there, too," Travis insisted.

"I think not," was my immediate reaction. My temper was bad enough without a hothead like Travis gumming up the works.

"I know the conditions here better than you. Better than you or Crockett. I know the law, and I know what the provisional government in Washington-on-the-Brazos is planning," Travis explained.

"The Declaration of Independence? Hell, Bill, everybody in Texas knows about that," Crockett said. "Besides, Santa Anna knows who ya are. Knows you've been causin' trouble since the ferst day you 'rived in Texas. How many times were you arrested for agitation? Two or three?"

"All I did was demand our rights under the Constitution of 1824," Travis defended.

"Say that 'til the cows come home, but Santa Anna ain't gonna negotiate with someone trying to steal Texas away from him," Crockett insisted.

"You're trying to steal Texas from Mexico. So is Custer," Travis said, waving an angry finger.

"Am I?" I asked.

"Damn right you are!"

"I haven't decided what my plan is. It's possible Santa Anna and I can reach an accommodation," I said, almost saying too much.

Truthfully, I had no specific plan, but the kind of Texas Travis wanted wasn't the one my men would fight for. It wasn't the Texas President Lincoln would have wanted us to fight for.

"Make a deal with the tyrant and we'll hang you," Travis threatened.

Curiously, General John Mosby, the Gray Ghost, had once threatened me with a hanging, too. Travis almost made me laugh.

"Wait until this is over, my lawyer friend, and we'll see who does the hanging," I jovially said, slapping him on the back. "Come on, David, let's see what the tyrant would have of us."

I ducked through the portal of the lunette with Crockett, Butler and Hughes. Corporal French kept Spotted Eagle back, for the young brave would only make the situation more complicated. We walked among the ruined adobes to the bridge, all the while prepared for treachery, for I had no reason to trust Santa Anna's honor. Especially after what Kellogg had told me about the massacre at Goliad.

"If they try a double-cross, kill the officers," Sergeant Hughes said, holding his Henry repeating rifle. I had Tom's Winchester, Butler had his Sharps. Crockett carried the Springfield I'd given him.

There were two officers waiting for us under the flag of truce, a colonel and a lieutenant. I recognized the colonel— it was Juan Almonte, the aide-de-camp to Santa Anna who had been thrown from his horse during the skirmish on the Cibolo. His shoulder looked stiff but not broken.

"*Hola, Coronel Almonte. Como esta el brazo*?" I asked, reaching to shake his hand.

"The arm is fine, General Custer. How is your leg? Have you been run over by a cannon lately?" he replied in English.

"It's a cold day. What can I do for you?" I said, realizing Santa Anna had received a detailed report on the Battle of La Villita.

"General Antonio López de Santa Anna recognizes your bravery and offers to negotiate an honorable surrender," Almonte said.

"Premature, isn't it? Your general still has a large army in the field," I said.

Almonte paused in surprise. His lieutenant frowned, insulted by my jest.

"No, it is not *my* general who wishes to surrender," Almonte patiently said. "If you will lay down your arms and surrender the fort, your men may depart with all honor. We will send the rebel leaders to Mexico City, where they will receive a fair trial."

"Generous terms. Please thank your master on my behalf. I will relay his terms to the rebel leaders. I hear Mexico City is lovely in the spring," I said, bowing deeply.

"Not the jail cells," Crockett remarked.

"I heard Steven Austin spent a year in Santa Anna's prisons. Was he a rebel?" I asked.

"No, Old Steven just wanted to present a peaceful petition," Crockett explained.

"Not the best way to treat an emissary," I remarked.

"Sir, I sense that you take His Excellency's proposal lightly," the lieutenant said, his accent not difficult to understand.

The lieutenant was a middle-aged man of high birth, but given his rank, low abilities. His white uniform was smartly pressed and decorated with more gold braid than I'd worn with the Michigan Brigade at Gettysburg. Streaks of gray hair were showing under his silver steel helmet, though the crest was nicely plumed with red feathers. I had to admit, these guys knew how to dress.

"Not at all, sir. I am honored that he would suggest terms to me when he has declined to do so during these past twelve days of siege. I offer him no disrespect."

"What should we tell him?" Almonte inquired.

"Tell your general that great men should discuss great issues face to face, and not through our inferiors."

"His Excellency will not meet with rabble," the lieutenant protested, his cheeks flushing.

"Now who shows disrespect?" I curtly demanded.

And my cheeks were getting a little red, too. I had met with President Lincoln and President Johnson. Cornelius Vanderbilt and Alexis, Grand Duke of Russia. I knew senators and congressmen on a first name basis. Who was Santa Anna? President of Mexico? I didn't recall the people ever voting for him.

"We will give him your message, General Custer," Almonte said, pulling his angry subordinate away.

We backed up slowly, guns ready but not aimed. A Mexican cannon crew in the battery to our right was watching, but there were only a handful of infantry. To our left, the remains of La Villita continued to smolder. I spotted a few sentries, but for the most part, the position had not been reoccupied.

"They're making the flank look empty, General. Bet they got cavalry back there," Hughes said, indicating the destroyed village.

"It's an ambush, for sure. Do they think we're that stupid?" Butler said.

As thick trees blocked our view to the south, there was no way of knowing how many troops might be hidden there waiting for us.

"They think the Alamo's garrison will try to escape," I guessed. "If I had my druthers, I'd rather take the town instead."

San Antonio was visible straight ahead, about a half a mile beyond the bridge. The presidio's walls weren't very high. Despite the occupation, the town would still have more food and better water than the Alamo. But I had to give up the idea. Moving the entire garrison, along with the women and wounded, was too complicated an operation for my resources.

A few minutes later, we were back in the Alamo surrounded by a dozen men asking questions.

"What did he say? What does he want?" Travis asked.

"How would you like a trip to Mexico City?" I answered.

By noon the entire garrison was hard at work. This was not so easy as it sounds. The Alamo had been under constant siege, hounded by a persistent artillery barrage, and left short on supply. The men were tired. Our eighty reinforcements helped, being fresh blood to the scene, but life on the frontier is always hard, and even the Seventh had endured many weeks of arduous effort. There is only so much you can expect from any group of men subjected to such hardships.

Fortunately, they had George Custer to lead them. Old Iron Butt, the martinet, and shooter of deserters. My reputation soon spread throughout the fort, and I did not disappoint.

The first order of business was the north side of the Alamo, the weakest position. Jameson had stationed five cannon on two elevated platforms, but the antiquated guns could not be pointed down once the enemy was below the wall. At a range of one hundred yards, the guns were deadly. At a range of ten yards, they were worthless. And the wall wasn't much of a barrier. Variously eight to ten feet high, it had been reinforced with an outer curtain of timber supports packed with mud. If a large attacking force congregated at the foot of the wall, they would be able to push over in overwhelming numbers. And according to Kellogg, that's exactly what happened.

"We must hold this wall," Travis said, repeating it several times. "Our entire defense is based on maintaining our perimeter."

I stood on the northwest bastion near two 6-pounders, the river to my left. Before us lay a vast prairie marked by a few small farms on the rolling plain. Santa Anna had established two batteries to the north that were slowly pounding the wall into submission. If I had brought my entire command into the Alamo, and if we had an inexhaustible supply of ammunition, the wall might be held. And even then, it would be a fruitless effort. With three thousand men, Santa Anna could shift entire battalions to the west or east. Or starve the garrison into submission.

No, I decided. This is the crucial position. Not because it is strong, but because it is weak. And the enemy knows it's weak.

Travis and Jameson were standing at my elbow, ready to make more arguments. I had enough of arguments.

"Mr. Jameson, I have not changed my mind," I said, trying to be gentle. "Have your men strip this entire half of the fort. Pull one of the guns back. Go into the houses along the walls and take out the timber supports. We'll sharpen them into stakes. Once the new ditch is dug across the center of the courtyard, we'll fill the trench with the sharpened timber. Take off the latches and hinges. Pull out the nails. We'll use them as canister shot."

"Fifty of our men live in these houses. Going to make the barracks awful crowded," Jameson warned.

"During the war I fought, we discovered our cemeteries so crowded that we buried the dead in General Lee's front yard. Which do you prefer?"

"We'll sleep in the long barracks tonight," he agreed, going to see it done. A competent officer. I hoped he would survive the battle.

I walked down the sloping dirt ramp into the north courtyard. The area may have been a garden at one time, or a cattle pen, but now it was just a large empty space for men to die in. All the buildings at this end of the fort were one story, made of adobe, and roofed with straw or rough wood slats. Only the long barracks had two stories, though the church was fairly tall, as well.

The long barracks, known to the Tejanos as the convent, was the compound's primary structure, the famous church being a half-finished ruin. About twenty feet wide and almost two hundred feet long, the barracks had once been used by padres to help the poor and treat the sick. The main courtyard lay on the west side, the horse corral and cattle pen on the east. For reasons I did not understand, Jameson had his men digging trenches *inside* the barracks. He called it a last ditch defense, but they may as well have been digging their graves. Once the enemy was over the walls, the garrison was doomed.

Being more optimistic, I had moved the diggers out into the courtyard, cutting a trench from the middle of the long barracks to the west wall. This trench would be filled with the sharpened stakes, much like Lee's defenses at Petersburg. In the daylight, such a barrier would be a joke. We did not have enough time to dig deeply. But in the predawn darkness, amid the smoke of battle, even a small trench might entrap some of the enemy.

The south side of the Alamo must be my stronghold. The left flank would be the bastion on the west wall holding the 18-pounder. The platform guarded approaches from the south or an attack from across the river. In a desperate moment, the 18-pounder could be turned around to fire into the courtyard.

Our right flank was the quadrangle in front of the church, screened on the south by the wooden palisade. The long barracks and a spur of the low barracks formed irregular walls protecting the area from a quick assault. We would throw up some boxes and barrels to complete the enclosure.

The log palisade between the low barracks and the church appeared to be the weakest position of all, but this was an illusion. Two 4-pounders loaded with canister shot protected the stockade wall, supplemented by a ditch and branches of thick tangled briars. The lunette on the right, and the church on the left, provided flanking fire. Crockett had been assigned this position, and I had no doubt he would hold it.

The center of the position was the low barracks. The L-shaped structure had thick walls for protection and space on the roof for sharpshooters. I had men extending a defensive line along the south end of the compound while adding another cannon to the lunette. Bobby Hughes was in charge of the modifications, ably assisted by Dickenson.

I walked up to the church. When I had first seen it in 1866, the U.S. Army Quartermaster had turned the building into a supply depot. A barrel roof had been built and a hump atop the façade added, which gave the structure a distinctive appearance. The Alamo of 1836 had no distinctive hump. Most of it didn't even have a roof.

Squeezing through the oak double doors, partially blocked by a mud-filled rawhide barrier, I found small rooms to the right and left. One was being used as the powder magazine, others for food storage or housing the families of Captain Dickenson and the Tejanos.

At one time in its history, I supposed the Alamo had contained pews and an altar for various ancient rituals. It was, after all, a Catholic church. But the pews were long gone, the central floor area now filled with a long dirt ramp leading ten feet up to the rear of the church where two 12-pounders dominated the eastern approaches. Because this portion of the church had no roof, the platform was damp and cold. A tarp had been strung up to protect the gunners from rain.

I walked up the ramp to stand between the guns in an area called the apse, looking east toward Powder House Hill. The land was partially occupied by a morass, cut with irrigation ditches, and generally poor ground for an attack. The cottonwood trees lining the Alameda were far off to the right.

The church certainly appeared to be a strong position. The walls were four feet thick and twenty feet high. There were few doors or windows, making it difficult for the enemy to scale the wall. But this was also its weakness. The garrison could not deploy its strength in such a confined area. For the purposes of a last stand, the church was inadequate.

"Captain Dickenson, your attention please," I summoned.

"Yes, General," Dickenson said, coming at a run.

Like Crockett, Dickenson was from Tennessee, a blacksmith by profession, though he dabbled in various small businesses. Much like my father did. Less than thirty, he was the best artillerist in the fort, and I had come to rely on his expertise with these antique weapons. Like most blacksmiths, he was a big man with large forearms.

"Sir, once it grows dark, I want you to withdraw one these guns," I politely instructed. "Pull it down into the courtyard and station it facing north between the long barracks and the redoubt. Throw up a barrier. Barrels, sandbags, whatever you can find."

"Sir, that would leave our eastern flank weak. The only other gun is the 4-pounder above the corral," Dickenson said.

My instinct was to command, not debate, but I liked this young fellow and did not wish to hurt his feelings.

"Almaron, I appreciate your concern, but I do not anticipate an attack from this quarter. Bring up one of the 3-pounders, enough to make extra noise. I also want you to mount two heavy logs on this wall. Cover them in pitch so they look like cannon barrels. The enemy will think our cannon are concentrated here."

"You want to fool them?" Dickenson asked, though it should not have been a surprise. The Quaker gun trick was invented long before my time.

"An ancient Chinese philosopher wrote that war is the art of deception," I responded, going back toward the courtyard.

At the bottom of the ramp, I was intercepted by Dickenson's wife and her baby, a little girl hardly more than a year old.

"Excuse me, sir. My name is Susannah Dickenson. This is my daughter, Angelina," she introduced. I supposed her to be twenty years old. Pretty, if not for the rugged frontier lifestyle.

"Yes, Mrs. Dickenson. I noticed you helping Mrs. Alsbury with my uniform. I should have thanked you sooner," I said, tipping my hat.

"Oh, no. No thanks necessary. Glad to help. General, do you think we kin hold out? I'm not askin' for myself, you understand. We heard Santa Anna murders the families of rebels. I don't want him hurtin' my little girl."

"Don't fret yourself. Stories get exaggerated. Just stay here in the chapel where it's safe."

"I will, sir. I will. God bless you," she said, standing on her toes to kiss my cheek.

I grew embarrassed and fled into the compound.

Our day remained hectic. I pushed the garrison hard, telling them to ignore the occasional cannon shot that hit a building or crashed into a wall. One man was killed by the shelling, four others wounded, including Private Madsen of F Company. Anticipating an attack the next morning, I knew the men would need rest. Better to work now and sleep once the sun went down.

John had started following me around. He was my age, if not a few years older. Calling me "sir" so often began to get uncomfortable. Not that I wasn't accustomed to such deference by persons of his race, for it is only natural, but it's not something you want to hear all day long.

"Is there a problem, John?" I finally asked.

"No, sir. No problem, sir," he answered, but it wasn't the truth. He shuffled his feet and looked down.

"Dijon threatening you?"

"Can't say that, exactly. Not exactly."

"Want me to shoot the son of a bitch?"

"No, sir! Don't want no killin'. Not on my account. Just wish I knew what will happen to me when this fightin' is over."

"What do you want to happen? Would you like to stay in Texas? If not, I'll book passage for you back to Africa."

"Africa?" he said, stunned. "Sir, I don't know nothin' about Africa. My daddy was born in Georgia. His daddy was born in Virginia, and his daddy before him. Ain't no one more American than I is."

"John, when this fight is over, you can do whatever you want. You're a free man. If something happens to me, Tom will help you, or Bill Cooke, or anybody in my command. We helped former slaves in my own country during a time called Reconstruction. Freedom is hard, but worth the effort. And if Dijon bothers you, promise to tell me. Okay?"

"Yes, sir. I promise," John said. "Sir, I ain't ever needed a last name before. Never seemed necessary. Can I have one now?"

The request caught me off-guard. Swapping names within families is common. My sister honored me by nicknaming her son Autie, but I'd never been asked to give anyone a name before.

"John, I was named after a family friend, George Armstrong. Old George was a minister. My father hoped I'd join the clergy someday. I'd be pleased if you took Armstrong on."

"John Armstrong. I like that. I like that fine. Thank you, sir, thank you," he said, bursting into a grin.

John rushed off to help dig the trench in the courtyard, leaving me feeling particularly proud.

"George! George, over here!" Crockett yelled as I strolled toward the south gate.

Crockett was standing on the mound where Travis had made his speech. Jameson was with him, along with a tall thirty year old Virginian named Bill Carey, captain of the fort's artillery. They had been busy.

"What do you think?" Jameson asked, eager for approval.

They had mounted an 8-pounder on the mound and two 4-pounders on the immediate flanks, all protected by a makeshift stockade. Jameson's men had piled stones to form a munitions bunker that was being filled with powder and canister shot. Carey now had men extending the barricade to the 18-pounder ramp on the left and to the southwest corner of the long barracks on the right. Two 6-pounders had been set in the courtyard facing north, and another entrenchment was being prepared for the 12-pounder coming down from the chapel. In effect, we were building a fort within the fort, the inner wall lined with artillery. Much of the defense was nothing but oak barrels, pieces of old wagons, and chunks of adobe ripped from the inner dwellings. Had we a few cotton bales, it would have looked like Old Hickory's lines at New Orleans.

"Got a good crossfire here, General," Carey said. "That is, if the Mexicans come from this direction. Travis don't think they will."

"Travis don't think about a lot of things," I replied. "Been in Texas long, Mr. Carey?"

"Just since last summer, sir," he said.

"Any military experience before that?"

"Not really, but seen plenty of fightin' since I got here."

"Well, you've done a good job. You all have," I said, seeking to keep their spirits up.

At the battle of Trevilian Station, my command had used similar materials while fending off desperate Confederate charges. Like the Alamo, we were under fire with little time to prepare. And like the men, I had been frightened that we could not hold. We had done our best then, and we would do our best now. I could not expect miracles.

"General Custer," Crockett said, taking me aside.

"Yes, Colonel Crockett?" I responded.

"Been talkin' to Travis. Think you two should shake hands. Put the hard feelin's aside," he said, using a firm but calm tone. It really wasn't a request.

"David, for your sake I'll try, but don't get your hopes up," I agreed.

We walked the length of the compound toward the north wall where Travis commanded forty men. A long ditch was on our left. It had been an aquifer supplying water to the mission until Santa Anna dammed the flow upstream. It occurred to me that if the enemy breached the outer perimeter, they might be able to take cover in the dry channel, much like the Rebs had done in the Sunken Road at Antietam.

"We need to post a cannon where it will flank this trench," I said to Crockett, turning to look for the best position. The bottom of the ramp where the 18-pounder was stationed seemed a good spot. It would compromise the entire length of the channel all the way to the north wall.

"Let's talk to Travis first," Crockett said, thinking I was stalling.

"Catch up in a minute," I promised, kneeling down to study the angle.

Crockett sighed and went to warn Travis that I was coming. I didn't know if Travis had initiated the contact with the possible intention of apologizing. Or if he expected me to apologize.

"Custer! Custer, you goddamned son of a bitch!" someone shouted.

I stood up and turned, finding Dijon coming towards me with a pistol in his hand. Before I could react, his raised the flintlock and fired. All I saw was a red streak and black smoke. And then there was a sharp pain in my neck. I instinctively put a hand to the wound as Dijon emerged from the black cloud, leveling another pistol. He pulled the trigger, but it misfired, white smoke swirling in his face. And then he was on me, a hunting knife thrusting at my heart.

I reached to grasp his arm, but my reactions were slowed by the sore leg and I lost balance, landing on my back with my head hanging above the dry ditch. Dijon jumped on top, trying to cut my throat. I grabbed a wrist, then sought to push him off with my other hand, but he had the strength of a demon, hatred burning in black-brown eyes. I could smell whisky on his breath.

The blade got closer, the edge starting to draw blood. There seemed little I could do to stop it, for I could not wrestle the man off.

"You goddamn swaggering Northern trash are done," Dijon grunted, pressing the knife harder. "And after I've carved your hide for a new hat, I'll flay that darkie's . . ."

Suddenly there was a spray of crimson. Blood everywhere, like a wet blanket. At first I supposed it to be mine, but Dijon grew limp. The knife fell from his clutch. His eyes blankly rolled back. A second spray blotted out the gray clouds as Dijon's body dipped down, only to be yanked back. A Sioux war cry filled the Alamo compound.

"Custer! My God!" Crockett shouted, appearing at my side.

As I sat up, I saw Spotted Eagle standing over Dijon, one hand gripped in his hair, the other holding a bloody hatchet. Dijon's skull was chopped open, the brains spilling out of the jagged hole. Spotted Eagle drew a knife to claim Dijon's scalp. I made no effort to stop him.

"George, are you hurt?" Crockett asked.

"I might be. My neck hurts."

Crockett probed the neck just above the shoulder. I flinched.

"Don't move. You've been shot," Crockett said.

Shot? I'd ridden though hails of bullets during the Civil War without ever receiving a serious injury, and now I had been shot by some dim-witted frontiersman? It made me angry.

"General, what have they done?" Sergeant Hughes asked.

I found myself surrounded by twenty of my men, Colts drawn. There were angry mutters. And a good deal of swearing. Crockett was pushed away. I heard Butler chamber a shell in his Sharps. The battle of the Alamo may have started right then and there.

"Relax, Bobby. It was just that idiot," I said, trying to get up. My legs felt weak.

"Easy there, sir. We'll get a stretcher," French said. "I wish Dr. Lord was here."

Dr. Lord said the life he could save might be mine. Was he right?

"It can't be that serious. I'm still breathing," I protested, for the indignity of being carried away would only weaken my authority.

"Let me have a see," Travis said, elbowing French aside.

Though not a doctor, any commander responsible for the welfare of his men learns to assess a wound. It's particularly important if you have slackers seeking to be put on the sick list.

"Odd. Crockett, take a look at this," Travis said, fingers entangled in my red scarf.

"I'll be damned," Crockett said, almost amused.

"We need Dr. Pollard," Travis said, motioning to one of his men.

Dr. Amos Pollard was already halfway across the compound. We'd had no chance to talk before, for the hospital was not my priority. I sincerely hoped the hospital would not become a priority now.

"Give us some air, sirs," Dr. Pollard said, kneeling down and opening a black leather medical bag.

Pollard was a New England man, about thirty-five years old, probably from Massachusetts. He was short, rather thin, and prematurely balding, yet had a presence that made him seem larger. Such is not unusual among doctors. He probed, squinted, and made doctorly sighs as if he wasn't one step removed from a corner butcher.

"Vermont College of Medicine," he said, seeking to assure me of his credentials. "And I hate slavery as much as you."

"It looks like . . ." Travis started to say.

"Yes, yes. I think you are right," Dr. Pollard said, taking tweezers from his bag to work on the wound.

Hughes frowned. If Pollard hadn't had that Northern accent, I'm sure threats would have been made.

"George, this is going to hurt. Are you ready?" Crockett said.

I gritted my teeth, hands gripping the butts of my pistols. Pollard pulled on my scarf, then pulled a little more. With a final effort, the scarf came free, followed by a generous flow of blood. Pollard shook the scarf and out came to musket ball.

"Good you had that neckerchief. The ball didn't penetrate the silk," Dr. Pollard said.

"Ancient Romans wore silk underwear for the same reason," Travis added, indicating he'd had a classical education.

I knew much of the Romans from my studies; I just never imagined such a benefit ever applying to me.

"Wait while we bandage this wound," Dr. Pollard said.

Before he moved, Mrs. Dickenson and Juana had arrived with strips of white cloth from the infirmary.

"Anyone have whisky?" Hughes asked.

I glanced up. There were fifty men standing around me gawking instead of working.

"Thought your general weren't no drinker," someone said.

"Here, I got this brandy," another offered, passing a green glass bottle.

Hughes soaked the bandage with the brandy, then let Mrs. Dickenson tie it around my neck. It stung like Black Death, but I tried not to let it show. Pollard looked surprised, wondering at the strange ritual. Though it was not certain that alcohol could stop deadly infections, it had become a common belief during the war. Even I subscribed to the strange theory after a British doctor wrote a book about it.

"Need a jolt, sir?" Hughes asked.

"No thank you, Bobby. Thanks everybody. Back to duty," I ordered, slowly standing up.

There was momentary dizziness but nothing worse. Twisting my head might be difficult for awhile.

"Mr. Custer, I can't express my dismay," Travis said. "I assure you, I had no hint this might happen. None of us did. No gentleman would tolerate such bad manners."

"You are above suspicion, Mr. Travis," I said.

Then, after taking a sideways look at Crockett, I extended my hand. Travis shook it. Our peace was made, for now.

"Spotted Eagle, my young friend, thank you for saving my life," I said. I started to shake his hand until seeing it covered in gore.

"Slow said you would find much coup and many scalps. Slow is never wrong," Spotted Eagle said, tying Dijon's scalp to his belt.

I could not let him walk around like that for long, for there were many angry stares from the garrison, but thought it best to give the youngster a few minutes to enjoy his prize. And if anyone had a problem that Spotted Eagle had killed a white man, they would need to deal with me first.

"What of the body, sir? We shouldn't leave it here," Hughes said, glancing around the busy compound.

"Dump it over the wall. When Santa Anna's troops attack in the morning, it's the first thing I want them to see," I answered.

"General, I know you don't wish to show weakness before the men, but this is still a serious wound," Dr. Pollard said. "Give me a quiet place to work and you might be back on your feet by tomorrow."

"I'll give you an hour."

"That's impossible, sir. This is a serious injury," Pollard said.

"Doctor, I expect the impossible," I replied.

They found a canvas chair for me to sit in outside Bowie's room where Pollard made sure the wound was cleaned before stitching it up. He thought me extraordinarily lucky the ball hadn't cut its way through to the spine, but between the silk scarf and the damp gunpowder in Dijon's flintlock, it was only a flesh wound. Custer's Luck, I thought.

"So you're opposed to slavery?" I asked.

"Many of us are. We came to Texas hoping to create colonies for freed slaves," Dr. Pollard explained. "Under Mexican law, our chances were good. I'm not so sure about this new constitution everyone is talking about."

"It's a harsh document. Worse than anything back in the States," I said, for Kellogg had much to say on the subject. "From what I hear, it will be illegal for a Texan to free his slaves, and freed black men won't even be allowed to live here."

"That's sad for Texas. This land could have been an Eden."

"It still can," I said.

Crockett, Jameson and Carey doubled their efforts in the courtyard, for we needed to be prepared. Unable to do more than advise, and be a nuisance, I ducked inside Bowie's room for a short visit. He was not in good shape.

"Hear everything, can't do nothin'," Bowie said, so ill he couldn't even sit up. His face was white, fever burning in his eyes. I guessed malaria or black lung.

"The men understand. You'll be up and around in no time."

His room was dark, the only window boarded up. There was a musty smell unlikely to help him get better, but a small hearth was keeping the chamber warm. A bowl of half eaten soup lay on the table next to him. I also saw his famous knife and a loaded pistol.

"Juana's doing her best. Won't be good enough," Bowie said. "If Santa Anna ain't already looted my house, parcel up the goods when this is over."

"Your house?" I asked.

"Veramendi Palace. Over on Soledad Street. Not really a palace, but nice. Make sure my people are taken care of."

"Even the slaves?" I asked.

"Specially the slaves. Don't have many left. Not since my Ursula died."

"I'll do what I can, after freeing them," I said.

"Do what's best," Bowie said, eyes closing.

Suddenly I realized he wasn't breathing. I felt for a pulse and peaked under an eyelid. Just like that, the man had died.

I sat for a moment, surprised. A man like Bowie, bigger than life, should have had a more glorious end. Perhaps propped up in bed, firing his flintlocks as the Mexicans burst into the room, and then fighting to the last with his Bowie knife. That's the way he'd want to be remembered.

I covered him with a blanket and went outside without telling anyone. With so much to do, there was no point in damaging morale.

"Rider coming in! Rider coming in!" our sentry on the old church yelled.

The 12-pounder in the apse fired, followed by a rifle volley from the corral. I hurried to the top of the long barracks, climbing the steep stone stairs with difficulty, to see a lone horseman riding like a madman over Powder House Hill and down toward our east wall, getting so close to the morass I feared they'd stumble into the swamp.

"Rides like a devil," Crockett said with a whistle. "Good he's so small. Mexicans can't seem to hit him."

A squad of Mexican troops were standing on the hill firing their muskets, but the horseman had dashed past them so fast they'd hardly had time to react. Not that they weren't trying. From the right, at the top the Alameda, another squad opened fire. And the roar of a 4-pounder was heard from the left, the cannon ball kicking up a plume of damp earth. It seemed the Mexicans were determined not to let any messengers reach the fort, no matter what.

And all were not shooting. Twenty lancers had taken up the chase, a brave sight in their red jackets and glistening steel helmets, flashing swords drawn for a quick kill. Their horses were not the best quality, but rested and eager for a run.

And then I saw it was not a horseman approaching the Alamo at all. It was a horse boy, and he was riding my horse!

"Come on, David, let's give him cover," I said, hiding a sense of desperation.

I raised my Remington hunting rifle, took aim at a lancer chasing down from the hill, and fired at a range of seven hundred yards, knocking the man from his saddle.

"Christ Almighty, no one's beatin' that shot!" Crockett exclaimed.

I wasn't interested in praise, firing three more times. When another lancer fell, the others slowed to a more cautious trot, finally giving up the chase. The horse boy veered around the morass toward the gate on the east side of the corral, entering below the raised battery emplacement. The garrison sent up a cheer.

"Slow! Goddamn it, what the hell are you doing here!" I shouted, storming into the corral only minutes later.

I'd run down the stairs so fast it was a miracle I'd not broken my neck, nor had I sworn so much since Benteen accused me of abandoning Joel Elliot at the Washita.

"Take it easy, General, nobody got hurt," Dickenson said, lifting Slow from Vic's back.

Good old Vic seemed excited by all the fuss, but he was always one for adventure, nudging Hughes with his nose and stomping a forefoot. French rushed to remove the saddle and sponge the horse down, for he'd had a hard run.

"My people's future does not lie in Goliad," Slow said, calmly even though he was out of breath. The lad looked worn to the bone, only the black eyes shining with any strength.

"It can't lie in the Alamo," I replied.

"The spirits focus in strange places. As I rode closer to Goliad, I felt only darkness. In the Alamo, I sense light."

"The Alamo will soon be a place of great death," I said.

"This is where the spirits dwell. This is where the spirits will be remembered," Slow insisted.

Even I remembered the Alamo, forty years after its fall. Maybe there was something in the medicine boy's words.

"You'll stay in my quarters. French, have Juana find him some food," I ordered. The lad started to follow my aide, but I stopped him, a hand on his shoulder, and then knelt down to look him straight in the eye. "Slow, that was the bravest ride I've ever seen. Your people are proud of you, and so am I. But don't ever ride Vic through a bullet storm like that again."

Slow smiled, quiet and pleased, and went to take a nap.

It was an hour before sunset. I had the 18-pounder fired so the world, particularly Keogh and Smith, would know the Alamo was holding out. We would continue working until the last sliver of light, preparing our defenses for the desperate struggle ahead, and then the garrison would be put to bed for a full night's sleep. If I were Santa Anna, I would attack in the predawn hours. I expected him to do the same.

There was a bugle call from across the river, and then a summons. I walked up the southwest ramp to see another Mexican delegation on the bridge under a white flag. This time I sent Jameson out to see what they wanted, and was astonished by the answer.

"Are you sure?" I asked.

"No doubt, sir. Santa Anna has invited you to dinner. A civilized forum to discuss your differences," Jameson reported.

We were sitting in my quarters, a coal fire burning in the old Franklin stove. The room was so small that Crockett and I sat on stools around an empty water barrel while Jameson, Travis and Carey sat on my bed. Butler, Hughes and Dickenson stood near the door. Slow slept on the floor in the corner, covered by a buffalo robe.

"I'll be . . . I'm surprised," I said.

"You shouldn't go. It's a trick," Butler said.

"Let's shoot the lying sons of bitches," Hughes added.

"All of them, or just the officers?" I inquired with a grin.

"We can start with the officers," Hughes said.

"The Mexicans are offering hostages, including Santa Anna's nephew," Jameson said. "I don't think it's a trick."

"They've always been good about respecting a truce," Travis said, anxious to accept the invitation but knowing I would forbid his participation. Travis was hated by our enemies; Crockett and I were enigmas.

"Think I should go, too," Crockett said.

"Along with me and Henry," Hughes said, hefting his rifle.

"Mr. Sharp is hungry," Butler was quick to say, propping the heavy rifle on his knee.

I rocked in my chair, a hand pressing the poultice Pollard had prepared for my neck wound. I didn't care for the smell, but a touch of morphine Butler carried in his saddlebags helped the pain. After Mrs. Dickenson washed the blood off my red silk scarf, I put it back on for good luck.

"Sirs, you will need to watch your manners," I said, tacitly approving. "Santa Anna may be a ruthless tyrant, but he is President of Mexico. And a gentleman. I'll not be embarrassed by your uncouth ways."

"You fart just like the rest of us," Butler said.

"I beg your pardon, Sergeant Butler, but generals do not fart. We pass wind," I corrected.

"My mistake," Butler said, poking Hughes with his elbow.

Travis smiled, something I'd not seen him do before.

"Mr. Jameson, you may tell Santa Anna's emissary that we accept his invitation," I instructed.

"I go as well," Slow said, sitting up with drowsy eyes.

"Of course," I agreed. "Who am I to stop you?"

We dressed in our best, such as it was, and had five horses saddled for the ride into town. I wore my army blues with a fringed buckskin jacket. The two sergeants were outfitted in clean uniforms and Crockett in a frock coat. Slow wore fresh leathers loaned by eight-year-old Enrique, the son of Tejano defender Gregorio Esparza.

"Try not to lose the fort while I'm gone," I said lightheartedly to Travis.

The man frowned. Jameson smiled. Both knew there was little chance of such an attack. The Mexican battalions moving to the north were not yet in position, while their entrenchments to the south were badly mauled.

"Listen. They've stopped firing their artillery," Jameson said.

The sun had just set a few minutes before. After twelve days of bombardment, the garrison was exhausted. They would sleep like babies.

"Bed the men down now, Captain. They need the rest," I said, a bit sleepy myself. "Warn them we'll be back up well before dawn."

"Bring us some leftovers, General," Jameson said, tired of boiled beef and corn.

We went out the corral gate and under the battery at the rear of the church, riding slowly toward the Alameda. Above us, what looked like three cannon were really one cannon and two black logs. We avoided a tangle of trees and brush screening the south palisade before reaching the main road. A dozen mounted lancers were waiting for us. At the same time, six hostages walked toward the lunette where they would await our return, for they would not be allowed inside the fort. One was said to be Santa Anna's nephew, another was a colonel named Morales. The other four were all prominent in one manner or another, though I hadn't paid attention to the details.

I saw Carey and Dickenson at the portal verifying the identity of the hostages, for the young lawyer was afraid of treachery. It seemed a prudent precaution, so my small party paused, hands poised on our sidearms. When Carey waved his hat, we proceeded. Colonel Juan Almonte was our escort.

"Good evening, general," Juan said, tipping his hat.

"Good evening to you, Colonel Almonte. You are looking better," I replied.

"And you are looking worse. Did one of our cannon balls find you out in the open?"

"Nothing so serious as that. You remember Slow, don't you?"

"Of course. The medicine boy. Do child warriors now defend the Alamo?"

"It saves ammunition. Rather than fight your army, Slow is going to cast a spell on you," I said. "We haven't decided which is better yet, the pox or leprosy."

Almonte laughed, but I heard his men whispering among themselves and looking at Slow with dread. None of them thought it was funny. I don't think Slow quite grasped the joke, but he glanced around with those dark eyes, and even I sensed a chill.

We rode over the old wooden bridge and down a dirt boulevard. The small houses to either side had been abandoned at the first approach of the Mexican army two weeks before. Though most of the towns east of San Antonio were Anglo settlements, west Texas was predominately Tejano. Especially Béjar. One should think the exodus of the local population would have alerted Travis and Bowie to Santa Anna's imminent arrival before February 23rd, but they had still been taken by surprise. Had the volunteers garrisoning the town been betrayed by the Hispanic citizens? Or had they simply taken the threat too lightly? I guessed the latter.

I knew Santa Anna had taken the initiative once Texas rose in rebellion. He quickly assembled an army and marched through northern Mexico in the dead of winter, invoking such terror in the locals that few dared oppose him. I had done the same in 1868, attacking Black Kettle's snowbound village on the Washita. Unpleasant business, but that's how wars are won.

A dog barked from a fenced yard, reminding me how much I missed my hounds. It was a furry white mongrel, more interested in making noise than trouble. I'd have thrown him a bone if I had one.

"The people fled so fast their pets were left behind," I remarked. "Does the dictator inspire so much fear?"

"Only among traitors," Colonel Almonte said. "But you need not worry. The white flag will be respected."

"Your master refused to treat with Bowie and Travis, and earlier he refused to treat with me. What caused him to change his mind?" I asked, not expecting a truthful answer. I was surprised.

"His Excellency likes to know his opponents. To understand them is to know their weaknesses. Travis and Bowie are not hard to understand, being pirates. General Custer is a mystery."

I gave thought to such mysteries. It was said General Lee thrived against McClellan, Hooker and Burnside because he knew them. Understood how they thought, and how they would react in a given circumstance. It wasn't until Grant arrived that Lee found himself perplexed by an unknown adversary.

What did I know about Santa Anna? The Texans called him a dictator and tyrant, but that didn't make it true. The South had said the same things about President Lincoln. I recalled reading an article in the *Army and Navy Journal* back in 1864, the memoirs of General Winfield Scott, who had fought Santa Anna in the Mexican-American War. Scott wrote that Santa Anna was energetic and vigilant, with unquestionable powers of organization. Scott thought him personally courageous, but a failure in his quickness of perception. Slow to adapt to changing conditions on a battlefield, and hence his many defeats. But was the Santa Anna of 1836 a better general than that of 1847? Was I in a position to know the difference?

As a commander, I had already recognized Santa Anna to be methodical. His winter march and sudden investment of the Alamo was decisive. The siege had been well-planned. Until the Seventh Cavalry arrived, there had been no problems with his line of supply. Santa Anna considered himself the Napoleon of the West. In every respect, it appeared I would soon meet a worthy opponent.

Custer rode tall on his white stallion, searching the path with the steady gaze of a mountain lion. He was not so confident as he pretended, but I would not have known this had we not shared the trail together. I rode beside him on Vic, for the general thought me well-suited to his favorite horse. Many of the Mexican soldiers looked at us with great curiosity, and I heard them whisper of the ghost riders. It was said we had died once. They believed we would die again, for they held great faith in their leader. I looked back at Hughes and Butler, who I had come to admire as fine warriors. They had great faith in their leader. Among the People, it is important to have faith in our leaders, for chiefs do not give orders, and the medicine men may not issue commands. Without belief in a leader's qualities, no one would follow. I thought back on the future. The future that would not see my people thrive. I realized we would need to walk a different path, following a leader who would take us to a different place.

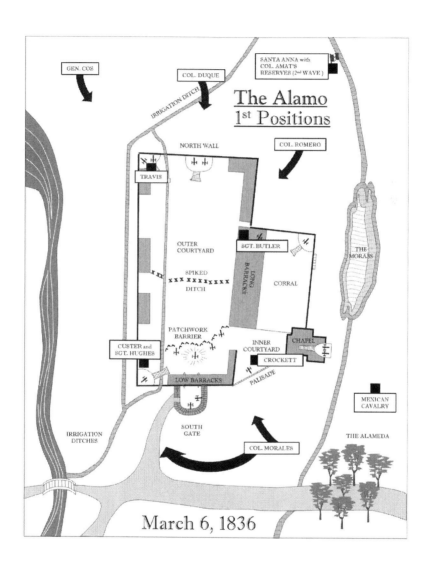

GEN. COS

COL. DUQUE

SANTA ANNA with
COL. AMAT'S
RESERVES (2nd WAVE)

IRRIGATION DITCH

The Alamo
1st Positions

COL. ROMERO

NORTH WALL

TRAVIS

THE
MORASS

OUTER
COURTYARD

SGT. BUTLER

LONG BARRACKS

CORRAL

SPIKED
DITCH

XXXXXXXXXX

PATCHWORK
BARRIER

INNER
COURTYARD

CHAPEL

CUSTER and
SGT. HUGHES

CROCKETT

LOW BARRACKS

PALISADE

MEXICAN
CAVALRY

IRRIGATION
DITCHES

SOUTH
GATE

THE ALAMEDA

COL. MORALES

March 6, 1836

.

CHAPTER TWELVE

SANTA ANNA'S DECISION

Though the main boulevard was dark and largely deserted except for a few detachments of soldiers, the town square was more crowded. A hundred campfires lit the plaza, which was paved, unlike the dirt roads we'd found every place else. The Cathedral of San Fernando stood tall over the surrounding shops and houses. Like most Mexican villages, the hundred-year-old church was the center of civic life. The red flag of No Quarter still flew from the highest steeple.

"Military town," Butler said.

"Comanche," Hughes said, offering the obvious explanation.

All of west Texas seemed plagued by Indian attacks. The Comanche were the worst, murdering and kidnapping at will, but they weren't the only perpetrators. The walls of the Alamo had been built for protection from hostile raids, and San Antonio had similar defenses, including the walled presidio behind the church almost as large as the plaza in front of it. The bells in the church did more than summon worshippers to Sunday services—they signaled danger, too. To the east, dozens of settlements were growing along the rivers that flowed south to the Gulf of Mexico, but to the west there was nothing but wilderness and Indians.

"Don't see how Cos lost this town to the Texans," Hughes said, referring to the fight four months prior. "He had a thousand men. Ammunition and food. We could have held this position until hell froze over."

"Guess his enemies wanted it more. That's the difference between winning and losing," I said.

"Bet Santa Anna wants this one bad, after the way these Texians humiliated his brother-in-law," Crockett said. "I weren't here, but they say Cos was chased out with his tail between his legs."

"He's back now," Butler said. "Travis reported seeing Cos leading an infantry battalion. Made him mad, too. Cos gave his word of honor not to fight in Texas again."

On the battlefields of Virginia, especially in the early years of the war, captured soldiers would give their parole not to fight until properly exchanged. This kept down the populations of the prisoner-of-war camps, but each man was bound by his most sacred honor to keep their word. To break such an oath was unthinkable.

We reached the plaza. Mexican soldiers in full uniform stood at attention. Most wore shako hats decorated with silver unit badges. The outfits were blue with white leather straps crossed over the chest. They held Brown Bess muskets, bayonets fixed. Only the footwear showed how difficult a journey they'd had. Some still had worn black boots but most wore sandals or moccasins. Not the best protection from the cold Texas winter. A marching band played a tune I didn't recognize, but it was a pleasant melody and well performed.

Beyond the town square, in the streets around the presidio, were the supply wagons and camp followers. Women in heavy wool shawls, a few old men, and even some children. Dozens of small fires were keeping them warm, the fuel of preference being buffalo chips or mesquite. A hundred or more gathered behind the rows of soldiers to see the strange Americans in their plaza. Pity showed in their eyes, for they thought us doomed men.

A smartly dressed major began barking orders, the soldiers crisply presenting arms before returning to attention. I dismounted my borrowed stallion and saluted.

"This way, General," Almonte said, pointing toward a low adobe residence on the north side of the plaza.

Several peasants in white sackcloth came forward to take our horses. They appeared nervous and underfed. I could not tell if they were impressed locals or camp followers. If I'd had two bits, I would have tipped them.

I walked with Crockett, Slow between us, Hughes and Butler a few paces behind.

"Should we guard the door, sir?" Butler asked.

"No reason, Jimmy. If it's a trap, better to be inside," I said.

"It is not a trap. Not as you suspect," Slow remarked in his mysterious way.

"Can you read Santa Anna's thoughts?" I asked.

"Not so well as the birds," Slow answered.

I glanced up to see a group of sparrows on the roof, but doubted any of them were mind readers.

We stepped on a covered porch and entered. The dwelling was large, lit with oil lamps, and nicely furnished with maple wood furniture and thick carpets. The home of a wealthy man, by frontier standards. Beyond the entry was a dining area with a long oak table and a dozen sturdy chairs. Above was a chandelier holding thirty candles, and more candles lit the corners. A bookcase held twenty or more books, all leather-bound. A fire burned in a great hearth, fighting off the cold winter chill.

"Very nice," I said, finding the quarters similar to the proud hacienda of Erasmo Seguin. I dwelled fondly on memories of Isabella and hoped I would meet her again.

"His Excellency expects the best," Almonte said.

I nodded to Butler and Hughes, who took up positions inside the doorway where several tall stools were set against the wall.

Before long the other dinner guests arrived, colonels and generals. Six in all. They acknowledged us in silence and took seats at the table, leaving the head chair vacant. They were dressed for the occasion in fine uniforms decorated with silver and gold braid, ceremonial sabers at their side. I clutched the stolen Spanish steel hanging from my belt, wishing it was the handsome Tiffany sword I'd lost at Trevilian Station in 1864.

Once everyone was settled, Colonel Almonte nodded to a servant, who ran into the adjoining study. Through the door, I saw another fireplace, colorful woven carpets, and several stuffed easy chairs. I also noticed a wooden cradle, now empty. Except for the cradle, it reminded me of my quarters at Fort Lincoln.

"Gentlemen, I have the great honor and privilege to present His Most High Excellency, General Antonio López de Santa Anna," Almonte announced.

Two soldiers entered carrying flags. One was the green, white and red flag of the Republic of Mexico emblazoned with a gold eagle. The other flag I didn't recognize, but assumed it was the dictator's personal banner. They were followed by six soldiers carrying Baker rifles who lined up single file against the wall, standing at attention. And then Santa Anna sauntered into the room.

The man did not look Mexican, which I generally took to be of Indian or mixed Indian blood. This gentleman was of pure European descent, average height and build, with dark hair and pale skin. A good-looking fellow, and from what I'd heard, popular with the ladies. There was a charismatic glint in his dark brown eyes as he gazed upon his adversaries. I didn't know whether to admire the man as a leader or hate him as a rival.

The officers stood up and saluted. Santa Anna smiled and gestured for them to reclaim their seats before sitting at the head of the table.

"Gentlemen, you may sit here," Almonte said, giving me the chair opposite his president at the far end of the table.

Crockett sat to my right, Slow on a pillow to my left. Hughes and Butler remained in the corner where they watched without getting in the way. Everyone in the room was armed.

"Your Excellency, I have the honor to present General George Custer, commander of the Seventh Cavalry. With him is Colonel Davy Crockett of Tennessee."

"*Saludos, Señor Presidente,*" I said, my Spanish improving with practice. He looked at me with studious eyes before responding.

"I believe my English is better than your Spanish, sir," Santa Anna said, the voice more causal than I expected. "And who is the Indian boy? The new commander of the Alamo? No doubt he will do better than those pirates, Bowie and Travis."

"This is Slow of the Great Sioux Nation. He studies to become a medicine chief," I introduced.

"Does he listen to the stars?" Santa Anna asked, his face lit with a grin. His officers smiled at his joke.

"Yes, I listen to the stars, just as I can read the hearts of white men who would steal the land of my people," Slow said, black eyes staring under bent brows.

"Then we have something in common, young Indian boy. I can also read the hearts of those come to steal the land of *my* people," Santa Anna said. "But we must not forget our manners. General Custer, allow me to introduce General Ramirez y Sesma, General Martín Perfecto de Cos, General Manuel Castrillón, Colonel Francisco Duque, Colonel José María Romero, and Colonel Estevan de la Mora. And you know Colonel Almonte, my aide-de-camp. I have many other officers, but they are occupied with their duties."

The colonels were generally in the late thirties, the generals in their late thirties to mid-fifties. By their dress and manner, I saw they were accustomed to traveling in style. Clean uniforms, polished buttons. Well-fed and unconcerned with trivial needs. During our stay on the plains, Libbie and I had used an old ambulance wagon with only Annie, our black cook, for help. It was all I could afford.

"It's my honor, gentlemen," I said, briefly standing.

Some of the officers understood English, but most did not. Almonte whispered a translation to the three generals.

"We have much to discuss, but first the formalities," Santa Anna said, apparently in a good mood.

The dictator smiled, glanced about, and clapped his hands. Four attractive serving girls entered carrying bottles of red wine. All the young ladies were fitted in white flowing dresses with wide blue belts and yellow trim along the hems, and each wore a delicate silver chain necklace. The wine was in elegant decanters, the glasses made of expensive crystal. Each person at the table was served, even Slow, and then my sergeants. The Mexican soldiers remained at attention.

"A toast to General Custer and the Seventh Cavalry, regardless of how short their stay in Texas may be," Santa Anna said.

"And to His Excellency, General Santa Anna. May his stay in Texas prove no longer than necessary," I responded.

Santa Anna laughed and drank deeply, as did his officers and Crockett. I sipped mine, not wishing to be rude, while Slow sniffed his wine and took a good swig, crinkling his nose.

"Are you hungry, gentlemen?" our host asked.

He clapped again. A middle-aged black servant arrived with large silver plates of roast chicken, rice and tortillas. I was surprised, for the man looked like an American.

"My name is Ben, sir. A free man. I cook for Colonel Almonte," Ben said, seeing my expression. "I is right pleased to serve you. Right pleased. Good to see you again, too, Colonel Crockett. We met once while you was in Washington."

"Glad to see an old friend," Crockett said, getting to his feet and warmly shaking Ben's hand.

I looked down the table at Santa Anna. He was enjoying himself, watching for my reaction. I had initially thought Ben a slave, and my presumption had been wrong. Just as Santa Anna intended.

"There are rumors of your cavalry," General Cos said, a man about my age, taller than average, with premature gray whiskers. He seemed intelligent but weary of his duties.

"What rumors are those?" I asked, for one never knows what strange tales are spread by the rank and file.

"That you are ghost riders," Cos said.

"We are flesh and blood," I said.

"Remade by the Great Spirit," Slow added, so quietly that only our end of the table heard him.

Nevertheless, the remark was repeated all the way down to Santa Anna. None chose to comment. I was served half a roast chicken and eagerly cut off a leg, tasting the salt and pepper seasoning. It was a marvelous thing, making me wish I was back at Delmonico's in New York, supping on sautéed asparagus and braised lamb chops.

"General Cos, should I welcome you back to Texas? I heard you took an oath not to return under arms," I asked, curious about his rationale.

"My president says a soldier must fight while he has the legs to walk and the arms to raise a weapon," Cos said.

"Then you blame President Santa Anna for despoiling your honor? In my country, a pledge of parole is a sacred thing. No man violating such an oath would be accepted among gentlemen of good character."

I noticed General Castrillón stiffen, and several others looked away. Our host seemed momentarily indignant at my remark, but quickly regained his composure.

"My sister's husband owes no obligation to the rebels who drove him from his assigned post," Santa Anna interjected, speaking with a practiced grace. "A pledge made to criminals is not binding by civilized law."

"And yet your subordinate made such an oath, which you have ordered him to disregard," I said, steeped in an irrevocable tradition. "An army's integrity can be no better than its leaders. Am I to think you hold yourselves to a lower standard than the rebels?"

"I value my honor as much as any man, but I love my country more," General Cos protested.

Cos looked toward Santa Anna. I had the impression there had been words between them regarding this sensitive subject—and Santa Anna had prevailed. The dictator appeared a willful and imperious leader, easily dominating the weaker personalities around him. I let the subject drop. I had only provoked the conversation to see how they would react, and I was not disappointed.

There were several courses, each better than the one before. Three of the serving girls helped Ben with the dishes while the fourth made sure everyone's wine glasses stayed full. The plates were of the finest china, bone white with blue and gold trim along the edges. The candlesticks were gold plated. It was by far the most elegant dining I'd had since visiting President Johnson at the White House following our Midwestern tour in 1866. President Grant had never invited me to the White House, but knowing Grant's habits, I had no doubt Santa Anna kept a better table.

"Mr. President, we are pleased to have such a luscious meal after the boiled beef in the Alamo," I said. "May I inquire why you have brought us here?"

"A better question would be what has brought the United States cavalry to Texas?" Santa Anna replied. "I rejected President Jackson's bid to buy my country. Are you here to take it by force?"

"We have not been sent by Andrew Jackson, and we are no longer United States cavalry," I replied, finding a reasonable explanation difficult. "We arrived in Texas by accident."

"Not by accident," Slow said, drawing everyone's attention.

"We did not come here on purpose," I quickly said.

"That is true. The Great Spirit brought you here," Slow said.

"Why?" I asked, for I had no clue.

"The future failed. It was necessary to find a new one," the boy said.

The table was silent. I'm sure the generals thought we were putting on a performance to confuse the situation. One of those fantasies so popular in the Paris salons, where intellectuals once met to discuss the works of Dante and Voltaire. Our hosts were not amused.

"The future is easy to predict," Colonel Romero said. "His Excellency will crush the rebels and free Texas of these vermin. Once the pirates are driven out, the land will be open for settlement by loyal citizens of Mexico. A few American cavalry will make no difference."

The Mexican officers tapped the wine glasses with their spoons in appreciation. Santa Anna smiled victoriously. They were a confident bunch. So was Burnside before Fredericksburg.

"I will be honest with you gentlemen," I said, thinking a bit of honesty wouldn't hurt. "The Seventh Cavalry was in Montana territory, far north of here, engaged in operations against hostile Sioux and Cheyenne Indians. And then suddenly we were here, in Texas. I can't explain it. I do not subscribe to the boy's theory about a Great Spirit, but something out of the ordinary occurred."

"I would say such a tale is well beyond ordinary," General Castrillón said, questioning without mocking.

I noticed that Castrillón's accent was different from the others. Possibly Cuban. He was also the oldest man at the table, bearing himself with the quiet dignity of a professional.

"Are we to believe such a fantasy?" Colonel Romero asked.

"Sirs, I am a soldier. I've been a soldier all my life," I sternly replied, for even a small amount wine goes quickly to my head. "It doesn't matter to me what is ordinary or not ordinary. It doesn't matter to me what is fantasy or not fantasy. All I want to know is who to fight, and when, and where, and not have some politician tell me how. In this, I have been successful."

"And who ordered you to attack Mexico?" Colonel de la Mora impatiently asked. A young hothead. In another time, I guessed he might have survived the battle of the Alamo. I doubted his chances this time around.

"History is yet to decide if this land is part of Mexico," I said, much to their anger. "Fifteen years ago, it was owned by Spain. It's claimed by the Comanche, and Kiowa, and many other tribes. Local Tejanos believe your government is remote and unresponsive. But having given the problem much thought, I don't think Texas should become part of the United States. Is there no way to resolve the grievances of the colonists short of independence?"

"They are thieves. They deserve nothing but death," Santa Anna said, the charm dissipating.

"In my own land, in the times I am accustomed to, liberty is held in high regard," I wearily said. "The men in the Alamo realize this. It appears the esteemed leaders of Mexico have not learned this lesson."

"Who are you to lecture the people of Mexico on liberty?" Santa Anna asked, rising slowly from his chair.

"I am George Armstrong Custer, commander of the Seventh Cavalry, and you are not the people of Mexico," I said, slowly standing. "You, sir, were elected by aristocratic elitists, who you promptly turned on and arrested. You swore to uphold the constitution of 1824, and then cast it aside once you took power. I will not say Andrew Jackson is any better, but he's certainly no worse. So I ask you again, is there no way to resolve this revolt of the Texans short of independence?"

Santa Anna seemed somewhat surprised by my question, slowly retaking his seat. I sat back down, taking a sip of water.

"General Custer, as an American, I should think you would favor independence," Almonte said, surprised by my attitude.

"Juan, if Texas wins independence, it will pass a constitution favoring slavery. I do not need to tell you gentlemen about the evils of that peculiar institution, though you tolerated it in this province while it suited your purposes."

"Sir, what do you mean by that?" Colonel Romero asked, his face flushed with indignation. He seemed an ambitious officer, eager for advancement. And fond of wine.

"When Stephen Austin said his new colony needed slaves, you cut a deal with him. Slaves would serve ten years before winning their freedom, but we all know their day of freedom will never come. For the Southerners, once a slave is always a slave. You needed a buffer against the Comanche, and Austin provided that buffer. The price was human bondage. Now there are a thousand slaves in Texas and you've done nothing to stop the trade."

"We tried," General Cos said. "Austin said the economy would fail without slaves. And Travis threatened a revolution if we tried to set them free. When we arrested the firebrand for his incendiary speeches, the colonists rose in revolt."

The exasperation was clear. Santa Anna's brother-in-law had not enjoyed his assignment in Texas.

"Gentlemen," I said, "there will always be those who claim the prosperity of their country depends on some dark atrocity. In the South, it's slavery. In the North, it's the urban slums. In Mexico, you suppress the peasants. I come from Ohio, where free men live by their own wits and their own labor. We pay no homage to the oppressions you find so acceptable."

"General Custer, what is it you want of us?" General Castrillón asked. The white-haired gentleman was genuinely interested, not merely looking for a fight. I liked him.

"I would like you to march back to Mexico City and let me deal with these Texans in my own way," I answered.

Some of the officers laughed, others frowned. I suppose it was too much to ask.

"Will you round up Houston and these other pirates for us? And do what with them?" Colonel Romero contemptuously asked, staring at me like I was trying to sell them rain.

"Most of the Texans don't want war. They came here to farm and ranch. But they won't accept oppression, either," I replied.

"What the Texans want will not matter once we've driven them back across the Sabine," Romero said, chin held high.

His brother officers nodded agreement. Santa Anna smiled.

"Your Excellency, the problem we got right here remains," Crockett said. "The boys in the Alamo are ready to fight, but if there's another way, we don't want no blood, neither."

"Congressman Crockett, what it war without blood and tears?" Santa Anna asked.

"Peace is a better way," Crockett answered without a blink. "I figure there's some hot heads bent on independence, but if the people's rights can be guaranteed, most would rather go back to livin' quiet. I came here to settle some land. Maybe bring out my family and start a new life. We would be good citizens and good neighbors."

"You are a sincere man, Davy Crockett, but I cannot allow interlopers to dictate terms to my government," Santa Anna said. "You Americans tried to buy Texas. Then Austin broke his word and allowed thousands of illegal immigrants to overrun our borders. Thousands more came when they heard your provisional government is offering free land to mercenaries. Should this continue, America will overrun all of Texas. Mexico's best hope is to stop you now, and it begins with the Alamo. It begins with setting an example that such impudence will not be tolerated. It is an example that will be made with blood and fire."

The three colonels nodded agreement, lightly tapping the table with their spoons. They were anxious for battle, ready to prove themselves. The three generals were more restrained. They knew storming the Alamo would be costly.

"Mr. President, a lot of what you say is true, but there's still got to be a better way than fightin'," Crockett protested.

"You need not die so uselessly. Stay here, as my guest," Santa Anna offered. "We can say you were on one of your famous explorations when you fell in with the rebels against your will."

"The boys in the Alamo know different," Crockett said.

"Do not trouble yourself on that. The Alamo will have no survivors," Colonel Romero said, a hand on his sword.

"Thanks all the same, but reckon I better stay true to my word. It's important to know what's right, and then go ahead," Crockett replied, his genial grin winning admiration from our enemies.

"What of you, General Custer? By your own admission, this is not your fight," General Castrillón said. "Why don't you accept His Excellency's generous offer and ride out with your men? No one will prevent you from returning to the United States."

Dinner was over and the girls were serving a sweet bread dessert. I had drunk a full glass of wine and part of a second. Less wine than anyone else at the table, but still a little too much.

"What do you think, Slow? Should we ride back to the United States?" I asked, rubbing the thick black hair on the boy's head.

"You will not," Slow said, enjoying a mouthful of the sweet bread.

"Then you admit Custer is a rebel leader?" Colonel Romero said, satisfied he had discovered the truth.

"General Custer is rebellious, but he is not a rebel," Slow said. "He knows that if he rides away, Texas will become a cursed land. White men will come who bring evil with them. General Santa Anna cannot hold Texas. He is not a wise leader."

Several Mexican officers were immediately on their feet, hands on swords, angry frowns adding to furious growls. Santa Anna rose last.

"If you were a man, I would cut out your heart for such words," Santa Anna said, chin held high.

"I agree with everything the boy said. Why don't you try cutting my heart out?" I said, standing with a hand on my saber. "I make challenge, Your Excellency. You and me, in honorable combat, with the fate of Texas as the prize. Let the blood and tears be ours alone."

"I will not risk my honor dueling with a foreign barbarian," Santa Anna replied. "Go back to your Alamo and prepare to die. There will be no mercy for pirates. No quarter. All of Texas will feel the wrath of my justice."

"I wondered if there was any hope of peace under your rule, sir, but now I see the Texans are right. Their only hope for freedom is to fight," I said, perceiving the dictator's true nature. He could be charming, if not beguiling, but at heart he was just a grasping politician with an army at his back. "My men and I, we know something about fighting for freedom. It's worth fighting for. It's worth dying for."

"Then you shall die. And you, too, Congressman Crockett. You are a pleasant fellow, but an interloper. After the battle, I will look upon your bodies before casting them on a funeral pyre. There shall be no graves to mark your passage," Santa Anna said.

"People will remember the Alamo. It'll be all the legacy we need," Crockett said, getting a bit touchy.

Santa Anna stood up, nodded in a most gentlemanly manner, and left the room, followed by all of his officers except Almonte and General Castrillón.

"Our president is temperamental," Castrillón said. "But he has the good of Mexico at heart. We did not want this war. There are factions at home seeking to overthrow His Excellency. Forces who seek wealth at the expense of the peons. Only a strong government can protect our nation's honor. These rebels, Austin and Houston, they seek to impose an Anglo tyranny on the native people of Texas. Are they any better?"

I looked at Slow, knowing the future his people could expect from white civilization, and remembered what Kellogg had said about the Tejanos. I knew Texas would soon impose a brutal system of slavery, for Tom and I had seen the remnants. Even the most civilized of non-white races, the Cherokee, would be robbed and murdered by the regime that replaced Santa Anna. And my own country would fight a bloody civil war, half a million dead, before the dreams of President Lincoln could be fulfilled. Was there no other way?

"General Castrillón, I'm not a statesman," I said. "Such wisdom is best left to greater leaders such as you. But Slow knows the world better than the men who sat at this table tonight. He sees a future that needs to be better. Do not expect the fall of the Alamo to resolve your country's problems."

"Perhaps you may be wiser than you know," Castrillón said, "but it changes nothing. His Excellency must crush the Alamo or lose the respect of his army. As a soldier, you realize this."

"I've seen many generals sacrifice the lives of their men rather than lose respect," I agreed. "Lee at Gettysburg. Grant at Cold Harbor. Custer at the Little Big Horn. Risking the respect of your army may be a reason for a bad choice, but it's not an excuse. Speak with your president, sir. Tell Santa Anna there is still time to make the right decision."

Our horses were waiting in the courtyard. It was a cold, damp night, the moon partially hidden by black clouds. I helped Slow up on Vic. Ben came forward with a large iron pot of steaming beef stew.

"Something to keep you warm, General," Ben said.

Hughes and Butler were already mounted, rifles laid across their laps, coats pulled tight against the frost.

"Guess we shouldn't have expected much from this," Crockett said, disappointed with Santa Anna's intransience. He pulled a bearskin blanket up over his store bought jacket, wrapping a fur around his neck.

"Surprised your charm didn't work on the dictator?" I asked.

"Works on most folks," Crockett said, climbing atop his brown sorrel. "Reckon we'll just have to fight."

"I reckon," I agreed, mounting last.

Troops had lined up, possibly a hundred in all, standing at attention. An officer barked and they presented arms. I saw General Castrillón standing with Almonte and several sergeants.

"I wish you well, gentlemen," I said, giving a sharp salute.

"We will remember you," Almonte answered.

We rode back through the muddy streets, past the empty adobe houses, and over the rough wooden bridge. The road leading up to the lunette still had too many burnt-out buildings for a good field of fire. Too much cover for an attacking force. Given more time, I'd have torn them down. We were dismounting as Dickenson's men threw some heavy planks over the protective ditch. The hostages were released, gratefully making a run for the south entrenchment. I caught a glimpse of Colonel Morales, who was still inspecting our works up until the last moment.

"We'll take care of the horses, sir," Corporal French said, a group of volunteers taking the mounts across the planks and through the gate. Travis and Jameson were waiting for us. So was John. I handed him the pot of beef stew.

"Give this to Mrs. Dickenson. Share it with the families in the church," I said.

"Yes, sir. Smells real good," John said.

"Have a taste for yourself, Mr. Armstrong," I suggested.

"Just a little, sir. Just a little," John agreed, carrying the precious gift away.

"Get any terms?" Jameson asked.

"Nothing we can accept," Crockett answered. "Better get ready, they'll be coming tomorrow. Day after at the latest."

"Sooner, I think. This dinner. The explanations. I think Santa Anna wanted to lull us into believing his strategy is still evolving. But it isn't. He's already decided to attack," I said.

"What should we do?" Dickenson asked.

"Make sure the men are getting their sleep now. We'll wake everyone up at four o'clock. Keep the powder dry from this mist," I ordered. "Crockett, Travis, Carey, officer's call. We need to talk. Bobby, Jimmy, I want you in on this, too."

The fort was eerily quiet, almost like a ghost town. Most of the men had already turned in, if nothing else, to escape the bitter cold. Only half a dozen guards manned the walls, and even they were less than alert. Though Santa Anna might have risked a midnight attack, I don't think it would have been successful in such weather.

"Finally finished the new trench," Jameson said, sounding tired as he walked at my side. "Set the stakes as best we could."

"Repositioned the artillery, too, but I still think our perimeter is weak," Carey added.

Carey was right, our perimeter was weaker than before, but the walls couldn't be held in any case. I didn't bother to argue.

French ran up as we approached the long barracks.

"How fares the command?" I asked.

"Tucked in, sir, except for Omling and Rudden. They have the watch," French said, curious about our mission. "Sir, is there going to be a battle?"

"A big one, Henry. Glory for everybody," I said, slapping him on the back. "Get some sleep. I want you here at three o'clock, ready and eager. Bobby, check on the men."

Hughes and French backtracked toward the low barracks where my men were bivouacked. The rest of us proceeded to the long barracks roof, the best observation post on our side of the river. A few chairs and a table had been dragged up over the past few days. There was a 2-pounder stationed at the end of the roof overlooking the north plain, but only one sentry on duty. The gun crew was two floors down, asleep. An oil lamp lit the narrow staircase. At the end of the roof near the cannon, a brazier glowed with a few red coals. A small source of warmth for the beleaguered night watch.

I walked to the end of the roof and studied the dark fields through my binoculars. There were a few campfires near the enemy's north battery. To my right, I saw the Mexicans had reestablished a battery on Powder House Hill. The river to the left was completely dark. Torches and lanterns burned in the town. Too many torches, as if they wanted us to believe the entire army were loitering about in the plaza.

"I can't see them, but I know they're out there," I said, sounding frustrated.

"How can you be sure?" Travis asked.

"Because that's what I would be doing. Getting ready to strike before dawn. That's why the artillery is quiet. Santa Anna wants everyone in this fort asleep when he launches the assault."

Hughes and French returned, along with Bonham, Brister and Captain Baugh. Spotted Eagle and Slow arrived last, keeping to the fringe of the meeting. I paced at the edge of the roof, nervous. I'd had the same feeling of foreboding the night before the Little Big Horn, which was not good for my morale.

"Gentlemen, I think holding this position will require some grit," I explained, trying not to be too grim. "When we're taking our stations in the morning, tell the men how important it is to obey orders. There can be no mistakes. Militia can run or fight, or do whatever they get into their fool heads. This is why militia often loses, and why professionals don't want to fight beside them. Soldiers stand together, brother helping brother. Brother defending brother. Brother dying for his brothers. This is what makes an army strong. This is the key to victory."

I pointed to the dark, shapeless mass of open ground north and east of the fort. We could see no movement, but occasionally, there was noise. A man stumbling. A clink of equipment. The creak of a cannon wheel.

"Santa Anna believes this position is vulnerable, and I said nothing to dissuade him," I continued. "We have added a gun to the lunette. He's thinks we've added a gun to the chapel. Crockett's wooden palisade looks weak enough to crawl over. That is why he won't attack from the south, but he may feint there to draw us off. When Colonel Morales was in our custody, did he say anything?"

"Yeah, come to think of it," Baugh said. "He claimed he could walk over our south wall like they was on parade. Made me want to add twenty extra men to Crockett's platoon."

"Very good. Then it will be Morales who leads the feint, probably the first to attack," I speculated, for such a tactic is not hard to fathom. "Once we've been distracted on the south flank, the main attack will begin. They'll come out of the dark in three divisions. Northwest against the corner. North against the center battery. Northeast against the cattle pen. Cos will lead one division to make up for the family disgrace. Romero will lead another. I could see the eagerness in his eyes. I don't know who will lead the third, but it doesn't matter. They'll eventually bunch up under the wall where our artillery is ineffective, and then pour over using superior numbers."

"We can hold that wall. Hold it all day long," Travis said, feeling insulted. Now I knew for sure how the Alamo fell.

"It will be your job to try," I said. "You and Bonham. But when you hear the bugle sounding recall, spike the guns and withdraw across the compound at a run. Don't stop to fight. Don't even look back, just run. But you've got to spike the cannon first. If the Mexicans seize your artillery, they'll turn the guns around to use against us. We won't win against those odds."

"Yes, sir," Bonham said, a smart young man.

Travis sulked a bit, but nodded.

"Crockett, your job is simple. Don't let Morales over the palisade. Jameson, I want you in the lunette. The men must stay focused on our south flank, regardless of what they hear behind them. They'll be scared and tempted to run, but if they do, our position will collapse. We are all in this together, every man doing his part."

"Yes, General. If anyone tries to run, I'll shoot them," Jameson promised.

"Now you've got the spirit," I said, grinning.

"Baugh, I'll need you in the church so Carey and Dickenson can command our artillery in the courtyard. Can your New Orleans Grays hold the long barracks?" I asked.

"The only openings in that building are the musket ports, and there'll be a gun in everyone," Baugh said. I thought him an unimaginative officer, yet capable of inspiring the men with his good humor.

"Jimmy, pick the ten best shots in our command and station them up here," I said. "In any attacking force, there are always a few officers and sergeants that keep the others going even when the situation looks bad. Your job is to target those leaders."

"I get to shoot the officers?" Butler said, bright-eyed.

Jimmy turned to look at Hughes, knowing Bobby would envy his assignment.

"Yes, shoot the officers," I agreed. "Take a bugler with you. If I can't issue the recall from the courtyard, you'll need to give the order."

"Mad at me, General? Not letting me shoot any officers?" Hughes asked.

"You'll be with me, Bobby. I need someone fearless at my side. Have I picked the wrong man?"

"No, sir. Not wrong at all," Hughes said, puffing up his chest.

"Does everyone understand their assignments?" I said.

"General, what do you think our chances are?" Dickenson asked.

I could tell Dickenson was thinking of his wife and child. Libbie had joined me during the Civil War, sometimes closer to the fighting than I wished. And she was my loyal companion on the Great Plains. I could sympathize with Dickenson. It also made me feel guilty that I had taken Libbie for granted so many times.

"Almaron, I won't lie. It's going to be tough," I answered, looking at my officers with a sturdy defiance. "We're outnumbered ten or fifteen to one. These walls lack a solid defensive posture. We're not flush with ammunition. But we've got advantages. Our enemy is overconfident. Our Springfield rifles are worth ten muskets. My men are well-trained. And this garrison knows that defeat means death. If everyone remembers his duty, stays loyal to the man fighting beside him, I think we'll prevail."

"Thank you, sir. Thank you for coming to our aid when so many others didn't," Jameson said, shaking my hand.

The other Alamo officers followed his lead, offering a handshake before going downstairs. Soon only Crockett and Travis were left.

"General Custer, I can't agree with your politics," Travis said. "I'm not happy you've stolen the command that was rightfully mine, and after this is over, we'll have issues. But I commend you as a fine soldier."

Travis reached to shake my hand. I accepted, hiding my reservations. What I suspected of the coming battle made me feel like a hypocrite.

Travis and Crockett followed the other Alamo officers down the steep steps. Butler and Hughes were gone, too, leaving me alone with Slow. I sat down on a barrel near the edge of the roof, wondering where the enemy army was forming. What strength? Was my theory of their attack correct? If I was wrong, we were all in big trouble.

I took out my pocket watch, found the key, and slowly wound the spring. It was almost nine o'clock. I remembered how Judge Bacon often toyed with the watch while talking, as he had when I asked for Libbie's hand in marriage. The Judge had died two years later. Now he wouldn't die for another thirty years. The watch I was holding wouldn't even be invented until 1857.

"You worry greatly," Slow said. "Were you dishonest with the white soldiers?"

"Less than truthful," I replied. "I had hoped to delay Santa Anna's attack for a few days. Give time for Tom to encroach on their flank. But it looks like my plan didn't work. If the Mexicans throw their whole force at us in the morning, I don't think we'll hold."

"Mr. Kellogg said this Alamo fought bravely. He said your people remembered it for many years. Is this not the glory you seek?"

"I'd rather not get everyone killed if I can help it. When the shooting starts, I want you to find Mrs. Dickenson. Stay with her until the battle is over."

"My place is at your side."

"You're a brave lad. I sense someday you'll be a great leader. It's not your place to die at my side."

"Death cannot be so certain."

"There was a time I didn't think so. I thought myself above such a fate, trusting in my luck. But my luck failed me at the Little Big Horn. Now I fear it might fail again."

I turned back to the open prairie, gazing at the darkness. How could so peaceful a scene be filled with death?

"We will bleed the enemy," I said, sighing deeply. "Bleed him so bad that Tom and Keogh will sweep up what's left. There will be a free Texas, but I won't be here to see it."

"The Great Spirit has not brought you this far for an early death. There is a plan."

"And what plan would this be? What is its purpose?"

"I do not know the answer," Slow admitted.

"Youngster, I'm afraid that's not much help," I said, warming my hands at the brazier before going downstairs.

I left Slow on the roof staring at the stars, apparently praying to his Great Spirit. Strangely, I heard birds chirping.

"Going to get some sleep?" Crockett asked as I entered the quadrangle before the church.

The small area had been transformed into a self-sufficient fort. One sentry stood near the palisade, everyone else having bunked down as ordered. I heard snoring from the long barracks.

"You've done good work here, David. Unless the enemy is able to seize our artillery, it will be a hard position to take."

"That's why you keep stressin' the 'portance of spikin' them cannon. We all got that."

"Nothing is worse than getting whipped with your own guns."

"This civil war you fought, sounds awful bad," Crockett said.

"Any sacrifice will be worthwhile if we can head it off."

"You know, if the people of this time knew what was coming, if they knew where this national division is taking us, maybe they'd think different on it," Crockett suggested.

"I wish that was so, but I doubt it. I'm no expert on history, but I know a lot of politicians. Once they dig in their heels, they'll take us straight to hell regardless of the consequences."

"Guess I'm not one to disagree. Told many a tall tale to get elected to congress. Only lost because I decided to tell the truth."

"If we make it out of this, what are your plans? Sell your land grant and head back to Tennessee?"

"That was my first thought. Only came out here to rebuild my fortune. Never did have much luck with money."

"I'm afraid my brother won't make it back in time to help," I whispered, not wanting the men to hear my doubts. "But a few might be able to hold out here in the church for an extra day. By then Tom will take what's left of Santa Anna's army to task. He's a bright young man, but to make Texas what it needs to be, he'll need your help."

"George, what are ya tryin' to say?" Crockett asked.

"Not really sure. Just thinking out loud."

"Just think about how we're gonna win this fight," he said, slapping me on the back. "When you're out huntin', and its dark, and you're startin' to feel alone, it don't help to wonder if the bear's smarter than you."

"Santa Anna isn't smarter than me. He just has more bears."

"Fer the last two weeks, I been a worrying that I'd die in this dry old rat trap. After ridin' out to find Fannin, I even wondered if I should keep on goin' until the Mississippi was at my back. I ain't so worried now. Live or die, I'm in good company. Wouldn't trade my place for nothing in this world, not even the White House."

"There were some who said my campaign against the Sioux was an attempt to win the Democratic nomination for president."

"Was it?"

"Hell, David, I'm only thirty-six years old. The presidency is for old men."

"Not *that* old," Crockett laughed, having aspired to the golden crown when he was forty-seven.

"I've never wanted political office. Too much politicking. Too much back-stabbing. The army has enough of that already. I just want to lead a force of good men and keep the peace. I like to read. I love the theatre. There was a time I thought to make a career as a writer. I could even teach at a military college, despite my academic record. Not everything young men need to know is found in books."

"I wrote a book. Well, wrote one with help from a friend. Wrote it about myself, and made some money, too. Maybe one day we can write a book together."

"I'd like that. I'd like that a lot. Custer and Crockett, written by themselves."

The Alamo was quiet as a tomb. As I thought, the Mexican artillery had gone silent to lull the defenders into a deep sleep. An effective tactic against amateurs. The moon had risen in the east, just two days past full. I guessed sunrise about 6:30. Time to get some rest, for I needed to be up in five hours.

"Good night, David. Sleep while you can. Tomorrow will be a long day," I said, shaking the old bear hunter's hand.

"You need it more than me," Crockett said with a grin.

I crawled over the makeshift barrier between the long barracks and the low barracks, going to my quarters near the room where Bowie's body lay hidden under a pile of blankets. A few suspected the famous knife fighter had made his last battle, but we all had other things to worry about.

Falling asleep wasn't a problem. I was bone tired and ready to close my eyes. Tomorrow would be March 6th, 1836. A Sunday. If Santa Anna decided to attack, it would be a bloody day. The bloodiest I had seen since Cedar Creek. As a youngster, I had eagerly sought battle against the enemy. Sought glory at any cost. Looked forward to reading my name in the newspapers, and losing myself in the passion of my Libbie's seductive embrace. Always the dashing young cavalier whose luck never failed. Now I only felt weariness. I was getting old.

I remained on the stone building after Custer left, realizing for the first time that he expected to lose his great battle. And in losing, the future of my people would be lost with him. This could not be why Wakan Tanka had reversed the course of history. But the enemy was vast, as large as a buffalo herd. The white general needed help. What help could I provide? What help would the Great Spirit allow? I sat near the fire of red coals and began to chant. The great knife I had found in the room of the dead Bowie lay at my side, a long blade much revered by the white-eyes. I cut a small flake of flesh from my arm, dropping it into the fire. And then another. The stars glowed brighter. The moon smiled. More strips of flesh were offered to the flames, but this was not the vision quest I had performed after the Rosebud battle, where a hundred pieces of my body had been given in sacrifice. That vision had revealed the white soldiers falling into our camp. A vision that presaged both victory and disaster. I needed no more darkness. I was seeking light. A solution to my people's woes. I prayed. And I saw blood.

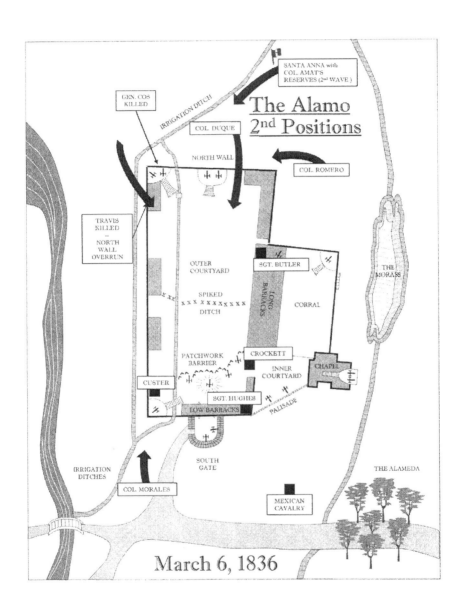

The Alamo
2nd Positions

SANTA ANNA with COL. AMAT'S RESERVES (2nd WAVE)

GEN. COS KILLED

IRRIGATION DITCH

COL. DUQUE

NORTH WALL

COL. ROMERO

TRAVIS KILLED -- NORTH WALL OVERRUN

OUTER COURTYARD

SGT. BUTLER

THE MORASS

SPIKED DITCH

LONG BARRACKS

CORRAL

CROCKETT

PATCHWORK BARRIER

INNER COURTYARD

CHAPEL

CUSTER

SGT. HUGHES

LOW BARRACKS

PALISADE

SOUTH GATE

IRRIGATION DITCHES

COL. MORALES

MEXICAN CAVALRY

THE ALAMEDA

March 6, 1836

CHAPTER THIRTEEN

BY DAWN'S EARLY LIGHT

I woke up from a strange dream. I was standing on a weed-covered hillside above the Little Big Horn, but there were no hordes of hostile Indians. A small village lay in the valley below, mostly hunting lodges, and all was peaceful. Women were curing buffalo hides, children were playing in the cold rushing river, and dogs guarded a herd of horses grazing in the tall green grasses. A red, white and green flag flew from one of the teepees.

My hunting rifle lay on a blanket at my feet. Near a picnic basket. The day was warm, cloudless. Late spring. I was not wearing an army uniform, but a checkered cotton shirt and buckskin breeches. And moccasins. Had I become an Indian?

I plucked at a stringy curl, finding a strand of thin gray hair. Not helpful. Then I remembered my watch, finding it where it should always be, in my breast pocket. The watch I found was not my father-in-law's, but something more modern, and engraved, *to Autie, with love, from I.* Glancing at the silver facing, I saw a reflection. Distorted, but clear enough to see an old white man wearing spectacles. I took the spectacles off, discovering myself nearsighted, and studied my wrinkled hands.

I was not an Indian. Someone waved from the river, a slender man with long black hair. It looked like Slow, only decades older. Others were coming from the village, gesturing. They wanted me to come down the hill and join them. Smoke was rising from the campfires. I smelled trout. Was I late for supper? I began to stand, but suddenly my knees grew weak. There was pain in my left arm. A shortness of breath. I fell back into the grass, one hand on my heart, the other on my rifle. A beautiful blue sky stretched from horizon to horizon.

It was morning, dark and cold. I had slept fully clothed except for my boots, which I pulled on with a grunt. I strapped on the Spanish steel saber, then my leather holster with the two Bulldogs. Fifty rounds of ammunition were tucked in my pockets for quick retrieval. I picked up Tom's Winchester and checked to be sure there was a shell in the chamber. Then I tied the red silk scarf around my neck, careful not to aggravate the deeply bruised wound, and tugged on my gray wide-brimmed campaign hat. If this was to be George Armstrong Custer's last fight, I'd go out the way I'd lived.

"Good morning, General," Corporal French said, waiting outside my door.

"Get some sleep?" I asked.

"A little. Hard to get too much," he explained.

"We'll sleep good tonight, one way or the other," I said with a grin.

"Yes, sir," French said, almost returning the smile.

John appeared. It looked like he hadn't slept at all. He still carried the flintlock pistol in his belt, but I considered him a noncombatant.

"Doctor Pollard and Mrs. Dickenson will need help in the church. I'd like you to stay there until the fighting's done," I said.

"Rather help you, sir," John protested.

"Not recruiting Buffalo soldiers today," I said.

"Not recruitin' who, sir?"

"An all-Negro cavalry regiment. The 10th. Maybe someday we'll make our own 10th regiment, but not now. I need you helping Mrs. Dickenson."

John reluctantly obeyed, walking slowly toward the decrepit old church while French and I went around the compound, quietly waking the garrison while reminding everyone to stay silent. I found Crockett first and roused his Tennessee boys, most of whom were not even from Tennessee. So much for the myth.

Hughes and Butler had already stirred, putting our men in position. Ten would go with Butler to the roof of the long barracks, eight more on the roof of the low barracks, and the rest would support either me or Crockett inside the south wall. Our internal defense line had been established from the platform holding the 18-pounder at the southwest corner to Crockett's position before the church. Spotted Eagle and Slow appeared out the darkness. The teenager was ready for a good fight, holding a Colt pistol. A steel hatchet was tucked in his belt. He'd painted his face with red and black streaks. He was also wearing a blue cavalry blouse, the one that had belonged to the late Private Milton of F Company.

Slow seemed a bit withdrawn, his eyes red and arms wrapped in thick fur. He did not look at me with his usual curiosity.

"Light the candles, my friend," I ordered, handing a torch to Spotted Eagle.

Some people say Indians can see in the dark. I don't believe it. Growing up in Monroe, nearly everyone was white, but the more I'd seen of different types of people, the more it seemed they were all essentially the same. Except for the defects of their character. Nevertheless, Spotted Eagle was half my age and likely to see better in the dark than I, so he had been given a special mission.

Two paths led from the north wall to our defensive line near the low barracks. Ditches and stake barriers had been placed across the compound to slow an enemy charge, but the obstacles would also hamper the retreat of Travis and his men. To make the withdrawal safer, small oil pots had been placed to mark the planks over the ditches. Once the retreat was complete, the planks would be pulled back and the pots kicked over. At least, that was the plan. Amid the smoke and chaos of battle, who could say what would happen?

Spotted Eagle took the torch and began lighting the pots. I followed, finding Travis in a gutted bungalow on the west wall close to his post. He was already awake but not yet armed.

"What time is it?" he asked.

"A little before four," I said, checking my watch.

Travis's slave was sleeping on a pallet in the corner. As slavery goes, Joe's could be worse. He dressed warmly, ate what Travis ate, and slept where Travis slept. But he was not free to go his own way. There was a time in my life when I wouldn't have cared. My father had told me that slavery was the South's problem, but I'd come to believe my father had been wrong about that.

"Morning, Joe. Mrs. Dickenson will be making breakfast in a few minutes," I said.

Joe looked to Travis, who agreed with a nod. I could tell Travis would prefer to have Joe at his beck and call, but he was not in command. Joe's ownership was one of the many issues to be decided after the battle. If we were fortunate enough to live so long.

"Thank you, sir. Can I fetch you some, Mr. William?" Joe asked.

"Wish we still had some coffee left," Travis said, sending Joe away with a wave of his hand. He was still sleepy, the Alabama drawl a bit more pronounced.

"Remember to spike the guns," I said.

"We won't need to. They'll never get over the wall," Travis replied.

"I need your word."

"We have spikes and mallets next to each gun. If I can't hold, we'll ram the touchholes before withdrawing."

"That's good enough for me," I said, offering to shake hands.

Travis appeared surprised, then accepted the gesture. He seemed the type of a man who would make a good friend or a determined foe.

We walked up the dirt ramp to the bastion on the northwest corner. The gun crew was yet to arrive, but the powder was safely stored under a heavy tarp, protected from the damp weather.

With dawn still two hours away, there was no glimmer of light from the east. If the moon was still up, it was hidden behind the clouds. The platform held two 6-pounders. Solid shot and canister loads were piled along the ledges. Fifteen yards to our right, another platform held two more 6-pounders. Between us, the wall was battered so badly that only a few adobe bricks and bent timbers were holding it together. Jameson had wanted to shore the wall up but I told him not to bother. We were joined a few minutes later.

"Morning, boys," I whispered, recognizing Bonham and a few others in the dim light. I pointed back across the compound where a dozen small trail markers were burning. "Remember, when you hear the bugle, come running."

"Won't need your bugle, sir, but thank you all the same," Bonham said, wrapped in a heavy fur coat and drinking some sort of warm porridge from a clay mug.

There was no point in arguing.

"Give 'em hell, boys," I said, going back down into the compound.

Hughes and Spotted Eagle were waiting for me, and the blond-haired youngster, Jimmy Allen, who I was using as a messenger.

"Everyone at their posts, sir. Some of the powder got a little damp," Hughes reported.

"Low grain, it will still fire," I said hopefully. "Jimmy, tell Crockett to watch out. They might be on us any time now. Spotted Eagle, make sure Slow stays with Mrs. Dickenson. He worries me. Bobby, check on the 18-pounder. It's the key to our position."

They dashed off, no questions and no debate. There was no more time for that. I followed the trail of firepots, not wanting to start the battle in a ditch impaled on a wooden stake. The long barracks lay on my left, a strong position if properly supported. The west wall was to the right, so weak it amazed me that anyone thought it could be held. The wall was barely nine feet high, had no parapets and no bastions. Only a day before, there had been two large holes cut in the adobe for cannon ports that I immediately ordered sealed up. Amateur engineers. Untrained militia. Undisciplined frontiersmen. And lawyers for officers. My God, what had I gotten into?

No, it wasn't the men. They were better than could be expected, under the circumstances. It was the waiting. My whole career had been spent as a cavalry officer. Sure, there was endless paperwork, tedious ceremonies, and the dreary boredom of life on a frontier post, but when it came time to fight, I was accustomed to probing the enemy, looking for an opening, and launching an attack. Through hard experience, I had learned that taking the offense was the surest path to victory. More often than not, the only path.

Now I was forced to wait behind these walls, on the defense, at the mercy of the enemy's next move. Just like Major Anderson at Fort Sumter. And John Pemberton, who lost his entire command at Vicksburg. In fact, I could not think of a single instance in recent history where the besieged had emerged victorious. Why hadn't I thought of that sooner?

I walked quickly about the compound inspecting the preparations, knowing it was too late for any significant changes. Crockett caught up to me near the south gate.

"Calm down, George. You're gonna make the men nervous," he said.

"Why don't they attack?" I said, looking at my watch. "It's almost five-thirty. What are they waiting for?"

"Maybe Santa Anna changed his mind?"

"That would be rich, wouldn't it? The goddamned son of a bitch."

"Now, now, remember what you always say about swearing," Crockett chastised. And he was right.

Then a shot was fired from the south side.

"To your post, sir. And good luck," I said.

Crockett needed no extra encouragement, rushing to his position at the palisade.

Another shot, then quiet. It wasn't a battle yet. I limped in the opposite direction, climbing the ramp to the southwest gun mount, one hand braced on the wall, the other on the 18-pounder. There was definitely movement out in the dark. A rustling of bushes. Shuffling.

"Jameson. Jameson?" I called down into the lunette.

"Yes, general?" he answered.

"Open fire."

The 4-pounder barked from its bunker, lighting up the prairie with the blast. I saw hundreds of Mexican soldiers, and far closer than any of us would have imagined. A few went down, but most were coming from the east beyond the gun's best angle. They were in full uniform, with tall shako hats and crossed white straps over dark blue tunics. A few carried ladders, though most were armed with their Brown Bess muskets. For the barest moment, I thought I saw Colonel Morales standing near a colorful banner, waving his troops forward.

"*Viva Santa Anna! Viva Mexico!*" the soldiers yelled, charging through the twisted monkey bushes toward the palisade.

The lunette's 6-pounder fired, somewhat ineffectively, but the shearing red light showed scores of cavalry along the south road. They could not attack the fort on horseback; their mission was to cut down any of the Alamo defenders who might seek safety in flight. Hopefully my men realized there could be no such safety.

"Give it to 'em, boys!" Crockett ordered, standing at the six-foot high wooden barricade with his 1873 Springfield. He put a foot up on the firing step, poked the rifle over, and shot the closest enemy, probably not more than twenty yards away. The man was thrown backward with such force that he knocked two of his fellows down, for at such close range, the Springfield has a devastating impact.

Eighteen rifles quickly fired in unison, a wave of enemy soldiers falling. Crockett ejected a spent shell, slid another bullet into the breach, and fired again. He had been practicing. Each of his men had two more muskets primed and ready, picking them up and taking aim. Effective, in the short term, but they could not maintain such a pace once they needed to reload. A difficult thing to do while someone is trying to run you through with a bayonet.

The palisade's cannon fired again, raking the front ranks of the Mexicans trying to cross the ditch. Crockett's men fired a second time, and then a third, each volley taking a toll. The flashes were bright enough to see there were only a few hundred Mexicans at our front, not the thousands Santa Anna might have sent.

Faced with such ferocious resistance, the Mexicans began to draw back, scrambling away from the ditch to firmer ground. Some stopped to return fire and I saw one of Crockett's men get hit, grabbing his head as he toppled backward. Then musket balls struck the top of the palisade, forcing many to duck the splinters. Blood was dripping from a frontiersman's eye, but he kept fighting.

Unable to reach the palisade, the enemy shifted to their left, moving parallel to the low barracks while shooting at the men in the lunette. A cannon stationed there fired canister shot, cutting down those who had lingered too close, but moans and cries rose from the lunette, indicating some of the men had been struck by musket fire. I would need to reinforce the gun crews if they took too many casualties.

My men on the roof of the low barracks had an advantage, for the frontiersmen had trouble reloading without getting up. And when they did, they were vulnerable to enemy fire. My men could reload their breech loading rifles while lying down. But in the dark, good targets were elusive. I was glad to see they weren't wasting ammunition on phantoms.

Suddenly rockets arched overhead with red and yellow tails lighting up the landscape. Despite deep shadows, the enemy could be seen more easily. And they could see us. Heavy fire erupted across the entire front as the Mexicans continued to move west, finding shelter in the burned adobes south of the main gate.

One of my men fell from the low barracks, landing hard in the courtyard. And then the gunner standing beside me was hit, collapsing on the platform holding his left arm, his eyes squinting in pain. I hoped the ball had not cut an artery, but a moment later it didn't matter. A second shot struck him through the forehead and he fell back against the gun mount.

"Dickenson, fire the gun," I ordered.

Dickenson had the 18-pounder turned, needing all six of the gun crew. He touched the charge and the cannon roared, tearing a gaping hole through the nearest hovel. The sound was so loud it blotted out the battle, the recoil so fierce we all needed to jump out of the way. Had the wheels not been secured with rope, the cannon may well have leapt entirely off the platform.

"Keep it up. Don't give them a chance to dig in," I said, seeing the enemy taking aim at us from their sheltered positions only fifty yards away. An effective range for a Brown Bess.

"Yes, sir. Yes, sir. Esparza, solid shot," Dickenson ordered.

He turned to pick up a powder charge, then suddenly stumbled to the platform, hit through the shoulder. He groaned, sat up, and handed the powder charge to Esparza. The crew reloaded the cannon and fired again, ripping through two of the broken down houses. One caught fire, a beacon to see the enemy by. Soldiers were scrambling in every direction.

"Tear them up!" I shouted, kneeling on the wall with the Winchester.

It was a target-rich landscape, much like a slowly moving buffalo herd. I fired eight rounds in rapid succession, probably hitting a few of them. Springfields and muskets followed, the fusillade so great the enemy was forced back to the edge of the darkness, only the cries of the wounded marking their trail.

"That'll teach 'em," Hughes said, standing at my side.

"They'll reform," I replied.

Hardly a moment later, a ragged but deadly storm of fire from the Brown Bess muskets killed and wounded several men on the walls. We hunkered down, matching shot for shot only because of our superior weapons. I could hear the Mexican officers issuing orders, trying to keep their formations together. The cries of the injured and dying rose from the darkness. The ground was too dark to see them.

The heaviest fire began to strike around the 18-pounder, the most obvious source of the enemy's distress. Esparza had the gun fired two more times before being forced to find shelter. Dickenson was wounded, two others were dead. Even I had stepped down from the wall, fearing an early death. If the lunette could not keep up a flanking fire, the corner of the fort might be stormed.

"Jameson!" I shouted.

"Yes, sir?" Jameson called back.

"To the right! The right!" I said, pointing.

A 6-pounder was fired, striking the dark areas between my bastion and the bridge. The powerful blast was quickly followed by the 4-pounder, causing the remaining adobe shacks to shatter. I suspect more men were wounded by deadly fragments than the cannon shots. I opened fire with the Winchester again, Hughes with the Henry, and the enemy was finally forced back even further. They were still within the effective range of our guns, but we were beyond the range of theirs.

With the pressure on the palisade relieved, Crockett and some of his men reinforced the low barracks. My men on the roof adapted to the murky warfare, selecting their best targets. The momentum of the attack had been halted, the Mexican officers unable to push their men forward. We heard a great deal of cursing, browbeating, and even a few threats, but marching frightened soldiers over the bodies of their slaughtered comrades is no easy task.

At that moment, had I mounted a cavalry attack, I'd have chased Colonel Morales all the way back to Mexico.

"Dickenson?" I asked.

"Alive, sir," he said, sitting with his back against the parapet.

"Gregorio, reload the gun. Canister shot," I ordered, for the next time I expected the enemy to get much closer.

Just as our portion of the fort grew calm, shooting erupted three hundred yards away at the opposite end of the compound. It was as I expected, but still a surprise. The attack on the palisade had been a diversion, just as Santa Anna intended, though his men had paid dearly for it. The cannon on the north wall opened fire, but it was too dark for me to determine the extent of the danger. Another gun fired, the cannon overlooking the corral at the east side of the long barracks, and then the gun at the back of the church. It sounded like the entire north and east sides of the fort were under sudden assault.

"Steady, men. This is our station," I said, limping down the ramp toward the redoubt. My neck hurt from all the physical activity. I tied the silk scarf a little tighter, hoping to relieve the pain.

"General, we can whip them," Dickenson protested, though his arm dripped blood and he could barely stand. Half the men were ready to charge across the compound to help the north wall.

"Our instinct is to rush to the new scene of battle. That is just what the dictator wants," I answered, reluctantly deciding militia need their strategies explained. "Don't worry, fellows. There's plenty of fighting coming our way."

"Maybe this one can go to the wall?" Spotted Eagle said, hatchet in hand. Driving the first wave back had denied him a scalp.

"Patience, my friend," I urged.

All four cannon on the north wall were engaged now, switching from shot to canister. We heard shouts of encouragement from the defenders, and once I even heard Travis. I briefly wondered if Travis had been right. Could the position be held?

More cannon fired, but these were not the Alamo's guns. Mexican artillery had been drawn forward, trying to blow a hole through the northeast corner of the fort. Plumes of dust rose from the weakened adobe bricks, some of the supporting timbers collapsing.

Tremendous commotion was heard as the enemy surged against the wall, and suddenly the defenders were struggling to keep the attackers off their bastion. Though I could not see them, I imagined the Mexicans gathered in strength, mounting their scaling ladders. Climbing up, being knocked down, and then climbing again. An unstoppable wave. More rockets streaked across the pre-dawn sky.

I looked up to my right. Butler and his hand-picked sharpshooters were maintaining a heavy fire, benefiting from higher ground and closer range, but it was impossible to see how effective their efforts were. Much of the fighting was a jumble of shadow and confusion.

"General, Captain Baugh's compliments," a messenger reported, a seventeen-year-old named Espalier who had been a favorite of Bowie. "Captain says the Mexicans are withdrawing to the north. His gun can't do no more."

"Thank you, Carlos. My compliments to Captain Baugh. Have him leave a guard in the church and send the rest of his men to support the corral," I instructed.

"Not the north wall, sir?" the youngster asked.

"Follow orders," I insisted.

Espalier saluted and ran back. The only attacking force east of the Alamo now was on horseback, and they weren't likely to make a twelve-foot leap into the church.

"What do you think, George?" Crockett asked.

With the enemy having withdrawn on his flank, the Tennesseans were getting a short respite. I thought Crockett looked tired, and scared. And excited. His face was smudged with gunpowder.

"There are two thousand soldiers trying to break through over there. Nothing we can do will stop them," I said, pointing at the growing breach to the right of the center bastion.

Another shell hit the wall dead center, the upper portion collapsing into the courtyard. In a few more minutes, the Mexicans would not need ladders to enter the fort—they could just charge over the rubble.

The last cannon on the northern bastions went quiet. There were no longer any encouraging shouts, only the grunts of desperate men as the enemy tried to storm the shattered wall. The hand-to-hand fighting would be intense now. No more time to reload the muskets. No way to use the artillery. Fifty men using knives and bayonets were trying to stave off thousands.

Another rocket revealed several Mexicans crawling on a workshop near the northwest corner, standing for a moment to look down into the courtyard. They didn't know the rooms along the west wall had been stripped of ceilings supports. Seconds later, the roof suddenly caved in. The surprised soldiers would find little but sharpened stakes to land on. Straw on the floors would allow Travis's men to burn the huts as they retreated.

"French, sound recall," I said, fearing even a few more seconds would be too late.

French blew the bugle, loud even in battle. Another bugle took up the call from the roof of the long barracks. It was Charlie Clark, one of the New Orleans Grays. He'd been studying with French.

"Covering fire!" I ordered. "Crockett, Carey, to your posts! Prime your guns, boys!"

The cannon crews pulled back the tarps keeping their power dry, lighting the matches. The hundred men assigned to this position knelt between the guns in a long line, hay bales and debris for cover. My soldiers on the low barracks turned their attention inward, relying on Jameson in the lunette to guard our rear.

The ghostly trail leading across the compound quickly filled with retreating men. They ran down the ramps from the northern bastions. Some jumped from the parapets. One slowed to torch the workshops, but the rest did not look back, arms waving as they tried to steal a march on the Mexicans. I did not see them spike the guns as ordered. They might have, I just couldn't tell. Fighting continued at the northwest bastion, and soon it became evident the defenders there had been cut off. It was the place I last saw Travis.

"Give 'em a hand, boys," Crockett said, shooting a Mexican off the wall. A fine shot, given the foggy visibility.

Hughes knelt and fired his Henry, hitting another. The first dozen attackers who climbed the north wall fell back just as quickly, taking fire from several directions. But more kept coming.

An explosion rocked the battered breach, opening an eight foot gap of crumbling rubble. Ten, fifteen, and then thirty Mexican soldiers charged though, bayonets fixed on their muskets. Santa Anna's attack force had been attempting to get a foothold in the courtyard, and now they had one.

"Rifles only!" I shouted, for our cannon would kill most our fellows fleeing for safety.

The smoke of battle was growing thick, obscuring the enemy. Only twenty or so of our men were making it across the planks, the rest missing and probably dead. One bringing up the rear was kicking over the firepots. A brave man. Crockett noticed and took aim at the remaining pots, shooting them over.

"The brown-eyes will cross the bridges," Spotted Eagle said, pointing with his hatchet.

He was right; the only man who tried pulling up a plank was shot for his trouble. I didn't think the planks would prove very helpful to the enemy. The boards were narrow and the compound dark.

That didn't matter to Spotted Eagle, who suddenly jumped from our line, running the hundred feet to the closet plank, and throwing it aside. When the last of the north wall defenders crossed the second plank, Spotted Eagle pushed that one over, too. And then he went down, shot in the upper body. I saw him crawl for a moment before tumbling into the ditch. None of the retreating men saw him fall, or if they did, chose not go back and help.

Within seconds, the dozen survivors reached the safety of our line, jumping over the bales with relief. I considered going after the young Indian, for I was quite fond of him, but the Mexicans were now approaching in strength. It would have been a futile gesture.

"Gun number one, fire!" I ordered.

When Captain Carey repeated the order, the cannon posted near the corner of the long barracks burst with red flame, raking the Alamo compound with canister shot. The black smoke swelled across our line, making it impossible to see anything more than bits of the action.

"Gun number two, fire!" Crockett ordered.

More black smoke. I tried getting up on the redoubt to see, but it was like being lost in a thick cloud. I heard Hughes order gun number three fired, Esparza number four. Dickenson ordered the redoubt guns fired. By the time the seventh gun fired at the left end of our line, the first gun had been reloaded.

"Gun number one, fire!" Captain Baugh yelled, having chosen to take his stand in the courtyard.

Many of my officers were yelling, aware the guns needed to be fired in succession, one following the other, to keep the enemy off-balance. Between the cannon, squads of riflemen were laying down heavy fire, sometimes finding targets. More often, they were just shooting into the murky darkness.

The courtyard filled with screams and shouts. *"Viva Mexico! Viva Santa Anna! Adelante! Adelante!"*

I could hear them coming, a few emerging here and there from the black fog. They came with bayonets fixed and even a few lances. One carried an ax. Blood was soaked in their blue uniforms, some their own, most from lost comrades. They were cut down by rifle fire before reaching our line, but our ammunition wouldn't last forever.

"Keep them cannon going!" Crockett yelled, shooting an officer waving a sword.

I saw the bear-hunter was frightened but not desperate, keeping his nerve to inspire his men. Maybe some legends are true.

The crews were working as fast as possible, few of them being professionals. Gun number two was firing again, then three and four. We were taking heavy fire in return. A dozen men now lay on the ground, bleeding from severe wounds. Many of the injuries were grievous, for a Brown Bess at close range can be devastating.

A bloody hand grabbed my boot. There was a wounded private curled at my feet, one of Bowie's Tejano youngsters, hardly more than eighteen years old. He'd been hit in the arm, a piece of broken bone showing through his sleeve. Frightened brown eyes stared up at me. I dragged him against the low barracks, whispered a few brief words of comfort, and returned to my post.

With our line fully engaged, I needed to find out what was happening on other parts of the battlefield. Butler would have a good view, but sending a messenger was too dangerous, so I moved left, going up the ramp to the 18-pounder. Firing was now general throughout the fort, but despite the hailstorm of musket balls, I sensed we were giving them a tussle.

From the top of the gun platform, I was finally able to see something of the battle. The enemy was trying to cross the compound through the smoke and darkness. With the north wall open, they no longer pressed the wall to the west, pouring into the breach like an unstoppable waterfall. Hundreds of soldiers had already swarmed through, and another thousand were coming behind them.

Crockett, Dickenson and Carey were shouting at the men, urging on the gunners, keeping the artillery hot. Blinded by the smoke, the Mexicans continued to move forward, like the Persians at Thermopylae, with no room to maneuver on their flanks. And like Leonidas at Thermopylae, I hoped to pile the enemy dead one upon the other, keeping them unaware of the danger until it was too late.

The courtyard was finally lost in smoke, the enemy's movements being anyone's guess. If they could overrun our line, the fight wouldn't last another twenty minutes. I hoped none of the men were thinking of fleeing the fort, for I'd ordered Hughes to shoot the first one who tried.

Suddenly my chest burst in agony. Spinning as I collapsed to the platform, my hands reached out to break the fall. There was a momentary lost of breath, then a dulling of the wits. I crawled behind the 18-pounder, finding my shirt damp with blood. Then I sat up.

"General, are you dead?" French asked, kneeling at my side.

"Not yet," I answered, feeling for the wound.

Custer's Luck again. It hurt like the dickens, but my pocket watch had taken the brunt of the musket ball. Pieces of the shattered crystal had cut into the skin, but it was not a serious injury.

French plucked out a few of the shards before using a handkerchief to sop the blood, handing me what remained of the watch—a bent disk of silver with tiny gears. I remembered Judge Bacon looking at it with impatience the first time I approached him about Libbie. The first time he had said no. It had taken patience to win her father's approval. Now he was dead these eight years, and my life might be measured in minutes.

"You're one lucky son of a bitch, sir," French said. "Sir? Sir?"

I glanced at him, not sure what he wanted. The noise was terrible. For a brief moment, the world seemed to swirl around.

"Sir, we've got to get down from here. Can't hold the wall in this crossfire," French urged.

I saw what he meant. Five men lay dead around the 18-pounder, the rest had retreated down the ramp.

"Let's get out of here," I finally responded, staggering a dozen feet before falling near the bottom of the ramp.

"Sir, are you all right?" Hughes asked, kneeling next to me.

"A little dizzy," I said, gathering my bearings. "We need some rifles on this ramp. If Morales bypasses the lunette and climbs the west corner, there will be no one to stop him. He'll overrun our flank."

"Well, sir, I reckon we had best stop the bastards," French said.

"Henry, you'll make great sergeant someday. Where's Allen?"

"Here, General," young Jimmy said, coming up the ramp on his hands and knees to avoid getting shot. His face was covered in soot, his pants torn at the knees. He carried a flintlock pistol but no powder horn to reload.

"My compliments to Colonel Jameson. Tell him the 18-pounder is out of action. If he cannot protect our flank, he must spike the guns in the lunette and withdraw. Do you understand?"

"Yes, sir," Allen said, scurrying off to deliver the message.

I looked back across the compound. Dozens of Mexicans had taken over the north wall, many shooting at Butler's men on the long barrack's roof. A few ambitious soldiers were turning a cannon around to fire in our direction. Down in the courtyard, three of our cannon had stopped firing. Some had lost gun crews; others had run out of ammunition. I couldn't see what most of the enemy was doing, though they had apparently been held back by the intense resistance.

Then I saw a scene both remarkable and tragic. The workshops along the west wall were fully engulfed, the flames traveling high in the dark sky. The light revealed the long dry irrigation channel that had once brought water into the fort, now filled with hundreds of Mexican soldiers. A few fired their muskets, but most were crouching down, waiting for the chance to advance. Why weren't more firing their guns? Had they attacked the Alamo with so little ammunition that they had already run out? A few officers were attempting to motivate their men, pointing swords at the long barracks. The channel was also filled with pitifully wounded men.

It could not matter. I had stationed gun number six overlooking this trench, knowing the enemy might use it for shelter. Now I acted.

"French, Hughes, Esparza!" I shouted, staggering down to the 8-pounder.

Two men were already there trying to turn the gun for a better angle. They had seen the enemy hiding in the ditch, too.

"We'll aim, you load," I told them.

"Already loaded, sir. Five sacks of buckshot," one said, a captain named Baker. I swear, these Texians had more captains than the Seventh Cavalry had sergeants.

"We've got it, sir," Hughes said, six men coming to help.

They angled the gun so it looked straight down the entire length of the trench. Rifleman kept the Mexicans closest to us at bay, a hot exchange that dropped several on both sides. At the last minute, one of the Mexican officers, a burly major, recognized the danger. I remember staring into his surprised eyes as he stared into mine, for we were only seventy feet apart.

"*Fuera de aquí! Fuera de aquí!*" he shouted, grabbing a soldier by the collar, but it was too late.

"Fire the gun," I calmly said.

When the 8-pounder bucked with the recoil, hundreds of tiny metal bits spewed a long bloody swath all the way to the north wall. When the smoke faded, nearly every man in the ditch lay dead or wounded, their bodies ripped in the most unseemly ways.

"My god, General," Baker said.

"I've seen worse," I replied. "Esparza, reload the gun."

To my alarm, there was suddenly an explosion behind us, a plume of dirt followed by a shower of debris. Bits of wood and mud fell throughout the south side of our position, covering us in dusty fragments. At first I feared the Mexicans had moved artillery up against the gate, but then I realized Jameson had decided to abandon the lunette, blowing up the powder he was unable to carry out. Of the twenty men who held that post, I only saw fourteen coming through the gate. Jameson came last, helping to close the heavy oak doors.

Only the few soldiers I'd stationed on the low barracks roof now protected our rear flank. In the original battle, Morales had climbed the wall, seized the

18-pounder, and turned it around against the long barracks. Had we spiked the gun before withdrawing? I didn't know. Confusion was everywhere.

"Jameson!" I called.

Green hurried over with a slight limp. He was blackened with spent powder, his clothes grimy from sweat and blood.

"I was afraid they'd overrun us, sir," Jameson reported.

"You did the right thing," I said with a nod.

"The north wall? Travis?" he asked.

"Enemy has the wall. Don't know about Travis," I said. "We need to consolidate our position. Pull these guns back into the churchyard. If your wounded can still fight, put them on the palisade, otherwise get them to Doctor Pollard."

"We can still hold, can't we?" Jameson asked, for it seemed we now had more wounded than not.

"Do we have a choice?" I said.

Then I slapped him on the back and smiled. I'd forgotten how exciting a battle can be.

"The 18-pounder. I should spike it," Jameson offered, seeing the abandoned cannon on the corner bastion.

He was right that the gun needed to be disabled. I should have done it myself when I'd had the chance.

"My job. You get going," I ordered, taking Hughes and French with me.

Most of the men were pulling back, ready to make a final stand in the church courtyard. We had several cannon there and flanking fire from the long barracks. A handful from Company F remained near the redoubt, but only my small band now held the left flank, the three of us kneeling around the 18-pounder. I wasn't sure what the enemy was doing, the waves of advancing troops having faded in moans and curses.

Some of the shooting seemed to slack off. I was sure the enemy had taken heavy losses, but so did we. Daylight crept up from the east, turning the black clouds of smoke to gray. The rockets had stopped streaking overhead.

"Can't find the spike, sir," French said, searching under bodies and dropped equipment.

"Let's roll the gun over the side," I said, refusing to let the enemy capture our most powerful weapon.

We put our shoulders to the big wooden wheels, though I was not much help. My chest wound ached. My arms felt like they had no strength. I finally had to give up, raising my Winchester to provide covering fire instead.

And then I saw him. As I kneeled on the southwest bastion, I spied General Cos standing on the northwest bastion five hundred and twenty feet away. He was in full uniform, silver buttons, gold braid, and a tall sea captain's hat on his head. A long saber waved in his hand as he directed troops into the compound.

"As long as I have arms and legs," I whispered.

"What's that, sir?" Jimmy Allen asked, having rejoined our team.

"Santa Anna's orders to his brother-in-law. The oath breaker. You will come back into Texas as long as you have the arms and legs to fight with," I said.

Though I sympathized with Cos, who clearly hated the task he'd been assigned, I could not forgive the breaking of his sacred word. He was now killing the very men who had generously spared his life the previous December, and I could think of no greater sacrilege.

I raised my rifle, took careful aim, and shot Cos in the upper right arm holding the sword. He pitched back, the sword flying over the wall. With luck he would lose the arm, for I was pretty sure I'd cut bone. But he could still walk.

It was not a difficult shot at such a range. I aimed for a leg and shot him through the thigh. He grabbed the wound with his good arm while falling over the cannon mounted on the platform.

"No more arms and legs for you, oath breaker," I grunted with satisfaction. I envisioned him being carried back to Mexico, a cripple. A lesson for others to learn by.

But Cos was not finished. I saw him straighten up, waving his men through the breach, giving orders to his staff. The man was no coward. And then suddenly Cos's head twisted around in a pink spray, his arms flayed out, and he dropped backward against the cannon, killed instantly. I looked up to my right, seeing Butler on the roof of the long barracks holding his Sharps. He had notched himself a general.

I heard a crash. The 18-pounder had rolled backward off the platform and landed upside down in the courtyard in a wave of dust. There were some powder bags to carry out, though most were empty. We left the eighteen pound shot behind. There wasn't another cannon this side of St. Louis large enough use it.

"I think the Mexicans are withdrawing," French said.

"Taking cover along the walls," Hughes corrected, for the enemy was still present in force.

"Fall back," I said.

Crockett and Jameson had withdrawn the men to the quadrangle before the church. The chosen ground for our last stand. The best cannon were repositioned facing into the courtyard, all three loaded with grapeshot.

"Come on, George!" Crockett yelled, waving us on.

My small group gathered the wounded as we retreated. There was no panic. No fear, beyond the ordinary fear one should expect. I was very proud of these men. When we crawled over a low adobe wall and took cover, I was finally able to catch my breath. Hughes and French drew their pistols. I felt for my Bulldogs and found them still in the holsters.

"What do you think, George?" Crockett asked.

"If the Mexicans were up against muskets, they could overrun us in a few minutes," I said, for there was simply no way the Texans could reload fast enough to stem such a tide. "They weren't prepared for our Springfields and Colts."

"If they keep pressing, we'll run out of ammunition," Hughes said, showing he only had a few shells left.

I still had two boxes of Winchester shells, but only one box of cartridges for the Bulldogs. I hoped the enemy wouldn't figure out how pressed we were.

The sun finally rose over Powder House Hill, and we were still alive. From what Kellogg had told me of the Alamo battle, the entire garrison had been put to the sword before the first glint of sunlight. In this respect, we had exceeded expectations.

As the smoke lifted from the courtyard, we had our first glimpse of the carnage our cannon had created. There were hundreds upon hundreds of

Mexican soldiers lying on the cold damp ground, most stacked up near our trench lined with stakes. The trail of dead led all the way back to the north wall where the parapets were filled with more bodies. Many of the deceased on those parapets were Alamo defenders, presumably Travis and Bonham among them. I hadn't seen such a thing since walking the ground at Gettysburg after Pickett's Charge.

"I'll need a count," was my quiet reaction. "Jimmy, my compliments to Sergeant Butler. Have him give me a report."

Allen ran off, happy to have no one shooting at him. Even though the enemy still held the north wall and much of the west side, only a few were visible. They would need time to regroup, just as I would. We still held the long barracks and the church courtyard, and maybe part of the corral, but not much else. Santa Anna wasn't running out of men, but we were running out of space.

"Crockett?" I asked, for he had been talking among the men.

"We got fifty, maybe sixty dead that we know of. Just as many wounded," Crockett said. "Still got a hundred men full of fight. Baugh went to see on the long barracks. Heard a few Mexicans managed to break in but didn't get too far."

"Same in the corral," Butler said, coming down from his roof top. "About twenty made it over the wall, but they didn't get much farther. After the officers went down, the rest broke off the other direction."

"Causalities?" I asked.

"Two dead, Omling and Knecht. Three more wounded," Butler said, referring strictly to our own men. "Santa Anna's got his red flag, we've got ours."

He pointed to the roof. Flying from a lance at the highest point in the fort was my personal guidon, the red and blue silk banner with crossed sabers that Libbie had made for me.

"And a mighty fine flag it is," Crockett agreed. "Men, let's hear one for General Custer. Hip, hip, hooray! Hip, hip, hooray!"

The men lustily joined the cheer, surprised to be alive. The cheer was premature, but good for morale.

"Sir, what about them?" French asked, pointing into the compound.

The field was a bloody mosaic of slaughtered Mexican soldiers. Some of the wounded were struggling to stagger from the battlefield, others were barely crawling. There were moans and the occasional curse. A few were attempting to comfort their dying comrades.

"As Christians, we must do something," Dickenson said, returned to duty with his arm dressed in a sling.

"Not while Santa Anna flies his red flag," Butler objected.

"Damn right. Let them rot," Hughes said.

"Naw, don't see how we can to that," Crockett disagreed. "We got our own wounded first, then we should see on it. Ain't that right, George?"

I needed time to think. Everyone knows how Santa Anna had ordered the murder of prisoners after the Alamo battle, and I recalled Kellogg's story of the Goliad Massacre. Which, in this time, had not yet happened. Could I hold the enemy responsible for a butchery that might never occur?

"War is a cruel business, and this battle isn't over," I decided. "If Santa Anna offers a truce, we'll let him retrieve his wounded. I'm sorry, friends, that's the way it must be."

There were no arguments. Dickenson had made the necessary offer and been refused by his commanding officer. Honor had been satisfied. And besides, there was still a good chance none of us would see another sunset. It did not stop the unease we felt at so much suffering.

"Santa Anna will regroup and attack again," I said. "We need to preserve this perimeter. Bobby, take eight men up on the low barracks. Drag the bales from the west end of the building and make a redoubt here at the east end."

"A castle in the sky, General?" Hughes asked.

Bobby had read Sir Walter Scott. I think it surprises people that many soldiers in the United States Army are actually literate.

"Protecting the high ground," I replied.

Holding part of the low barracks roof was crucial to my plan. A redoubt above the palisade would give us a strong point overlooking the south side. And every general wants to hold the high ground. Wellington at Waterloo. Longstreet at Fredericksburg. Every castle ever built was designed for high ground advantage. Of course, the Alamo was no castle, but it was all we had.

"General, I think your boys are doing enough already. How 'bout givin' me that chore?" Baugh asked, possibility feeling left out.

"As you wish, Captain. Sergeant Hughes will assign you rifle support," I agreed.

"Can I have my turn on the long barracks? I ain't shot me a general yet," Hughes asked impertinently.

"Okay, Bobby, you've earned it. But keep your head down. It's daylight now, and Santa Anna has sharpshooters of his own," I reluctantly answered. "You, too, Mr. Butler. Take ten men. Shoot anyone wearing gold buttons."

"Yes, sir!" they both responded, saluting smartly.

I sensed it wasn't a question how many officers they would kill, only who would kill the most. My money was on Jimmy Butler.

"Crockett, your job is to hold this position," I ordered.

"Shouldn't it be your job?" Crockett said, eyeing me with suspicion.

"We need more powder and shot. Once my men run out of .45 calibur shells, we'll all be firing flintlocks," I explained. "Gentlemen, I need volunteers. I'm going among the enemy soldiers to gather what ammunition we can find."

"Someone will stick you with a sword, sir. Let a few of us boys do it," Allen said.

"I'm going. Jimmy, you're my first volunteer. Anyone else?"

Everyone within earshot raised their hands. I took a dozen of the youngest and strongest, for the older men were invariably more experienced marksmen. Our feeble position needed all the veterans we had.

"What about me?" Jameson asked.

"Keep an eye up there," I said, pointing to the empty platform where the 18-pounder had been mounted. "The left flank is now our weakest spot. If they come over that corner in strength . . . Green, do whatever you can. That's your job."

"Thank you, sir," he said, saluting.

I had won the man's respect, as he had won mine.

I crawled over the barricade, struggling to keep my balance. Dickenson had suggested a stiff shot of whisky to kill the pain, but I had declined. Probably unwisely. Once again, I wished Dr. Lord had come with us, and wondered how the rest of the command was faring. Tom in the south at Goliad. Keogh somewhere across the river. Smith in the north, and young Harrington holding the Gonzales Road. I'd certainly done a fine job of spreading the Seventh Cavalry all over the countryside. Would it have been better to keep the command together?

No. I hadn't thought so at the time, and still believed myself correct. Cavalry needs to move fast, strike unexpectedly, and harass the enemy. That can't be done behind stone walls.

Led by Allen and Esparza, my brave volunteers entered the compound slowly, stepping carefully among the field of death. There was still enough smoke to burn the eyes, the smell of gunpowder almost overwhelming.

"Watch out for possums," I warned. "There's always one wounded soldier looking for a final blow against the enemy."

The youngsters surrounding me carried Brown Bess muskets with bayonets for a quick dispatch. I held a Bulldog in one hand and my saber in the other. Riflemen on the long barracks were watchful.

I immediately regretted exposing these young men to the atrocities we found, for many of the bodies were mangled beyond human understanding. Arms and legs ripped off. Heads torn in half. Entrails spilling out. The ground was so soaked in blood that red mud clung to our boots.

"Powder and shot, boys. Powder and shot," I urged, anxious to grab what we could.

We spread out, digging into pouches for lead balls and powder horns that might be full. Several hundred feet away, I noticed Mexican soldiers watching from beyond the breach. Some realized what we were doing, others didn't care. I was sure there were a thousand or more soldiers I could not see, all preparing for a second assault. We would not have the cover of darkness this time.

"Hurry, boys," I said, feeling anxious.

The search was fruitless at first. It appeared Santa Anna had sent his men into battle with little or no ammunition. A staggering error, in my opinion. Our search of the officers proved more satisfactory, finding British made pistols and pouches of ammunition. Many of the wounded mumbled to us in Spanish.

"*No problema*," I said many times.

One of the mangled bodies was a colonel I'd met at Santa Anna's dinner. I did not remember his name, but it wasn't Almonte. I hoped Juan wasn't one of the pitiful remains, for I'd grown fond of him.

We went as far as the ditch. I wanted to go all the way to the north wall, maybe discover the fate of Travis and Bonham, but it was folly to venture so far. And the ditch was gruesome enough for any man, filled to the brim with twisted corpses, the faces frozen in deathly surprise. They had not seen the deathtrap in the dark. Had not seen the spikes. Could not stop with the press of men coming up from behind.

I reflected on Tennyson, paraphrasing the experience. "Cannon to the right of them, cannon to the left of them, cannon in front of them, volleyed and thundered. Into the Valley of Death, charged the six hundred."

And charge these brave men did, right into my guns. Strange. When I was a young man, I had not thought war so sad.

"Yellow Hair?" a voice whispered.

I knelt at the edge of the ditch. It was Spotted Eagle. He had fallen near the bottom with several dead soldiers piled over him. The battered bodies had protected the brave youngster from the deadly fire that raked the field.

"I need help here," I shouted, sheathing the sword to dig the youngster from the trench.

Allen and two others came running, dragging the dead Mexicans off until I could pull Spotted Eagle out of the blood-soaked mud. He had received a serious wound in the lower back, but hopefully not fatal. I did not have the strength to carry him, so I raised a Bulldog to cover our retreat. I'd had enough of this particular battlefield.

"Let's get the hell out of here," I ordered.

We hurried back to our line, stepping over torn bodies. Allen and Esparza carried Spotted Eagle into the church where Dr. Pollard was tending the wounded. The youngster had passed out, and when a reluctant patient refused to make space, I gave the ungrateful man a kick.

"Spotted Eagle is a member of my command," I said to Pollard, so they'd be no mistakes.

"Every patient is equal to me, sir," Pollard replied, sounding offended.

"Don't worry none, General. We'll do for yours, as you've done for ours," Mrs. Dickenson said, kneeling at the boy's side and tearing open his jacket. It looked like the ball had passed completely through. With luck, he'd survive the battle. If any of us did.

I noticed Crockett had followed us in, watching from the door. Having many friends among the Cherokee, he knew how I felt.

When I returned to the courtyard, I saw the Mexican army was taking their time reorganizing. In his memoirs, General Scott had said Santa Anna was not good at adapting to new conditions, and apparently this still applied. The dictator had relied on the assault to carry the fort, and having failed, now needed a new strategy.

As we waited during the next several hours, women began appearing at the north breach. They were young and old, largely dressed in white cotton, though some wore black. They moved among the fallen Mexican soldiers, helping those who could still be helped, wailing for those who couldn't. A few dozen were carried from the field. We let them go, quietly watching from our stronghold.

"That could be us out there," Crockett said, kneeling next to the 12-pounder as he cleaned his rifle. "But we won't have no women cryin' over our bodies. What do you figure Santa Anna's up to?"

"He would be smart to starve us out. He's got us cooped up without much food left, but he won't. The Napoleon of the West is massing his troops to the north and along the river. Probably bringing up his artillery. Then he'll order everyone in at once."

Crockett looked around our small fort. We had less than a hundred men still on their feet. Thirty of those were needed to crew the cannon. David didn't require any more explanations. He knew we were reaching the end.

I walked with Crockett as we prepared for the final onslaught, talking to the men, trying to keep up their spirits. And our own. The small amount of ground we had left was filled with wounded, many who could barely sit up. Our ammunition was low. We were all streaked in blood. Our blood. The blood of friends. The enemy's. But there could be no surrender. Santa Anna's red flag had seen to that.

"Fellas, keep all your guns loaded," Crockett said, standing before the church. He face was blackened with powder, his buckskin jacket torn, but he cut a gallant figure. He patted young Allen on the head.

"Flintlocks at long range, then use the Brown Bess, and then your bayonets," Crockett continued. "We got more cannon than the Mexicans. We ain't just a bunch of farmers drafted by a dictator. We ain't criminals and castoffs freed from some prison. We're Texans, and Americans. Our heritage is liberty. We fight for the better world we know is comin', and God is on our side. Don't have no fear. Form up around the cannon and we'll do fine."

Crockett didn't mention we were still outnumbered fifteen-to-one, but it was a good speech. Even I felt encouraged.

"General, isn't there anything else we can do?" French whispered.

"It *has* been done," Slow said, emerging from the long barracks with John at his side.

The two of them had formed a unique bond, the former slave and mysterious Indian boy. Slow's brows were bent in thought, his hands clasped before him. John pointed up, indicating they had been on the roof. He had a quiet, grim smile.

"What's been done?" Dickenson asked.

Dickenson's wife and several of the Tejano women appeared with pots of soup and clay bowls. A thoughtful gesture.

"Thank you, Susanna," Crockett said, for we were all hungry.

"Okay, boy, what's that you were saying?" Dickenson continued.

"The Great Spirit will not abandon his chosen," Slow answered.

"And just what do you expect this Great Spirit to do? Descend from the heavens with avenging angels?" Baugh asked.

"The Great Spirit has no need of the white man's angels," Slow stiffly said, for he did not care to be mocked.

Suddenly there was an explosion. We looked to our right where a large portion of the north wall abruptly caved in. Another explosion opened the gap even wider. Then the west wall exploded, exploded again, and exploded a third time, leaving huge holes large enough for an army to march through. Smoke filled the courtyard, but not enough to hide what was happening. Santa Anna had figured out how to assault our position en masse.

"Gentlemen, to your posts," I said, cocking the Winchester. The women retreated, but Slow remained at my side.

"Into the church, lad. This is no place for a medicine boy," I said, pointing to the door only fifty feet away.

Slow took one of the Bulldogs out of my holster, checked the chamber to see it was loaded, and knelt on the ground behind the low wall.

"I will fight at your side," Slow said.

"Slow—" I tried to object.

"No point in arguin'," Crockett interrupted. "Boy's made his decision. We all have."

Crockett looked me in the eye. All around me, the men appeared just as resolved.

"Keep your head down, and keep my guns loaded," I said, handing Slow my other pistol and last box of cartridges.

Butler and Hughes began shooting from the long barracks, having the best angle, but they were forced to stay low, a hundred Mexican sharpshooters returning the fire. I looked back over the palisade to see if we were being flanked. There were a few infantry far out on the Alameda, but no cavalry. Was Santa Anna tempting us to breakout to the south? It hadn't worked before.

Then the Mexican army appeared in the new breaches, bayonets fixed and ready to charge. A few slipped in, forming a skirmish line. The attack would need to trample their dead fellows. Not that Santa Anna cared.

"Mr. Dickenson, open fire, if you please," I said, standing just behind the line to control the action.

The 8-pounder barked, mowing through a rank of enemies while blowing chunks out of the west wall. There would be little left of this fort once the fighting was over. I waited until Dickenson's crew had started to reload before firing the 12-pounder, for it was important the Mexicans not catch us with all three guns inactive. And then they started pouring through the gaps in earnest, shouting with renewed energy, wave upon wave.

"*Viva Santa Anna! Viva Mexico! Cos! Cos!*" they exclaimed.

They came on like devils, and we met them with every gun in the fort. The first rank went down, and then the second, but more kept coming. More and then more, stacking up in ghastly, writhing piles. Sporadic fire emerged from their lines, the bayonets gleaming in the weak sun. A young Kentuckian went down beside me, and then French took a hit, falling at my feet with a grunt. My Winchester was out of ammunition.

"Fight on, boys! Give 'em hell!" I shouted, drawing a Bulldog.

It was like the Hornet's Nest at Shiloh. Crockett was at my side, firing into the oncoming ranks at such close range that I could see their expressions as the bullets struck.

Kneeling at my side, Slow took one of the pistols to reload as I emptied the other. I should have ordered him back into the church, but I needed his help. I emptied the revolver and reached for the other just as Slow was handing it up. His black eyes showed neither apprehension nor resignation. He simply accepted our situation with a quiet bravery. Then I drew my sword, suspecting it would be needed soon. Another wave of desperate foes almost reached our barricade, pushing forward with fixed bayonets.

I wondered again what had happened to the Mexican cavalry. Were they about ride through one of the breaches? I had charged entrenched positions during the Civil War, a dangerous but effective tactic.

That's when I saw the new threat, infantry suddenly appearing on our left. The southwest bastion had been unoccupied since we'd made our retreat, but now soldiers were climbing over the corner, forming a skirmish line to protect those coming up behind them. Once they had gathered in force, they could rush down the ramp into our weakest flank. I looked up at Baugh on the low barracks. Why weren't they shooting? Were they all dead?

I handed Slow the other Bulldog and picked up French's Springfield, aiming at the commanding officer. He was a young man in a heavy coat, bearded, and not carrying a sword. But instead of pointing his men toward our exposed position, he raised his rifle and fired into the compound, hitting a Mexican sergeant. The bearded officer ejected a spent cartridge, reloaded, and fired another. The man was firing a Springfield!

That's when I belatedly realized it was Bill Cooke on the platform. I recognized Tom standing next to him, and Sergeant Major Sharrow. And Corporal

Voss, now shedding his coat to blow his bugle. It was a charge. The charge of the Seventh Cavalry! I had never heard more beautiful music in my life.

In less than a minute, a dozen men on were the bastion, some firing rifles, others using their Colts. And more were crawling over to join them. The platform became so crowded they began moving down the ramp, firing into the flank of our attackers. The enemy assault was thrown into confusion.

"Carey, quick! All three guns," I ordered.

Carey was a step ahead of me, as were Dickenson and Crockett, the gun crews rushing to load what little was left of our shot.

"Now, boys," Carey said, touching off the 12-pounder himself.

All three cannon roared, spewing broken nails and any other deadly piece of scrap that was available. When the smoke cleared, we saw nothing but broken bodies. It was if a summer storm had taken vengeance upon a field of wheat.

"What hath God wrought," Crockett devoutly whispered, quoting the Book of Numbers. I had not thought him so well-acquainted with the Bible.

I heard a new sound. Artillery. But these guns were not firing into the fort. The sound was coming from across the river, the shells striking the west wall where hundreds of Mexican troops were still trying to enter the fort.

"Captain Baugh! What's going on?" I shouted.

Baugh came to the edge of the roof, staying low so he wouldn't be a target. A bloody rag was tied around his head.

"Cavalry in the town, General. Flying one of your flags," Baugh shouted, red-faced with excitement. "They captured the guns near the bridge. Givin' the Mexicans hell, I'll tell you that!"

The artillery across the river fired again, forcing the enemy outside the west wall to stop their advance. Many tried to take cover among the brush, turning to meet the threat to their rear. Officers were yelling at the soldiers to regroup. Yelling at them to stand their ground. Yelling at them to retreat. Suddenly it became difficult to know who was surrounding who.

I was frightened by the shouting and gunfire, but staying close to the white general helped. The man knew no fear. He was either blessed by the Great Spirit or too stupid to be afraid. The Mexicans came in huge numbers, sacrificing themselves for their country's honor. I thought it strange that they would do this, for Texas was not their land. Most of the soldiers lived far to the south, beyond the deserts, but they came to die in this foreign place because their leader said it was their duty. To die for one's home and family is a great thing. Such an honor is a warrior's gift. But it is foolish to die for an ambitious chief who wants something that is not his.

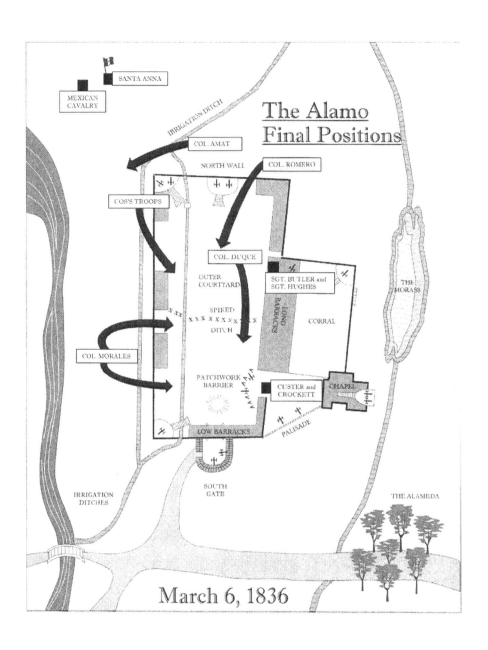

The Alamo
Final Positions

SANTA ANNA

MEXICAN
CAVALRY

IRRIGATION DITCH

COL. AMAT

NORTH WALL

COL. ROMERO

COS'S TROOPS

COL. DUQUE

OUTER
COURTYARD

SGT. BUTLER and
SGT. HUGHES

THE
MORASS

SPIKED
DITCH

LONG BARRACKS

CORRAL

COL. MORALES

PATCHWORK
BARRIER

CUSTER and
CROCKETT

CHAPEL

LOW BARRACKS

PALISADE

IRRIGATION
DITCHES

SOUTH
GATE

THE ALAMEDA

March 6, 1836

CHAPTER FOURTEEN

THE PRICE OF GLORY

The surprise reinforcements were too much for the Mexican assault to continue. A few who were trapped in the courtyard threw down their muskets, realizing retreat was impossible. Most ran for the breaches in the north wall now that the west wall was being battered by their own artillery.

"Cease fire," I ordered.

"Quit firing, boys, they's a runnin'," Crockett agreed.

"God be praised," Dickenson said, barely able to believe it.

"God and the Great Spirit," I said, giving Slow a hug. The boy was full of quiet smiles.

The men let out sighs of relief, most leaning against a wall or dropping to the ground in exhaustion. We were a ragged bunch now, blackened with smoke and grime, but there was much to do. I needed casualty reports, estimates of our remaining ammunition, and scouts to track the enemy's retreat. But for the moment, that could wait. The sun peeked out from behind a gray cloud.

"How are you, Henry?" I asked, helping French to his feet.

"Could be worse, sir," French answered.

He'd taken a musket ball through the forearm, but no bones were broken. I pulled out a handkerchief to wrap the wound.

"Reckon this is glory?" Crockett asked, coming to my side carrying a flintlock.

The dead of both armies lay all around us. Far more than were still on their feet. I glanced up to the roof of the long barracks where my guidon still fluttered in a light breeze.

"It may not feel like it now, David, but yes. This is glory," I answered without the slightest doubt.

Santa Anna's army continued to withdraw, gathering their wounded. Women and camp followers appeared, helping who they could. Good riddance, I thought. We'd have trouble enough tending our own.

"Looks like you did it, Autie," Tom said, marching down the ramp into the charred courtyard.

"Tom!" I shouted, rushing to greet him.

Bill Cooke and Voss were with him. A few horses appeared at a breach in the west wall, but they weren't chasing the enemy, merely watching. Lieutenant Smith was in command.

"Don't get too excited, Autie, there's only a hundred of us," Tom explained. "Most of the reinforcements from Goliad won't catch up 'til tomorrow."

"Fannin?" I asked.

"Decided to stay behind, but sent two hundred men."

"How'd you work that? Put a pistol to his head?"

"Something like that," Tom said with a sly grin. "You said to do whatever it took. I made our case to Fannin. Bill held the pistol to his head." Though said lightheartedly, I suspected he wasn't joking.

"It's a miracle you got here so soon," I said, giving him a heartfelt hug.

"We've got Bouyer to thank for that. Bouyer and Morning Star," Tom replied.

"Morning Star?"

He pointed back. I looked past Tom to a gap in the wall. Morning Star was entering through the breach, walking her horse between Smith and Harrington. She was wearing a blue cavalry tunic, gray campaign hat, and high rawhide boots, looking delicious.

"Bouyer found a shortcut through the woods," Tom explained, "but it was Morning Star and the Tejanos who showed up with fresh mounts. Once we got within striking range, we each took two horses and rode like hell."

I saw it was true; their horses looked exhausted.

"Glad you boys could make the main event," I said as everyone gathered around.

"Good to see you, too, General," Cooke said, coming down the ramp. The men looked like they'd ridden all night. Their uniforms were filled with mud, the sleeves and pants frayed. Tom's face was chapped from the cold wind.

"The Mexican cavalry?" I asked.

"Algernon drove them off the hill this morning," Cooke explained, slapping Smith on the back.

"Didn't you know your flank was clear?" Smith said. "We saw Slow and John waving from the roof."

"We were a little busy down here," I said, trying not to sound irritated.

"Harrington brought the relief force up from the Cibolo. Tejanos, Texian militia, a few of the locals. Even Walking-In-Grass. It was a good brawl," Smith added, so proud he was ready to burst.

I looked past him to see Sergeant Sepulveda and Francisco Sanchez, each mounted and well armed. Their small regiment of patriots had finally struck a blow against the tyrant. A few of the Gonzales Rangers and Chenoweth's men had joined them.

"I've got more work for you," I immediately said.

"You're not going to divide the command again, are you?" Tom asked, the rascal.

"No. Far from it. How strong is Keogh's hold on the town?"

"He rode in while the Mexicans were on this side of the river. Hard to say how long he can hold if they come back," Smith said.

"We can't stay in this graveyard," I decided. "Smith, have E Company screen our retreat. Harrington, cross the river and reinforce Keogh. Sepulveda! Sanchez!"

"We are here, General Custer," Sergeant Sepulveda said, offering a salute. It may have been my imagination, but their numbers seem to have grown.

"Can your boys gather up some wagons?"

"*Si, señor*," Sepulveda said, dashing away.

"We're abandoning the Alamo?" Crockett asked.

"No choice, David. We're still outnumbered. The walls are wrecked."

"We got lots of wounded," Crockett said.

"And where will they be more comfortable? In Béjar's haciendas, or crowded into that godforsaken church?"

"I'll start rounding up the boys," Crockett said.

"Mr. Carey, take charge of our cannon. Destroy what can't be taken into town. Mr. Jameson, load up the small arms. Mr. Dickenson, prepare the wounded to be moved," I ordered.

Carey, Dickenson and Jameson jumped to obey. They were part of my command now.

Dr. Pollard came forward just as Dr. Lord walked through the south gate. They would have much to talk about in the months ahead. With Pollard's connections in Massasschuetts, we might even establish a medical facility here in Texas that would rival the hospitals in Boston. If we survived the next twenty-four hours.

I issued no more instructions. These were good men who knew their business, but I had one more task to finish.

I've heard veterans speak of battles where one could walk across the hallowed field from body to body without ever touching the ground. The Alamo's courtyard was not quite that bad, but close. Baugh and some of the New Orleans Grays were gathering equipment while making a count, but that wasn't my interest. I went up to the battered ramparts on the north wall. The middle bastion held the bodies of eight defenders. Both cannon had been spiked, preventing the Mexicans from using them against us. I'd been worried they didn't have time.

On the northwest bastion, I found the bodies of Travis and Bonham. Travis had been shot through the forehead, probably in the early minutes of the battle. He'd fallen next to the cannon where General Cos lay, the two of them side by side. I picked up Travis's sword, thinking his son might want it someday.

Both of the northwest cannon had been spiked as well. Bonham lay next to the corner gun, a hammer still clutched in his hand. He'd done his duty to the last, and I saluted him. A true man, good as his word. And I appreciated the irony. In life, Travis and Bonham would have been opponents of my plan to end slavery in Texas. In death, they were martyrs to a glorious cause.

I walked down the ramp, crossed the bloody courtyard, and went out through a hole in the west wall. With any luck, I would never set foot in the Alamo again.

"Afternoon, Gen'ral," Bouyer said, meeting me just beyond the destroyed lunette.

He'd come up with Harrington's command. Spotted Eagle sat in a two-wheeled cart, ribs wrapped in bandages. Slow was holding hands with Walking-In-Grass. Our Sioux contingent was reunited at last. Troops in cavalry blue were coming down the Alameda in column of twos, their pace jaunty with victory, and E Company's flag flew proudly from the small building on Powder House Hill.

"Good afternoon, Mr. Bouyer. Thank you for such excellent service," I said.

"Still expectin' my reward," Bouyer replied.

"You and everyone else in the Seventh Cavalry."

"There's gold waitin' for me in California, sir."

"Waiting for *all* of us. Don't worry, Mitch, it's not going anywhere."

I embraced Morning Star, expecting her to be part of the family soon, and hugged Walking-In-Grass, the mother of our army. The old woman seemed especially pleased, stroking Spotted Eagle's hair while she walked next to him. That's when I noticed seven scalps hanging from the back of their cart.

"We've got food and warm beds across the river," I announced, for it finally occurred to me that Santa Anna's quarters were unoccupied. I wondered what Ben could make us for dinner.

No one needed extra encouragement to leave the Alamo. After thirteen days of siege, the men were thoroughly sick of the place. Our dead were laid out in the side rooms of the church, to be buried once the fighting was over. The Mexicans were left where they lay, stripped of arms and ammunition. There were too many to bury anytime soon. Baugh's preliminary count was eight hundred and fifty, but there were more lying beyond the walls. The final count would certainly exceed a thousand. Our losses appeared to be seventy-seven dead and a hundred wounded.

On a sinking ship, tradition says the captain is supposed to be the last man to leave. Fortunately, I'm a general, so I departed right after issuing the appropriate orders.

"Sir! Sir!" Corporal Voss shouted.

I turned to find a pleasant sight. Voss had brought Vic from the corral so I could ride into town, saving me the embarrassment of limping. The noble steed looked no worse for wear, having been sheltered near the long barracks. I rode over the old wooden bridge with head held high.

The road into San Antonio was cut with afternoon shadows, most of the houses still empty. The presidio was lit with several bonfires, Keogh's men having taken up positions on the low walls surrounding the town square. The burly Irishman rushed forward to shake my hand.

"Congratulations, General," Keogh said.

He'd lost some weight, but otherwise looked fit. I knew he would enjoy raiding behind Santa Anna's lines, and now he'd gone and captured the entire town right under the dictator's nose. I was green with envy.

"Looks like you're the one who deserves the congratulations, Myles. Casualties?"

"Six dead, fourteen wounded. We got most of the Mexicans' supplies," Keogh bragged. "Thirty wagons. Hundred horses and mules. Three cannon. Found some food. Not much, but some."

"Prisoners? Did you catch Santa Anna?"

"Naw, didn't find no officers. None worth shootin'. We had some prisoners at first, but we let most of 'em go after the fightin' stopped. Not sure how far they'll get without their boots."

I glanced toward the presidio, seeing a large pile of shoes, boots and sandals. If the released prisoners came back to attack us, they would need to do it barefoot.

"If you find any enemy doctors, send them to the cathedral. Crockett's bringing in our wounded," I said, pointing to the big church. I noticed the red flag had been taken down from the steeple.

"No doctors, sir. Not even an ambulance. Can you believe it? I guess Santa Anna didn't expect any of his men to get shot."

"Santa Anna didn't expect a lot of things," I said, shaking Keogh's hand again before crossing the street to the dictator's headquarters.

Ben met us at the door with a big smile. He had served Colonel Juan Almonte after meeting him in New York City, and then Santa Anna, and now he was ready to serve us. Practical, as well as talented.

A fire burned in the great hearth and I smelled roast chicken in the kitchen. Slow entered first, followed by the rest of our party. It's good the hacienda was large, for much of my staff would be using it in the days that followed. Warm quarters on a cold night are more than a blessing. And after what we'd been through, they were a necessity.

I cleared off the main table, gathered quill pens and parchment, and sat down to work. Messengers would be dispatched to nearby towns, for the army needed provisions. And more importantly, I would order the rebel convention on the Brazos River to disband, for I had no intention of recognizing the constitution they were writing. But the next thing I knew, it was the next morning. I'd fallen fast asleep the moment my butt hit the chair.

––––

"Monday, March 7th, General," John said, shaking me awake.

I was lying on a padded bench near the fire, a fresh poultice on my neck wound, a cold pack on my bruised chest, and a pillow under my sore leg. Tom and Morning Star were having breakfast, eggs over easy and fried bacon. The whiff of fresh biscuits filled the room. A bustle in the outer chamber indicated people were gathering to see me. The kitchen was no less busy. I sensed a relaxed mood.

"Tom, I've been meaning to ask you, whatever happened to Kellogg? Seems a star reporter from the Bismarck Tribune would want to have seen that battle," I asked.

Tom smiled, taking another bite of eggs before answering. One of the pretty servant girls in a yellow dress offered maple syrup. And maybe a little more.

"Went to see Houston. Wanted to tell him about the Cherokee," Tom said.

"What about the Cherokee?"

"You know, they signed a treaty with Houston in good faith, but after Houston left office, their land got stolen by Lamar and his band of cutthroats. Mark thinks Houston will see the situation differently if he knows what's going to happen. Maybe come over to our side."

"I didn't know Houston was our enemy," I said, not having given it much thought.

"Hell, Autie, we're making so many enemies, the Civil War is going to look like a picnic," Tom exaggerated. At least, I certainly hoped he was exaggerating. "From what I heard, you pissed off Dijon so bad he tried to kill you, and every other slave owner's gonna feel the same way. Better start making all the friends we can."

"So you think you're a better judge of men than I am?"

"Come on, Autie, there's never been any doubt about that," Tom said, going back to his breakfast.

Morning Star laughed and took Tom's hand. I would be insulted if they didn't name their first son after me.

"Excuse me, General Custer. Colonel Crockett will be here in a few minutes," John interrupted. "And Ben's got somethin' to say. Real important, he thinks."

"Thank you, Mr. Armstrong," I said, finding my uniform and boots.

Both had been washed, my guns polished, and the silk scarf scrubbed clean of blood. I was grateful, but didn't know who to thank.

Ben intercepted me before I left the room, his manner secretive. He put a finger to his lips for silence and led me to a study off the main room, closing the thick oak door behind us. A Mexican flag still hung on the wall. The desk was covered with Santa Anna's correspondence.

I hadn't gotten a good read on Ben during my previous visit, the room being filled with distractions. I guessed him at fifty years old, short for a black man, but not stooped, as so many were from bowing to white men. Ben didn't seem the bowing type.

"I got's respect for you, General, and I knows what you want for my people," Ben said. "Something here might help."

He knelt down behind the big pinewood desk and pulled out a steel strong box. A heavy steel strong box.

"President Santa Anna left this behind, sir," Ben said.

I knelt down, finding a padlock that had been pried open, and slowly lifted the lid. The box contained enough gold and silver coin to keep an army in the field for two months. There was also a fair number of bank notes. Most were drawn on Mexican institutions, but I noticed a letter of credit from Lloyds of London and several Spanish bonds. Given the deplorable condition of Santa Anna's impoverished army, it seemed to me the money could have been better spent on food and shoes rather than hoarded for his personal use.

"You could have kept this for yourself, Ben," I said, surprised.

"No, sir. I reckon I couldn't," he replied.

I took a long look at him as he hovered over the treasure. A free black man with an independent gleam in his dark brown eyes was a rare bird in this part of the world. He had been a sailor, world traveler, and such an excellent cook that he personally served the President of Mexico.

"Are you good with your numbers?" I asked.

"Don't just cook aboard ship, sir. Keep books and do some navigating."

"Then I'm going to ask you do some navigating for me. The Seventh Cavalry needs a paymaster. Interested in the job?"

Now it was Ben who was surprised. For a person of his station to be offered such an important position defied contemporary conventions.

"Reckon I is," he said.

"We'll get you a uniform. Welcome to the Seventh," I said, offering my hand.

He was glad to shake it. I was glad to make the gesture. If I was going to have a chance against the gathering storm, I'd need the help of honest men. Tom was right about that.

I went out into the busy street, filled with wagons, marching troops, peddlers, and returning Tejano families eagerly wanting their homes back. They would need to share, for a while.

The day was cold, crisp and clear. A good day to be alive. A Monday. In another time and place, the Alamo fell on a Sunday, all of its defenders being killed. In another time and place, on a Sunday, five companies of the Seventh Cavalry had died on a forlorn hillside, killed by a mistake of their commander. Few can truly understand how good a Monday can feel.

"Mornin', Gen'ral," Bouyer said, saluting.

As a civilian scout, he did not need to salute, nor was it appropriate. The rogue didn't care. He now wore a Spanish sword on his hip and a black silk scarf around his neck, no doubt taken from a dead Mexican officer. Had we fought a Sioux village instead of Santa Anna, I had no doubt his belt would have dangled with fresh scalps.

"I'll have dispatches for you later. Can you find this Washington-on-the-Brazos where the convention is being held?" I asked.

"Hardly more than a ghost town in 1876, but I kin find it," Bouyer replied. "Nice to have a Winchester, though, case I runs into some Comanches."

"Not a problem, Mitch. After those arrogant sons of bitches read the letters I'm sending, you're going to need that Winchester."

"That bad?"

"I'm telling them that their declaration of independence is invalid, that slavery is illegal, and that anyone opposing the legitimate government of Texas will suffer confiscation of their property."

"An' I kin take it *you* are the legitimate government of Texas?"

"Until God says different."

"Hell, Gen'ral, that all?" Bouyer laughed, his weather-beaten face crinkling with delight.

"After April 21st, anyone found in arms against my provisional government will be hanged."

"Can't wait to see that," Bouyer said, not sure if he believed me. And I could not be sure of my resolve, for hanging a man is grim business. Time would tell.

Bouyer went off to see if he could steal a good horse. Crockett sauntered up the street, smiling to all and shaking hands.

"Morning, George," Crockett said with a grin.

He was wearing a coonskin cap and carrying a fiddle. His fringed leather jacket hung to his knees.

"Good morning, *Davy* Crockett," I said, almost laughing. "What brings on this transformation?"

"Reckon you're gonna form a new government for Texas. Figured I'd start running for office now. Get me a good spot."

"I thought we might share the burden," I suggested.

"Share?"

"Ancient Rome had two consuls. Why not Texas? You can be president, I'll be the lieutenant general."

"Which of us will be the most important?" Crockett asked.

"I'm keeping command of the army."

"The people are gonna want democracy some day."

"And someday we'll give it to them, but not today," I said, hands clasped behind my back. "There's one thing I forgot. I've got big plans for this country of ours. Really big plans. I'm afraid Texas is just too small for what I have in mind."

"Texas is bigger than any state in the union. Bigger than any five states," Crockett said.

"It will be even bigger once we add New Mexico and California. And what's that Mexican state that wants freedom so bad? Coahuila? We'll round up Francisco Sanchez and his friends. See if they want to join up."

"George, you never fail to astound," Crockett said, shaking his head.

"David, I think it's time you called me Autie. Have you seen Slow this morning?"

"Over in the cathedral. Don't think he's ever saw a Catholic altar before. Some of the Irish boys are lightin' candles."

The San Fernando Cathedral was already a hundred years old, the tallest structure in San Antonio, and a grand example of the old church architecture I'd read about in *Harper's Weekly*. It was in the middle of San Antonio, the center of the town's business and spiritual life. It was a telling sign that the square had been deserted when Santa Anna's troops arrived, and was now crowded again once they were gone.

I found Slow sitting in the second row of pews as the village priest performed a sacramental ceremony. The priest wore long white robes trimmed with gold lace, his novices wearing blue. Dozens of candles gave the cathedral a holy reverence. As a rule, Catholics are not well thought of in Michigan, being servants of the Pope and prone to idolatry. The Methodist churches of my upbringing had brought us close to God without so much rigmarole, but like many soldiers, I'd learned to tolerate other beliefs during my long years of travel. Thank God none of the worshipers were Mormons.

"What are you thinking?" I asked, sitting next to him.

"The white men are still much in ignorance of Wakan Tanka, but they seek to discover the Great Spirit's mysteries. This is a good thing," the boy said, sounding like an old man.

"Do you still believe Wakan Tanka sent us here?"

"Without doubt."

"And he did this strange thing to help your people?"

"There can be no other explanation. None that I can think of," he answered.

The boy had a puzzled expression, looking down at his leather boots. He fingered the Bowie knife tucked in his rawhide belt.

"Lad, I'm sorry to say it, but I don't think you know anymore about this than I do. Maybe someday we'll figure it out," I said.

"I will ride at your side until we do."

"Yes, I know."

The church bell began to ring. Men were running outside. Officers shouted. I heard the big wheels of the 18-pounder in the square as it was turned to face east.

"Autie! The Mexicans are back!" Tom yelled from the door.

I followed him down Commerce Street toward the river, limping as fast as I could. Dozens of men ran with us, grunting with the weight of their weapons. Women and children were scrambling in the other direction, taking shelter in the cathedral. Cooke appeared on horseback with twenty mounted cavalry, passing us with ease. Harrington and Keogh were hot on his heels. I'd spent so much time in that damn fort that it hadn't occurred to me to find my horse.

Near the river's edge, we saw hundreds of Mexican soldiers on the open ground south of the Alamo. The small guard we had left behind had already retreated, leaving the ruins to the enemy. And good riddance. The Alamo had no food or ammunition, just a mountain of dead bodies.

"Hold the bridge," I ordered, for I saw no reason to advance beyond our position against superior numbers. We had the river on our flanks, trees for cover, and four cannon trained on the opposite bank.

"I count seven hundred," Tom said, studying their formations through his binoculars.

"Seven hundred and fifty," Cooke reported, having been at it a few minutes longer.

"Our strength?" I asked, looking to the right and left.

I only saw sixty men.

"Smith's coming with E Company, and we'll have a hundred more in another ten minutes. And the men from Goliad are on the trail behind the Mexicans. Should arrive by midday," Tom said.

He was careful not to say Fannin's men, but even if the illustrious Colonel Fannin had chosen to stay in Goliad, he had still sent the bulk of his force forward. Something to the man's credit.

"General Custer, we are reporting to battle," Mario Sepulveda said, arriving with the Zacatecan militia.

Francisco Sanchez and the other volunteer teamsters soon joined us, all carrying Brown Bess muskets or Kentucky long rifles.

"If you don't wish to fire on your own people, I understand."

"We would have the tyrant pulled down. You promised we could help," Sanchez said with determination.

"It's a promise I won't break. Take positions here among the trees, but don't fire unless given the order."

"It will be as you say," Sanchez agreed, directing his men.

Tom returned after placing F Company near the bridge, using Santa Anna's abandoned entrenchments.

"They'll never cross the river," Tom said, holding his Winchester.

Hughes and Butler were at my side, and most of my officers. We didn't have much ammunition left for the Springfields, barely three hundred rounds, but enough to blunt an attack.

"Myles, assemble I Company. Be ready to ford the river downstream and strike them in flank," I reluctantly said. "Harry, spread your troops out to hold this riverbank. Captain Baugh, please gather a mounted patrol to guard our rear, we don't know where the Mexican cavalry is. Dickenson, Jameson, draw up more powder for the cannon. Let's move, everyone. What we do here in the next few minutes may decide who wins this war."

As my staff hurried to carry out their orders, I hunkered down in the trees above the river to study the enemy's battle plan. I didn't need my binoculars; they were only two hundred yards away.

"What's wrong, George?" Crockett asked, kneeling next to me.

Crockett was once again carrying a Springfield, a bandolier with twenty shells slung over his shoulder.

"I didn't want another bloodbath," I said, unhappy with the enemy's return. With flags flying, they still made a fine impression. Worthy foes. Was I getting too old for battle?

"They're hardly likely to carry the bridge lined up like that," Cooke pointed out.

And he was right. The Mexicans were formed in squares, standing at attention, banners flapping in the breeze and drums beating. It reminded me of that time just a few days before when I had marched into the Alamo on parade. Is imitation the sincerest form of flattery?

Two officers walked toward the bridge under a flag of truce. I recognized General Castrillón and Colonel Almonte.

"Voss, sound the parley. We'll hear what they have to say," I ordered, going to the bridge before the bugle even sounded. "Tom, Jimmy, Bobby, you're with me. Myles, if it's a trick, kill them all."

Keogh would have killed them anyway, but it felt good to say.

We walked to the middle of the bridge, meeting the Mexican officers half way. Without ammunition for my Bulldogs, I carried a standard issue Colt .45 revolver. My brother and the sergeants were armed with repeating rifles. General Castrillón carried a fancy dress sword. Almonte appeared to have no weapons at all.

"*Buen dia, señores. Estoy contento ver que ustedes sobrevivieron el dia desa-gardable de ayer,*" I said, meaning every word.

"We appreciate your good will, General Custer," Castrillón replied in English, acknowledging me with a bow of his head.

"We heard you were wounded," Almonte said.

"Lost a valuable pocket watch," I answered, tapping my chest where the musket ball had almost struck my heart. My tunic had been sewn where the hole had been, the fabric still stained with blood.

"Maybe it's as the men say. You are favored by the gods," General Castrillón said, giving me a strange look.

It would seem rumors of ghost riders not only spread within an army, but between armies as well. Even Almonte eyed me with a reserved awe.

"It will be time for lunch soon. May I offer you gentlemen the hospitality of my headquarters? As you know, Ben is a wonderful cook," I suggested with a mischievous twinkle.

Castrillón grimaced. Almonte almost smiled.

"I'm afraid we must deal with the situation at hand," Castrillón said.

"I would not recommend an assault on our lines. There has been enough blood," I warned.

"We have not come to wage battle," Castrillón said.

He nodded to Almonte and stepped back. Juan took a deep breath. This was a painful experience for him.

"General Custer, General Santa Anna has left Béjar," Almonte reported. "He took the cavalry and most of our supplies. When he ordered yesterday's attack, the men were not allowed to bring their winter coats. We were given only five rounds of ammunition per man, which is now gone."

"Five rounds?" Tom said in disbelief. Having inspected the bodies in the courtyard, I suspected it was true.

"His Excellency did not wish the men to rely on their marksmanship, believing the bayonet more expedient," Almonte explained. "Now we have no food. We have no doctors and no medicine."

He paused, waiting to see if I would offer a comment. Tom started to speak but I held him back. This was for Almonte to explain without interference.

"Sir, if you may give honorable terms, we have come to surrender the army," Almonte finally said.

Needless to say, we were stunned. Outnumbered better than three-to-one, it didn't seem possible, but the condition of Santa Anna's abandoned army was indeed lamentable. They had no ammunition for an attack, and they had no resources to retreat. Their spare food and winter coats had been captured by Keogh.

When I had been a young officer, full of beans and ready to spit, I'd have challenged them to come forward with their bayonets. Taunted them to die like men. Four years of civil war, and ten years on the plains, had taught me better. And if I wasn't more humble now than in my youth, at least I was a bit wiser. And I remembered what Tom had said earlier that morning—we needed all the friends we could get.

"Sergeant Butler, my compliments to Sergeant Major Sharrow. Instruct him to prepare sufficient rations for our honorable foes. And tell Dr. Lord to expect more casualties," I ordered.

"But General . . .?" Butler started to object, for we were stretched thin.

"Jimmy, do as I say," I whispered, adding a touch of urgency.

"Yes, sir," Butler said, backing off.

"Sergeant Hughes, fetch Crockett, Morning Star, and Slow for me. On the double, if you please," I said. "And bring our band forward."

"The band, General?" Hughes said.

"We should have some music."

"Yes, sir. Right away, sir," Hughes acknowledged.

I turned my attention back to Almonte and Castrillón, who appeared cautiously optimistic.

"Gentlemen, I would like to inspect your troops," I said, catching them off guard.

When my party came up, I crossed the bridge. I wanted Tom with me, for he was a good judge of perilous situations. And I had plans for him that went beyond commanding a cavalry troop. Slow would pique their interest, for a Sioux Indian boy is not common in Texas, and his searching black eyes would enhance my own reputation for mystical powers. As for Morning Star, it never hurts to have a beautiful woman hanging on one's elbow.

I posted my band on the Alamo side of the bridge, mostly drummers, horns, and Private Engle on his flute, giving Voss orders to play a variety of pleasant tunes to put the Mexican soldiers at ease. I suggested *Oh Shenandoah*,

Ashokan Farewell, and *Bonnie Blue Flag,* but the final selection would be up to him. Whatever the nationality, we soldiers love our music.

"You are a clever man, General Custer," Castrillón said as we approached, for he understood what I was trying to do.

"Not so clever, sir. But I've had good teachers."

I saw the long lines of troops staring. They were cold, hungry and curious. They had attacked under a flag of no-quarter, and most would not expect to receive any now. But I remembered how gracious Grant had been at Appomattox. And I recalled the advice President Lincoln had given to his generals at City Point to "let them up easy."

The long rows of Mexican soldiers straightened as I walked along their line, heads held high. They had been defeated, but not beaten. Had Santa Anna not fled with their supplies, they might still be a force to be reckoned with.

The inspection only took half an hour, for the day was still frosty and I didn't wish to try anyone's patience. After the first few minutes, the rank and file began to relax, smiling at my unusual menagerie. I made some small jokes in Spanish, complimented them on their valor, and then made my offer.

"General Castrillón, I will accept the surrender of your men on the following terms: those who choose to accept service in my regiment will remain in Texas, be well-paid, and given grants of land. Those who decline will be allowed to go home on condition that they never return in arms again."

Slow tugged on my shirt. I knelt down, letting him whisper so that no one else could hear. My eyebrows went up in surprise.

"Are you sure?" I asked.

"The birds would not lie," Slow answered.

I stood up and took a deep breath, which hurt a little, and turned back to General Castrillón.

"And there is a final condition. I want Colonel Almonte to serve as my liaison until all the conflicts in Texas have been resolved."

"All? That might take years!" Almonte protested.

"It will take a lifetime," Slow said without hesitation.

Castrillón retreated with Almonte and two officers I didn't recognize. None of the other gentlemen who had dined with us at Santa Anna's dinner table were present. At least two had died in the fighting. For the others, I had no clue.

"Your terms are acceptable, sir. And I thank you," General Castrillón said when he returned, for he was a true gentleman and concerned for the welfare of his troops. Far more than his president.

When Castrillón offered me his sword, I declined. And I had made a friend.

———

The days that followed were the busiest of my life. Messengers came and went from San Antonio with amazing speed, given the hundreds of miles that separated the various towns. Crockett was just as busy, for all letters were issued under our joint signatures. But it didn't mean David and I neglected our hunting, for we went out one day and returned with a buffalo. Slow thought it a good sign.

The convention at Washington-on-the-Brazos was not pleased with our nullification of their declaration of independence. The slavery faction swore to raise an army, retreating east to friendlier country. Most of the towns in central Texas shrugged with indifference, as only a handful of colonists actually owned any slaves.

Seven days after the Battle of the Alamo, Isabella Seguin rode in with fifty Tejano reinforcements and good news from her father. Erasmo Seguin had found craftsmen in Victoria who could make .45 calibur ammunition for our Springfields, and they were already producing brass-jacketed rounds. Crockett and I appointed Señor Seguin Quartermaster of Texas, meaning he would need to stand good for our supplies until we had a government to reimburse him.

But we had not been lazy in Béjar. Young boys from the town had been sent to search the battlefields for copper cartridge casings. Those that were still in good condition were brought to the Presidio where Sergeant Major Sharrow supervised the manufacture of new shells. In this manner, we had produced nearly a thousand rounds. The quality of the gunpowder was a problem, but I could not expect perfection.

I was especially glad to see Isabella again. The fire of our earlier meeting had not gone out. She was beautiful, intelligent, had lovely brown eyes, and though a widow, young enough to bear children. And her family was among the wealthiest in Texas. I would always love my Libbie, but life goes on.

Ten days after the surrender of General Castrillón's army, a quarter of who were now in my army, we received an urgent dispatch. Voss sounded the officer's call, and by mid-afternoon, twenty subordinates were gathered around the long oak table in my headquarters. We were a varied bunch: white settlers from the east, native born Tejanos, allies from Mexico, and my own men from the Seventh, who would always be nearest my heart.

Between the various elements, I now commanded eight hundred men divided into seven battalions. Three cavalry, three infantry, and one artillery. All the units were socially mixed, each learning from the other, just as the Union forces had done toward the end of the Civil War, when it no longer mattered what state a man was from, so long as he was loyal. It was Tom's idea.

There was some good-natured bantering as we sat down to our meeting, the pretty maids serving fresh bread and wine. I was drinking water. Ben was no longer the cook, sitting to my left with our account books in hand. John had decided to stay on as my valet, and I made sure everyone knew he was well-paid. Or would be, once I could afford it.

"Gentleman, this letter has just arrived from Goliad," I said, standing to read, "To President Crockett and General Custer. Honorable sirs. I am surrounded by a thousand enemy troops under General José de Urrea. He has called upon Fort Defiance to surrender at his discretion or the garrison will be put to the sword. We have answered with a cannon shot. I appeal to you, as the only true government of Texas, to send help with all possible speed. We are determined to hold this position to the last. Signed, Colonel James Fannin, commanding."

"Well, how to you like that?" Tom said, for Fannin had not been generous when called upon to support the Alamo.

"Let him rot. We're still short of supply," Dickenson said, no fan of Mr. Fannin.

"We can't let him rot. It's a matter of honor," Crockett disagreed, for he knew the rest of Texas would be watching.

"With deference to President Crockett, we've got a Mexican army to the south, raiding Kiowa in the north, and slavers drawing recruits from New Orleans to the east. Seems we're already surrounded," General Keogh said, proud of the new stars on his shoulders. A wise appointment for a deserving officer.

"What do you think, Colonel Almonte?" I inquired.

All eyes turned to Almonte, still wearing his Mexican uniform, but rapidly winning the confidence of my officers.

"First, I think we should refer to Urrea's army as a Centralist force, not Mexican, for many of us here *are* Mexican," Almonte said, glancing to Keogh. "You will not win the love of my people by portraying them as foreigners in their own country."

"Colonel Almonte has raised a good point. One I heartily agree with. All in favor?" I said.

Everyone raised their hands. Almonte was surprised, and flattered, by the unanimous support. Slow had told me he was a man to watch. With Mexico on one side and the United States on the other, Texas would need powerful foreign allies to thrive. And Juan had visited England before. He would again, as my ambassador.

"General Urrea is an intelligent and dedicated officer," Almonte continued. "He will take La Bahia if he can, but he may back off if challenged. Or he may not. We don't know if he has received new orders from Santa Anna."

"Our claim to govern Texas could depend on answering Fannin's plea," Bill Cooke said, now promoted to colonel.

"Losing Goliad would cut off our access to the sea. We should not show such a weakness," Juan Seguin said, having returned from Gonzales two days before.

The younger Seguin knew I had an interest in his sister, and though suspicious, he was also ambitious. I remembered Kellogg saying the Seguins had suffered under the bigoted governments that followed the revolution of 1836. I was determined not to let that happen again. If Jim Bowie could win the respect of the Tejano community, then I would do the same.

"I think we've reached a consensus," I concluded, and though not precisely true, it didn't matter. I'd made up my mind before the meeting started. "We will ride to the relief of Goliad at dawn. Harry, you'll hold San Antonio."

"Damn it, George, how come I always have to hold your rear?" Captain Harrington protested.

Everyone laughed, for his protest was awkwardly expressed.

"Harry, you're right. Never let it be said George Armstrong Custer can't change his mind. Colonel Jameson, you'll hold San Antonio with the artillery unit. The defenses still need work and you're our best engineer."

"Yes, sir," Jameson said, and gratefully so.

I had learned that Green Jameson was much more interested in building things than fighting battles. And I was content to let him be a builder.

"Questions, gentlemen?" I asked.

There were no questions.

———

The next morning the command was drawn up in column of fours, cavalry at the front, wagons in the middle, infantry bringing up the rear. We were short on supply but strong in spirit. Voss and French were close by, acting as orderlies. Bobby Hughes carried my personal guidon. Jimmy Butler had new the flag of Texas sewn by Susannah Dickenson; red, white and green vertical stripes with the black silhouette of a buffalo stitched in the middle.

"Command ho," I ordered, seated on a white stallion that I had named Traveler.

The scouts went first, followed by F Company. The people of San Antonio turned out to see us go, lining the road and waving. Our band played *Gerry Owen* on drums and fife, the old Irish ballad stirring our hearts.

Riding on my right was Slow, still mounted on Vic, for the two of them got along well. Tom rode on my left.

"Taking the youngster with us?" Tom asked.

"Yes. Tom. I'm a great man now," I replied, glancing toward my youthful companion. "And every great man should have a conscience."

———

I would ride with Custer to another battle, and more battles after that. The white men of the east would never give up their ambition to conquer all the western lands. The Americans of the South were loath to surrender their slaves. The Mexicans still had dreams of an empire. The Comanche would not cease their raids, nor the Kiowa, the Cheyenne, or any of the wandering tribes. The wars of my previous world were small compared to those now witnessed in the creation of a new one. But in time, Wakan Tanka's vision finally became clear to me. It was not my people who had been given a second chance. It was I who had been given a second chance. A chance to forge a better life for my people, and for peoples who had never before dwelled in my thoughts. For this task, the Great Spirit had granted me two powerful tools: Texas would be the anvil for creating this new world, and General George Armstrong Custer would be the hammer.

ACKNOWLEDGEMENTS

It would be nice if I could take complete credit for this book, but any work based on so much historical research must pay homage to those who have come before. And like many baby boomers who grew in the years following the Davy Crockett craze, I owe Walt Disney and Fess Parker a huge debt for instilling in me a love of history, if not theater.

The first Alamo book I remember reading was Lon Tinkle's *13 Days to Glory*, still one of the best on the subject. I would also have to include Walter Lord's *A Time to Stand* as required reading. Other books that are very popular would be *A Line in the Sand* by Randy Roberts and James S. Olson, and *The Blood of Heroes* by James Donovan (which I read after completing this novel). Stephen Harrigan's novel, *The Gates of the Alamo*, is also worthwhile.

For books about George Custer, it's hard to beat *Son of the Morning Star* by Evan Connell and *Custer's Luck* by Edgar Stewart. We are also fortunate to have much of Custer's story written in his own words, for he supplemented his meager army pay by writing articles for various publications, and even had a book published before his death called *My Life on the Plains*. *The Custer Reader*, edited by Paul Andrew Hutton, is filled with numerous contributions by historians and contemporary observers. I may also recommend *The Custer Story*, which provides great insight into Custer's character and the times he lived in. It is a collection of personal letters exchanged between Custer and his wife, Elizabeth. Edited by her friend, Marguerite Merington, the letters follow the couple's correspondence from their courtship in 1862 to his death in 1876.

There are two books I need to pay special tribute to, hopefully without too much controversy. Devotees of the Alamo story can be a prickly bunch, passionate in their opinions, and intolerant of anyone who slights their heroes. I wouldn't have it any other way. Nevertheless, there are some who may take issue with my adventure story, and in acknowledging two sources of my inspiration, I assume the risk of taking them down with me. Let's try to be forgiving.

The first book I must mention is *Alamo Traces* by the late Thomas Ricks Lindley. Mr. Lindley was a relentless investigator who theorized that the Alamo was reinforced several times prior to its fall, and that dozens of the defender's names have been lost to history. His conclusions are not generally accepted by the Alamo community, but I found his book thought-provoking. His research also proves that there is much about the Alamo that still needs to be studied.

The second book I must acknowledge is *Sleuthing the Alamo* by James E. Crisp. Professor Crisp was born in Texas, and in his marvelous prologue, he speaks of the prejudices common to white children growing up in Texas in the 1950s. It was while reading *Sleuthing the Alamo* that I realized my original concept for *Custer at the Alamo* required serious revision. Soldiers who had fought for the Union in the Civil War, having lost fathers, brothers and friends, would not fight to make Texas a slave state. Thank you, Professor Crisp, for sending me back to the drawing board.

There is a list of preferred reading at the end if this book, most of it from my personal library, but not everything in this novel can be found in history books. Fiction occasionally has to take some liberties, and I've taken a few (though not as many as my critics will claim). Erasmo Seguin is a real historical character, but I invented his daughter, Isabella Seguin. Likewise, the character of Renee Dijon was created for dramatic emphasis. Most of our Native American friends in this book are also fictional, with the exception of Slow. Though Sitting Bull did have a sister, she was much younger than Morning Star.

I will also offer a final thank you to my friend and advisor, Professor Matthew Bernstein, whose persistence made the completion of this book possible.

REFERENCES

The Custer Reader, edited by Paul Andres Hutton, University of Oklahoma Press, 2004

The Custer Story, edited by Marguerite Merington, Devin-Adair Company, 1950

Sleuthing the Alamo by James E. Crisp, Oxford University Press, 2005

Alamo Traces by Thomas Ricks Lindley, Republic of Texas Press, 2003

13 Days to Glory by Lon Tinkle, McGraw-Hill, 1958

With Santa Anna in Texas by Jose Enrique De La Pena, Texas A & M University Press, 1975

The Alamo Remembered by Timothy M. Matovina, University of Texas Press, 1995

A Time to Stand by Walter Lord, Bonanza Books, 1987

Eye Witness to the Alamo by Bill Groneman, Republic of Texas Press, 1996

David *Crockett, Lion of the West* by Michael Wallis, Norton 2011

Custer, A Soldier's Story by D.A. Kinsley, Promontory Press 1992

Custer's Luck by Edgar I. Stewart, Univ. of Oklahoma Press, 1955

Custer by Jeffrey D. Wert, Simon & Schuster, 1996

Custerology by Michael A. Elliott, Univ. of Chicago Press, 2007

Custer Victorious by Gregory J.W. Urwin, Associated Univ. Presses, 1983

ABOUT THE AUTHOR

An avid reader of history, Gregory Urbach has been writing science fiction for nearly 30 years. From his days working for a campus newspaper at CSUN, he has also pursued an interest in politics, sociology, and popular culture. His degree in Urban Studies proved useful when writing the nine-book Tranquility science fiction series. Last year, he published his first fantasy novel, Magistrate of the Dark Land. All of the author's books reflect alternate worlds where the concepts of good and evil are challenged by grim realities.

Additional novels by Gregory Urbach

————

Magistrate of the Dark Land
"A cowardly lawyer seeks two kidnapped
girls in a war-torn medieval land."

The Waters of the Moon Series
"Born on the moon and raised by computers, young Grey
Waters struggles to survive in a world ruled by machines."

Tranquility's Child
Tranquility's End
Tranquility's Heirs
Tranquility Besieged
Tranquility In Darkness
Tranquility Down
Tranquility Divided
Tranquility Under the Eagles
Tranquility's Last Stand

Slave of Akrona
"He was Earth's greatest hero, sent to die
in the mining camps of Akrona. But this strange
visitor from another star-system is no slave, and the
Arikhan Empire will never be the same again."